DEMON
SPEAR

THE GODDESS PROPHECIES

BOOK  FOUR

ARAYA EVERMORE

DEMON SPEAR

StarFire
Published by Starfire Epic Fantasy

Paperback Second Edition
ISBN: 978-99957-917-2-8

Also by Araya Evermore:

The Goddess Prophecies:

Night Goddess

The Fall of Celene

Storm Holt

Demon Spear

Dragons of the Dawn Bringer

War of the Raven

Acknowledgements

Thank you to Jon whose patience and support over the years have enabled this work to come to fruition. Thanks to Kathy and John for their excellent editorial work and advice, and to Milo, Kim and Darja for their superb cover art.

Thank you to my precious Reader Team who make this work that much more fun. A special thanks to Ian for his unending enthusiasm and help in spreading this story to other fantasy readers.

Thanks to the Cosmos for making this work possible. I would also like to thank you, the reader, for joining the adventure.

For Joy

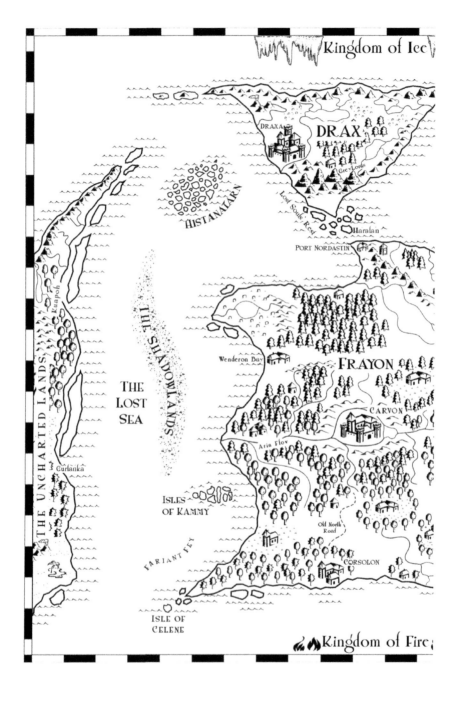

Kingdom of Ice

DRAXA

DRAX

Grey Lords

Lost Souls Reef

Haralan

PORT NORDASTIN

HISTANATARN

THE SHADOWLANDS

THE LOST SEA

Wenderon Bay

FRAYON

CARVON

Arin Flow

THE UNCHARTED LANDS

Kuapoh

Curlanka

ISLES OF KAMMY

Old North Road

FARIANT FEY

CORSOLON

ISLE OF CELENE

Kingdom of Fire

MAIORIA
THE KNOWN WORLD

MUNLAND

Ocean Kingdom

LANS
HIMAY

TERAMIDES

INTOLANA

MAPHRAX

Mountians
of Maphrax

Everlight Mountains

ISLES
OF
Myrn TIRRY

ILALLANSTARYX

DAVONO

REDBEN

OSTASIA

TARVALASTONE

VENOSIA

JUNOS

ATALANPH

CHAPTER 1

World's End

DEMONS made of black smoke clustered before Issa.

They fed upon the shadows, drawing them into their form, becoming larger and more solid. One materialised fully—black skin slick and smooth, slanted red eyes narrowing, wings stretching high before folding back.

She retreated, thinking if she moved slowly it would not see her. But its eyes fell upon her, pupils widening sickeningly. A clawed foot stepped towards her. The other demons turned, looked at her and followed the first.

She tried to think of a spell that would save her and reached for the Flow. It wasn't there. A smoke demon reached out, its deathly cold hand clamping onto her forehead. She screamed and tried to shake it off.

'Issa, relax,' a familiar voice spoke and the demons faded away. 'You have a fever, nothing too bad, and quite usual after the Storm Holt.'

For a moment Freydel's smiling face came into view with the fire-lit, comforting darkness of her room in Castle Carvon.

'But I'm still here in the Storm Holt,' she murmured. Her voice sounded all weak and croaky. Was this really her room or a demon trick? But Freydel's pupils were normal and not slitted like a demon's. She remembered leaving the Storm Holt; Maggot had been there with her. She was free of that place. A wave of relief washed over her and she sank back into the fever.

The demons were waiting for her—a crowding cluster of shadow-shapes, red eyes flashing, fangs gleaming—ready to devour her soul.

'Raven Queen,' one called. Its voice deep and hollow like wind howling through a chimney—a voice she dreaded hearing. The demon grew larger, its head becoming a three-pointed helmet, its chest the body of a huge man. Her heart skittered and she slammed her eyes shut, not wanting to see the horror of Baelthrom.

The sacred mound, think of the sacred mound. Reach for it.

With all her will she formed a clear picture in her mind and reached for it. The sacred mound loomed before her, driving away the demons and the half-materialised form of Baelthrom. His voice echoed away into nothing.

She sobbed in relief. Why did the demons still haunt her? Why did the Abyss still have a hold on her?

Her feverish dreams abated and the serenity of a vision engulfed her. The calmness of the standing stones and ancient trees of the mound soothed her and she wiped her face, taking a deep breath. It was night and myriad stars twinkled above, their brightness unrivalled in the absence of any moon. The Blaze of Eight—a distinctive, curving line of eight stars—trailed overhead. The great stones stood still and silent like watchful guardians.

She stepped towards the liquid black entrance of the mound, no longer afraid of entering it but curious. Her reflection stared back at her. The mysterious warrior woman dressed in Dread Dragon scale armour and armed with swords, whilst she stood unarmed in a nightshirt that barely reached her knees.

She looked into the woman's eyes and, for the first time, thought she no longer seemed so different or frightening. Better skilled, more experienced and harder perhaps, though that iron determination in the warrior woman's face was the same she felt in her own heart. But was she merciful or utterly unyielding? Was she empathetic and kind, or just a cold-hearted warrior? Could she even love?

"The warrior who shows no mercy will be the one still standing at the end of the battle." Grast'anth's words echoed in her mind, and made her sad. Did she need to give up love and empathy to become the Raven Queen?

'But what about love?' she whispered to the warrior.

A faint smile broke across the woman's face, followed by a look of wonder that took Issa by surprise. She did not want to let go of love and become something else. She lifted her hands and so did the warrior woman, and stepped forwards into herself.

A moment of intense cold froze every cell in her body before the darkness faded into light.

Everything was hazy and surreal as in a dream, and yet she was wide awake. Warmth spread through her and then the arms of a woman cradled her tiny baby body—a woman with long dark hair and intense blue-green eyes. There was nothing but love in her face and it made her squirm with joy. *Mother*, she thought, knowing it was true beyond any doubt.

Beyond her mother another face came into view. A man's. His hair was darker and he was tall and broad. His tattooed arms were folded across his chest. He was smiling at her. *Father.*

She remembered her parents profoundly and longed to find them and be with them again. The world began to blur and fade. She tried to hold onto it, wanting with all her heart to stay with them longer, but it melted away.

A warm breeze blew and she stared wide-eyed as a fascinating world took shape.

She stood in a courtyard made of gleaming white crystal. Four gigantic pyramids surrounded the courtyard, their white tips rising high into the night sky. Beyond them were more pyramids, the tops of which she could just see. She sighed in relief, feeling as if she had finally returned home after a long and difficult journey.

Stars twinkled above, far more than she'd ever seen on Maioria, and she recognised none of the constellations. There were two moons—one reddish in colour and the other yellow—slowly coming into alignment, one behind the other. Beyond them a bright star shone, and then several dimmer ones. The moons and stars were all moving into one straight line.

'How incredible,' she breathed, realising what a monumental event it must be.

In her hand she held the raven talisman. It seemed lighter than usual and gleamed beautiful indigo. She gasped as her hand began to tingle and glow blue. The colour spread up her arm and over the rest of her body until she was covered in a subtle shimmer of indigo extending an inch above her skin.

What is this? Where am I? She stared at her hand before glancing up at the crystal pyramids.

A low hum started and the ground began to rumble. The pyramids burst into light, illuminating the night. The tips of the pyramids grew brighter and brighter, light flaring up from all of them towards the moons.

The ground shuddered and rocked, forcing her to catch her balance. The sound of people yelling came from all around her; tall, beautiful but very strange looking beings appeared, filling the courtyard as if they had been there all along but she hadn't been able to see them.

They had pale gold or silver skin, elongated, bald heads, very large slanted eyes like an elf's, only much bigger, and small mouths. They had six fingers and toes—just like the Ancients—and they seemed to flow gracefully above the stones as they moved. They were obviously in a panic, running this way and that, and totally oblivious to her as if they couldn't see her.

The vibrating earth intensified and she fell to her knees. The crystal flagstones began to crack and separate. Waves of immense energy began to roll through her. It felt like magic passing through every cell in her body, turning them upside down—a tumbling feeling that utterly disorientated her.

She screamed along with the strange people as the flagstones began to lift and drop and lift again. People fell and rolled, tripping others over. The pyramid stones began to rise and separate yet still maintained their pyramidal form, as if each stone was being moved by magic and suspended in the air. The entire planet looked and felt as if it was fragmenting as great waves of energy smashed through it.

A burst of devastating light was followed by a boom. Everything disintegrated; even her hands in front of her face burst apart—too fast to see or feel any pain.

I'VE been surrounded by people all my life, and yet I've felt utterly alone for most of it.

Asaph hunched lower on his stool and watched the people throng in the packed tavern. Nobody paid him much attention. Finding an empty beer barrel for a table, he'd wedged himself into the corner of the dingy bar. In the gloom he hoped he looked like any of the other patrons drinking their ale.

On previous visits he'd glimpsed the locals eyeing him up—he stood half a foot taller than most—and could almost hear their thoughts about his heritage. He wanted nothing more than to be a nobody and blend in.

Smoke wafted upwards from pipes and collected at the ceiling where it created an interesting, rippling, indoor cloud effect. Light from the front windows spilled in but barely reached the back of the room where he sat. Being lunchtime and market day, the tavern was filled to brimming.

He sipped his ale. It was warm and bitter and not to his liking, but the warm fuzzy feeling it brought was very welcome—a respite from the dark mood that seemed to blacken his days lately.

"There simply is no time for us."

The argument with Issa played out in his mind time and again. He'd stormed off and spent the rest of that night wondering if she actually loved him. Sure, the anger had calmed, but all he felt now was rejection, just as he had been rejected by his Kuapoh kinswomen. It seemed his love would always be unrequited, and he wondered if she wanted to be with him at all.

If she liked him, why did she clam up as soon as he touched or kissed her? She seemed warm and loving sometimes, but at others cold and shut off. She never came to him for anything, not even for help, and she never seemed to want him by her side. He didn't doubt that she cared for him, but was it any more than that? Would it ever be any more than that?

If she says there's no time for us, then what is there time for? I must find time for myself.

He had avoided her since the argument, and was certain she was avoiding him as well. He'd also tried to avoid everyone else too, not that that was difficult since Coronos and Navarr were busy with the Wizards' Circle. No one noticed whether he was there or not and no one needed him. He may as well not exist.

The days had become monotonous, just as they had been with the Kuapoh. At dawn he went for a run around the city walls—this made sure he avoided everyone at breakfast. Then he disappeared into the city for most of the day.

It was an amazing place. The pale grey stone of the buildings seemed to gleam in the sunlight. Bridges and walkways traversed the two great rivers that ran through the city (or one river divided cleverly into two to nourish the north and south) in a complex yet beautiful manner of ornamental stone, wrought iron and carved wood.

The place was so large it had taken him a week to explore it, and there were gardens and back streets he had yet to discover. People from all over the Known World filled every street, busy about their business. Usually his travels would take him to one of the many taverns that littered the city.

He had never felt anonymous before, and he was growing to like being a stranger. He wondered if Coronos even noticed he wasn't around. His father was either in deep discussion with the wizard Freydel, or completely absent at the Wizards' Circle.

He sighed. He didn't even know when Issa would go into the Storm Holt or when she would return. Perhaps she'd already gone. Even thinking about it twisted his stomach, and the thought of her not returning made him feel ill. But what could he do? He couldn't force her to stay.

She was right anyway, so was Coronos. He couldn't stop her doing what she wanted, that would be wrong, but he only wanted to be with her and to protect her—something which she would not let him do. Whatever happened, he couldn't lose her the way he had lost his mother.

He gripped his tankard. His feelings frustrated him, making him feel useless and pathetic. He was so besotted with her, he couldn't even think about his own life. But what was there to think about?

I'm an unknown, exiled prince of a lost land. And a damned shapeshifter at that! I'll remain hidden and forgotten and alone my whole life.

He took another gulp of beer, wishing Kahly, Jommen and Tillin were here, bantering and laughing with him. He felt more alone now then he had before he'd left them. Had he made the right decision to leave his home? He'd made no friends here at all, and though King Navarr had invited him on scouting parties, he had declined, feigning illness. He should have gone, it would have helped. His life had been boring and meaningless until he'd saved Issa from the Shadowlands, but now it seemed boring and meaningless once more. Did he exist only to help her, or did he have a divine calling of his own?

The Recollection expanded in his mind. He saw the Sword of Binding surrounded by a great many people. The blood-red pommel and blue-grey blade gleamed. Whisperings came from it, asking him to wield it. In the distance he heard the roar of dragons, and then the sky was filled with them. Majestic, pure-blood dragons of red, silver and green flowed over the mountains and circled above in a dazzling wave.

The people cheered, their voices mingling with the roaring dragons. He knew instinctively what the celebrations were about; the Dragon Wars had ended, and for the first time ever there was peace between human and dragon.

Something whispered to him and the cheering din of The Recollection and garbling noise of the tavern fell away to silence. Far away a voice called in his mind—a dragon voice filled with all the sorrow of a caged animal.

Out there, somewhere, dragons slept. He had to find them and awaken them. And to do that he had to find the sword—*that* was his destiny. Excitement and urgency coursed through him. He had to do this with or without Issa by his side. His sanity and sense of self-worth depended upon it.

The noisy tavern crowded around him, again became stifling. He drained the rest of his pint, left some coins on the table, and squeezed past the crush of people to the door.

Coronos had given him a small pouch of coins from his chest in Castle Carvon, but Asaph still found the whole notion of using bits of metal to purchase things very strange. The Kuapoh did things because they needed to be done, and everything was shared. If someone was in need, the whole tribe saw to it. They didn't need to exchange bits of metal to do anything.

A hand caressed his bottom. He started and looked back at a heavily painted woman, all bright, curvy and fleshy. She winked at him from her kohl-ringed eyes. Her lips were made fuller by red paint and she pouted seductively at him.

She was pretty and young, but Coronos had warned him away from the "painted women" and told him everything he needed to know. He had been shocked at the time. The thought of paying for sex made him feel deeply uncomfortable. He smiled uneasily back at her, and moved faster out the tavern, hoping she wouldn't follow.

Stepping outside, he breathed in the cool air, relieved. People bustled past, and it seemed as busy outside as the tavern was inside. At least it wasn't stifling.

The leaves of the trees lining the street, and those of the forest rising above the city beyond its walls, were beginning to change to the beautiful yellows and oranges of autumn. He smiled. At least some things weren't so different here compared to the Uncharted Lands; the trees acted the same.

'My, he's a big one,' a man's squeaky voice came from somewhere, cutting through the sound of the noisy street and catching Asaph's attention.

'Oi, Draxian. Fancy a fight? There'll be gold in it,' said a deeper voice soon after then guffawed.

He searched behind for the owners of the voices, his eyes settling on a short, wiry man who folded his arms and looked ready to take on anyone. He grinned, showing one gold tooth that gleamed in the light, and several missing ones.

The guy next to him was as wide as he was tall, although he was still half a foot shorter than Asaph. He looked more fat than muscly under his grease-stained T-shirt. The big man also folded his arms across his huge chest in the same challenging manner. Both were smirking.

Asaph pointed at himself and they nodded.

'Next fight starts soon,' said the big man, and rubbed his stubble.

'A silver piece for the winner of each fight and a gold piece if you can win all three in a row,' said the skinny man, his half-toothless grin widening.

'That's if you're not scared, of course,' the big man said and rolled his eyes.

Asaph shook his head, a little confused. Why would anyone fight for gold?

'It's not quite my thing,' he said, waved his hand and turned to go.

'All muscle, but no fight.' The skinny one laughed.

The words made Asaph bristle and he stopped, his mind buzzing.

Actually, yes, now that he thought about it, he *did* want a fight, a big one. He didn't care about the gold, but he wanted to punch and to be punched—to feel pain and blood and sweat. He felt wound up and coiled tight with a sudden desperate need to release whatever it was inside. He *had* to release his pent up anger and a fight was *exactly* what he wanted. He'd prefer one with his sword and to the death, but maybe today it was safer for everyone that he didn't have it.

Surprised at his own actions, he rolled back his shoulders and turned back to the men who were walking away down a side street.

'All right,' Asaph called out. The other men stopped.

'All right what?' said the big man.

'All right, I'll fight. What are the rules?' Asaph said and walked towards them, wondering what he was getting himself into, but feeling reckless and free, all the same. He would be the ruler of his own destiny and no one could tell him what to do.

The men looked at each other and laughed loudly.

'There ain't no rules, Draxian. You just win or lose,' said the little man.

'It's until the first one can't get up. If you win you get to fight the next one soon after. If you lose you get to pick your teeth up,' the big man explained. 'Three fights in total and they must finish before sundown.'

'Are you game or are you chicken?' The little man chuckled. Asaph didn't trust the gleam in his eye.

'I'm game,' Asaph said firmly.

He could prove his worth in a fight, if only to himself and his opponent. It was recognition, of a certain kind. He grinned hard at the small man.

CHAPTER 2

Guardians

THERE was nothing, only her mind suspended in a gentle sea of indigo.

Understanding and unfathomable sadness filled her. The planet she had been on only moments ago, and all its people, were gone.

'Yes, Aralansia was destroyed,' a soft, female voice answered her thoughts. Zanufey's voice.

Issa searched for her, but nothing was distinct in the flows of indigo.

'That's why you came, isn't it? To help?' Issa asked, her own body forming around her as she spoke.

'Yes.'

'If Baelthrom is not stopped, more planets will die like that one?'

'Yes.'

Issa had many questions, but also the sense that time was short. She had to ask the most important ones before everything faded.

'Are you really a goddess?' She felt blasphemous.

'As your race currently understands the concept, yes. But I, like all things in existence, was created by the benevolent One Source of All—as you call it. Beings like myself were created to create, and so we brought into being other life forms, beings such as yourselves. Source made us, guardians as you might call us, and we made you.'

Issa blinked. 'We? There are many of you?'

'For every planet and every star, there is a guardian, a keeper of the house if you will—sometimes more than one. In the beginning, we are all created with, by, and through love and hold only that intention. But through the desire to explore, some choose the opposite of love, to see and learn what that it is like and what their choices bring. In the end, we all come back to love, one way or another, and there is only pure vibrational harmony—which is love. In this universe, the journey from beginning to end is one of free will choice.'

'In this universe? There are other universes where things might be different?' Every answer Issa received made her want to ask more questions. Why had she never thought to ask these things before?

'There are other cosmoses, yes.'

Other cosmoses? What did that mean? She got the sense that creation was much larger than she had thought, unfathomably big.

The air became denser, and soft, blue sand formed beneath her feet. The familiar, endless desert took shape around them, the trilithon standing to her right and the hooded figure of Zanufey to her left. The wind was warm and comforting.

'You were the guardian of the planet that I saw destroyed?' Issa asked. Had it really been destroyed? It wasn't how she imagined it would be, witnessing a planet annihilated.

'Yes. Once it was a beautiful planet filled with life and oceans and flowing rivers. What we stand on now is all that remains of Aralansia. A barren rock stripped of its mantle and devoid of life and the ability to hold life again.' There was sadness in Zanufey's voice, and that sadness grew exponentially within her.

'Couldn't you save it?' Issa's voice was barely a whisper. If the goddess Zanufey could not save her own planet, what hope was there?

'Free will must always be honoured. The people of Aralansia, the Aralans, chose to help heal another falling race, but the Aralans unwittingly let the darkness into themselves and their world. In the end, they were not able to save themselves or the other race.'

'Knowing that frightens me. The loss and…hopelessness. But why am I seeing this planet? And why do you talk to me of all people? Why do you tell me all this now and yet remain silent most of the time? And why is your face hidden?'

The questions sounded pertinent and sulky, but she had a heartfelt desire to understand.

'All your questions can be answered by yourself if you cultivate the skills to look deep within. It's hard for you to understand because there's much your race has to learn. It will come, in time.

'You are seeing Aralansia before it was destroyed. You are seeing it because it's in your blood, and because, long ago in another lifetime, you were there. As your power increases, and what you call the dark moon calls to you, you are remembering the past. You were young when it was destroyed.'

Issa caught her breath, unable to believe what she was hearing. There was a cacophony of thoughts clamouring in her head as Zanufey continued.

'Maioria called out for help as the darkness of the great rift reached her. The darkness had already consumed many planets. Her call was answered by many. Your courageous spirit spoke to me; you wanted to return to help because you were not able to complete your mission and help Aralansia.

'It may be too much for you to understand, but you had chosen to come and stop the darkness before, to stop it spreading on Aralansia, but sadly you were too late. You promised to come and try again, for the darkness still spreads, and so your soul incarnated into a human body upon Maioria. I can see this is a lot for you. In time you will come to feel and know what I tell you as the truth.

'I was gifted with the pre-creative force, and I gave this gift to those I created—the Aralans. You also carry some of this gift, which is why you can do things most others can't. This gift cannot be taught or learnt, it can only be discovered.

'This pre-creative force flows through the eyes. The eyes are the windows to the soul and through the eyes the soul shines. Light from the highest dimension is too bright for your species to look at and would harm you. So I conceal that light, the light that flows from my eyes. I could choose any form but I choose this form to appear to those of your planet as it's one they'll most easily identify with. If I were to reveal my true form to you, I would appear only as light so bright you would not be able to look at me at all.'

Issa imagined Zanufey removing her hood and awesome, divine light flooding from her eyes, blinding everyone in its purity. Could she really choose any form? Her mouth hung open at the thought. 'Is that why some call you the Goddess of Death? How can you just choose any form?'

Zanufey smiled. 'Perhaps so. I come from the highest dimensions to collect all those I can reach, all those who have not fallen too far into darkness and still wish to return to the light. I do not bring them death, as such, but reach for them across the void.

'All of those beyond the realms of matter can choose any form. Our natural state is light and sound, not material bodies.'

'And the guardians of Maioria called for help?' Issa asked, keen to return to topics of which she had a better grasp.

'Yes. And also those from the many planets threatened by the Dark Rift. So you see, you aren't alone in this struggle. Just as there are many planets, there are many guardians. We are not one, but many.'

'Who are they? The guardians of Maioria—' even as she asked it, she suddenly realised. 'Doon and Woetala. Two guardians?'

Zanufey smiled. 'The male and the female are strong polarities in your world. In other worlds there is only one gender, and on some there are five. Perhaps in other cosmoses there are more; even I do not know that.'

Issa's eyes went wide as she struggled to comprehend five genders. 'And Feygriene?'

'The guardian of your sun,' said Zanufey. 'In the next dimension above Maioria, your sun is a planet just like Maioria. The darkness spreads there too. So you see again, Maioria is not alone in her struggle.

'Asaph was sent by Feygriene to assist Maioria and help you, my chosen. Just as you have come from Aralansia and are imbued with gifts from me, so too is he from Feygriene. And there are many others who have incarnated upon Maioria to help her—but you must be the strongest, for you carry the encryption of Aralansia and the pre-creative force within you, and it was from Aralansia that Baelthrom came too. It's a divine calling you have chosen.

'However, Baelthrom isn't the only one to spread the darkness. There are those amongst you who still choose dominion over others, and many who help him.'

Issa took a deep breath, trying to hold onto her spinning mind and wondering which of the thousand questions she should ask next.

'Can we win?'

Zanufey held out her hands. 'That depends upon what the collective beings of each planet choose. It is the job of the guardians to assist those who ask for help, who desire the light. Free will must always be honoured.'

'But why don't we know any of this?' She didn't disbelieve anything Zanufey said, as far-fetched as it was to the point of madness, but how could such important information just not be known?

'You did, a long time ago. But your race desired to explore the darkness and so things were forgotten. Some even destroyed the sacred teachings, and that is when you began to fall from the light. When you let the darkness in, Baelthrom came. He destroyed the rest of your sacred scriptures and relics until no one remembered anything anymore.'

'Why are you telling me all this now? Why not before.'

Zanufey's lips curled into a smile. 'Because you did not ask. And you did not ask because you were not ready to know. There is a divine order and a timing in the universe, despite how chaotic it might seem in the outer worlds of creation. It is not my right to reveal to you those things for which you are not ready to understand.

'See, your spirit is tiring. This is already a lot of information for you to understand.'

Issa nodded. She was feeling exhausted, but the questions still burned within her. The desert began to disappear and she felt herself floating downwards. For all her desires to have her questions answered, she welcomed it when the light faded.

The men led Asaph down a side street and through two alleys to a shabby part of the city he had never explored. The houses here were old, and though they may have been rich once with their two stories and dark wooden beams, they were in dire need of repair. Even as they passed, a slate tile fell off and smashed on the ground, making them jump.

They emerged out of another alley to the back of a row of houses where people, mostly men, were gathered around a fenced-off area about fifteen-foot square. Through the jeering men hanging over the fencing, he glimpsed two well-toned men stripped to the waist, rolling in the dust and straw-covered ground.

The smaller, younger man kicked and rolled to his feet, spitting blood and teeth at his larger, slower opponent. The larger man's left eye was swollen shut, but he still managed to dodge the younger man's punch, which came so fast Asaph could barely see it. Another fast, left-handed punch sprayed blood from his mouth and he staggered.

The bigger man caught his balance, swept a leg and punched at the same time, completely flooring the other. His opponent folded with a gasp and lay unmoving. Asaph resisted the urge to run and help him. Seeing the fallen man's chest rise and fall set him more at ease.

Half the crowd erupted into cheers whilst the other half scowled and grumbled. He rubbed his stubble, finding the whole thing a bizarre spectacle. What people were willing to do in this city for bits of metal was very strange, and yet people wanted to pay for it and be paid to do it.

Feeling it wise to refrain from laughing out loud at his thoughts, he kept his face blank and watched as coins and papers were exchanged between those gathered. The winner was tossed a silver piece from a man he couldn't quite see through the crowd.

'All right, laddies. We have another tough guy,' shouted the half-toothless man who had led him here.

Everyone turned, cheered and eyed him up and down. Some nodded approvingly and began to count their coins.

Surprisingly, he wasn't nervous and stood tall as they measured him up. Perhaps the beer earlier had helped settle his nerves and made him bold, but he was still incredibly pent-up.

Another painted lady sauntered into view, her gaze lingering long on him. She had dyed-red hair and pushed-up breasts that were all but exploding out of her dress. Her huge skirts pushed the men back from her. She ignored their hungry looks and stared only at him. She winked and turned away, placing herself a position from which to view the next fight.

'You'll be ready to fight within the hour,' the fat man at his side said, jabbing him in the ribs.

'I'm ready,' Asaph growled, scowling a warning.

The fat man barked a laugh and walked away.

Asaph glanced over the crowd, wondering who he would be fighting. Most of the men were dressed simply in dungarees and straw hats—perhaps they were farmers and labourers—but some were dressed in the finer clothes of merchants: pressed white shirts, black blazers and round hats. Whatever their class, most seemed too old or too unfit to fight, not that he had done much fist fighting to be sure. He'd been taught by the Kuapoh how to fight with his hands against goblins if he ever lost his weapon. Other than that it was mostly play fighting with Jommen.

Being tall, he watched the next fight over the heads of those gathered. It ended much like the first with the winner bloody and the loser unconscious. His father would never approve. Purposeless fighting was completely frowned upon by the Kuapoh and he had never seen a heated, physical fight break out amongst his kinsfolk.

Knowing he was doing something wrong made him feel good. Who cared what they thought? He didn't belong anywhere or with any people. What did it matter what he did with his pointless life? This was rebellious and fun. He was finally taking control of his own life.

CHAPTER 3

Fighting for Gold

ASAPH stared at the lanky, wiry man who growled back at him.

His hair was dark and shaved close, as was his thick stubble, and there was a subtle sheen of sweat already on his brow. They were both stripped to the waist.

The man lifted his fists and circled, his eyes never leaving Asaph's. He twitched, as if with nerves, and his breath was shallow and tense. Asaph lifted his own fists and focused, his senses beginning to heighten. There was a slight breeze, a welcome thing in this claustrophobic, crowded city, and it blew cool across the flame scar on his chest, making it tingle.

The warm smell of cooking mixed with the fresh smell of laundry lay heavy on the air. Spectators shouted, urging them on, but he pushed the noise away, letting it fade into the background. Even their faces became lost in a blur as his eyes fixated only on his opponent.

The man struck first, lightning quick. Asaph dodged it faster, and stepped sideways. A wave of interested murmurs spread across the crowd. His eyes remained on the other man as they circled. Asaph was still unfazed and totally focused.

The man moved in and struck again, twice, once with his right then his left. Asaph dodged them both just as easily, but this time, before his opponent had a chance to complete his left swing, he smashed his fist into his face, feeling all his pent-up anger surge forwards.

There was a still moment as the man shuddered, then staggered back, blood and spit dripping from his mouth. Then he fell, stiff as a plank, to the floor.

Alarmed, Asaph dropped down beside him. The man was breathing and moaning a little, but he did not open his eyes. Confused murmurs spread through the crowd, then they cheered. Two burly men jumped over the fence, pushed Asaph aside and dragged out the unconscious man.

A flurry of activity descended upon the crowd. Amongst the shouting and jeering, coins were exchanged as new bets were made. Bets on him, the newcomer, he supposed.

He looked at his fist and then at the man sagging between the burly men. Perhaps this wasn't such a good idea. He'd never deliberately harmed anyone who wasn't his enemy before. He started towards the fence, intending to get out, only to find it was too late. Another bare-chested man was climbing into the square, glaring at him; a keen, predatory look in his eyes.

Asaph gave a silent sigh and turned towards his corner of the fence where a mug of water was thrust into his hands. He downed it and eyed the new man. He was facing the crowd with his back to Asaph and his arms raised. Most of the crowd cheered at him. So, the man was known, maybe even famous.

As if sensing his gaze, the man turned and grinned at him. His two front teeth were missing and his nose was bent and flattened, but that wasn't the most frightening thing about him. This guy had huge muscles that bulged and rippled under his tanned and tattooed skin. His head was completely shaved, apart from an inch-high crest of fair hair running from front to back.

Asaph stepped forwards. The man sniggered as he raised his fists and began to circle, slow and deliberate. He seemed completely sure of himself, showing none of the nervousness of the previous guy. Asaph swallowed. This would be a harder fight. His confidence had oddly been rocked because of his victory. Perhaps he didn't actually want to hurt anyone, nor did he want to lose his teeth.

The other man came on strong, throwing a meaty punch that brushed past his hair as he dodged. He sensed the tattooed man had expected him to dodge and was testing him whilst warming up. He circled the man cautiously with his fists raised.

'Come on, Draxian. Let's see how tough you are,' the man said, his voice deep and rasping.

Asaph was curious about the man's strange accent—one he hadn't

heard before—and it definitely wasn't Frayonesse. He wondered if the
man was from Lans Himay, since Davonians were generally dark-haired.
His musings were cut short as the man lunged for him, faster than he
expected. Rather than punch, the man's arm reached past him, circled
around his neck and plunged him down into a headlock.

Asaph gasped, gripped the arm, and heaved uselessly back and forth.
He bucked and kicked, but the man's hold was unbreakable. Breathing was
hard and soon he was panting.

The man's fist slammed into Asaph's stomach like a battering ram,
winding him perfectly. He gasped for air as his head was crushed against
the man's chest. Another fist in his face made him dizzy. Fury surged
within and the dragon opened its eyes.

Not now, I'm busy, Asaph prayed, desperately hoping that the dragon
wouldn't come upon him now, in the middle of all these people, in the
centre of the biggest city in the Known World. Why on Earth had he
agreed to these stupid fights? He should never have listened to those
lowlifes.

More blows hammered into his face and stomach as he wheezed and
struggled. He punched his left fist into the man's rock-hard gut, then his
right into the man's equally solid back, to no avail. He couldn't reach a soft
or sensitive spot. Feeling as if his head would explode, he was vaguely
aware of the crowd jeering and shouting. His opponent rasped a laugh
that made him even more furious.

Asaph growled, slammed both fists and his leg into the other man's
legs and hurled backwards. They crashed to the ground together, sawdust
and straw spraying into his face. He used the surprise to pound the man's
side just below his ribs. The headlock loosened and he jerked free, landing
a solid punch into the man's face just as he was getting up. The tattooed
man fell back on the ground, only to fling himself back up with a roar,
spitting blood.

Asaph punched him again and the man staggered. Sensing victory,
Asaph drove on, punching left then right, never pausing. He knew his
blows were fast, his hands even blurred in his own vision. For a moment
he felt release come as he fought. For a moment he was enjoying
himself—the pain, the blood, the dirt. There was just him and his fists,
and the fight before him.

The audience fell back as the tattooed man plunged against the fence nearly breaking it. Blood dripped from a number of cuts and his eyes were glazed. Asaph paused, fists high and ready to strike, but the man slumped down onto his knees.

The crowd cheered.

Asaph grinned and wiped away the blood from his own split lip and bruised cheek. His knuckles were sore and his crushed throat hurt, but he was far from wounded.

He'd hoped for a pause, for a sit down and some water, but already another bare-chested man moved towards the ring, the crowd parting eagerly to let him through. Perhaps there was no rest for the winner. His victories just seemed to spur more fighters to come and test him—the newcomer. He was tired but not done in, though he didn't want to fight so much anymore.

The next man was slender and shorter than the other two, but his body was covered in sinewy muscle and he moved silently, gracefully, like a cat. Coins and papers were exchanged and the crowd hushed. Many nodded approvingly at the man—and that got Asaph concerned. The last thing he wanted to do was fight the city legend. With a good amount of uneasiness, he eyed up the calm, quiet man who came to stand before him.

The man was grey-eyed and fair-haired—like most northern Frayon people. He wore his shoulder length hair like Asaph, tied back in a cord. His nose was straight, chiselled almost, and certainly had never been broken. Unusual for a fighter.

The man said nothing as his gaze locked onto him. He didn't even raise his fists yet, and instead seemed to measure him up by looking at only his face.

The silence deepened around them and, unlike the other two, this man held no malice towards him. It seemed as if he was there simply to do a job, enact his craft, and move on.

Asaph calmly held up his fists, but he did not even see the first strike come. It hit him straight between the eyes like a hammer, luckily just missing his nose. The world wobbled alarmingly before the pain came, and he only just managed to keep his balance. He expected the man to come on relentlessly but, almost honourably, the sinewy man let him recover.

Asaph shook his head and blinked back into focus, suddenly feeling the weariness of the first two fights bearing down on him. He worried that this man was an experienced fighter, possibly excellent, at least far better than he was. And he could probably tell that Asaph was inexperienced. As the world focused, he noticed the man still had all his teeth, unbroken. Had this man ever lost a fight? Asaph swallowed.

The man did not move and circle, but instead remained still as calmness settled around him once more. Asaph found himself being captivated by the man's actions and instinctively mirrored them. He sorely wished he'd had all the training Dragon Lords used to have, but without that he had to learn from whoever crossed his path, and he felt he could learn a lot from this opponent.

The man came on fast and Asaph found himself parrying desperately, his own arms moving faster to block than even he thought possible. He barely managed to knock back the blur of his opponent's strikes.

The man stopped his rain of fists, a glimmer of surprise and respect in his grey eyes. Asaph, too was surprised at his own ability. He had never fought like this and yet he seemed to know instinctively how. Did his dragon blood give him greater speed? Surely it must. He wondered if the Recollection gave him shared skill and knowledge as well as memory.

The crowd was strangely silent. Those watching appeared spellbound by these seemingly well-matched fighters.

The man came on, raining blows upon him again before he even had a chance to hit back. Again he parried desperately—never able to find the time to land his own blow, but managing to block or dodge every one of his opponent's strikes. The fists stopped and again they looked at each other.

Asaph went in for the same attack, copying exactly his opponent's technique since he had no experience of his own to draw upon. His fists were blocked equally superbly and with just as much speed. He stopped for breath and fell back.

They circled once and he noticed the other man was finally sweating and breathing harder. However, Asaph's own breath still came easy and only a light sweat covered his chest. It was surely his dragon blood giving him speed and stamina. He hesitated; perhaps this wasn't really a fair fight. Perhaps he could have easily killed the other two fighters too. The feeling made him uneasy and, seeing his hesitation, the other man attacked fast.

Asaph blocked him, felt a leg curl around his calf and was flung to the ground, the breath knocked out of him. A pummel of fists fell on his face and blood burst from his nose before he could shield. He kicked hard, landing his foot solidly in the other man's stomach and hurling him back against the fence.

Asaph jumped up, winded and breathing heavily, but surged forwards as his opponent launched himself off the fence. Asaph ducked the blows and rammed his shoulder into the man's stomach, hurling him against the fence again.

The man ran back, slower than before. Asaph stepped to the side, jabbed his elbow into the man's ear and followed it up with a solid punch to the jaw.

The man went down silently, gracefully almost, just as he had been graceful in the fight. Stunned silence covered the crowd and then half of them were cheering whilst the others looked on dismayed.

'He downed Leaper,' one man said in shock.

'That's the first time in a decade,' said another.

The fat man and skinny man Asaph had originally met were grinning at each other.

He looked down at Leaper, saw his chest rise and fall and relaxed. The man's nose was bloody, but still remained unbroken. Part of him was pleased he hadn't ruined the man's face just for a fight. He turned and climbed out of the square as the burly men came to collect his opponent. The crowd parted to let him through, nodding at him respectfully.

'Nice work, Draxian,' said the fat man. 'We expect to see you again. Everyone will want to fight you now.'

Asaph nodded and took the two silver pieces the skinny man gave to him—the first money he'd ever earned.

'But the first gold,' the skinny man said, holding up one shiny gold piece, 'is the price newcomers must pay to enter the fight,' he grinned slyly.

'That wasn't the deal,' Asaph growled.

'It's always the deal,' said the fat man, stepping closer.

Asaph lunged for the gold then felt something solid crack down upon his skull. He fell to the floor, hot blood trickling down his face. He blinked through stinging blood up at a heavy man holding a club. He'd seen the man collecting money from the crowd earlier. Now four men bunched close around him as he got back onto his feet.

The world swayed. The skinny man laughed. The dragon opened its eyes and stood up. Asaph snarled and lunged for the gold again, daring them—wanting them—to attack him. A meaty fist punched him in the stomach, winding him painfully and sending him back into the dirt. He gasped, the pain of three fights making him groan. The dragon within growled impatiently, and he felt his temper rising out of control.

He jumped up, swung a punch randomly, felt it connect with soft flesh and heard a gasp before the club crashed down on him again. The dragon roared as he spat out dirt and rage flowed through him.

'Asaph,' the relatively quiet, commanding voice cut through the noise of the crowd and the laughing men around him. The dragon snapped its mouth shut and the rage lulled. The same voice continued.

'When the mind is unclear, seeking the Fire Sight is better than brawling like an idiot.'

Asaph blinked and wiped away blood, sweat and dirt. Silence descended and the men surrounding him melted into the crowd. Onlookers began to disperse too, as if fearing the arrival of an authoritative figure come to report them to the king. Had the city guard come to arrest them? He recognised that voice, but his bludgeoned brain couldn't quite make the connections. He blinked through the grime up at the man in the grey cloak carrying a staff and walking towards him through the disappearing crowd.

'Father?' he said, struggling to his knees and wiping at the blood that continued to flow from his head into his eyes. He felt like a little boy again, and this time he knew he'd done something very bad. The dragon within sighed and curled up. His father looked down at him with a disapproving frown.

'And besides, I thought you'd like to know that Issa is finally awake.'

Coronos' voice rebounded off the walls of the dining room.

'You fool. What were you thinking?' he demanded. 'Did I bring you up to be a dull-brained brawler? You are a prince, Asaph. No, actually, you are a king!'

Asaph guffawed and adjusted the bandage on his head. 'King of what? Who gives a damn?'

'I do, Asaph. And so should you.' His father whirled away with a disgusted look that made Asaph hunch.

Coronos stared out of the window. Outside it was darkening with the oncoming dusk. 'I know you've been angry with Issa and that you've argued, but you can't stop her doing what she chooses, and you can't vent your pique in street fights with local thugs.'

'I've learned more today about being a man and fighting than I ever have before,' Asaph retorted, chagrined that his voice was weak and his throat raw from his recent stranglehold.

Coronos sighed and spoke as if to himself. 'Yes, you should have been trained in fighting to an elite standard. I guess you have seen that much in the Recollection. But what can I do?'

He turned and faced him. 'Anyway, to keep you out of trouble, I've arranged for you to join Prince Petar's hunting party. That way you'll meet better quality men and fighters. And I suggest we ask King Navarr if you can train with his men in the armoury, as all princes are expected to do.'

'I met a great fighter today, probably one of the best,' Asaph mumbled. Coronos cast him a warning look.

'Anyway, how is Issa?' Asaph changed the subject, thinking it wise not to anger his father further. He had been arguing with him for nearly an hour and his already sore head was beginning to throb.

'She was gone for days.' Coronos frowned and shook his head. 'She hasn't left her bed yet. It was bad. The demons are up to something; we're sure of it.'

Asaph's heart lurched and he suddenly felt sick. He jumped up. 'I must see her.'

'But she survived,' Coronos added, wonder in his voice. 'Somehow— and I don't understand this or what it means—the lesser demons of the Murk helped her. We'll learn more when she's up, but I think it's high time we had a woman on the Circle again. I think she'll become a Master Wizard.'

'Where is she? In her room?' Asaph stalked to the door.

'Yes. The healers have left her to rest. She was asking for you but when I couldn't find you I went searching through the whole city.' Coronos scowled at him. 'It didn't take me long to find you. Don't think for a moment that a Dragon Rider cannot sense dragon kin nearby.

'Anyway.' His father sighed, reached into his robe and pulled out a gold coin. 'You're a fool for thinking they wouldn't rip you off. But at least they won't be ripping anyone else off too soon. Let's just say what goes around comes around.'

Coronos tapped his nose.

'I think this belongs to you?' He flipped the coin to Asaph. 'Don't ever brawl again.'

Asaph caught the coin, his first ever earning, and grinned.

Asaph quietly opened the door to Issa's room and walked over to her. His heart pounded as he watched her sleeping. She was pale and had dark rings under her eyes. He stroked her hand folded over her chest. Her eyelids fluttered and she looked up at him with those big, sea-green eyes he'd first fallen in love with what seemed like so long ago.

'I didn't mean to wake you,' he whispered apologetically.

'It's all right.' Her voice was faint. 'I've been sleeping too much anyway, and yet I still feel tired.' She pushed herself into a sitting position and smoothed the hair back from her face.

'Coronos said it was bad.' He frowned, half not wanting to know what had happened.

'It was. I thought I was dead. I chose to die.' Pain passed across her face. 'I saw you, only it wasn't you, and you were with another... You were with Cirosa, the High Priestess of Celene, only it wasn't her either. You both had eyes like a demons. It was awful...' She shook her head.

He sat down on the bed beside her.

'It wasn't me and I've never met this Cirosa,' he blurted. 'I've never wanted to be with anyone but you.'

Memories of the beautiful pale woman in the forest floated into his mind, making him feel guilty. He pushed them aside. 'It was all part of the test. Father told me some of it, but we don't have to talk about it now. Maybe later when you're well.'

She nodded and gave a faint smile. 'I'm sorry we argued.'

'Me too.' He leaned forward to hug her. She hesitated, as if she were afraid, and then hugged him back, albeit weakly. He hated how frail she seemed.

'Things are very...complicated. I wish there was more time for us,' she said when they pulled apart. She chewed her lip, then started a different conversation.

'In the Storm Holt I met the demons who've been plaguing my mind. It may seem strange, but they saved my life when I was lost in the Abyss. They call themselves Shadow Demons, and they desperately need our help.

'Hear me out,' she said when he scowled. 'There are many types of demons.' She shivered.

'To put it simply, the lesser demons are being invaded and destroyed by the greater demons. The greater demons want to invade here, Maioria—and they most certainly will unless we do something to stop them. If we help the lesser demons close the gates to the Pit, then they cannot take the Murk and they cannot come to Maioria. That's what my dreams have all been about. That's why they've contacted me.'

'But what can we do about it?' Asaph said. 'Why are they asking you?'

Issa shrugged. 'I don't know, but I'm sure it's to do with Ehka going to them, and the fact that I can enter the realm of the dead, like ravens can. I think.

'There's a spear we have to find and a man who can use it. It's all so confusing. I don't know any more about it than that. But if we don't help them, then there will be Maphraxies *and* demons to fight, and I don't think anyone will be left alive on Maioria if that happens.'

'Never trust demons.' Asaph shook his head. He didn't like what he was hearing.

'Quite, but I've been thinking about it a lot… If we decide to help them, we can ask them to fight with us against the Maphraxies, in return,' she said.

'You'll never get them to do what you want.' Asaph scowled. Perhaps she had gone a little crazy in the Storm Holt.

'Maybe, maybe not. I'll only agree to help them, if they agree to help us. Imagine, if we did join forces, we'd be formidable against the Maphraxies,' she said, her eyes alight.

'I don't know, it sounds very dangerous…' He shook his head again. 'Perhaps you should rest more and I'll bring you some food.'

'But still, it's worth thinking about, isn't it?' She grinned.

The look in her eyes worried him. 'I just can't imagine ever trusting a demon, let alone fighting alongside them as allies,' he said. 'You relax now and I'll bring you something nice to eat.'

She nodded and smiled as he got up and closed the door. On the other side he let out a long sigh.

CHAPTER 4

Zorock

'I saw a green beast,' Issa said to the King of the Shadow Demons.

She swallowed and shivered, recalling her time in the Storm Holt when the hideous green devil had appeared. 'He beckoned to me. He could have killed me if he wanted, but he chose not to.'

Its face had been long and green, unlike any animal she could think of, and its black horns straight and shiny. But it *had* come to her aid. Apart from Maggot's voice, it was the only thing that had reached for her in the darkness of the Abyss. Maybe the only being that *could* reach her. Why had it helped her? She doubted if she'd ever know.

'Almighty Zorock,' whispered the demonic voice within her raven talisman. Gedrock's voice was a low rumbling sound filled with awe. The image of the crystal shard glowed green then dimmed, pulsing slowly.

'God of the moon of the Murk?' She was unable to keep the shock from her voice. Why would Zorock come to her, much less help her?

Gedrock, the king of the Shadow Demons, remained silent.

'Why did I see Baelthrom?' Everything about her experience in the Storm Holt was a confusion of unanswered questions, and just the memory of the place filled her with dread.

'That wasn't Baelthrom,' Gedrock's voice rumbled. 'Demons beyond the Murk can take any form they wish. Down there they have no solid body.'

Issa yawned and felt herself sinking. Communicating to the demons was incredibly tiring. She had become quite good at scrying through the raven talisman; its shiny surface proved as good as any still water, but to scry between dimensions was exhausting. Her eyes drooped and she felt herself slumping back into the pillows.

'Rest, Raven Queen. Remember our deal. Find the Cursed King and retrieve the white spear. Do not fail us,' Gedrock's voice rumbled into silence and she fell asleep, the raven talisman still in her grasp.

Even when she wasn't scrying for them, the demons still came to her in her dreams, either talking in disembodied voices or appearing as shadowy shapes with wings and yellow eyes. It was becoming very clear that they wouldn't leave her alone until she had fulfilled her word.

Several days had passed since she'd returned from the Storm Holt and most of that she'd spent in bed fighting a fever that had descended upon her immediately. Only today had she managed to pull her still weak and tired body out of bed. Freydel told her earlier, when he'd brought her breakfast, that travelling inter-dimensionally took a lot out of the body and required much rest after. Sometimes an illness comes along to force the body to do just that.

She sat on the edge of the bed and watched the autumn sun spread its rays across the forest beyond Frayon's city walls. *What has the Storm Holt taught me?* She pondered, not for the first time. Words could not really describe what she had learned. Though she had returned from the Storm Holt weak and sick, her magic reserves had completely recovered, and to greater levels than before. Mentally complicated tasks involving magic, such as scrying, were easier now, and the Flow came to her more readily. With intuition alone she found she could use the raven talisman to do many things, such as giving light or heat, and it no longer seemed such a mystery.

The wizards were right, it had made her stronger, but on the inside, not the outside. She had prevailed against terrifying powers and beings that were beyond her skills in magic and sword—she had prevailed, barely, through strength of will, faith and spirit. And *friends*. She frowned at the thought. Could demons ever be considered friends?

It worried her how easily weak and deceived she, and likely most humans, were. That hadn't been Asaph down there with Cirosa, but it had hurt her as much as if it had been. Demons were true masters of form, they could change into and mimic anything. It frightened her how much they knew about and understood the beings of Maioria in order to copy them so precisely. She clenched her jaw, determined not to fall victim to demon trickery in the future.

So, that hadn't been Baelthrom, and yet she had believed it utterly. She shivered. The darkness and intelligence that had seeped from him...a consciousness that had become utterly twisted, and yet part of her wondered how and why. She had glimpsed his plan and now she understood Baelthrom and what drove him: to make what he saw as a broken and pathetic world stronger, and to get rid of all beings he deemed as weak.

She couldn't simply stop him because she knew his plan. Why did he want to control all beings, even planets? What was in the Dark Rift and why did he want to return there, taking everything with him? The thought made her go cold.

The demons wanted her to find the Cursed King, but how? Maybe if she asked Ehka, he would find the man again. But how would they get the spear? They would have to go to the Murk and into that awful black spire—and that's *if* the man agreed to come with her. Not many people simply walked into the Murk, and willingly at that. Maybe if she first found the Cursed King, Gedrock would tell her what to do. Being in cahoots with demons did not sit well with her.

She got up and washed herself in the water basin. Her meeting with the Wizards' Circle was soon. Besides a brief visit from Freydel at her sickbed, she had yet to see the wizards after her return—and one thing was sure, she was still furious at them for what had happened to her in there. They should have warned her that the Storm Holt led to other places and that it could go wrong, very wrong. They could at least have told her that there was no magic down there. None that she could use, anyway.

Why didn't they teach her more about demons? They had said nothing. How could anything like that be called a Wizard's Reckoning? She yanked on her trousers, going over everything she planned to say to them. When she had finished brushing her hair, the Orb of Water began to pulse. She picked it up and took a deep breath.

'Now then, wizards, you deserve a piece of my mind,' she scowled and accepted the translocation.

'Call that a Wizard's Reckoning?' Issa had barely materialised in the Wizards' Circle before she was screaming. Somewhere in the few seconds it had taken to translocate from her room in Castle Carvon to the Wizards' Circle, her fury had exploded.

'What the hell has it got to do with magic?'

The shocked faces of the wizards materialised. They all looked taken aback, Freydel particularly so. Perhaps she had never lost her temper in his presence before. She didn't care.

'What bit about it could even constitute a test of a wizard, hmmm?' She eyed each of them critically.

'Uh, hang on,' Freydel began, clearly trying to form some ordered thought under her onslaught.

'Hang on to what? There's nothing to hang on to. I nearly died in there. Not because of any magic failure, but because that bloody gate doesn't just go to the Murk, does it?' she shouted.

The wizards looked at each other and frowned.

'You saw the green moon of the Murk?' Averen began. Issa nodded. 'The black rock spire?'

'Yeah, yeah, all that shit.' Issa waved her hand. 'I couldn't stop myself. I was being sucked straight through. I fell through the spire into layers of darkness and out into a red world, red like blood, and still I fell.' The wizards looked increasingly concerned as she powered on breathlessly. 'Beyond that there were more layers of darkness—utter emptiness. It exists, whatever it is. I know, I was there.'

'The gates to the Pit have been opened.' Panic tinged Freydel's voice and his knuckles gripped his robes.

'The greater demons are trying to break through again,' said Haelgon.

'I went beyond the Pit,' Issa said more quietly. The tangible memory of it and her dissipating fury made her feel faint. 'I don't know how far I went, it was such a long way down, but I wouldn't have returned if…'

'If what?' Domenon said when she failed to continue, his dark eyes watching her unblinking.

'If the Shadow Demons hadn't saved me,' she said with a sigh.

Luren laughed in disbelief, but a stern look from Haelgon silenced him.

'She's not lying,' Averen said, his eyes gleaming in surprise.

'Yes, the gates *have* been opened,' she said. 'That's why the lesser demons speak to me in my visions and dreams. They saved me because they need my...*our* help.' Whether they believed her or not was up to them. There was no point dressing up what had happened down there.

'Why should we help those bastards?' said Drumblodd. He growled and gripped his axe.

'If we don't, then the Murk will fall to the greater demons, and then they will attack Maioria.' She hunched her shoulders. 'That's what their demon lord Karhlusus plans. The Shadow Demons want our help to kill this demon lord and close the gates to the Pit.'

'And how on Maioria do they think we're going to be able to do that?' Haelgon looked incredulous.

Issa stared into the distance where the sea sparkled in the sunlight. 'They say I must find the one who can wield the white spear. An ancient king reborn to lift his curse and that of his knights. He has come here to destroy Karhlusus anyway, whether he knows it or not. I don't know this man, only that he's called the Cursed King.

'The Shadow Demons talk to me because Ehka, my raven friend, showed them a vision of what will come to pass. They talk to me because of my ability to move between the world of the living and the dead, like ravens can.'

No one said a word. The wizards looked at each other.

'As if we don't have enough on our plate,' Freydel broke the silence and rubbed his eyes.

'I told you the Storm Holt was unstable,' Domenon said to the others. 'I said the energy felt strange and erratic, that the demons were up to something.' He smiled at her faintly, not an unkind smile.

'I would have gone anyway,' Issa admitted. 'I had to know why the demons plagued my mind. But you could have warned me it went beyond the Pit.' Anger tinged her voice again.

'We simply didn't know,' Averen said, raising his hands. 'Although it may not be obvious right now, perhaps you've already felt some of the strength the Reckoning has given you?'

Issa nodded slowly.

Averen continued. 'Knowing about all the power in the world doesn't mean you know how to use it.'

'Yes, but, I wasn't ready for it. I guess I'd never be ready for it.' She sighed. 'So what happens now?'

The wizards looked at each other then laughed. She felt her cheeks colour. Surely they had some idea of what to do.

'I think it's you who needs to tell us that,' Freydel smiled warmly. Issa frowned.

'Right.' She shrugged. 'Well, I've given them my word that I'll help because in helping them, I believe they will in turn assist us against the Maphraxies.'

Surprise flickered across his face.

'Demons help no one.' Drumblodd's scowl deepened.

'If she's made a pact with them, they'll never let her be,' Averen said, rubbing his naturally beardless chin.

'You should never have spoken to them.' Luren shook his head.

'Perhaps, but if I hadn't then I wouldn't be standing here now.' She stood tall and jutted her chin out. What did these wizards really know of what had happened, or of what was going on down there? Her soul would have been trapped and tormented at the bottom of the Abyss forever had Gedrock, Maggot and Zorock not helped her.

She spoke louder to cut through their chattering. 'They're only lesser demons and they mean me, and us, no harm. But I *can* see the strength of a demon army driving back the Maphraxies, can't you?'

'To fight alongside demons when we've fought them like a plague since the dawn of time?' Haelgon shook his head.

'What choice do we have?' Issa said.

Coronos nodded and looked at the ground thoughtfully. 'That's if they agree to help us *and* stick to their word. A pact with demons is a double-edged sword.'

'If we don't help them, then the greater demons *will* invade Maioria,' Issa said. 'If they don't help us, then Baelthrom will invade the Murk. The stakes are the same even though we reside in different dimensions.'

'That's if we're even able to defeat Karhlusus and his greater demons,' Freydel said. 'But first, before we decide to do anything, you must tell us all that happened in the Storm Holt, if you can bear it. It seems we can no longer stay silent about the things that happened to us in there. Our very lives depend on it.'

Issa nodded and swallowed. For the next hour she told them

everything that had happened, glossing over the part with Asaph and Cirosa. It wasn't easy remembering in detail all that she had suffered, and no words could describe how she'd felt. How she'd given up everything that she was, even her soul. How she would have perished had Maggot's voice not found her.

The wizards listened and patiently waited until she had finished before speaking all at once to each other.

'I warned that the Storm Holt energies were erratic,' said Domenon.

'How could it lead to the Pit?' growled Drumblodd.

'We must document this,' said Averen.

'No one has gone so far,' said Navarr.

'And returned,' said Freydel, a look of awe in his eyes.

'The gate must be sealed and protected by magic. What if the demons break through again?' Haelgon said, scowling.

'They won't break through, they can't and they're too busy,' Issa said, hands on hips. The wizards stopped talking and looked at her. 'They are worried humans will invade *them.*'

Freydel nodded slowly though worried his beard. 'And what about the green devil?'

'Zorock,' she said simply.

A look of horror and wonder was shared between the wizards.

'I would not have got out if he hadn't helped me. Why he did, I don't know.' She shrugged.

'I would be very wary indeed to accept the assistance of a demon god,' said Domenon. 'Your life is indebted to it now.'

'Indeed,' said Issa holding his gaze coolly. 'But when not to accept means death... We shall see. He would not have helped me without a reason. I think he knows the peril his demons are in.'

Again, the wizards began talking at once, mostly about the technicalities of how the Storm Holt could have been changed energetically. She agreed with them that it could only have been through Karhlusus' meddling demonic magic. Freydel sat back with a sigh then pointed at the raven talisman tucked in her belt.

'Whilst you were gone, we had a good look at that, but even now we're none the wiser. It's like an orb, only its power is not separated but whole. We couldn't touch it for long without feeling unwell. It's bound to you, like the orbs are bound to their Keepers. We have, as yet, discovered no scripture mentioning it.'

The wizards shook their heads, apart from Domenon who rubbed his chin and stared at the talisman. She wondered if he knew something but was keeping it to himself.

'I can use it better now, since the Storm Holt, but all I know is that it's very old. Arla found it, but from where I don't know. Perhaps she can tell us more?' The thought excited her.

Freydel gave a pained look and shook his head. 'She's been bed-bound since the day I returned. She lives in a permanent fever that no healer or wizard can break.' The worry in his voice infected her and her heart lurched. What had happened to the poor child?

'I must see her,' Issa said, her voice stricken.

Navarr's expert healers quietly closed the door to Arla's room, leaving Issa alone by her bedside. The room was much like her own: large and decorated with wooden wall panels. The curtains were half drawn, leaving enough light to see, but not enough to wake Arla.

Issa knelt down beside the child. Her face was as white as the sheets that bound her and her breath was noisy in her throat. The girl did not stir even when she touched her cold hand. She blinked back tears. Arla was dying and she had no idea how to help her.

'You know, I remember another who was bed-bound?' Issa whispered, thinking of her mother, Fraya. 'I couldn't help her no matter what I tried. But I want to help you, if you'll let me.'

She closed her eyes and focused her mind on Arla, just like she used to do when treating sick animals at the smithy on Little Kammy. In her mind's eye, the child's aura was very faint and drawn close to her body. She got a real sense that Arla was only half there, whilst the other part of her was somewhere else.

She's trapped between two places, Issa realised. Maybe part of her was stuck where Freydel had been trapped in the ethereal planes. That was where Arla had found him, so he'd said. How had he returned all right and she hadn't? Issa chewed her lip. She had no idea what to do. Could she reach Arla in the realm of the dead? But Arla wasn't dead, so it wasn't likely.

'Arla, can you hear me? I know you can. Tell me how I can help you.'
Issa took the talisman from her belt. 'You gave me this. I don't know
where you found it but, from your note, I think that retrieving it
weakened you. Maybe I can use it to make you stronger.' She tucked the
talisman under Arla's arm and closed her eyes.

'Arla, reach for the talisman; it has power,' she said in her mind.

Arla's aura grew brighter and larger. The child stirred. Issa bit her
nails, praying that the girl would awaken. Finally her eyes fluttered open
and Issa gasped. They were brilliant blue with the Sight.

'Issa?' the girl croaked.

'Arla.' She hugged her gently.

'I can barely see… My spirit is trapped,' Arla wheezed. 'I feel my body
dying.'

'Arla, how can we help you? Please tell us what to do,' Issa pleaded.

'I don't know,' Arla whispered. 'Take me to him. Take me to the
boatman.'

'The boatman?' Issa asked. 'Murlonius the Ancient? How do you
know of him?' But Arla's eyes had closed again and her aura was
shrinking.

'Arla, come back.'

There was nothing she could do as the girl descended back to sleep.
Whatever strength the talisman had given her was gone. Blinking back
tears, Issa stood up, tucked the talisman into her belt and slumped in
defeat. How did she know of the boatman? Freydel said she talked to the
Ancients. Could that be how she knew him?

She bit her lip, feeling utterly helpless. Arla confirmed she was
trapped. She needed to find someone who could reach the ethereal planes.
Perhaps Murlonius knew how. Reluctantly she left the sleeping girl and
went to find Coronos.

He wasn't in his room. She eventually found him in the library where he
sat on a plush velvet couch with a huge book resting on his knees. He was
too engrossed in his book to notice her until she was right next to him.
He looked up startled and she smiled and bent to hug him, feeling as if he
was the grandfather she'd never had.

'Ah hah. How is my favourite daughter-in-law?' he said as she sat down beside him, a mischievous gleam in his eyes.

'Asaph and I aren't married.' She sighed, then grinned.

'Well, you know he loves you very much,' he said, taking her completely by surprise. 'You don't need to be afraid of love and you don't need to close yourself off.'

His sudden frankness and insight startled her and she floundered. 'I didn't know I was. I thought *he* was being distant. I don't want anyone else getting hurt because of me. I can't lose another…' She left it hanging.

'You cannot know what the future holds. You can only live in the moment. If you shut love out now, then how can it find you in the future?' Coronos gave a grandfatherly smile and she realised how not having a grandfather, or even a father, had left a big hole in her life.

'Love lets go. Love opens up. Fear holds on and closes in. If you live in fear, then Baelthrom has already won,' he said.

She had come here to ask him something but instead he had laid her heart bare. Was she so easy to read?

'I'm afraid of losing those I love,' she admitted. 'But I'm so angry… I want revenge for those who were murdered and taken from us. When the dark moon rises again, I want to devastate them. I want to end him and this stupid war now.' The anger boiled up as Ely, Rance and Fraya's faces flashed in her mind.

'We all do, Issa. We all do,' Coronos said gently. 'I long to see peace. I enjoyed it in the Uncharted Lands, but now I think I'll only find peace when I rest eternally.'

'I think you've got a good number of years left to go.' She grinned, trying to lift the dark mood she felt she had created. 'You don't get out that easily.'

He laughed and set his book aside, patting the couch beside him for her to come closer. 'You have come looking for me for some reason? I can see the worry in your eyes.'

She nodded. 'It's about Arla. She's trapped. Her physical body remains here where it weakens, but her spirit is trapped beyond. I tried to help her with the power of the raven talisman. She came around for a short while and said to take her to "the boatman"—I guess she means Murlonius. Then she slipped away again.'

Coronos' eyes widened. 'Murlonius the boatman? Asaph called his name and he came, but back then he had divine intention and a mission. I'm not sure if he'll come just like that.'

'We have to try, for Arla's sake. Otherwise she'll die.' Issa worried the hem of her tunic dress.

'Indeed.' Coronos stood up abruptly. 'Let's find Asaph. He's called the boatman twice before. Perhaps he'll be the best person to call him again.'

They couldn't find Asaph, much to Coronos' surprise. He'd apparently taken his advice and accepted King Navarr's invite to join his son's scouting party. The stable master informed them that they would be gone for two days hunting the forests for ogres, foltoy, thieves and anything else unsavoury in close proximity to the city.

'Well, I feel there's nothing we can do except wait,' Coronos said as they made their way back to the castle.

Issa nodded, worry for Arla churning in her stomach. She didn't feel right calling the boatman herself, but she couldn't wait for Asaph to return.

She decided to go for a walk alone through the castle's water gardens to try to take her mind off Arla. Her meandering steps brought her to the river.

'The City of Rivers,' she murmured, admiring how one river flowing through the castle grounds had been split into myriad streams, channelled between beds of yellow, orange and tiny pink flowers.

One part of the river flowed through a miniature stone city complete with connecting bridges, towers and a castle. She realised it was an exact replica of Carvon City. There was even a tiny stream flowing through a green patch, marking where she stood now in the water gardens. But the beautiful castle grounds could not distract her for long, and soon she was thinking about what to do with Arla, the demons and the Cursed King.

Before dinner, alone in her room, she pulled up a chair to the open window where Ehka was perched on the sill.

'I remember what Edarna told me,' she said, stroking his feathers and making him croon. 'She said that you were searching for the Cursed King. Now I understand why. I also know now why you went to the demons, though I'm not sure why Zanufey would care about them. Perhaps she knows this is the only way to stop a demon invasion of Maioria when her people are so weak.

'Our hope lies in this strange Cursed King. Together we'll help the demons, as I promised. I know they'll help us fight against the Maphraxies; they'll have to. But first, I must meet this king, wherever he is. Can you find him again and bring him here?'

Ehka cooed and nodded his beak.

'Go to him, no matter how far away he is. Tell him that we must meet. Tell him about the demons and Karhlusus. Bring him here if you can, or come back and lead me to him. As soon as the demons are on our side, we'll have a greater force to fight against the Maphraxies.'

Ehka cawed.

The sun was setting and its orange rays cast the forest ablaze. She looked straight up. The sky was darkening to deep blue. Out there, somewhere, she felt the dark moon moving. She closed her eyes and felt the faint touch of its pure power. It was coming closer and soon it would rise again. She didn't know when, but she had to be ready for it. When it rose, she would use its power to her fullest potential.

'You feel it too, don't you?' She opened her eyes and looked at the bird. He fluffed up his feathers. 'The dark moon will rise again, and soon. We must be ready. Go now, find the Cursed King as fast as you can.'

Ehka croaked and stood up, flattening his feathers and looking ready for business, but he didn't fly away immediately and instead looked at her.

She smiled. 'You needn't worry about me, I'm not going anywhere outside of these walls. I'll watch and wait for you. Now, go on.'

Ehka crowed, turned and launched himself from the window. She watched him fly low over the city then the forest, heading west until he was lost from view.

CHAPTER 5

Banished

JARLAIN tossed and turned in a half-sleep, reliving the moment when Marakon lifted his eyepatch.

This time, rather than events unfolding at lightning speed, everything was slowed down, forcing her to take it all in.

Her vision was a bird's eye view, looking down at the turquoise bay and the jungle beyond. Black ships swayed in the sea, too many to count. Fear shuddered her heart as their hulls thudded the shores of her homeland.

Huge, deformed, man-beasts devoid of any living aura swarmed from the decks onto the white sand—a scurrying mass of black-metal-clad terror heading straight for her people. She tried to go down to warn them, to help them, but the vision would not let her, holding her captive in its bird's eye perspective.

The beasts spread fire; screaming filled the air; warriors howled. She tried to scream with them but nothing came out. She watched helpless as parents were slaughtered and their children ensnared in huge nets. People tried to flee but four-legged beasts, that were neither living nor dead, chased them down.

Helpless in its grasp, the vision carried her away, travelling north along the coast. More ships landed far into the distance. They spread for miles and miles in seemingly inexhaustible numbers. Wherever there were people, the black ships with their man-beasts attacked.

They came because of Marakon's white eye; she was as sure of it now as she had been the first time she'd seen it. If he had not come to them, this undead horde would never have known her people existed. Why didn't he know the horrors he carried behind his eyepatch?

A terrifying screech ripped through the air. Flying beasts bigger than anything she had ever seen blotted out the sun. They flew on featherless wings and breathed fire down upon the people. The roaring flames drowned out their cries and the smell of burning flesh made her wretch. She screamed and tried to flee, to close her eyes—anything to get away from here, but the vision refused to let her go.

In the sky a face formed. A face made of black metal within which triangular eyes glowed all colours. She couldn't look away. Weakness flooded through her and her heart shuddered. Those eyes were sucking the life out of her soul.

Jarlain bolted upright as the yell left her throat. She clutched the sheets to her chest, trying to calm her thudding heart. *They're coming… Soon.*

It was still dark outside and a long way from dawn. She wiped the sweat from her face and lay back down with a long sigh. Her wounded leg throbbed with a dull pain. That wasn't all she'd seen in Marakon's eye; it hadn't been all bad. The faintest smile curved her lips and the terror left her heart.

I saw us together, Marakon, as lovers. What she'd seen had frightened her because she hadn't known him then. At first he'd seemed strange and alarming, with his terrible wounds, his weapons and his covered eye. *I guess I wasn't ready. But in my heart I knew it was true and that I would love you.*

Was that why she hadn't told the elders what she had seen when she was oath bound to do so? Was she afraid of telling them that she and this stranger would be lovers? That he unknowingly brought danger to their people? She was more afraid of believing it herself. But the visions never lied and told her only what would come to pass, regardless if she agreed with it or not. How could she possibly describe to them the coming undead man-beasts and flying black monsters that breathed fire? Of the face in the sky who stole souls with his gaze?

Ever since the day Marakon had lifted his eyepatch and changed her world forever, she had tortured herself about whether or not to tell the elders about it. As a potential High Elder, she was oath-bound to tell them about every dream and vision she received with the Sight. The Hidden Ones communicated with her in that manner, and for the safety of the entire Gurlanka she had to tell the elders what the Hidden Ones shared with her. And she always had, until now.

She could not bring herself to tell them that this man brought their destruction and she would be his lover. She was tortured and torn; unable to betray Marakon and yet unable to betray her people either. Deep down she knew she had done something terribly wrong.

She got up and went about her day, but for all of it she deliberated on whether to tell the elders. She'd feared for Marakon's safety at the hands of her people had they known, but now he was gone, could she tell them? They couldn't harm him now. They already knew he was cursed, but they didn't know the danger he had brought to them.

I'll tell them tomorrow at dawn. I must tell them. That evening the Hidden Ones came to her.

She saw them first as humanoid figures of pale blue mist surrounded by diffuse yellow light. They had no faces or any distinct features that she could make out. With long, pale arms they beckoned to her and she followed. They disappeared and a different, nightmarish world took shape—one she hadn't seen since she was a little girl.

Fear slithered through her as she crouched upon the orange earth of a planet so small she could see it curving on the horizon. The planet convulsed, pitching her forwards. She gasped, her hands burning as they scrambled in the hot dirt. She pushed herself back onto her haunches. Wind blasted her, tearing at her clothes and body.

The sky was a paler orange than the earth and the sun was huge in the sky, burning her flesh with its furious rays. Heat rose from the baked ground in wavering mirages. Sweat cloyed her face and glued her clothes to her back. She staggered to her feet, struggling for balance as the world tilted and quaked.

In the distance beyond the plains, blood-red mountains reared up into the sky. Poisoned clouds clustered together and a face formed within them. That face made of black metal and triangular slits for eyes. The eyes started to glow and molten red tears dripped down to the earth, setting the ground on fire where they fell. Jarlain screamed and ran.

The face followed, flames spitting out from its terrible eyes. There was nowhere to hide on this tiny barren planet, she could only run and run until her legs burned.

She stumbled over a pile of rocks and found herself back in the place where she had started. Ahead, shimmering in the heat, a village appeared. It seemed a strange mock-up of her village, only without the jungle surrounding it.

The face in the sky swung before her, its lava tears falling upon the houses and setting them on fire. Tears rained upon the people and their screams filled the air as they tried to flee. Wind swept the fires high and soon an inferno blazed.

'Help us!' the people screamed, running towards her with outstretched hands, but the flames engulfed them, drowning their screams. Their charred remains were spat out upon the ground.

The tears fell harder, coming towards her and the ground turned into flames. She tried to dodge them then a wall of fire blocked her path. The face descended, engulfing her in its molten eyes. She screamed as her flesh caught fire and agony filled her body.

Cold hands gripped her arms. Blessed cool soothed her burning flesh. They pulled her from the flames. She blinked up into a face she had longed to see.

'Marakon!' She gasped, embracing him. 'Great Goddess, how I've missed you.' She pulled back to look at him, but his face was twisted with an anguish she could not fathom.

'I did this,' he cried.

'No Marakon, you can't have.' She shook her head and grasped his hands. 'I love you, but we must run and hide from the burning eyes. Please come with me.'

'We can't hide.' He shook his head. 'I can't hide. Not now, not ever. I'm damned to a life of agony.' He gripped her arms painfully.

'Look at me, I am damned!' he screamed and raised a hand to lift up his eyepatch.

'No, don't,' she cried, but couldn't stop him. Beneath his patch his eye burned molten lava like the eyes of fire in the sky. She screamed as the whole world turned into flames.

Jarlain got out of her chair covered in sweat, her heart pounding again and her head splitting in pain as the vision released her. She blinked out of the window at the rising sun, half expecting to see those awful lava-dripping eyes staring at her.

The Hidden Ones had given her a warning. Something terrible was coming, and when the visions were that bad, they were fulfilled soon. She had to tell the elders about everything immediately. She pulled on her clothes, the feeling of panic almost overwhelming her.

Running to the Elders' House, she took the stairs two at a time. She found them already up, seated in a circle and in deep discussion. They weren't alone and Hai, the High Elder, was staring intently at a young, paler-skinned man who could be no more than seventeen. His hair was dark brown rather than black like the Gurlanka, and he was wearing little more than a loin cloth, a torn shirt and bloodied bandages. The young man was clearly distressed, stammering as he spoke and his hands trembled. His accent was from the north.

It was highly disrespectful to walk in upon the elders, especially during a meeting, but she couldn't wait and stepped forwards. They all paused and turned to stare at her breathless entrance. The look of anguish on her face roused the closest elder, Elan. She stood up and led her into the circle, motioning her to sit silently with them.

'Elder Hai,' Jarlain began between gasps of breath, 'I—' but he held up a wrinkled hand to silence her and gave a solemn look. The words died in her throat.

'Young Jarlain will speak once our honoured guest has spoken, and not before,' he commanded.

She understood the right of guests, but she couldn't wait, it couldn't wait, their lives depended upon it.

'But Elder Hai, it's so urgent—' was all she got out before he made a slight gesture and she found her tongue would not move, as if held by some invisible hand.

'No matter how urgent it is, Jarlain, we will not lose our respect and dignity. This man's word is as important as your own right now. Guests always speak first. Feel privileged to sit amongst us Jarlain, and hold your tongue and your mind chatter—which I can hear quite clearly even if my physical ears are gone,' he said, giving her a disapproving look which was echoed by the others.

She didn't need to hold her tongue for someone else appeared to be doing it for her, so she sat silently, impatiently, and waited.

The young man looked at her and his eyes were filled with fear—not a fear of her, but of the things he'd experienced. What had he seen and why had he come? Had he seen what she'd witnessed in her dreams? His fear fed into her and she looked away.

'Please, Tayle of the Yaso Peoples, continue,' Hai said and motioned respectfully.

Jarlain had met members of the Yaso frequently when they had visited their village. Being excellent with their hands, they were boat builders—which was how they managed to travel so far south so quickly. They were courteous and good singers too; she remembered them singing at the feast—their voices pure and enchanting.

Hai closed his eyes, as he often did in communion. Jarlain knew his inner senses were so sharp he needed no ears to hear or eyes to see; he just focused his mind. She wondered if he could actually see everything Tayle had seen.

The young man spoke in short, sharp bursts, his eyes wide as he recounted events. 'As I said, the sea devils came in great numbers on fast boats. They were at least five times our number, maybe more. We fought them, as we always do, and many of us were killed. Then the sky was filled with huge flying beasts that blocked out the sun and breathed fire upon everything. This scared the sea devils back into the ocean.

'Then came huge ships filled with people-like beings, though they were huge and deformed with muscle, and no life lit up their eyes. Some of us they killed. Others, our children mostly, they tried to capture.

'We couldn't fight them, there were so many, so we fled into the jungle, where we remain. I'm a runner, so my people sent me to warn our cousins. Because there were so many ships, we believe they'll attack everyone. I don't know if any of my people are alive; I haven't stopped running for two days.'

He stopped to gasp and swallow water before rushing on. 'High Elder Hai, there's more. Just before the beast-men came, the Animal Listeners were visited by ravens. They were given a terrible vision of a dark force coming from across the sea. Our High Elder, Iolan, spoke with the Hidden Ones and they told her a strange thing, almost like a riddle. They said, "First comes the king to betray, second the enemy to slay, third the dead to enslave."

Jarlain shivered at the words. Hai opened his eyes and stared into the middle distance, his face expressionless.

'Zanu's ravens came to us also, Tayle,' Elan said gently.

Jarlain wondered when; the elders hadn't told her about any ravens, but then she hadn't spoken to anyone since Marakon had left. Elan continued.

'We've all seen the rising dark moon that warns us of great changes. We were forewarned long ago, but had little ability to do anything about it.'

Tayle continued speaking. Jarlain closed her eyes like Hai and tried to envision his words, but all she saw was a black face crying molten tears of death and destruction. She tried to shake the vision from her mind, but those awful eyes wouldn't leave her be—mocking her, hating her, burning her. She could feel the heat on her face; it was so hot, sweat beaded her skin. Hotter it burned and she screamed, clawing at her face and trying to put out the flames.

Cool hands gripped her arms, just as Marakon's had, and pinned her to the floor. The heat was pushed away and cool air blew over her. She opened her eyes and stared up at the five white-haired elders. A cold cloth wiped her face. Her cheeks stung from her own clawing. They helped her sit and waited patiently for her to speak.

'I saw a black metal face. Its eyes cried tears of fire,' she said, her voice hoarse. Hai was reading her lips. 'Fire that destroys us and burns our souls to nothing but dust. What Tayle says is true. I have seen it.'

The elders took her hands as she continued in a shaking voice, telling them her visions. When they closed their eyes, she knew they could see all that she had seen. Speaking about Marakon was a struggle, but she could not shut the elders out and dared not try.

'I knew Marakon would be our salvation against the sea devils, but also our destruction against a darker enemy,' Elan said, a pained look on her face as she let Jarlain's hand go. 'They wouldn't know we were here if it weren't for him, and they wouldn't have come.'

'It's not his fault,' Jarlain pleaded. 'He doesn't know the danger he brings. He's been tricked, cursed to be his own undoing.' She dropped her head into her hands as the tears came.

Hai spoke next, his voice quiet but commanding, and his face harder than Jarlain had ever seen it. 'You saw our destruction in Marakon and yet you said nothing to us? You have known from the start that something was not right with the half-elf, yet you still told us nothing?'

Jarlain wiped the tears away as she spoke. 'I didn't tell you what I saw because I didn't understand its meaning.' Her voice dropped to barely a whisper. 'I also saw us together as lovers and I was afraid and confused. I worried what you all would think and I needed more time.'

'It doesn't matter that you were afraid,' Hai's normally soft voice grew loud. 'You are ordered to deliver your visions, your messages, to us as soon as they happen—you are commanded and bound by oath to do this. Our lives, the lives of our people, depend on you and you said nothing?'

Jarlain flinched and shrank from him as he shouted. She had never seen him angry.

'High Elder, I...' but she could think of nothing to say. He was right, she should have told them. She had done something terribly wrong. She glanced at each of the elders, but they looked only at Hai, their expressions blank.

'Our very lives depend upon such warnings. Your silence may have brought our downfall, but only time can decide that.' Hai stood up. He seemed even more frightening as he stared down at her, his long, red beard moving in the breeze, staff gripped in his wizened hand.

'I've felt the swell of a mighty power in the east and it rushes towards us like a storm upon the sea,' Hai said, looking into the middle distance again, his wrinkled face solemn. 'The things that attacked Tayle's tribe are coming here, of that there's no doubt. Now we're forced to leave our home and join with the survivors of the other tribes for safety. We must become one people as we were once before, a long time ago.'

He sank back down to a cross-legged position. Jarlain couldn't look at him, only at the floor. She knew she would be punished for breaking her oath and the punishment was usually severe. She shivered despite the heat.

The elders spoke quickly about what they should do now but Jarlain was not listening. Marakon was gone and he had unknowingly betrayed them all, and she had broken her oath and knowingly betrayed her people.

The elders stopped talking and looked at her with solemn eyes. In the silence, Hai stood up, his face hard as he spoke.

'The oath-breaker must be punished. As we have done in the past, so shall it be done now. Evil will reach us because Marakon was here, and many of us will die because of your silence.'

She wanted to protest, to say she hadn't willed anyone to be harmed, but she dared not even open her mouth.

Hai continued. 'So you will be cursed as is he. The hair from your head will be shorn and the clothes from your body taken so all will know what you have done—that is as standard. You will be naked just as you have left us naked without knowledge.'

Jarlain hung her head in the shame; her hair would grow back, but to walk naked like an animal amongst her people was a terrible disgrace. She suddenly felt desperately alone, an empty shell of a person. Her breath came short and shallow in her throat as she tried to survive the next few moments.

'Your eyes will be blindfolded to show others the nature of your crime, for you have received visions from the Hidden Ones but refused to share them. Blind and naked you will stand amongst us before setting out to follow Marakon's path. Find him, end his treachery, and only then may you return as one of us.'

Jarlain stared in shock at the floor. She wished then that the burning face in the sky had been real, wished she had died, burning alive in those eyes, for nothing was worse than what had been decreed to her. To walk blind and naked was bad enough, but to follow Marakon's path, even to find him, was surely impossible. How could she end his treachery even if she did find him?

Like a dead person, she let them pull her to her feet and lead her to another room where they sat her down. She stayed silent and stared at nothing as they cut her thick, black, curly locks from her head. Hair that Marakon had so recently run his hands through as they made love. With a sharp knife they shaved her head until it was smooth. She felt ugly, cold and already naked without her hair.

They undid and took the clothes from her body that she had so hastily put on that morning. Finally, they tied black cloth around her eyes, thick enough to shut out all the light. What did it matter? The light had already left her heart and she was simply living in a nightmare. She felt the tingle of magic as Hai bound her punishment to her like a yoke.

'For a day and night you will stand naked by the well and afterwards you will be given lesser clothes. Then you will follow the betrayer's path. The cloth around your eyes will burn and blind you forever if you try to remove it. These things will come undone when the betrayer has been found and his betrayal reversed. We pray to the goddess that you find a way to do this, lest our people perish forever. Now go.'

She was led stumbling outside and left to stand naked in the scorching sun by the well. Her only saving grace was that no one saw her tears since her blindfold soaked them up. She prayed for the night to come so the darkness would hide her shame.

With her eyes bound, her ears became sharper through the day. Soon she could hear the soft footfalls as people passed, their laughing voices dropping to shamed silence. She could almost feel their shocked, embarrassed stares. Usually the centre of the village was bustling with noise. Not today, not while she was here.

The sun got hotter, and her bare skin began to burn, but she welcomed the physical pain for it was nothing compared to the pain inside. Anger and shame rolled through her. She longed for the dawn, when she would leave this place and go into the jungle, following the path of the man she loved. Each moment moved by so slowly, each hour felt like an age.

Her body began to sag with the fatigue of standing for so long, but she would not let herself sit down, she would not show any sign of weakness. Sometimes she thought she swayed to and fro for everything became distorted in the sweltering heat without her eyes. She began to lose sense of her own dimensions and felt as if she had become a part of the ground she stood upon.

One of the elders brought her food and drink. She was so deep in her own mind that she didn't immediately recognise Sharnu's voice. "Food and water," she had said. Jarlain's throat was parched and her stomach empty, but she refused it with a single shake of her head. She decided then that she would no longer speak to any of her people again. It was her only way of fighting back.

Blessedly, the heat of the day began to wane.

As night fell the cool breeze of the evening offered her some relief. She heard the soft footfalls of someone approach—from the heaviness of them she concluded it must be a man. A strong, warm hand touched her shoulder and squeezed. She knew it was Tarn even before he spoke.

'Dear Jarlain, my half-sister. I'm so sorry for what has happened to you. If I could help you, you know I would. I know Marakon would never betray us willingly. Some great evil has been done to him and he is cursed still. Maybe you're the only one who can truly save him.'

Jarlain choked back a sob, but she could think of nothing to say even if she would have spoken.

'I know these are terrible times for you, and terrible times for us all ahead, so the elders have told us. I feel the changes in the air, in the forest, like no other. I see many things I do not tell others. Know that I've seen light at the end of the tunnel, and we can all find strength in that.' He gave her shoulder a final squeeze before turning away. She listened to his footfalls fade and felt the loneliness descend once more.

As the night drew on, the cold came and she shivered, hugging her bare arms around her, hoping she would die from exposure but knowing she wouldn't. With the darkness to hide her, she found a little peace within, a small space inside herself in which she could dwell, in which she might survive—just.

She wasn't sure if she slept standing up; intense weariness befuddled her mind. Her body was sore and aching all over but she wouldn't let it lie down, not this night.

When she felt the first rays of warmth touch her cheek, she finally moved her stiff and swollen legs. Her grasping hands found the edge of the well. Someone had left rough material upon it. It felt like sackcloth—what they used to store root vegetables. There were three holes cut into the base, for her head and arms, she supposed. The final insult, she thought, but she knew she deserved it.

She scrambled into it, desperate to hide the shame of her nudity. It barely came to mid-thigh and the material was horribly scratchy. Still, even this small amount of clothing gave her some strength. There was a long thin stick left there too and she realised someone had given it to her to help her find her way like a blind person.

Silently, emotionlessly, swinging her stick left and right like Ella the blind elder, she left the village she had lived in all her life. Even if she'd had eyes, she wouldn't look back. To be cast out felt ruthlessly unfair and a part of her was furious at Hai for shaming her so severely. The other part was riddled with guilt, forcing her to accept her punishment and leaving her in a state of confusion. She didn't know if she longed to return home or if, out of her own pride, she would never return again.

So many times had she walked this path from the village that it was easy to follow at first. As soon as it narrowed into jungle, she found herself veering left and right in confusion. Wherever she swished her stick there was something in the way. Roots tripped her over and branches scraped her face so many times she was soon bleeding and out of breath.

Every time she fell, her wounded leg throbbed painfully. She wanted nothing more than to curl up and die, but she forced herself to go on, desperately needing to be far away by nightfall from the people who had cast her away.

Her progress was painfully slow. Hunger and dehydration made her weak and delirious. The tinkling stream was a welcome noise. Scrambling low, she cupped her hands and did her best to swallow the muddy, grainy water. After, her groping fingers found the fallen fruits of a tallen tree and she tore the soft flesh away, gulping down the sweet insides.

Blinking back tears, she remembered Marakon telling her how he'd first fearfully eaten the strange fruit. Thinking of him made her smile. He was the only light in her life, leading her on. She would walk as far as she could, and then she would call the boatman, just as she had seen him do. Only he would know where Marakon had gone; only he could take her to him. Finding Marakon was all she existed for.

As the heat of the day faded, she searched for a place to sleep away from the predators and insects. It was virtually impossible to find anywhere suitable without her sight and she didn't dare try to remove the blindfold. Bushes were no good; they were too low and covered in ants, and she dared not sleep in any clearing either.

Finally, she climbed the gnarly boles of a tree she thought might be a bellon and, feeling like an animal, lodged herself into one of its wide, scooped branches. Most insects didn't like the acrid smelling bark of bellon trees, so she would be left alone by the worst of them. She hugged herself and fell into an exhausted sleep of vivid dreams, as if they sought to replace the sight that had been taken from her.

CHAPTER 6

A Witch in the City

'WHAT is it, Edarna?' said Naksu.

'That's the fifth time you've sighed in half an hour.'

Edarna turned from staring out of the window at the milling crowds on the streets below and looked at the seer sat. The albino woman was sitting on her bed reading a book in their small, shared room. The traitorous Mr Dubbins was asleep next to her. The cat was actually snoring, not purring, laying on his back with his feet in the air.

Edarna had found them a room to rent, complete with a fire and a tiny stove and oven, at the top of a rickety old shop just north of Carvon's main market square. Their shared room had seemed spacious at first, until they'd squeezed both beds in.

There was another room leading off from it, barely more than a big wardrobe, where Edarna had put her chest of witching items and a small sewing machine she'd purchased at the market. Cramped as it was, the rent was the cheapest she could find, and they were safe from prying eyes.

After so many years spent living alone on a tiny island, she found the huge bustling city gave her more vigour than she could remember. It filled her head with dreams of the riches she would make selling dragon scales.

'She's in the city, so Mr Dubbins said, but why have we yet to find her?' Edarna sighed again.

'We'll find Issa when the time is right,' said Naksu, putting down her book.

Edarna shook her head. 'Time's running out. Something's amiss. I should have found her already. Unless she's sick and bedbound, making her aura weak. If that's the case, then that's a worry.'

'I think you're more worried about meeting the Oracle than finding Issa,' Naksu replied soothingly.

The seer was correct. Even mentioning the Oracle raised Edarna's heart rate and she scowled.

Naksu smiled reassuringly. 'There's nothing to worry about. No harm will come to a witch whilst a seer is by her side, and the Temple is bound by the law of the land.

'No one outside the Temple, neither seers nor common folk, agree with what they did to the witches of Maioria. Indeed, what has been done in the name of religion is utterly despicable and should never have happened. Although it's wise to remember that it did happen a long time ago now.'

'It happened only yesterday, in the grand scheme of things.' Edarna snorted. 'Though few women have enough magic to be a seer, many women have a little talent with the arcane arts, enough to be a witch and help the people of their villages and towns. Why should they be denied to use the skills they *do* have?'

Naksu nodded. 'You know, we seers are convinced that the world got sicker when witches were persecuted and driven away. But there will come a time when witches are in good standing again.'

'Hmph, only when that corrupt Order of the Temple is gone.' Edarna sneered at the name. 'Order indeed. Forced upon the people. Hmph. Nevertheless, I *shall* be donning my banned green robe tomorrow, *and* I'll have Wandy at the ready for any nasty priestess tricks.'

'Well, I advise you to keep said Wandy hidden. You know how they are about weapons in the Temple,' Naksu said. 'The suspicions of the people worry me. Rumours that the Oracle will be assassinated are deeply unsettling, possibly because they could be true. Hykerry has been the Oracle for so long now, and she's been going mad since she was first anointed. There is another reason for my long journey from Myrn, you know.'

Edarna eyed Naksu critically. There was more this seer kept concealed than she revealed.

Naksu raised her hands. 'I don't tell all my missions to just anyone. Anyway, I was also coming to visit the Oracle. You know she thought her late daughter was the Raven Queen? She even sent letters to us by personal courier when her daughter was conceived in sacred ritual. She said she had been given a vision—that the child she carried would be the Raven Queen of prophecy.'

Edarna's mouth dropped. 'That old nutter? The Oracle? I know her child died soon after birth, though I didn't know the cause.' The Oracle really *was* mad then.

Naksu nodded. 'No one knows how she died. I was coming to speak to her about it as soon as we saw the dark moon of the Night Goddess rising. It's possible her daughter may have been one of Zanufey's chosen—for there can be three Raven Queens, though only one will survive to adulthood. Three chances to bring the light back into the world.'

Edarna worried the hem of her shawl. 'Then I don't think she'll take kindly to Issa, or what I'm about to tell her.'

Naksu brushed her hair in the mirror then smoothed her shirt. Today they would be meeting the Oracle, as arranged. She wasn't anxious like Edarna, only deeply curious as to what had happened to the woman's child; that she'd come to term at her age was enough of a surprise, as it was.

She'd visited the city taverns to discover the local gossip. Rumours were rife that the Oracle had gone completely mad since the attack on Celene had seen the disappearance of the High Priestess—who everyone knew really ran the Temple.

Cirosa was next in line to the Oracle, and now she was missing; the Temple had plunged into disarray and unrest. The struggle for the High Priestess's position had begun in earnest as ambitious priestesses vied for the ageing Oracle's favour.

She shook her head. Such enterprises that built themselves upon hierarchical power structures and control, always set themselves up for rivalry and fractures from within. Eventually they would tear themselves apart and crumble.

On Myrn, the leaders of the seers were more like wise advisors than rulers. They were called the Trinity—three seers superior in age, experience and service, chosen from amongst them by all the other seers.

Her friends said that she, with all her worldly experience, skill with the

Sight, and extensive travels, should one day be of the Trinity. But she wondered if that was what she really wanted. It would mean less travelling, which she loved, and staying on Myrn teaching others, managing and supervising.

Sometimes she wondered what kind of Seer of the Trinity she would make. Would she be powerful in magic like others had become? Would she live twice as long, as a handful had? She smiled at that. She was approaching her thirties and was still several decades too young to even be considered for the role.

Edarna emerged from her tiny workroom with a satisfied smile on her face. Naksu eyed her suspiciously. The witch often shut herself away, thinking no one would notice what she was up to, but Naksu could always feel her earthy witch's magic working away, even when she was sitting in the tavern next door listening to the local gossip.

The witch sneaked out of bed in the night, and that was when Naksu could feel clearly the movement of witch magic, coupled with the awful whiff of a witch's potion. She didn't mind what the witch got up to. Her magic, earthy and substance-based as it was, simply wasn't powerful enough to be of concern to her. Besides, Naksu was not one to pry and the witch meant no harm, working hard in her own way to help people. If it made Edarna happy, that was all that mattered.

'Honestly, Edarna, you're as secretive as you say seers are. What on earth are you up to in there?'

'You'll just have to wait and see, and no peeking when I'm not around—I'll know if you do. It's a surprise for someone, that's all.'

Edarna frowned and looked around the room. 'Hmm, we're going to need a bigger place and on the high street where I can set up shop. I've already got someone making posters to put up around Carvon. You wait and see, every witch in her right mind will be coming out of the woodwork to find me and what I've got to sell.' She grinned and rubbed her hands.

Naksu half smiled, half frowned. 'Nevertheless, we'd better get going. We don't want to miss our appointment with the Oracle.'

'Oh goody,' Edarna said with a scowl and busied herself getting ready.

Naksu watched her pull on her forest-green, velvet robe. The witch had a mixed look of pride and sadness on her face that moved her to speak.

'You may not know this, but the seers shielded many witches who sort refuge with us while the persecution raged. One or two even became seers.'

Edarna gave a half smile, her eyes glistening, but said nothing.

'We may have our differences, but witches and seers alike dislike the way the Temple has gone, all about order and control and turning religion into a business when it should only be about the spirit,' Naksu continued, pulling on her own sky blue robe.

'The more I think about it, the more I'm beginning to think the Ancients were wrong. Despite all their power and wisdom, it's clear to me that the orbs should never have been split. It may have kept Maioria's life-magic out of Baelthrom's hand for longer, but in the end all it did was make us weaker and divide us against each other—priestess against witch, wizard against seer, man against woman, elves, humans and dwarves against each other—the list goes on. It seems our fate was ready to play itself out regardless.'

'As much as I want to believe in the power and wisdom of the Ancients, I cannot help but agree with you,' Edarna said, slipping her wand into her belt and patting it.

'Ready?' Naksu said, picking up her white birch staff.

'Yup,' Edarna said with a scowl.

CHAPTER 7

Walking in Darkness

AS the warm light of dawn spread over the village, old Hai stood watching their future High Elder from the top room of the Elder's House. But the dawn held no warmth for him this morning. He'd not slept last night, and now he wondered if his punishment had been too severe—and yet it was no more severe than any of their punishments, for oath-breaking had been in the past. Indeed, it was far less, given the consequences of what may happen now Marakon had betrayed them to a nightmare beyond their shores.

But still, his heart was heavy and his bones weary. It wasn't easy being High Elder at his age, and he was keen for someone else to take over the role. But he was afraid; there was only darkness ahead—the great unknown that was the domain of the Night Goddess. And even he, with all his long years on this earth, could not advise his people or shelter them from the coming storm.

He watched with a heavy heart as Jarlain pulled on her sack clothing and blindly stumbled into the forest. He hoped and prayed that she'd return to them one day—he knew if she did, she would be more powerful and learned than he had ever been. But he also knew, in his heart of hearts, that there would be nothing for her to return to. The Hidden Ones had shown him the truth—that soon the people called the Gurlanka would be no more, but from the survivors would come another people. Jarlain would be part of the new people and, in a way, he felt as if he had exiled her for her own survival.

The sunlight spilled over the trees and hit the ground where she had stood. A shadow darted overhead and moments later a huge raven landed in the sunlight. It turned and looked directly up at him, waiting.

Hai left the window, leaning heavily on his twisted Halen Palm staff, and went outside to commune with the messenger of Zanu. He came to stand beside the bird. The weight of the world pressed down upon him and he felt as if he stood on the edge of a great chasm that separated knowledge with all its painful wisdom, and ignorance with all its painless bliss. Did he really want to know what the raven would reveal to him if he communed with it? *One must never fear the truth,* he reminded himself, and with a sigh he opened his mind to the bird.

The ground fell away and roaring filled his suddenly clear ears. He stood above a raging ocean, waves smashing and churning against each other in all directions as far as the eye could see. There was no land. Thunder cracked and lightning flared across a sky filled with smouldering clouds. Wind howled around him. Powerful magic moved. The storm was unnatural.

The winds of change and the seas of destruction, Hai thought, recognising the vision he had witnessed before.

The storm abated. Clouds flattened, the wind dropped and the sea calmed until it was no longer savage but still and brooding. Upon the horizon black dots appeared. They approached quickly and became large, black ships with sprawling masts and complex rigging so that they looked like spiders crawling upon the ocean surface. They moved so fast it would have been a sight to marvel at had they, and the beings they carried, not looked so terrifying.

They wore black metal that shone like beetle carapaces and they swarmed the decks just the same. Their faces were from nightmares: grey, wrinkled or taut skin pulled unnaturally back over deformed faces, and their eyes—their eyes he couldn't forget for they had no life in them.

Praise the light, they are dead! Soulless. Yet some unholy force moves them.

'Is it ended?' he spoke aloud whilst the vision gripped him.

Beyond the storm clouds the raven croaked. A face formed in the sky. Pale, flawless skin framed by long, black hair and eyes the colour of the sea. Those eyes watched him and he felt as if they looked into his soul.

She opened her mouth and seemed to be calling to him, but he couldn't hear what she said. Then the vision was gone.

Hai stood blinking and bathed in bright sunlight as the vision left him. He looked at the raven. It cawed, jumped into the air and disappeared above the jungle canopy.

'Go swiftly and deliver your message to all the peoples of this land,' Hai said. He gripped his staff, his soul heavy. They were coming. How long did he have? Days? Hours? What must he do now? Leave. They must go, all of them, and find their way to the Centre.

Jarlain continued to stumble through the jungle. She used her stick, tapping the ground and swaying it left and right. It had stopped her falling several times. Days must have passed. The only way she could tell the difference between night and day without her eyes was the drop in temperature and the sounds the animals and birds made. When the songbirds hushed and bats squeaked, she knew it was dark.

She stopped little, despite the weariness in her legs, the hunger in her belly, and the thirst in her throat. She was desperate to get as far away from her home as she could. Always she kept the sound of the sea within earshot to her right. It gave her a sense of direction and a feel of familiarity.

Even when she did stop, her sleep was short and restless, filled as it was with Marakon and Hai. She ate little, nibbling only on the fallen fruit she could find with her hands and feet. Her hands had become adept at feeling the bark of trees and recognising them. When she found a fruit-bearing tree she felt the ground for its fallen nourishment. Some of it was delicious but without her eyes to find the ripest ones, most she bit into were rotten.

Initially terrified of the dark, she was surprised at how quickly she overcame her fear of it. She supposed it was because her days were as dark as her nights, so why be afraid of the night?

She didn't think about much else other than her own survival; it took up all of her existence, and for that she was grateful. She didn't want to think about Hai or Marakon, or of how she had lost everything: her hair, her home, her heart... Her senses had become tuned intensively to her surroundings. The feel of leaves beneath her feet, the wind across her bald head, the sounds and smells of the forest, so full and so sharp. It was only when she slept that she was haunted by those she knew.

It was foolish, but in the beginning she talked to herself purely to hear the sound of her voice, a human voice, and to drive away the worry that she would forget how to speak. As the days wore on, she no longer spoke or feared going mad. Loneliness and darkness, these were her solitudes, her reality.

She was keenly aware of her body changing from within, becoming stronger, leaner and fitter than ever it had been. With no distractions and keenly heightened senses, she found all these changes happening rapidly. It was only when she stopped being afraid of the dark, of going mad and of being alone forever that she embraced her new existence.

Having accepted her predicament, a sense of power filled her. And with that sense of empowerment came a new level of insight, a new type of vision. In the past her visions of the future had always come spontaneously, usually when she least wanted them, showing great changes.

This new insight was far subtler. She received simple, smaller visions of the future—utterly mundane happenings most of the time, if not all of the time. When her mind was still and calm, the visions were clearest.

She had them now. If she rounded the next tree, there would be a fox and she would startle it. In her mind's eye she could see the fox sat blissfully unaware and licking her shining coat.

Her stick slapped a tree and the leaves rustled as the fox bounded away. She focused her mind again and the vision came. Ahead, through the ferns and five paces to the left would be a tallen tree and there might be ripe fallen fruit. She could see two perfect fallen fruits.

Though the image was blurry and faded into a strange red hue, she could make most things out, such as trees and rocks and other objects in her path. She wondered why everything was tinged red, as if she looked through red glass at the world. Some things were dark red, almost black— perhaps these were shadows—whilst all else varied in shades of red ombre. Had these little visions always been there, or had she somehow unlocked a greater skill within her?

She stopped and focused on her inner vision until she could just about make out the path directly ahead of her. As soon as she started walking, the vision of the path would waver and disappear, but her memory of it would remain, enabling her to walk forwards unhindered. She smiled.

In the old days, the elders said people could see without seeing. Was this what they meant? It was a level of insight she'd never have thought possible. A skill she would never have tried to learn, had not necessity and survival forced her to do so.

When the birds stopped singing, signalling that the day was ending, she stopped walking and wiped the sweat from her forehead. She hadn't washed in days and knew she must stink and be covered in dirt, but she didn't care. Her appearance was as it should be for an oath-breaker, a betrayer of her people, an exile—she was almost proud of it.

She straightened her back and took a deep breath. It was time to call the boatman; Marakon had told her his name. Could just anybody call him? Was she worthy enough? If he did not come, then her life was as meaningless as it was hopeless, and she would swim away into the ocean until she drowned.

She turned to her right and clambered over roots towards the sound of the sea. Now she had a destination, it seemed to take an age to crawl through bushes to get there. She smiled when her bare feet, cut and bruised in a hundred places, touched hot, soft sand then cool ocean water.

The salt water stung her scrapes as she waded in, but the healing pain was welcome. She slipped her head under, feeling the freedom of her shorn head, feeling the sea wash the dirt and tears and shame away.

After she had washed she stood in the late evening sun to dry. It didn't take long in her thin sackcloth. Being salty felt better than being dirty and stinking.

What if he doesn't come? What will become of me? He must come. He must. There was no point waiting any longer.

'Murlonius,' she spoke the name slowly, loudly almost. 'Murlonius,' she repeated louder, and then more quietly, 'Murlonius.'

She chewed her lip, her heart pounding offbeat, reminding her of the desperateness of her situation. If he didn't come, she would die. *Great goddess, please make him come.*

An age seemed to pass until she distinctly heard the waves stop lapping. The wind dropped, and everything fell still and silent. She could hear nothing but her own heart, even her vision was empty.

'Jarlain,' an old man's voice said beside her, making her jump.

Murlonius looked at the sorry sight before him—the woman with bound eyes and shaved head, barely dressed in sackcloth and cuts covering her feet and legs. Every bare patch of her skin was either bruised, muddied or scraped, but more than this he saw a broken woman whose heart bled like an open wound. He could see clearly what stained her aura.

'You have been cursed and banished, just like the one you love, the one you want me to take you to,' he said. 'When you became one with this man, you helped him heal by sharing the burden of his curse.'

'Can you see so much?' The woman's voice was hoarse, maybe with disuse, but he detected wonder there.

'That's as much as I can see.'

'I love him, regardless,' she whispered, quivering fearfully like a deer.

'That's the only thing that can save him and you, and save anyone.' He sighed. He thought of his own love, Yisufalni, and his heart grew heavy.

'Do you have a hand in his fate?' she asked.

'No more than a man can hold back the tide,' he said. 'I help when I'm called and I do what I can, but no more. Why are you cursed and banished?'

'I committed a crime against my people by withholding information about Marakon, the man I fell in love with. I didn't do it out of malice, but out of fear. I was afraid of what I saw in the future, and now it may mean the death of my people.'

'Those few who can see anything in the future at all should be very afraid,' he said. 'It may mean their death...or their beginning. No ill ever came of love.'

She was silent, pondering his words. 'Only time will tell,' she replied finally.

The depth of her sorrow and her wisdom moved him. He gave a half smile.

'Take me to him,' she said and stepped closer. She clasped her hands in front of her. 'There's nothing for me here now. If you leave me here I'll die.'

'I can take you only where your deepest, heartfelt desire dictates,' he said. 'The passenger decides upon the destination; I but guide the boat.'

'That's good enough for me.' She gave a weak smile and reached forwards. He took her hands, helped her into the boat and sat her down.

'Whom do you serve?' he asked, picking up his oars as she settled herself. She took a long moment before answering.

'I serve no one, sir. But if I did, it would be the darkness, for since my heart was broken and my eyes bound, there is nothing but darkness.'

He smiled down at her and replied, 'Then you would be wrong. It's only in darkness you walk, but you serve love, the only true light.'

He pushed the boat from the shore and watched as the mist and the glittering Sea of Opportunity became their world.

CHAPTER 8

The Temple of Carvon

EDARNA in her green robes, and Naksu in her white, caused some commotion in the city as they walked the streets of Carvon towards the temple.

Naksu forced a smile over her grimace as the people stopped to stare and point at them, whispering to each other their surprise. There seemed no malice in their stares, only genuine shock.

Edarna grinned and stood proud, basking in the attention, whilst Naksu pulled her hood lower. By nature and by training, she always preferred to avoid drawing any attention herself. She thought it strange, especially since witches were the ones that had been persecuted, and not seers.

Beyond the chaos of chimneys and rooftops, rose the pristine white turrets of the Temple of Carvon. Ordered, confident and unyielding, the temple unabashedly dominated the rest of the city it looked down upon. Even the pale grey walls of Carvon Castle, complete with its dazzling white-water rivers cascading around it, seemed dulled of splendour in comparison.

Sunshine glinted and sparkled off the gilded gold that rimmed the temple's roof. It was the biggest and most impressive Temples of the Goddess, and as such was the home of the Oracle. Despite its majesty, the temple seemed as cool as this morning's autumn sun.

Naksu couldn't help but notice that the buildings this end of town seemed poorer than the rest. The roofs of the houses were in desperate need of repair. Front doors were old and shabby, and where windows had broken, rather than be mended, they had been hastily bricked or boarded up—their owners unable afford the cost of fixing them.

Here, people dressed poorly. Ripped trousers stayed ripped, with many a patch holing up another patch. Tatty shawls wrapped around thin, hunched shoulders. Some shoes were mismatched and most had clearly never seen a cobbler.

Few smiled. Most looked at the ground as they walked, bent over with the burden of their lives. The streets were littered with garbage and the smell of rotting was almost overpowering.

'It's as if the temple is sucking the money and the joy out of the people surrounding it,' Edarna muttered, echoing Naksu's thoughts.

'The love of the goddess should light the people up, not spread darkness and poverty.' Naksu scowled.

The dark, huddling streets opened up onto the wide bridleway ringing the temple, but they could not get any closer because it was surrounded by a ten-foot high white stone wall. Between the wall and temple were extensive gardens filled with magnificent trees from all over the Known World.

'The place must have fifty gardeners,' Edarna said, staring up at the huge branches and yellow leaves of a golden maple from Intolana. 'There's more money in the gardens here than in Carvon Castle,' she added as they approached the huge entrance gates.

Naksu pursed her lips. The beauty of the trees was marred by the ugly poverty that surrounded them. 'Why is there a wall here? One would think a religion serving the people would let them inside at all times.'

The tall, double gates were also ten feet high and a masterpiece of metalwork. The metal was moulded and woven into intricate flowers and ivy, and finished off with a layer of gold that shone in the sunlight.

'The "Golden Gates,"' Naksu said, noticing Edarna shiver and pale.

It was rumoured that many witches had met their death beyond these gates. She wasn't quite sure if it was true or a metaphor used for the loss of their livelihood and dignity. One thing was for sure, despite their beauty, the gates were meant to keep the common folk out.

Two priest guards towered above them, eyeing them up and down disdainfully. Over their chainmail they wore sleeveless white robes, distinguishing them from the city guard. Both held long spears, the tips of which looked deadly sharp.

'We have an appointment with the Oracle,' Naksu said.

They looked at her and she detected a hint of unease. She remembered in her travels that no initiate of the Temple seemed to enjoy being in the company of a seer; perhaps they were taught to fear them and their greater powers.

'No witches allowed,' said one and sniffed.

'Witches are allowed because the Oracle arranged the meeting,' Naksu said, finding with surprise that her temper was already rising.

If *she* was having trouble even entering the temple with an appointment, how many common folk had been denied outright? These priests were supposed to be looking after the spiritual needs of the people and instead they lorded it over them. And it's not like it was free either. Any meeting or services rendered by the Temple cost a pretty penny. Even so much as confessional talk was expensive, and they should always be free, as it was decreed in the past.

'No witches,' said the other and looked away.

'We are guests and invitees. Let us pass,' Naksu commanded.

She had spoken quietly but the air stilled at her voice. The guards shifted uncomfortably and she caught a nervous glance from Edarna. Perhaps the witch could feel the subtlest movement of her magic in the air. She glared at the guards silently. The minutes passed.

'No witches' robes then,' said the first guard scowling, clearly determined to walk away with something from this quiet battle.

'I'll never be de-robed again,' Edarna hissed.

'Edarna, do as he says.' Naksu sighed.

'Over my dead, rotting body,' Edarna replied, her gleaming eyes never leaving the guards, her hand feeling for her wand. She was ready for a battle to the death, or so it looked to Naksu.

Naksu spoke again in a quiet voice, but a voice that could not be disobeyed. 'Edarna, don't do it for them, do it for me—your friend.'

Edarna looked at her incredulously and opened her mouth to protest.

'You can put it back on inside!' Naksu all but shouted the mind-speak to the witch.

Edarna blinked. In stunned shock she took off her robe, much to Naksu's relief. She grasped the witch's arm.

'Let us pass,' she commanded the guards, keeping her face hard as stone. Without a word the guards opened the well-oiled gates and shuffled sideways. The witch and the seer walked through, Edarna with her nose in the air and Naksu scowling.

'You said that *in my mind?*' Edarna whispered loudly when they had passed.

Naksu looked at the shocked witch. 'I used mind-speak to get through your stubbornness!'

'You can use *mind-speak?*' Edarna hissed.

'Yes, many seers can, to varying degrees, but we don't use it often and only in emergencies. After all, it's not so rare. Many non-seers have the mind-speak, Daluni talent—not least of all elves and Karalanths. So it's not to be trusted as a secret way to communicate. It's also rude and disrespectful to others who don't have the gift. Seers are often reminded in their training that they must never be afraid to speak their truths aloud, even if it costs us our lives—especially if it costs us our lives.'

'But, but, you're not Daluni and only the ancients had mind-speak like *that*. Are seers trained in it?' Edarna stuttered.

'Yes of course, but it only goes well if they're young enough and their brains aren't full of nonsense already,' said Naksu.

'So, that's all part of a seer's secret training?' said Edarna.

'It's not really secret, we just don't advertise to the world what we do. Anyone who comes to Myrn can find out anything they want about us. We're only secret and hidden to the eyes of Baelthrom and his horde. You must remember that Myrn is the closest country to Baelthrom's advance that's still free, and long may it stay that way. He knows about seers, of course, but he does not think we have much power—the result of us keeping to ourselves and leading relatively secret lives.' Naksu held her hands to her chest, silently praying that the Immortal Lord would never find their hidden islands.

'Now,' she said, looking around. They were alone on a path surrounded by trees. 'It's safe to put on your robe.'

Edarna nodded and, with her head high, proudly slipped back into her green robes. She smoothed her front with a satisfactory sigh and set off at a pace towards the temple.

Naksu followed, hiding a grin. To Edarna, the witch's robes were their usual deep green, but to anyone else they looked grey and a little worn as any traveller's might. It wasn't completely right to pull a magic trick on someone else, but she consoled herself that her barest magic was there to protect the witch until she had felt the Temple out and decided it was safe.

They walked through the ornate gardens filled with late summer flowers and carefully pruned bushes, to arrive at the sweeping white steps leading up to the temple doors. Young Temple Initiates, priests and priestesses in a mix of grey novice robes and middle-ranking brown robes, huddled in groups chatting.

Others flowed in and out of the temple, all under the watchful eyes of a handful of white-robed priestesses who scowled at Edarna and Naksu as they passed. Perhaps that's how they treated anybody they deemed to be "common people." Other than that, they entered the Temple without trouble.

Inside, the reception hall was a similar affair with groups of initiates gossiping in hushed voices. They turned and eyed the witch and the seer as they passed. It didn't seem that they were used to having many visitors at all, thought Naksu.

'Everyone's so young. Where are the adults?' said Edarna.

'Quite. I guess they're busy doing other things, though what, is beyond me,' Naksu said, looking up at the silver-gilded chandelier above their heads. Beyond it, the domed ceiling rose to a magnificent height. The walls were pristine white, and in places decorated in beautiful gold filigree. Huge windows of stained glass rose from floor to ceiling, and though they were closed, the Temple seemed cold.

Naksu shivered and pulled her robes closer. The place just felt so empty of the divine, the opposite of what it should be.

'A long time ago, these temples were open to the people and filled with joy. Now I see only Temple Initiates,' Naksu said.

'Women like us were once all priestesses of the Temple,' Edarna nodded, 'and the people came from miles around. Now there aren't even chairs to sit on. Look, they seem so lost here.' She nodded to a young couple dressed as ordinary folk in a skirt, trousers and shirts.

The woman held parchment in her hands, a worried frown creasing her brow. The man squeezed his flat cap in his hands as he looked around. They looked out of place and humble amongst the proud priests and priestesses. The woman was pale-face and when she turned, Naksu noticed she was pregnant. She went over to them and Edarna followed.

'Who are you looking for, kind people?' Naksu smiled warmly at the couple. They seemed to relax a little.

'We wanted to bless our child and organise a baptism, but the Oracle cannot see us, not until it's born,' the man explained. 'But even then we don't think we can afford two silver pieces…'

'Two silver pieces?' Edarna exclaimed. 'Just for a baptism? It's a crime,' she said loudly.

Priestesses looked in their direction and Naksu shot her a warning look. The witch shut her mouth. Naksu pursed her lips and turned back to the couple.

'I'm Naksu Feyrin, a Seer of Myrn. I can bless your unborn child should you wish, and I don't charge—'

'I'm Edarna Higglesworth, Witch of the Western Isles,' Edarna cut in. Naksu sighed as she rattled on. 'I can tell you if your child is breached or sick, or will be healthy and strong. I can tell you the sex if you wish,' she ended with a little bow.

The couple looked at each other and smiled.

'Please, we wish it. Both. When can we do this?' the woman asked breathlessly.

'Right here and now. The goddess requires no fancy ceremony or special time for blessings of love. May I?' Naksu raised her hands.

'Yes, please,' the woman said and Naksu placed her palms gently upon the woman's swelling belly.

She closed her eyes and cleared her mind. She could see the beating heart of the baby, and beyond it the soft, pale light of the soul who was coming in. She smiled at the soul and emanated feelings of peace and love to it. It responded back with the same feelings, as all unborn souls did. She could see a long thread of silver-gold stretching forwards and backwards from the soul and its aura shimmered gold like sunlight.

'It will live a long life,' she said quietly without opening her eyes. 'An old, gentle soul awaits to come in. Feygriene is strong with this one. You will have a loving child.'

She focused on the golden-silver thread stretching forward. Clouds of darkness surrounded the soul's future, but the soul itself remained silver and gold and untainted by the dark. She had seen those clouds of darkness surrounding unborn souls before and it always left her feeling uneasy.

'There will be turbulence, for we live in uncertain times, but your child has known these before. Your child will weather them.

'Great Source of All, bring love and happiness to this child.' Naksu smiled and opened her eyes, seeing the familiar shock on their faces as the blue of the Sight slowly dissipated from her corneas.

There were tears of happiness in the young woman's eyes.

'Eh-hem, may I?' Edarna said and raised her hands. The woman nodded eagerly.

'Hmm, yes,' Edarna said, bending close to the woman's stomach. 'Hmm, a girl for sure. Hmmmm, she's healthy so far, though she'll be small. She is upright at the moment, but in a manner in which she will turn easily as she grows,' Edarna stood up smiling triumphantly. 'If you want to assist her turn, then find yellow fallow blooms just before the first frost comes. Take it steeped once a day until the birth.'

'Thank you,' the woman said, grasping both Naksu's and Edarna's hands.

'It's a pleasure.' Edarna bowed. Naksu inclined her head with a smile and the happy couple left.

'What on Earth could the Oracle have done for them anyway?' Edarna tutted.

'Quite,' agreed Naksu.

They made their way along an exquisite turquoise marble floor until they came to an oak door. Outside, standing proud with her white staff, was a tall, thin, white-robed priestess. Her grey hair was scraped back from her scalp and her hawk-like nose and cold blue eyes accentuated her bird-like appearance.

'We have an appointment with the Oracle. I'm Seer Naksu,' said Naksu.

The priestess eyed her disdainfully then spoke. 'The Oracle is busy today. Your meeting will have to wait until next week.'

The witch and the seer glanced at each other then back at the priestess.

'There must be a mistake. We received a letter from the Oracle herself. Tell her that the seers she has been requesting for so frequently are here.' Naksu gave a subtle flick of her wrist as she spoke, lending weight to her command and her refusal to be sent away.

The priestess shuffled uncomfortably as if wondering what to say. Then with a nod she disappeared back through the door. Before she had time to close it, the sound of women giggling could be heard and the smell of perfume wafted out.

'Busy, is she?' Naksu arched an exasperated eyebrow at Edarna who shook her head.

The minutes passed and Naksu and Edarna shuffled restlessly.

The priestess emerged, more red-faced than before. 'The Oracle will see you now, as long as it's quick,' she said tightly.

Naksu huffed. 'She sent for us, not the other way round,' she muttered, stalking through the door.

Edarna scowled at the priestess as she passed, her expression turning to one of intrigue as they entered the next room.

The room was huge, at least thirty yards square, with a domed ceiling towering above them. Tall, stained-glass windows, in sets of three, rose from floor to ceiling. Directly beneath the centre of the dome was an overly ornate, white dais, larger and more opulent than the King of Frayon's throne room.

With all the light, the room was very bright. The plush red sofas and cushions lining the white walls stood out starkly, like blood staining silk sheets. Cushions were discarded upon the floor and most of the chairs looked like they had recently been in use. Wine bottles and glasses—some empty, some half-full—also littered the floor amongst the fallen cushions.

A giggling gaggle of young, heavily made-up and brightly costumed men and women were quickly leaving the room at the back via a small door. The door shut, leaving Naksu and Edarna alone in the now silent, massive room.

Before the dais, a great, black marble flower with a white centre decorated the floor. Naksu knew that, given the correct magical command, the flower's petals would descend one under the other to create a winding stairwell down into the Mother's Chamber—the most sacred and blessed part of the temple.

The priesthood thought this was a secret known only to them, but seers and witches were also aware of the Mother's Chamber, for it had once been a part of all their knowledge a long time ago. That was until the Order of the Goddess decided to hide away sacred knowledge and decreed only those of the Order would be allowed to know such things.

Naksu's eyes came to rest upon the dais that dominated the room beyond the marble flower. Long, smooth, white marble steps flowed up to a large, gold-gilded chair, draped in velvet and richer than a king's. Besides the chair on a slender iron pedestal was a clear crystal ball, half a foot in diameter.

Naksu closed her eyes and focused upon the crystal ball. It had magic, powerful magic, but it was being used strangely. Almost as if energy was flowing out of it even though there was no one obviously there.

Her concentration was broken as the door at the back was flung open. Three people emerged talking loudly.

'Stop fussing, Jen, I don't need a rest!' A red-faced woman with long, greying-brown hair said. Naksu immediately recognised the Oracle, Hykerry, though she had not seen the women for well over a decade. The middle-aged, black-haired woman called Jen apologised and stopped trying to adjust the Oracle's neck ruffle. Instead she led her to the dais by the arm.

Walking the other side of the Oracle was a tall, slender man who also led her by the arm as if she were infirm or drunk. Indeed, she did seem to wobble as she walked, but whether she was old or filled with wine, Naksu couldn't be sure. Her huge skirt and overly fancy ruffles were obviously not helping her progress.

Naksu and Edarna composed themselves silently as they watched the doddering Oracle climb the steps and plonk herself on the chair. She pushed her large spectacles up her nose and squinted down at them, her pale brown eyes made huge by the thick glass.

'Now then,' her high-pitched voice grated. 'Who are you?'

CHAPTER 9

Night Watch

ASAPH was roused from his deep and enjoyable sleep by a loud knocking on his door.

He groaned, stretched and rolled over. The twins, Thane and Bayel, were peering into the room.

'What do you want? It's not even dawn yet.'

'Come now, Asaph. Your horse is ready and the others are waiting,' they whispered.

Damn, he'd forgotten the scouting trip today. Staying in bed a few more hours sounded perfect, and now he wished that he hadn't signed up to it. From what he'd overheard the cooks saying of the king's son in the kitchens, Prince Petar was an annoying, self-obsessed fop who looked down on everyone else. He didn't fancy meeting royalty, but there was no getting out of it now.

With a sigh, he dragged himself out of bed. He couldn't keep them waiting, not when he'd agreed to join them, but why did they have to get up so early? Having dragon blood in his veins, it seemed utterly illogical to do anything without Feygriene's light warming his body.

Dressing quickly, he pulled on his boots, slipped out the door and followed the broad backs of the brown-haired twins silently through the hallways of Carvon Castle. Most people still slept and it was dark but for the odd dim lantern. On the ground floor a side door lead out to the stables. He stepped out into a crisp autumn morning and wrapped his cloak closer, missing the warmth of his bed.

The twins rubbed their hands together, their breath rising as mist in the cool air. He'd met them only last night after dinner. Apparently King Navarr had asked them to specifically invite him on their scouting party. His daily run alone, outside the city walls, had clearly not gone unnoticed. Whether the king thought he needed some company or just a job to do, Asaph would never know.

Initially, he was reluctant, preferring to keep his own company than be bothered making new friends, but the thought of getting outside and away from the increasingly boring castle and the loud busy city was very appealing.

Issa was back, and he was happy about that, but she seemed even more distant—as if what happened in the Storm Holt had made her wary of him or worse. He dreaded to know the details, but it's not like he'd much time to ask her since he'd barely seen her.

She was busy with her own life and he felt like a dolt waiting on her every word, wondering what she would like to do that might involve him. He needed time to himself to be himself and live his own life. Joining a scouting party—like he used to do with the Fearsome Four—was one way to do it. Fist fighting was another. He often thought about sneaking off and trying to win fights for the fun of it, but the thought of disobeying his father didn't sit well.

The smell of horses and hay filled his nostrils as they approached the stables. The twins grinned at him, their identical white teeth gleaming in the dawn light.

'Ready to ride fast?' Thane said—or at least he thought it was Thane.

'You bet.' Asaph smiled back, though he felt otherwise. He still didn't feel comfortable riding horses and wondered if he ever would. The twins slapped him on the back. So far they seemed to be the most amicable and easy-going young men he'd ever met.

Holding the reins of two horses was Yusov. A black-haired, swarthy-skinned young man with slicked-back hair and an impressively sculpted thin beard and moustache. His clothing was as groomed as his beard: black leather and tight-fitting with an expensive-looking, claret silk scarf wrapped around his neck. He had an earring too—a single, black onyx stud that glistened in the light. He bowed slightly to Asaph and passed him Ironclad's reins. Yusov, as much as Asaph had seen of him last night, was a man of few words, but his dark eyes were sharp and appeared to miss nothing.

Duskar stuck his head out of the stables and neighed at Asaph, surprising him.

'I think that one is missing his mistress,' Yusov said. He had an accent Asaph still couldn't place.

'Yes, aren't we all? She seems too busy for anyone.' Asaph sighed.

'Women.' Yusov shook his head, then winked. Asaph laughed.

'Yusov! Where's my saddle? My favourite saddle with the little red embroidery on it?' A well-spoken, commanding voice came from within the stables.

The twins grinned at each other and Yusov sighed, rolling his eyes.

'Coming, Your Royal Highness.' Yusov disappeared into the darkness of the stables.

'Don't call me that, you know it vexes me,' the voice muttered sulkily. 'I'm only trying to find my lucky saddle.'

'Prince Petar is not a mean man,' whispered Bayel.

'But he's not that good at much,' added Thane.

They grinned and waited patiently for the prince Asaph had yet to meet in person.

The man who emerged from the stables was tall and lanky with a big flop of sandy-coloured hair that he brushed back from his face. His blue eyes rested on Asaph and looked him up and down, considering him thoroughly.

'My father's spoken a lot about you. What is it, Aphas?' he said. There was a hint of disdain in his voice, maybe even jealousy.

'It's Asaph,' Asaph said. He noticed the desperate look on Thane's face and quickly added, 'Your Highness.'

Petar seemed to relax at this. 'Right, Asaph, good to have you along. Just don't hold us up any longer.' He turned away to mount a huge bay horse.

'Yes, your highness,' Asaph muffled, feeling a mix of indignation and guilt. He wasn't the one delaying everyone by looking for a fancy saddle. Still, he daren't say anything back to the heir of Frayon. He gripped Ironclad's reins. The palomino mare looked at him, unblinking.

'Now don't you show me up,' he whispered. She snorted.

She didn't prance as much as she used to when he was near, for which he was grateful. Hoping no one was watching, he clambered uneasily into the saddle. The last thing he wanted was to look like a fool. He turned

Ironclad and she followed the others.

Once outside the city gates, the men set off at a gallop towards the forest. Asaph clung onto Ironclad for dear life. The horse, now with the other horses, seemed determined not to fall behind. He prayed the others didn't see the desperate look on his face.

The forest loomed dark and foreboding in the dull dawn light. The air was chill at speed and he was glad he'd snapped up his gauntlets on the way out. They blessedly dropped to a canter and then a trot as the forest closed in around them. The prince turned and looked at him, as if to check he'd kept up. Asaph smiled back at the look of surprise on the prince's face, but he turned away. It was clear he was going to have to prove his worth to the young prince.

The path through oak trees narrowed, forcing them to trot no more than two astride. Asaph sat in the centre with the prince and Yusov leading, and the twins trailing behind.

'So, what are we scouting for?' Asaph asked cheerily.

'Father said you were used to scouting for goblins,' said Petar. 'Well, the things here are much bigger than that. Recently we took down a foltoy and several death hounds—there always seem to be some lurking about. We also make sure wolves and bears don't get too close to our farms.'

He turned around to give Asaph a good hard look down his nose. 'Hopefully you know how to use that sword you carry; who knows what we might find.'

Asaph smiled tightly. Retorting harshly to the condescending prince would not go down too well, and he was already in his father's bad books.

'I know how to use it,' he replied softly and looked away.

'We took down the foltoy not a week past,' Thane explained. 'Gave Petar's uncle a nasty gash on his leg. We were lucky to get a clear shot.'

Asaph remembered the carnage after the attack on the Karalanth's village—the corpses of friend and foe littering the ground, the blood soaking into the earth. He didn't fancy witnessing that again. He wanted to tell them about the Dromoorai and Dread Dragon he had faced and taken down alone—it would certainly earn him respect—but couldn't bring himself to reveal his dragon self. They probably wouldn't believe him anyway.

'We faced foltoy, death hounds and a Dromoorai,' he said quietly.

'No way,' Bayel said, his brother mirroring the shock on his face. Petar guffawed in disbelief.

Asaph nodded. 'South of here in a Karalanth settlement. It attacked us. We were lucky to survive.'

He took a deep breath and described how they'd fought and defeated the Dromoorai and Life Seekers without mentioning his dragon self. The twins and Yusov listened enthralled whilst Petar kept his face blank, though Asaph was sure he caught a hint of wonder there. Perhaps the prince would respect him now, at least a little bit.

'Karalanths are savages,' Petar scoffed when Asaph finished.

Asaph straightened, controlling his anger. He opened his mouth to explain how brave his friends were, but Yusov spoke first.

'They're warriors, like those of old.'

The prince smirked. 'They're uncivilised, uneducated and rut in forests.'

'The ones I knew were the bravest people I've ever met,' Asaph spoke softly, feeling his face colour. He decided to say no more and they rode in silence.

The five men travelled for hours riding deep into the forest. Asaph revelled in the aliveness of it, the rich smell of pine, the endless stretch of dark trunks, green canopies and rich earth. Nothing but the sound of birds and animals filled the air. He could almost imagine he was back with the Kuapoh, and a pang of homesickness hit him. He was on a scouting party again and it felt good to be with others of a similar age outside the stuffy walls of the castle and overcrowded city. He wondered how Jommen and Kahly were. Did they miss him? Would he ever see them again?

The rain came—a brief shower dripping through the trees, but heavy enough to soak them. He enjoyed it, the cold drops invigorating him. The prince hated it, however, and soon began to grumble.

'I hate these outings. I wish father wouldn't send us on them so often. They're mostly boring and especially annoying when we have to camp out. I'd rather be back in my room reading or fencing with Gerald.'

'We're camping?' Asaph said brightly. Sleeping out in the open after being in a stifling bedroom for so long was very appealing. He could watch the stars if the clouds cleared and listen to the sounds of night animals.

'For two nights,' said Thane. 'That's how long it takes to circulate the Outer Perimeter.'

They'd explained last night that the Outer Perimeter was a very rough pathway that circled Carvon, serving to mark the city's rural borders. It was many miles long and took two to three days to travel on horseback.

'I miss my bed already.' Petar scowled.

An hour later, the rain stopped and the sun came out to dry everything. The hairs on Asaph's neck prickled. He glanced around and his eyes fell on a black shape hunched and hidden in the bushes ahead. His hand dropped to his sword and he hissed at the others to stop.

'What are we stopping for now?' huffed the prince, then squealed as the black shape stood up.

The horses whinnied and pranced; weapons were yanked from their sheaths and crossbows raised. The foltoy stood up and faced them, standing half again as tall as a man and more fearsome than a bear. Staying out of range, its pointed ears twitched and yellow eyes gleamed. There was a deer carcass at its feet and blood and gore dripped from its teeth. It snarled, dropped on all fours and readied to pounce, utterly fearless despite being outnumbered.

The prince was closest but Yusov, his protector, jumped his horse in front of him. His rapier was drawn. Asaph's sword was also drawn but it was Thane who attacked first, leaping his horse forwards into range and firing an arrow from his crossbow. It hit home in the beast's shoulder but its tough skin prevented it from going deep. It roared and lunged.

Not knowing how to fight on horseback, Asaph jumped off Ironclad and bounded forwards, reaching the creature just as Yusov did. The foltoy went for Yusov's horse first, allowing Asaph to sink his sword between its ribs. Yusov danced his mount and sliced the foltoy's face. Black blood sprayed over them, barely halting the beast. Two more arrows thudded into its neck. It fell to the ground with a gurgling sigh and lay twitching in a pool of black.

The twins and the prince cheered. Yusov and Asaph clasped each other's shoulders grinning, breathless and blackened by the foltoy's blood. They stood there for a moment, senses sharpened, waiting for more to attack. None did and they relaxed.

'Well, that was close. Well done Yusov,' the prince said, his hands shaking as he wiped the sweat from his face. 'But now we appear to have lost a horse.' He glared at Asaph.

Asaph looked around, but Ironclad was nowhere to be seen. He sighed.

'Crap.'

'Don't worry. It takes quite a bit of training to fight from horseback, and only those in the King's Court train to be knights,' Yusov explained. 'You'll also need a proper bred and trained horse for that.'

'She might have run all the way back home. Horses spook easily and run far,' the prince said.

'Come up beside me. My horse is strong enough to carry two.' Bayel offered him a hand and he swung up onto the man's heavy black stallion.

They searched for Ironclad for hours and were just about to give up when Asaph caught a neigh in the distance. Yusov's horse also heard it and neighed back.

'That way.' Asaph pointed into the trees.

They found Ironclad in a thicket, covered in sweat and her eyes wild as she pranced. Her loose rein had caught around a branch and held her fast.

'There, there, easy now.' Asaph slipped off Yusov's horse. She rolled her eyes in panic. He'd watched Issa talk to horses and noticed how they always calmed at her soothing voice, but Ironclad eyeballed him fearfully as he approached and he was keenly aware of the other men watching him. The horse did stop prancing as he untangled her reins, but her shoulders still quivered and she tossed her head as he mounted. He prayed she wouldn't buck him off.

'Right then, enough time has been wasted,' said Petar. 'We'd better move fast if we want to reach Hanging Rock before dark.' Without waiting, he set his horse off at a canter.

They moved too fast to carry conversation, but they did make it to Hanging Rock before full dark.

As its name suggested, Hanging Rock was a huge overhang of rock on the lee side of a craggy hill.

'It provides the perfect protection against the wind and rain, as well as against beasts and vagabonds trying to sneak up on us,' Thane said as they tethered the horses.

The twins set up camp whilst Asaph went with Yusov to collect firewood. The prince busied himself with his own numerous packs. He seemed to have twice as many as anyone else. Perhaps Frayon princes weren't expected to help on excursions and instead got others to do everything for them.

Firewood was plentiful and they soon returned with armfuls of it. The prince was still busy with his own stuff. Asaph had his sword, his cloak, a flagon of water and a small pack of food. He considered it all he needed in the world—apart from Issa, who didn't seem to feel the same, and Coronos, who had forgotten he existed.

The prince unrolled a thick ground sheet and two soft fleece blankets, smoothing them down carefully under the most protected part of the rock. His bed looked rather comfortable considering that all Asaph would be sleeping on was his horse's blanket and his cloak. Asaph set about building the campfire and forgot the preening prince. Soon it was blazing and he settled himself beside it, enjoying the roar of the flames and the heat on his face. He was in the forest under the stars, far from civilisation. He was free.

Their simple dinner of hot, smoked beans and bread was delicious. Afterwards, Bayel brought out his silver flask of rum with a grin.

'The finest Atalanph rum,' he said and poured a shot into five small silver cups.

Along with the others, Asaph downed it in one, feeling it burn down his throat and fill him with warmth. Bayel poured another and they sipped it slowly as they chatted late into the night.

When yawns spread, Asaph lay back and looked up at the stars. Just above the horizon he could see the edge of the empty blackness of the Dark Rift. It wasn't always visible. Coronos had said it was growing larger and getting closer, and that it had nearly doubled in size since he'd been a lad. Asaph looked to another part of the sky where a thick cluster of stars twinkled. He wanted to enjoy tonight, not be reminded of the darkness spreading over the world.

'We'll keep watch, an hour at a time like usual,' the prince said as he snuggled down in his blankets. 'Yusov, you go first and show Asaph how it's done,' he added sleepily.

'Yes, my prince.' Yusov accepted his task without question.

Asaph bit back a retort that he'd kept watch many times since he could walk. He was beginning to think proving his worth to the prince was futile. He was a prince himself, maybe even a king, so why should he have to prove himself to anyone? Instead he admired Yusov's quiet tolerance and dedication to his liege and cast a grin at the dark-haired man.

Yusov set about polishing his knives. He carried several about his person, and they gleamed in the firelight as he worked.

A gentle squeeze on Asaph's shoulder dragged him up to consciousness. He blinked up at Yusov, then yawned and sighed. Ignoring his protesting body, he dragged himself up to take the watch. The fire was still burning but low and he put another log on it as Yusov silently settled down to sleep. He sat staring into the fire, blinking constantly to keep himself awake and trying to keep his senses honed for anything lurking nearby. The rum had made him sleepier than he would have liked. Night watch, he decided, was dead dull.

He considered stepping through the dragon door, but the prince disliked him enough and if something happened whilst he was gone, that dislike would turn to hatred, and he didn't need any more enemies.

Sword on his lap, he sat cross-legged before the fire, thinking of the Sword of Binding and the pact between human and dragon. Was he really the last Dragon Lord? He couldn't quite believe it, found it too depressing to consider. There were Draxian refugees all over the Known World; surely some of them or their children would be Dragon Lords?

How many pure-blood dragons were alive out there? In his mind he'd felt lots of dragons somewhere far away to the north, north beyond Drax. They had fled—he knew that from the Recollection—and they had hidden deep in the mountains wherever they could escape the Dromoorai. Could he find them and awaken them? Would they hate him for being a Dragon Lord, for being of the kind that were turned into Dromoorai and then persecuted them? It was a thought that bothered him, as if his kind had betrayed both human and dragon. They might hate Dragon Lords, he thought sadly. But if he could retrieve the Sword of Binding they would remember their oath. They would remember the days when dragon and human lived together in peace.

'I must find the sword,' he whispered into his reflection in the sword's blade. He tried to imagine where the dragons might be—somewhere in the Kingdom of Ice, frozen and sleeping. He focused harder, his eyes staring into the metal. There they were, a dull presence, a faint feel on the mind, barely there but there all the same. Tears blurred his vision.

Blessed Feygriene, tell me how I can reach them. Help me find the Sword of Binding. Simply knowing the dragons still lived gave him hope, gave him purpose. He had to find them; it was the only thing he knew he had to do.

Sleep driven from his mind, he stood up, belted on his sword and decided to scout the area around their camp. Silently he padded through the trees, just beyond the reach of the firelight, but careful to always keep it in sight. The high-pitched squeak of bats came from overhead; something small scurried away into the bushes and the sound of owls hooting came in the distance. He could sense nothing but the night and her creatures.

He skirted a thorn bush and the hairs on the back of his neck rose. He stopped, hand dropping to his pommel, eyes wide, ears pricked. Something was watching him.

Opposite, in the trees beyond the campfire, a smooth white hand pushed the branches aside then disappeared. His breath caught in his throat. He'd almost forgotten about the pale beautiful woman in the woods, but now the memory rushed back to him, along with an intense desire to see her again.

As quietly as he could, he ran through the trees to the other side of the campfire. He glimpsed her again: a long, smooth leg disappearing away from the light of the fire and deeper into the forest. He glanced back at the others sleeping then back to where the woman had gone. She was watching him now, half hidden behind an oak tree. This was what keeping watch was about: checking out danger or other strange things. He'd only be gone a minute, perhaps he could get her to come to the camp with him.

He stepped towards her, moving slowly, letting his hand drop from his sword, not wanting to frighten her. She didn't move, much to his joy, but continued to watch him with beautiful, ice-blue eyes. Her long, platinum hair flowed around her bare shoulders, and her perfect face was angelic.

'Hi, er. I…' he began awkwardly. 'Who are you?'

She smiled and he found his heart pounding at her beauty.

'Are you hurt? Lost? Can I help you? What's your name?' His voice sounded loud and discordant in the silence. He felt awkward and clumsy under her gaze.

'Come closer,' she whispered and beckoned with a graceful motion of her hand. Her voice was like soft bells tinkling.

Asaph stepped closer until he was only a few feet away. Her skin was so smooth, he longed to stroke it and her hair shimmered like a fairy's as it spilled down her back. Now he was near he could see she was not naked but wore a short, flowing chemise so fine and thin he could see the curve of her breasts and hips. His breath caught in his throat. Somehow the chemise was more enticing than if she had been completely naked.

He reached out to touch her arm, needing to know if she was real. His fingers touched her skin and static tingled. Her flesh was cold but smooth and he trembled, suddenly afraid as intense desire overwhelmed him.

'You're frozen,' he said and unbuttoned his shirt, intending to wrap it around her, but she held up a hand to stop him.

'I'm not cold, but so tired,' she whispered and seemed ready to faint. He grasped her shoulders and pulled her close.

'Rest against me,' he said, his voice husky.

She looked up into his eyes and heat flooded through his body, driving straight to his loins. For a moment he was completely bewildered; he had never felt such intense need before. The feeling seemed to descend upon him rather than come from within himself. But now it was upon him he could not control it.

Her lips trembled and he wanted to kiss them. Just one kiss would not hurt. He felt his head being drawn down and his lips sought hers. A part of him felt he shouldn't kiss her, that this was wrong and dangerous and that he really loved Issa, but the desire was so strong it overwhelmed his reason. Another voice reminded him that Issa did not want him, but this woman did. This woman had time for him. He drove his lips down onto hers.

She kissed him hard, which surprised him, almost bruising his lips in her hunger. Passion exploded within him and he found himself pushing her down to the ground, her lips never leaving his as she let him. His passion was overtaking him and he struggled to master it. He felt like a boat tossed in the storm of his desire that he couldn't hope to control.

He fumbled for her breasts, tearing her chemise in his haste. She giggled—it seemed strange that she did—then dug her nails into his back. He gritted his teeth but found he enjoyed the pain, though something about it felt wrong. She bit his neck, almost painfully as he struggled with his trousers. His groin ached in desperation and then the passion ended, as if it was suddenly shut off. He gasped in confusion, his head pounding and his body trembling. He looked down at the pale woman beneath him, noting her torn chemise, and fell to the side of her, exhausted and panting for breath.

'What happened?' What had he done? What had overcome him to make him so desperate? 'I'm sorry I-I don't know what came over me.'

The pale woman rolled lithely to standing and loomed over him, her cold blue eyes capturing him so he couldn't look away. She smiled but her smile seemed cruel.

'You will want me more and more,' she breathed. 'Will you follow me?'

'Follow you where?' Asaph frowned, a fog of confusion clouding his mind. 'Yes, I'll follow you anywhere,' he said, knowing he would go anywhere and do anything just to be with this woman.

A yell in the distance cut through the fog in his brain, and he jumped up. The pale woman pulled her torn chemise up and scowled in the direction of the yell.

'Thane?' he shouted.

'Come to the safety of the camp—' He turned back to the woman but she was gone, along with the fog in his mind. A man screamed in the distance.

'I'm coming!' he yelled and pelted back to the camp.

Hidden in the bushes, Cirosa grimaced as she turned into an owl. She had almost netted him. Still, she grinned, the seeds had been sown fully. His mind was weakening and filled with desire. Just a little more and he would be as a dog on a leash, her leash, and ready to be dragged to her lord. He wouldn't be able to get out of her sight. She would snare him completely tomorrow night.

CHAPTER 10

Chasing Blue Tails

'SHE sprained her fetlock bolting from a snake,' the farmer said, scratching his balding head then slapping his cap back on it.

He was shorter than Issa, and fat to the point of being completely round. They were standing in the sunshine outside Zeb's smithy within the grounds of Castle Carvon. The yells of fruit sellers could be heard beyond the castle walls and the smell of animals filled the air.

'Did the snake get a nip at her?' she asked, stroking the strawberry roan's neck.

'Nope. She's a fast one, but she was off balance and stumbled.'

Issa nodded, relieved. She couldn't heal poison, and snake bites often festered.

'Gently now,' she mind-spoke to the horse, placed her hands upon the mare's nose and neck and closing her eyes. The horse, unused to such communication with humans, took a few moments to relax. Issa smiled when she began to see pictures coming from the horse as she communed with her. Sometimes animals wouldn't speak, and they were the hardest to treat.

Issa could see the snake hidden in the grass, then it rose to strike. She felt a wave of panic and stomped down, killing the snake but smashing her hoof on a rock. Pain shot up her leg. The rock had splintered under the force of her stomp.

Issa opened her eyes and lifted the horse's leg. Dried blood caked the skin and she tenderly pressed the soft flesh under the hoof. It was hot and swollen.

'There's a stone shard embedded here, as thin as a needle and as long,' she said, feeling around the hard prick of stone. She reached into her apron and pulled out a huge pair of tweezers.

'I can reach it to pull it out but it's going to hurt.'

The farmer nodded and gripped the horse's reins as if to steady her.

Issa formed images in her mind what she was going to do and shared this with the horse. The mare calmly allowed her to lift her hoof again. She gripped the shard end in the tweezers, working fast to spare the horse unwanted pain and anxiety. With a smooth firm pull the shard came loose with a spurt of blood. Issa felt the horse's shooting pain in her own arm. The mare snorted and jerked away. The farmer strained against the reins.

'There there, it's out,' she soothed and stroked the horse, calming her.

The farmer bent down to wrap it with a cloth.

'No, don't try to cover it. Let it bleed the toxins out,' she said. 'It won't bleed for long. Look at that, two inches long.' She held up the mean stone shard covered in blood, and both the horse and farmer peered at it curiously.

'Well, thank the goddess I brought her to you.' The farmer beamed.

'See, the bleeding has already stopped and the swelling will come down in the next few days,' Issa said. 'Rest her for a week and let the healing take its course.'

'Aww, and I thought I'd have to lay her to rest. My best horse made whole again. The goddess bless you, gal'. You've a fine healer's hand on you.' He grinned and shook her hand. 'I'll tell all about you, so expect a lot of work.'

She laughed. He pressed a silver coin into her hand, half more than the price she had charged.

'Take this and get yourself something nice.' He winked, then led his limping horse away. The mare turned to look at her; she got the faintest feeling of gratitude, and then they disappeared through the smithy gate.

Issa smiled and went to wash her hands in a bucket of water. This is what she should be doing—healing animals just like she used to. She'd started working at Castle Carvon Smithy yesterday morning. Already she'd treated three sheep, one pig and two horses. They'd all had minor problems, this mare being the worst, but she'd healed them all and already had several silver pieces for her work. It turned out the city folk paid a good price compared to the poorer folk of Little Kammy.

King Navarr had protested that she do such things, being, as he said, "a queen of sorts." But working at the smithy was a balm to her soul. She sighed, remembering home, Laron and Tarn and all the normal things she'd done and been and loved. If she stopped to think about it too much, she always began to cry. Already the tears were welling in her eyes. Silly really, especially when she had been bored with her life back then. She just didn't realise what she'd had until it was gone.

'You can't take the country out of the girl,' a familiar voice said behind her. She whirled around.

'Freydel!' She blinked back the tears and went over to give the Master Wizard a hug.

She hadn't seen him since their last meeting at the Wizards' Circle a few days ago. Asaph had been missing as well, on some scouting party apparently, and wouldn't be back for a couple of days, King Navarr had said. So she'd been mostly left to her own devices. She hadn't meant to be so cold with him and now he was gone she sorely missed his company. As beautiful as the castle was, without a purpose she quickly grew bored and listless. It hadn't taken her long to find work at the smithy alongside Zeb, and he welcomed female company and someone to help clean the place up.

'I had to find something to do. I need to earn my keep and have a purpose in my life. Besides, working here reminds me of home, of the life I might have had,' she said, pulling off her apron and following him into the yard.

'Do you wish you were still back there?' he asked, his hazel eyes twinkling in the late afternoon sun.

'Sometimes, yes. I miss the peacefulness. I miss knowing exactly what kind of life I would lead, one just like everyone else's. But it's funny because when I was there I didn't feel any of those things. I found it boring. Although I felt different to everyone else and I wanted something more.'

Freydel laughed. 'Yes, things are always very different with retrospection. Without the changes that have happened to you, to me and to everyone—all the hardships and loss—we would probably never appreciate much at all. I've been thinking a lot lately...' he trailed off and looked into the distance, the smile leaving his face.

'What is it?' she asked, immediately worried. 'Have the Maphraxies attacked? Surely the Feylint Halanoi have reached Western Frayon by now.'

He looked at her and frowned, as if he had forgotten she was there. 'The Feylint Halanoi? Yes, yes. They'll be well on their way to Western Frayon. No, I wasn't thinking about that. I've been thinking about time. That it isn't really rigid at all… It's hard to explain.'

Issa shook her head. 'What happened when you were trapped in the astral planes? I've heard only snippets from Coronos, and a brief account from you. We must help Arla. I've thought of and tried everything. Do you think you could try to find her? I don't know how to break her fever…' She chewed her lip. Arla had asked to be taken to the boatman but she had been delaying because Asaph had not returned yet. Time was running out. Perhaps she could call him on her own—there was no harm in trying—but she really wanted Asaph with her.

'A lot happened in the astral planes,' Freydel said. 'And yes, that was part of what I was thinking about. I've been thinking I should return, to see if I can help Arla and…' He left it hanging and stroked his beard, lost again in his thoughts.

'And what, Freydel? Why are you being all mysterious? Is it a "wizard thing"?' She smiled.

He muttered to himself then sighed. 'I haven't told anybody, and still don't know if I should.'

'Well, what harm can telling do? There are no enemies listening here,' Issa said, looking around and pretending to be scared.

Freydel took a deep breath. 'Yes, you're right and, if she recovers, Arla knows what happened there, anyway. The truth is, I wouldn't have made it back without her help. I travelled back in time, Issa.' He looked at her, his hazel eyes intense.

She blinked in shock. 'Are you sure? Is it even possible?'

'Yes, very much so. Especially with the power of the orb. And I went further than that. I went so far back in time that I arrived in a different time and place entirely. I asked the orb to take me somewhere safe from Baelthrom and it took me there. It was a totally different planet because I recognised none of the constellations. And there were these amazing beings that were beautiful, graceful, tall—they had powers far greater than our own. They were so far back in time and yet far more advanced.'

Issa listened, spellbound, as the wizard spoke, his eyes shining with the memory of it. He stopped suddenly and looked around as if someone might be listening.

'Come, come to my chambers this evening where we can talk in private and I can show you in the orb.'

She nodded and with that Freydel turned and left. She stood there staring at the wizard's back as he disappeared around the stone wall. He was telling the truth, she was certain, but believing one could travel back in time and to another planet entirely was stretching her mind to its limits.

Issa helped Zeb sweep the floor and tidy tools away, her mind a complete whirl. The stocky blacksmith was a man of hard work and few words so she was left to her thoughts as they cleaned up. No matter how much she thought on it, she couldn't work out what Freydel was going to say tonight.

'See you in the morning, Zeb,' she said, turning to go.

'Right-o missy. Been a busy day today and expect the same tomorrow.' The fair-haired man waved and disappeared into the tool shed.

She walked the short path from the smithy to the castle. Just as she turned the door latch, movement caught her eye: a fluffy blue tail disappearing around the wall. She blinked in surprise, dropped the latch and went to investigate.

Sitting a few yards away before the gate leading into a courtyard was Mr Dubbins, the blue cat. She gasped. He looked at her with big golden eyes and, as always, he seemed to be smiling.

'Mr Dubbins, what on earth are you doing here? Where's Edarna?' She went towards him.

He meowed and then, in that special cat way of being able to fit into anything, wiggled under the tiny gap at the bottom of the gate.

'Wait,' she called and hurried after him.

The little-used gate was stiff and took some heaving to force open. Beyond, she caught a blue tail disappearing over the top of another gate that led out into the city. She raced after the cat.

'Miss Issa,' the startled guard said as she flung open the gate. He bowed.

'My apologies, sir, I'm in a rush.' She smiled, suddenly realising she was covered in dirt and sweat from work. She swallowed, smoothed her green trousers, made especially for her by King Navarr's seamstresses, and adjusted her shirt.

'Which way did the blue cat go?' she asked with some composure.

'Over there, I think.' He nodded towards a side street. 'Stupid thing must have fallen in paint. Never seen a blue cat before.'

Issa grinned at him and hurried along, just fast enough to glimpse a blue tail disappearing down another street.

'Mr Dubbins, will you hold up a minute?' She huffed, doing her best to ignore the raised eyebrows of the people she ran past.

The street she stepped into was empty and the cat nowhere to be seen. She took a chance and went left along East Street which would eventually take her into the market square. The blue cat disappeared round a corner on her right. He didn't look like he was moving fast, trotting as he was, but she couldn't seem to catch up with him. He looked back at her, gave a loud meow, and turned down an alley.

'Mr Dubbins, wait!' She raced on.

How could a sauntering cat get so far ahead? He must be running when she couldn't see him. With a forlorn sigh she watched him vanish into the crowd-filled market square. She'd never find him in there. Still, she didn't fancy giving up so easily. Where in Maioria was he going? If the cat was here then so was Edarna. And how she longed to see the witch's friendly face. It would be good to have a chat.

She pushed through the crowds. Everyone was bustling to and fro, each thinking that their business was far more important than anyone else's. They were even too busy to notice the strange blue cat. Though it was market day, as it seemed to be most days in Frayon's busiest city, it was late in the afternoon and the square was emptying as people and merchants made their way home. She wiggled this way and that, trying to spot the cat through peoples' trousers and skirts, but after a while she gave up.

She stopped short by a tankard seller. Tankards in copper, silver, pewter and gold plate hung at the entrance, gleaming in the sunlight. The blue cat was several marquees away, sitting happily on top of a purple fabric roof at the edge of the square. He licked his paw and grinned at her as if this was all great fun. Sighing through pursed lips, she squeezed through the crowd towards him and, as she knew he would, watched hopelessly as he jumped away and disappeared up a wide empty street.

The next street was long and straight as an arrow. At the end of it was the gleaming white wall surrounding the Temple of Carvon, its pristine spire rising up into the sky. She'd passed the temple once before on her walk through the city with Asaph. Again she marvelled at its size and beauty—it was at least four times the size of the Temple of Celene. The opulent building was so out of place when the houses surrounding it were positively miserable; some looked like they would fall down at any moment. The richest temple was in the shabbiest, poorest part of town.

She finally lost Mr Dubbins for good when he leapt onto the ten-foot-high wall and disappeared into the subtropical gardens surrounding the temple. After all that chasing, there was no way she could follow him now. The walls were smooth, with no foothold or anything to grab onto, and there were guards watching everything outside the gates, and probably guards inside too. The cat suddenly appeared above her and meowed.

'There you are. You know I can't get up there. Where's Edarna?'

He meowed again, louder.

'I can't follow you in there. Look, there are guards at the gate.' She pointed all the way to the end of the wall where two guards stood watch. Behind them, gold gilded gates shone. It occurred to her how strange it was having guards guarding a place of worship. 'They won't let me in without an invite, and I'm not sure I even want to go in there, beautiful though it is.'

She'd asked the guards before if she and Asaph could walk around the gardens, but with a look of disdain they were refused entry without an invite. On asking if she could make an appointment to talk to the Oracle, they'd said she was too busy and booked up until next spring. They were dismissed and sent on their way and she didn't fancy approaching them again.

With a bit of magic she could probably jump it, but somebody might detect her magic. And what if there was a magical shield protecting the temple that she couldn't see? She looked up at the cat then back at the guards. Guards notoriously saw everything. One glanced in her direction and narrowed his eyes.

She nonchalantly walked in the opposite direction, stepping down a narrow, dirty alley. Black covered the walls and the smell of soot was heavy in the air. Ahead was the burnt out remains of an unfortunate person's house, never torn down and rebuilt like it should have been.

Making sure she was alone, she slipped off her shoulder sack and pulled out the raven talisman. She tried to have it with her at all times. 'Objects of magic,' Freydel always reminded her, 'should not be left lying around.' So, armed with his advice, she treated the talisman like an orb and kept it close.

Without thinking about it too much in case she lost her nerve, she loosened her shirt and pressed the talisman against her chest. In the next moment she was leaping into the air and spreading her raven wings wide. In the past, turning into a raven only happened when she was in dire need. Now, with the raven talisman, it happened at her will and with the barest amount of magic.

The guards didn't even look up as she flew over the temple wall. She landed on the branch of an unusual tree. Its thick, purple-green leaves fluttered against each other in the breeze and its smooth trunk flowed elegantly to the ground.

A meow came from below and she looked down at Mr Dubbins. He was staring up at her, not fooled by appearances. He turned and trotted towards the sweeping, white steps leading up to the entrance of the temple. Gaggles of grey-and-brown robed priestesses and priests milled under the watchful eyes of a few white-robed priestesses. Issa took a deep breath and flew silently into a cluster of bushes.

Edarna and Naksu looked at each other, eyes wide in exasperation, then back at the Oracle. The woman's face was flushed red and she fanned herself furiously.

'Veren! Open a window, will you? Can't you see it's stifling in here?' she commanded and with her fan wafted the tall, thin man towards the closest window. The man obediently did as he was commanded and cool air rushed in.

'Now then, Edarna who? And a seer, hmm? Hmph. I sent for a seer ages ago. Years, in fact. Where have you been? Useless. My dear, sweet child passed away because of you.' She glared down at Naksu as if it was her fault.

'Hykerry—' Naksu began and stepped towards the dais.

'I am the Oracle!' she squealed.

The two assistants scowled at Naksu.

'Oracle Hykerry,' Naksu tried again, her voice taking on a commanding tone as she controlled her rising temper. 'The Seers of Myrn are at nobody's beck and call. We are in service to Maioria, the Goddess and the Great Source of All. For everything there is a divine right time and a divine right order in which it must occur. Just because we don't come immediately when summoned, does not mean we don't know what is going on or don't care. When we arrive, we arrive at exactly the right time and no sooner. Now then, please tell me about your daughter, the one you mentioned in your letter.'

For a moment the Oracle opened and closed her mouth, making Naksu wonder if anyone ever spoke plainly to the priestess, or did they all treat her like a queen?

'My only child...' the Oracle began, then turned to her assistants. 'Leave us,' she commanded. They looked at each other, confused.

'Come on, go. Tsk tsk.' She wafted them away with her commanding fan. They backed down the steps and with awkward bows, disappeared through the door.

Naksu looked at Edarna, seeing the same surprise on the witch's face. They really did treat the Oracle like a queen. Something Navarr would not be too happy about, Naksu was sure. Only when they were gone did the Oracle speak.

'She was born blue.' She sighed and sank back into her chair. Her red face drained of colour, becoming stark and bony in the light, and there were shadows under her eyes. She suddenly seeming like nothing more than a skeleton swathed in huge skirts and ruffles. Her half-moon glasses perfectly reflected the crystal ball in front of her.

Naksu felt the faintest magic move and an image of a tiny pale blue baby appeared in the crystal ball. Naksu forgot her surprise, reminding herself that this Oracle had mastered some control over the Flow—not as much as a seer might, but enough to do something with it. Perhaps Hykerry could have become a seer, with the right training.

'Children born blue have special powers,' Naksu agreed. Edarna nodded silently, her eyes locking on to the crystal ball. 'But it doesn't mean they are Goddess Chosen.'

'What?' said the Oracle, flashing an angry look at Naksu, but her eyes were drawn inexorably back to the baby in the crystal ball. The intense longing in her face struck Naksu.

'I had visions,' the Oracle whispered, still staring into the ball. 'So many visions… They were messages. I know higher messages when I receive them. I saw that my child would become powerful in magic and powerful in the sword. She would surely become the fabled Raven Queen of prophecy.'

In the ball, images of a muscled, tanned woman with short, brown hair formed. She held a sword and the Flow moved at her command.

'I saw her build an army and face the Maphraxies. Under her might the enemy fell. I saw the Forest Goddess, the Sun Goddess and the Night Goddess bless her.'

Naksu did not disbelieve the Oracle, but there was more to this that Hykerry either didn't know or was choosing to ignore.

'Indeed, your child may have been *a* Raven Queen—' Naksu began.

'*The* Raven Queen.' Hykerry glared.

Naksu continued, keeping her voice gentle but firm.

'You should know this: that there can be three possible Raven Queens, according to prophecy. That your daughter, sad though it is, is no longer with us, then she can no longer be the Raven Queen.'

The Oracle shook her head, dropped her eyes and fell into muttering to herself. Edarna frowned at Naksu.

'She's a little mad,' Naksu whispered to the witch.

'Just a little?' whispered Edarna, raising an eyebrow.

'My beloved daughter might be dead, but these others are impostors,' she hissed and sat forwards, her face reddening again. 'I see them, these *impostors*, I see them. But my daughter, the only *true* Raven Queen, is dead. She's gone and all is lost. There's no one who can help us against… *them!*'

'Oracle Hykerry, as I have just said,' Naksu drooped her shoulders, 'there can be *three* possible Raven Queens, but only one of them will survive to adulthood; only one will be strong enough. I'm sorry for your daughter, truly I am, but all is not lost.'

The Oracle began muttering to herself again, her eyes darting around the room as if she saw ghosts fleeing there. Every now and then she would shake her head as if in conversation with someone, and laugh shrilly like a little girl. Naksu frowned. Who did the Oracle think she was talking to in her head? The seer walked closer to the dais and took the first step. Edarna shuffled along beside her.

'Oracle Hykerry, who are you talking to?' Naksu asked mildly.

'Shhh.' The Oracle held a gold-ringed finger to her lips. 'If we cannot fight them,' she giggled, wild-eyed, 'then we must join them.'

Naksu suddenly felt very strange, as if her energy fields had turned to water. Everything slowed down. She had the awful feeling that they were being watched, watched by something very bad. A piercing headache hit her and she scrunched her eyes. Edarna gasped. Her usual apple-red cheeks were pale and she swayed. Naksu reached to steady her and entered the Flow. It drained away from her like water disappearing down a drain. Everything sounded eerie and filled with a strange whirring noise.

Edarna wiped her brow and took out her wand with a shaking hand. Naksu gripped her staff in two hands and with a word it burst into light. The Flow was horribly weak, but her staff held enough magic of its own to protect them if needed.

The Oracle continued to giggle throughout it all, her laugh growing louder and more insane. Her two assistants peered around the door. The Oracle snapped her mouth shut and sat up straight, horror on her face as she glared into the middle distance.

'She's here. The impostor is here!' Hykerry howled.

Issa hunkered down in the dense bushes as two novice priestesses walked by chatting. They glanced at her, saw a bird and carried on by without interest. She shifted back into her human self and shuddered. The change always left her feeling queasy and crawly just under the skin. The more she changed, the more she attuned herself to the subtleties of shifting form. Brushing the leaves from her shirt, she wished she'd had a wash and put on some clean clothes. She probably stank of horses and didn't even have a comb to brush her hair.

Mr Dubbins meowed from the top step. The priests and priestesses paid him no attention, which Issa still found strange. Did no one but her think a blue cat was odd? Maybe they didn't even notice, much less care.

She hovered at the tree line and smoothed her clothes. She was obviously not a priestess and would stand out whether she was clean or not. She'd have to pretend she had an important appointment—why else would the guards have let her in?

'I have an appointment with the Oracle,' she whispered to herself, trying to calm her racing heart.

She glimpsed two women in the crowd dressed more shabbily than she. One wore a shawl with holes in it and a fraying skirt. The other wore a simple, brown dress stained with mud at the hem. Both had frowns of worry on their faces as they left the temple and walked towards the golden gates. She wondered if everyone in the temple was morose.

No one paid the women any attention and she began to relax. Guests were mostly looked down upon and ignored. Why were the common folk so sparse here? Surely the place should be filled with weddings, funerals and baptisms—all the normal proceedings expected of the Temple of the Goddess, and which she was brought up believing still happened on the Main Land.

She stood tall and walked towards the temple, following Mr Dubbins as he trotted inside. She moved past the priests and priestesses, making sure not to catch their eyes and maintaining the same determined, purposeful look on her face. A few glances came her way and looks of disdain followed as they saw her stained clothes.

Once inside, the first thing that struck her was the size of the place. Great ceilings towered above her and beautiful gold filigree expertly decorated the white walls and dome. She dared to gawp only briefly, or risk losing the cat again.

She had trouble making her way through a large crowd of sombre-looking novices clustering around a door. Obviously they were waiting for a class to start. Surely the young people should be smiling and giggling at that age, but life seemed far too serious for them, or perhaps it was the dull lessons they were being taught. They proved no obstacle to Mr Dubbins, however, who wound easily through their legs.

By the time she emerged into the corridor, the cat was nowhere to be seen. Seeing no other way, she carried along it and came to a winding staircase that lead up. At the top, the wooden door was ajar and she slipped through, hoping she wouldn't bump into anyone. The next corridor was empty, apart from Mr Dubbins' tail disappearing the other end. She padded after him, wondering if these were the dormitories.

'Mr Dubbins!' she hissed in exasperation as she followed him down another winding set of staircases. She came to a stop before a simple oak door. Mr Dubbins finally stopped and sat down, smiling up at her.

'Why have you led me here?' she whispered, bending to stroke his silky soft fur. He began to purr. 'And more importantly, why are you here? Shouldn't you be with Edarna?'

Voices came from beyond the door, making her freeze. Nobody came through, however. She placed her ear against the door but couldn't make anything out other than muffled talking. Suddenly the Flow jolted around her and magical energy electrified the air. Instinctively she entered the Flow only to see it drain away. The Under Flow swirled and surged around her in nauseating waves. Her head pounded with her heartbeat and she felt faint. Terrible danger was near.

Shouting came from the other side of the door. She grasped the handle and flung it open.

CHAPTER 11

White Feather

PELTING towards the campfire and the sound of screaming, Asaph was on the foltoy in seconds.

The beast had Yusov's arm in its slathering jaws and the man's blood dripped from wounds. The others were grappling with their weapons. He noticed the prince had left his sword in his horse's saddle and was now running away from the fight to get it.

The foltoy spun left away from his sword and, without a thought for his own safety, he jumped on its back. Gripping its matted fur with one hand, he plunged his sword down, severing its spinal cord at the neck. Both man and beast fell to the ground. The beast made a horrible gurgling sound and released Yusov's arm before lying still. He gripped his arm, grimacing in pain, pale and panting.

Asaph bent to look at the wound. It was bleeding heavily and possibly the bone was broken.

'You can't do anything; I need a trained healer.' Yusov gasped, his face scrunched. 'A wound from one of them always becomes infected.'

'Let's wash it in the river and bind it tight,' Asaph said, wrapping the man's good arm over his shoulder and helping him up.

'Where the hell were you?' the prince all but screamed at Asaph as he stalked over, his face red and pinched.

'I was investigating a strange noise,' Asaph retorted angrily, heat creeping up his neck, knowing he had been with the beautiful pale woman.

'You should never have strayed so far from camp. We could have been killed!' the prince screamed on. The twins looked at the ground with worried expressions.

'I'm sorry, I-I had to investigate the noise. I thought there was danger,' Asaph stammered, keenly aware that he was talking to the heir of Carvon.

He told the truth, but the prince was right, he shouldn't have wandered so far and left them to danger whilst they slept. There was nothing more he could say. He was furious with himself as well. What had come over him to wander off after a woman like that? And then he had…he had been rough with her. His head began to pound horribly.

'You won't stand night watch again. Nor will you join us hunting. You're nothing but trouble.' The prince scowled and turned to Yusov. 'Now my protectorate is injured. At first light we must return home and get the wound seen to before it festers with the poison of the undead.'

In silence they carried Yusov to the nearest stream several yards down from Hanging Rock and washed his wounds. The twins had a small first aid pack and they used all the bandages within it to bind his arm. Without much talk, they bedded down close to Yusov to make sure the man would stay warm. He was pale but already asleep.

Thane kept night watch but Asaph couldn't sleep. He was too angry with himself and confused by what had happened with the woman. Coronos would be furious and King Navarr would no longer respect him, that was obvious. He wouldn't be surprised if he was thrown out of the castle, maybe even out of Carvon, for risking the heir's life.

If it hadn't been the pale woman, would he have investigated a noise so far away anyway? Probably, but it did little to ease him. Why had she come to him? Why couldn't he seem to get her out of his head? She had an effect on him like no other; he was bewitched and yet the feeling didn't bother him—he loved being enchanted by her. The way the light had curved around her smooth breasts and long white legs, her platinum hair shimmering in the dark. His head pounded harder and his throat went dry. He felt as if he was getting a cold again.

After an hour spent trying to sleep, he got up, nodded silently at Thane and went to the stream to fill up his water canister. He wandered slowly back but found his feet taking him back to the spot where he had been with the woman.

What had happened to make him desire her so frantically? How would Issa feel? He sighed, the guilt weighing heavy. He remembered thinking that if she didn't want him at least this woman did.

Something gleaming in the grass caught his eyes and he bent to pick up the white feather, marvelling at its perfection and beauty. It seemed to shimmer in the night like an enchanted thing. Maybe it was lucky. He could certainly do with a bit of luck right now. He tucked it into his pocket and with a heavy heart headed back to camp.

Cirosa nestled herself on a high branch. She had specifically told the dumb foltoy to wait for her call. It had attacked too soon and she'd barely lured her prey away from the others. Such half-wit creatures were hard to work with and never to be relied upon.

Still, not all was lost, she thought, watching as her prey pocketed her feather. It would be too difficult to attack again in the same night, and she'd already lost one foltoy. She watched the man leave and flew down to a thick patch of ferns. Her form shimmered and became human.

'My prey has been snared, Lord Baelthrom,' she breathed into her amulet, feeling the power of her lord emanating from it.

'*My* prey, Cirosa.' His voice was so deep it rumbled even the amulet.

'Yes, my lord,' Cirosa conceded sullenly.

'Where, then, is the Dragon Lord?'

'I have a noose about his neck and have but to prise him away from the other humans. But the noose will hold no matter where he goes now. Only death can break it,' Cirosa said.

'Well done, Cirosa. When I have him, you will be rewarded.'

Cirosa grinned, basking in her lord's favour.

'How shall I bring him to you, my lord? It's a long way to Maphrax.'

'When you have him alone in your grasp, use the amulet and leave the rest to me. Be ready; he'll be violent, but I can subdue even the most powerful Dragon Lord.'

'Yes, my lord,' Cirosa said. 'Soon you'll have another Dragon Lord in your ranks.'

The amulet dimmed and she sat alone amongst the ferns. In the darkness before dawn she considered for a long while how to separate Asaph from the rest of his friends. When the sky began to lighten she turned into her owl form and found a hole in a tree in which to sleep.

Very little was said as the four men headed back home. Everyone was tired and shaken by the attack and Yusov looked very ill. His face was grey and his hands trembled. The journey seemed to take forever too. They had to go slower because Yusov could only ride one handed and, whilst he was an expert horseman, galloping with one hand was hard and dangerous. He kept quiet about his pain, however, making Asaph worry all the more.

Asaph spent the entire journey cursing himself for his blunders, in between thinking about the blond-haired woman. He saw her naked body whenever he closed his eyes, which sent him into an annoying state of arousal. His thoughts could barely think about anything else but her.

Every slightest movement in the forest caught his eye and always he looked to check if it was her. She had to be following him to find him so easily, but why was she? If he saw her again, he would have to hold her down, tie her down if necessary, and demand she tell him who she was and why she followed him.

His head pounded the whole time too and no matter how much water he drank he could not seem to quench his thirst. Even the amicable twins chatted little amongst themselves and not at all to him. He *had* heard a noise and he *had* gone to check everything was all right, that was what the night watcher was supposed to do. He guessed that no one wanted to be seen siding with him against the prince.

Would he ever win back the men's friendship or respect? That he single-handedly killed the foltoy seemed to be totally forgotten.

He let go of his breath. Why did his life seem to be so hard and complicated no matter what he did? Was he destined to fail at everything? As soon as he was alone, he would go through the dragon door and seek out Faelsun. He needed advice, answers, and to get away from this world in which he just didn't seem to fit.

Though they'd hoped to make it home before dark, the night closed in, forcing them to camp out in the woods several miles away from the city. The prince helped Yusov dismount.

'We needn't worry about foltoy this close to the city,' Bayel said and cast a half smile at Asaph. Simply being acknowledged made him feel better.

'That was quite a move back there,' Bayel added. 'It was unfortunate, what happened.'

Asaph nodded and tethered Ironclad. 'I was a fool. I heard a noise but should never have investigated it so far from the camp.'

'We're rarely attacked at night, not even by a wolf or bear,' Bayel said louder, and Asaph wondered if it was deliberate so everyone could hear. 'It's almost like the foltoy was already there, waiting. Usually they attack in full daylight and in twos or more. Like I said, it was unfortunate.'

Bayel went to collect firewood.

Asaph considered the man's words. It certainly did seem unfortunate. He rubbed his throbbing temples and swallowed water down his parched throat, thinking on the man's words. *"It's almost like the foltoy was already there, waiting."* Could it have been? Could it be following that strange pale woman? He touched his sore back where her nails had dug into his flesh, feeling a mix of pain and suffocating desire.

He sat down by the fire to eat a tasteless dinner of dry bread and spread, the last of their food and there wasn't much of it. Forbidden the night watch, he went to bed early, leaving the others to chat and drink into the night.

Sleep came swiftly but his dreams were filled with hundreds of white owls hunting for him. He was a tiny mouse running from their shining talons and hooked beaks. He couldn't seem to hide from them; they found him wherever he went and ran him to exhaustion.

Cirosa woke late to discover the men were no longer travelling the route she had anticipated. After some time searching she found their trail. They were moving slowly but directly back to the city. The dark-haired man's arm was infected, she could smell it a mile away. Pity the foltoy had not done its job. She should have lured the dragon man farther away from the others.

She tried and failed to rouse her prey that night. He slept too deeply under her spell and she could not get close enough for the watchful eyes of the man who stood guard. She gave up when dawn came and sought a safe place to sleep. She would not disappoint her lord.

The next day she followed the men all the way back to the city, screaming her frustration as they disappeared through the city's gate. She would have to lure him back into the forest, or find another way to get close to him.

In the morning Asaph was positively sick. His vision was blurry and his muscles were so weak he had trouble mounting Ironclad. He managed to hide it well enough and soon they were trotting through a thinning forest just a mile or so from Carvon.

They made it home by midday. At the first opportunity he slipped away and staggered up to his room, collapsing on his bed fully clothed.

He awoke just as the sun was dipping into the trees, feeling a little better. He downed the water in his canister and sat back against the headboard. Something odd was happening to him, but his brain was too full of fog to reason it through. He should tell Coronos. But then his father had probably already learned about what had happened. He couldn't cope with his father's disappointment right now, and he was too sick to be thrown out of the castle just yet. He felt weak from lack of food but the thought of eating made his stomach churn.

Sweat slicked his skin and he flung open the window to get some air. He pulled off his clothes and boots and sat in his underwear, enjoying the cool breeze blowing over his body. He tried to clear his foggy mind and focused his inner attention upon the dragon door. It took a long while to come into his mind but finally he saw the mahogany dragon head reaching forth majestically through the wood.

Tears of relief filled his eyes; he didn't think he would find it. A wave of clarity, calm and wellness spread over him. In his mind, he reached to open the door but it would not budge. He tried again and again, but the door was not opening and there was no way to force it.

What if it no longer opened for him? Panic gripped him. Had he been banished from there too? Was he disgraced everywhere and by everyone? All he wanted was to speak to Faelsun. He desperately needed to talk to the Guardian of the Dragon Dream about everything, especially the dragons he had felt sleeping in the north.

He sighed and lay down. The whole world and beyond had shut him out.

Coronos worried his beard as he looked down at his pale-faced son. Asaph had not come down for dinner, so he'd brought a tray up only to find him sleeping deeply. The red embers in the hearth gave the room the barest glow, but even then Asaph's face seemed to reject that glow and instead looked grey and drawn.

For a moment, he was horribly reminded of how similar he'd looked after his near fatal battle with Keteth. Something was making his son sick and no matter what that spoilt brat of a prince said, and he'd said a lot, there was more to this ambush story. Asaph would not have wandered off without purpose.

Coronos let go of the breath he'd been holding. His son had embroiled himself in street fights with unsavoury brawlers—and his name had spread too as men sought out the fighter who had beaten the best. They would all want to fight him now.

And now he'd jeopardised the lives of four young men. They could easily have been killed in their sleep without Asaph raising the alarm. He had never failed on a scouting party before, so why now? It was certainly not a matter of courage; Asaph had enough for two men.

He'd barely seen his son lately, and when he had he was morose and remote. He noticed that Issa had been cold towards him since their argument and her return from the Storm Holt. Could that be what was eating him? It was no wonder she was remote; she needed time to recover, if indeed she could. Whatever she had experienced in there would scar her for life. But even so, the man before him needed direction and purpose, and nothing Coronos did seemed to help.

'My son, have I somehow failed you?' he whispered. 'If I have, then I've failed your parents too. I don't know how to help you but to love you and guide you. You need your home, your Drax, your dragons—and I cannot give you that.'

Tears filled his eyes. Asaph stirred but did not wake. Coronos looked at the flame scars on his chest.

'The goddess put that mark on you, and it's not without a reason. Go to the Dragon Dream and go there often. Only there will you find true guidance.'

He turned to the small hearth and put a log on the embers. Autumn was moving swiftly towards winter and the room felt cold. The log began to smoulder then flames licked at it. He pulled a cushion from a chair and sat before it, rubbing his stiff knees so he could bend them more. Settling himself comfortably, he stared into the dancing flames, trying to banish the worry from his heart and mind.

His thoughts calm, he took the Orb of Air from its pouch and sat there for a long time, staring into the flames. In his mind he recited the Fire Sight then was still.

'Mother Feygriene, embrace me,' he whispered.

The fire began to move in an ordered manner, the flames flowing to the left and then to the right. In them a beautiful, otherworldly face formed, no bigger than a Draxian copper half-piece. She smiled at him and the rest of her golden body materialised. She danced, lithe as a fairy, but utterly divine. Her ribbon dress of flames flared around her as she moved to a song he could not hear. Her graceful arms of gold twirled above her head of flowing hair and always she smiled that knowing benevolent smile.

She held her arms open to him and he reached forwards. The fire engulfed him and then he was dancing with her upon a golden floor and in a room made of yellow fire. His back was straight and the aches gone from his body. He danced with her as if he were a young man again, strong and agile. Joy spread over him, sending his worries scurrying.

The roaring fire became a concert of a thousand stringed instruments. For a long time it seemed they danced—the cares of the world unimportant in this eternal place. Then the rhythm slowed and they became still.

'I want to dance in the everlasting flame forever,' he whispered. He was having trouble beholding her light and her beauty.

'Soon,' she said, the smile of knowing never wavering.

'I'm afraid for Asaph, always,' he admitted.

'Change is coming. Fear not,' the voice flowed around him in silken waves. Coronos nodded. She began to fade.

'Wait,' he said, not wanting to be alone, needing that all-knowing, benevolent voice to tell him it would be all right. But the fire began to turn back to its usual chaotic burning.

'Beware the white owl,' she whispered as she disappeared.

The golden floor faded to the dull red rug before the hearth and the walls of flame became the dour wooden panels of Asaph's room. The heaviness of the world descended upon him.

A flaming ember leapt out of the fire onto Asaph's crumpled coat lying on the floor. Coronos jumped up and brushed it off before it could set light. As he did so a feather of the purest white fell out of the pocket.

Dark energy moved, thick and cloying. With a gasp, he fell back from it, the orb flaring in his hand. A strange hissing whispering scoured his ears; it seemed to be coming from the feather. In the Flow he could see the enchantments upon it—dark and twisted and made by the Under Flow.

He snatched at the feather but as his fingers touched its soft fronds, pain shot up his arm and a dull pounding began in his head. He clenched his fist around the feather, all the strength flowing out of his arm. Gritting his teeth he strained to lift it and threw it into the fire.

The feather hissed and exploded. Coronos shielded his eyes as fire flared out in a violent burst of white sparks, then settled back to mellow orange flames. He leaned against the bedpost and wiped his sweaty brow.

Asaph stirred and he went to his side. The man moaned but did not awaken.

'My son, something foul has had its clutches upon you.' He laid a hand on the man's hot, clammy forehead. 'Rest now. The feather is gone, whatever it was. We shall speak in the morning when you are up.'

Feeling exhausted but not wanting to leave Asaph alone, he settled himself on the couch beside his bed. What had really happened in the forest just the other night? Whatever it was, the foltoy was not working alone. He was sure of it.

CHAPTER 12

Strange New World

JARLAIN had many questions she wanted to ask the boatman about Marakon—where he had gone and why he was cursed, but the rocking of the boat and the soft slapping of the waves made her sleepy.

Free from worrying about predators, insects or the weather, she finally relaxed.

She awoke with nothing beneath her but damp earth. There was no sea or rocking boat either. Her searching hands found she slept between two trees, the species of which she did not recognise. Their bark was extremely rough and their leaves were strange, not wide and flat but long and thin like needles, and prickly. The ground was covered with them too, making it spongy to walk upon. Where was she? She tried to reach her inner vision but it eluded her and she began to worry she might have lost it.

'Hello?' she called out.

There came no reply. The boatman was gone and she was completely alone in a place she did not know. She shivered and rubbed her arms. When had she ever felt this cold before? It never got this cold at home, even in the stormy season. Home—her warm little house filled with food, fresh water and clothes. She forced the homesickness away angrily. She was shamed. Hai and the elders had banished her. It was not her home anymore.

Groping around, she found her hardwood stick—at least she still had that. She took a few unsteady paces, feeling the rocking of the boat in her legs. Her stomach rumbled but she found no fallen fruit nearby, only dead leaves and sticks. She tried to reach her inner vision but maybe she was shivering too much for it eluded her again. She gave up looking for food and moved towards the sound of rushing water.

The noise grew louder and became a roar in her ears. The river must be huge. She wished she could see its beauty with her own eyes.

Her stick splashed at the river's edge. She knelt and scooped the cold crisp water to her mouth, drinking long and deep, hoping to drown out her hunger. Despite the cold, she slipped off her sackcloth and stepped into the freezing shallows, feeling the pull of the current. Kneeling, she washed the sea salt off her body.

The sun came out as she worked, but it was weak and lacked so much warmth that she wanted to cry. This land was not her home and she tried not to hate it. Blinking back tears, she thanked the goddess for the sunshine anyway, stood up and let the weak rays dry her as best it could.

Shivering, she pulled on her sack and set her mind to hunting for trees with long flat leaves. At home they wove the wide fronds of jungle ferns to create canopies. There had to be something here she could use to weave simple clothing from, anything to keep out the chill.

Her hands found nothing.

She followed the river upstream and her feet trod upon a carpet of round, waxy leaves with long stems. It would be possible to weave the long stems together, but how warm they would be was questionable. She began collecting leaves anyway.

She hadn't woven since she was taught the skill as a child, but even blindfolded, it came back to her easily. How little she'd cared for weaving, until now. Were these her lessons? Gratitude for the simplest of things that might just save her life? She would do anything to be warm again.

She created just a simple small cloak out of the leaves, draped it over her shoulders and closed the weaving at the front. She wondered how she must look, like a Hidden One revealing itself in the forest, all covered in leaves and dirt. The thought made her laugh, a hollow sound in the quiet wood. Her leaf cloak was warmer but still she shivered.

Now she needed food but how could she find it? She tried not to let the panic of hunger and of being somewhere foreign and seemingly inhospitable overwhelm her. *Panic breeds chaos,* as her people said.

Every place with trees had food, always; she just had to find it. At least she had water and a little warmth. She could cover herself in fallen leaves at night. Predators she could do little against except pray to Woela to protect her.

The boatman said he would take her as close to her heart's desire as he could. Wherever she was, she was as close to Marakon as she could be and that brought happiness into her heart, enough to give her hope. All she had to do was find him.

Calm of mind and filled with purpose, her inner vision returned. She saw a red-tinged world of tall trees. Some were rounded and their leaves hung head-height off the earth. Others were very tall and straight, narrowing off to a point at their peaks. Ferns, like those at home but smaller and more delicate, covered the ground between the trees. There were no nuts or fallen fruit on the ground. Her inner vision wavered. She would find food, she had to. She began to forage in earnest.

Hours must have passed and the sun had gone now, but her stomach wouldn't let her give up.

A bush, flat and dense with dark round things amongst its leaves, loomed into view.

'Ouch,' she yelped and sucked her pricked finger. The bush was covered in thorns—which meant the bush was protecting something. Its delicious fruit, no doubt.

Careful to avoid the thorns, she pulled a soft berry off and warily bit into it. A burst of tart sweetness filled her mouth and she almost groaned with relief. Sweet meant edible, at least she hoped the old teaching was true. Hunger won over caution and berry after berry she pushed into her mouth, stripping the whole bush bare before she stopped. She wasn't full but at least she was no longer starving.

She had the sense that evening was already approaching and thoughts of a fire to warm herself filled her mind.

Collecting wood, leaves and twigs turned out to be much easier than foraging for food in this place. Setting her material down, she began rubbing two sticks together. Like weaving, it was something she had not done for a very long time. It was painfully slow.

She smiled when she felt heat then smelt smoke. There came a soft crackle and the intense heat of fire. Deeper red appeared in the red of her vision. The sound of flames and the warmth it gave offered her a calming sense of familiarity in this foreign world. But still, just surviving had taken all day. What if Marakon was on the move? What if she lost him already before she'd even started?

Gathering leaves around her, she lay down before the flames. For a moment Hai's face hung disembodied in her mind. His eyes were sad as he looked at her and her hatred of him wavered. He opened his mouth and seemed to be calling to her and then his face was gone. Was he thinking of her? What did it matter?

She was afraid of this cold new world in which she found herself. Only thinking of Marakon gave her strength and purpose. She didn't care that he had a wife. She didn't even care if he didn't want to be with her. All that mattered is that she saw him again, to be in his company for a short while, if only to end the curse laid upon her by her own people.

Was he north or south of here? How would she find him? She'd given him a keepsake—a lucky stone with a bear on one side and a sun on the other. Something of hers in his possession linked them together, but was that link strong enough to guide her?

She could survive like this for a little while but it was hard. She existed but she did not live and her soul was silent. Only when she was with him would she be alive again.

Brown eyes and yellow fangs in an open mouth filled her dream. Giant paws, complete with thick claws, walked. The beast made her freeze. A growling roar ripped through the air, making her whole body tremble awake.

The dream went, leaving her blinking against the cloth that bound her eyes. Had the roar been in the dream, or was it a warning vision? Knowing better than to ignore her dreams, she grabbed her stick and strained uselessly to see through the blindfold. What could she possibly do against a hungry predator hunting her?

She hunched into a crouched position, shivering with cold and vulnerability. She went over the beast in her dream. It was one of them— a bear—just like the one on the stone she'd given Marakon and like the ones the elders drew on their sacred instruments. They'd seemed majestic then, but now they were terrifying.

Her sharpened hearing picked up movement in the forest behind. Using all of her senses and training, she tried to determine where it moved or what kind of creature it was. A foot fell, soft but heavy. Twigs snap under its weight. The animal sniffed the air noisily—smelling her, no doubt, since she was upwind. Whatever it was, it was big.

Her heart pounded in her throat but she remained still. She was completely exposed and unprotected. If she moved slowly she could maybe climb the tree behind her. Sitting here, just waiting for death, was stupid.

Soundlessly, inch by inch, she stood up and reached for the tree trunk. There were no lower branches, only smooth bark. It would be fatal to climb blindfolded anyway.

It ran then, heavy footfalls pounding the earth, making the ground shudder. A gasp exploded from her lips and she clung to the tree and froze. Pain would come at any moment.

The animal stopped.

With the Sight she saw it. A bear. It was black, or appeared to be in her inner vision, and it was big—bigger than the bush pigs of home. Its fangs were over an inch long and a long pink scar ran up its lip, pulling it up slightly. She didn't stand a chance.

It roared, baring its flesh-ripping fangs. She whimpered. The roar faded into a low growling sound as it walked closer, swinging its great bulk, heavy muscle rippling under thick fur.

She wished she didn't have her inner vision, but now she couldn't seem to turn it off. Sweat beaded her forehead. She shouldn't show fear—all animals could sense it—but she may as well try to stop the sun rising for the fear engulfed her.

The bear snorted, fully scenting her, then stood up to a giant height. A sob escaped her throat. The bear raised its head back and snorted.

Finding the courage to move, she began to back away. She inched herself around the tree, hoping to place it between it and her.

'I mean you no harm, Great Bear,' her voice was a trembling whisper. 'Please let me go.'

The bear dropped back onto all fours and came towards her until it was barely two yards away. She shuffled backwards, letting go of the tree. Her heel caught on a root and she sprawled onto her back, the breath knocked from her lungs. She lay gasping, waiting for the bear to rip out her throat.

Instead it just watched her. Seconds passed like hours. Then the bear turned and lumbered into the forest, back the way it had come.

She let go of her breath and sank down into the roots, body

trembling and heart racing. For a good while she lay there until calm returned. Why hadn't it attacked? Maybe it had sensed no threat from her or maybe it had decided she wouldn't make a nice lunch. She thanked Woetala for sparing her.

Remaining alert for the bear, she sat on the forest floor and focused her mind upon Marakon, feeling for the bear stone she had given him that linked them together across hundreds of miles. It was such a small thing, she thought with a smile, and now for her it held so much power. She had only given him the luck token to help him in the Drowning Wastes and guide him back to her should he become lost. How funny it was that she would need it now.

The stone was clear in her mind as she let her senses expand, feeling out where it might be: north, east, south or west. She felt a faint pull.

'North,' she breathed. Was it enough to go on? It had to be; it was all she had. She'd have to leave the river and hope she found another one before she got too thirsty.

It felt sunnier today and she thanked Fey the Sun Goddess for giving her the warmth she so needed—its warmth would help guide her north.

With her belly full of berries and the sun almost hot on her right shoulder, she set off, stick swinging left and right. Her bare feet had become so hard she barely felt the sharp needle-leaves on the ground, or the jagged edges of stones. The roaring of the river disappeared behind her and the trees crowded in, making it harder for her to feel the guiding sunlight on her skin. It was slow going and she stopped often, feeling for the bear stone.

By the time the sun began to set, she heard the tinkling sound of a stream. Besides the stream her feet trod on hard round balls about the size of her fist. She bent down and felt the ground.

The balls had a rubbery texture. Could they be fruit? She picked one up. It smelled sweet. Tentatively she took a bite. It was sour with some sweetness. She bit into the fruit, revelling in its crisp juiciness. It seemed now that the less she had the more she appreciated. The thought humbled her. Was this the hardship that all elders endured? Did they need to realise the bounty of their lives before they were worthy enough to become elders? She was thankful just to be alive.

The next morning it was cold and she awoke stiff and sore and ungrateful for her lot. Even her old wound from the Sea Devil knife throbbed painfully. She refused to imagine being in her warm house, eating her rich and varied food. What good would dreaming of things lost do?

Why hadn't she found Marakon? The boatman was supposed to take her right to him, but then he was in a boat and perhaps could only go as close to her destination as his boat would allow. A wide river inland was maybe all he could do.

She rubbed her arms, hoping the sun would come out. Her shoulders felt thin. Her stomach was no longer soft but firm and slim and her hipbones were easily felt under her fingers. Her curves were mostly gone and replaced with muscle. She scratched her scalp. Her hair had grown to almost a fingers' width. She wished she had her long thick locks to keep her warm in this cursed place.

She scowled, resenting Hai again. He must really hate her for punishing her so harshly. Maybe she deserved to die—death would certainly be easier than this. Hadn't she served him and the elders faithfully and willingly since she'd learned to speak? Not one of the elders had stood up for her, and that had hurt. If what she had done was so unforgivably bad, why did the Hidden Ones still give her visions? Even here, so far from home, they could reach her.

She got up and went to the stream for water. Her feet crunched on something cold, so incredibly cold it burned. She stepped back and felt her feet. They were unharmed. Reaching down she touched the grass. It was solid stiff. Frozen—the northern tribe's name for something this cold, came to her. She had never experienced frozen things before, but she'd heard stories from the northern tribes. In the cool season the ground would turn white and sometimes frozen rain would come. The frost melted into water in her hand. She licked it. It was pure and tasteless, like water. What a marvel, she thought, wishing she could see it with her real eyes.

What she thought was beautiful at first soon became painful as she walked. Her feet turned so cold she could no longer feel them. She did her best to wrap leaves around them but they soon broke. Half a day must have passed before the sun came out and melted the frozen ground. There was nothing to do but continue until she died of hunger, exhaustion or exposure. She didn't much care which one.

She would later wonder why she didn't see the ravine, or why the Hidden Ones had deserted her vision just then. Blindly she felt with her stick, swinging left and right. It clacked against another sloping wall of rock and there seemed to be no way round it. Cursing, she felt it with her hands, found footholds and began to climb, as she had twice before today.

The rock levelled and she stood up straight, catching her breath and searching for the inner vision. The rock beneath her shuddered and she froze. It tilted alarmingly and she screamed suddenly sliding forwards. She spun onto her belly and frantically scrabbled for a hold but found only loose rubble then air.

Another scream tore from her throat as she fell. Her left side struck a jutting rock. Panic blotted out the pain, then solid stone jarred her whole body, her breath exploding out of her lungs. Her mind flickered between pain and dark and then there was nothing.

In his silent world, Hai watched the storm of black ships reach their shores. The vision he had been given became a reality unfolding exactly as he had seen it. In the little time he had, he'd gathered those he could and led them up to High Rocks where they looked down upon the beasts who'd come to enslave and destroy. The black-armoured, man-like beings were as he had seen them in his vision: huge, deformed, lifeless—and there were thousands of them. Maphraxies, Marakon had called them.

The elders and tribes-people gathered around him and watched, each and every one of them steeling their hearts against what was to come. Hai gripped his staff and watched the abominations swarm up the beach to their homes. Even from this distance he could sense an emptiness in the man-beasts that made him shiver to the core. They were alive but not like he was.

'They're soulless.' Hai pointed out to the others, waving his staff at the Maphraxies below. His people looked pale, the children—so small and innocent—wanted to cry, but he admired their strength when their tears did not fall.

'The Hidden Ones have shown me they are attacking all the way up the coast, destroying our brothers and sisters. They'll burn our village and hunt us down.'

Unearthly screams ripped through his mind. Hai fell to the ground with his people. Everyone lay or knelt trembling. He looked upwards and locked onto the beasts in the skies. Riders, twice the size of a man, sat atop the flying lizards, their eyes glowing red. Hope died in his heart; he could not protect any of his people from them.

As if to complete the nightmare, fire spewed from their mouths as they dived low, igniting the jungle and their homes. Sobs shuddered through the Gurlanka. The Elder House burst into flames. His stomach lurched. The jungle that had fed, clothed and housed them all their days was burning alive.

The people scrambled to their feet, fighting against the fear the flying lizards spread. A strong hand gripped Hai's arm. He tried to shake it off, refusing to leave his burning village. The hand was stronger. He succumbed to it, turning to see Shufen's ashen face. The young man dragged him away from the horror, into the dark of the jungle.

They could not outrun them, Hai knew. The Maphraxies were fast despite their lumbering size, and soon they spotted them, black abominations bolting through green. The tribe ran on, old and young, but the undead did not tire. *Why did they bother running?* Hai thought bitterly.

One came alongside them, a stinking, helmeted beast with an ugly black blade. Shufen paused and loosed two arrows, dropping the Maphraxie and wounding another behind it. He was joined by other archers. It would not be enough, Hai knew. They had to run and run and never stop.

The flying lizards screamed and the bone-shaking terror ripped through the people again. Fire exploded in the trees ahead and to the right. With the Maphraxies behind, they were forced left. Hai caught Shufen's glance and shook his head. A mix of anger and fear passed across the younger man's face, but in the end he turned away and followed the fleeing Gurlanka. There was no defeating this enemy.

Hai, along with the old people, began to fall behind. Fit as he was for his old age, his legs were no longer made to run through the jungle like he once had. The enemy was closing in all around. Fire blocked the path ahead and nightmares swarmed the jungle behind.

'Up,' Sharnu mouthed and nodded to a big Halan Palm. She was breathless and trembling.

They began to climb, shaking hand over shaking hand. The Elders who saw them began to climb too.

An orange tidal wave of flames flooded through the jungle beneath them, engulfing all who were on the ground or not high enough. Some screamed; he could hear their souls crying out in his inner hearing. Then there was silence and he knew they were gone. Only he and Sharnu had climbed high enough to escape the flames.

The fire receded. Beneath the trampling boots of the Maphraxies were the black, smoking bodies of his friends. Hai looked away. He closed his eyes and held his staff high, mentally calling on cool winds to protect his tree from flames, and to shield himself and Sharnu from the eyes of the enemy.

More people came but there was no hope for them. All he could do was watch them fight, burn or flee. He wanted to burn with them but duty held him. Nothing must be lost of this day—the end of his people. From his protected visual amongst the canopy, he would be the recorder of his people's demise, committing it all to perfect memory. He would be the one to survive and tell others what became of the Gurlanka.

The enemy swarmed beneath him now, a carpet of black beetles. Wherever there were children, they hunted in earnest, nets drawn. Marakon had said they'd taken children. The horror of it had been distant until now. Hai watched, helpless, as the children were ensnared, as the young men and women were beaten, killed or bound. Sick as it was, he noticed a pattern. Those gifted with abilities from the Hidden Ones were spared. They wanted them and the children only.

Sharnu reached up and clasped his hand. Did hers tremble or did his? They said nothing, looked only at their people being slain. It was a silent agony. What could he do to help them? Even had he been a young man, he would have been killed or ensnared already. It was his duty to record all that happened this day. Had he been given the choice, he would be down there fighting and dying with his people, but the choice was not given to him.

Sharnu caught his eyes, reflecting the horror he felt. He was very glad, then, that he could not physically hear his peoples' screams.

The dead mounted; the battle waned. The enemy receded, taking their children, taking their gifted. The fires burned out and the flying lizards went. Sharnu and Hai remained on their perch. For the rest of the night they stayed there, and for all that time Hai prayed to the goddess that some of his people had survived.

She must have heard his prayers for, before dawn, the rain came heavy, dousing smouldering fires and soothing the earth. He let it fall on his face, wishing it would cleanse his mind and soul of all that he'd witnessed.

In the morning a blackened world appeared, one where smoke rose in stinking billows. A warm hand touched his wet cheek and he looked at Sharnu.

'The noise has stopped; the screams have gone,' her lips said. 'There's only silence. Even the birds have gone.'

Hai nodded. It was time to go.

'Is that why you sent Jarlain away?' Sharnu said.

Hai smiled at her insight and nodded again. 'When she was born, I saw the death and rebirth of our people. Only now do I understand what I saw all those years ago. Our destruction was coming one way or another, whether Marakon came here or not. And for that I feel bad for punishing Jarlain so severely. I'm a foolish old man. I still don't forgive the High Elder before me for the punishment I received, why ever would Jarlain?'

'But perhaps it made you strong enough to be High Elder. You have saved Jarlain, Hai, so that our people can live on. And for that she will forgive, in the end,' Sharnu said.

He nodded but did not agree.

'Pray that we can make it to The Centre.'

CHAPTER 13

The Oracle

THE scene that met Issa was chaos and confusion.

She entered a parlour that was as long as it was wide, with a ceiling so high it was at least two storeys above her. In the centre was an extravagant raised dais. Red light pulsed across the room in the sickening waves. It was coming from a large crystal ball beside the dais. Her head throbbed with the light and she felt woozy.

Next to the crystal sat what Issa could only describe as a mad woman. She had wild, grey-brown hair, wore half-moon spectacles and a strange kind of overly flouncy white robe with ruffles at the neck. She was pointing and screaming insanely at two women standing below her.

Issa stared at them. How was Edarna here? She was dressed unusually in her green witch's robe and holding out her wand which was pulsing white flares into the red pulses coming from the crystal.

Beside her stood a completely calm, small woman with white hair and skin, and wearing blue robes. She held, above her, a thin staff that glowed white. Issa's gaze lingered upon her. She commanded magic just like a wizard did and it was just as powerful. *A seer, she must be.*

An awful screeching cut through the air. She covered her ears and cowered, then grappled for the raven talisman in her bag. A window exploded and a huge white owl flew into the room. The Under Flow flowed towards the owl as it screeched and swooped at Edarna and Naksu, its talons swiping. Both women ducked. It arced towards the woman on the dais.

With the Flow drained from her command, Issa called upon the raven talisman in her hand. Indigo magic exploded from it, pushing back the red. The blue light reached the crystal ball, shattering it and showering the room in glistening shards. The white owl swooped high and darted back out of the window. The Under Flow fled. Calm descended on the room.

Shouts and banging came from behind the closed door beyond the dais as people struggled to get in. Edarna looked at her wand; it had stopped pulsing white light. She shook it as if trying to get it working again, then looked at Mr Dubbins sitting by Issa's feet.

'I've been looking for you for a day! Where have you been, cat?' she hissed.

Mr Dubbins meowed and bounded over to the witch. He jumped into her open arms and purred loudly as she cuddled and crooned over him. 'There, there, all finished. Nasty magic's gone now, Mr Dubbinsies.'

Issa smiled, wondering if the witch had noticed her yet.

The albino woman looked at Issa with faintly pink eyes that were as pretty as they were unusual. She smiled at her. Issa nodded back, still unsure as to what had happened. The woman on the dais was shaking and slumped in her chair. She suddenly seemed very old and frail as she wiped a shaking hand across her face.

'Oh my.' The woman gasped.

A man, woman and a guard fell through the door as it was kicked open. They stared in shock at the splintered glass covering the parlour then ran to the moaning woman.

'Oh my crystal ball, my magic!' The mad woman looked up and her eyes fell on Issa. She raised a shaking finger and pointed at her.

'You,' she rasped and began to shout. 'You! It's she, the charlatan. She's come to trick us all.'

'Oracle Hykerry,' the white woman's commanding voice rang out, her face pinched, 'have you completely taken leave of your senses? That magic coming from your crystal ball was no magic of Maioria but the magic of the Immortal Lord! No use of the Under Flow will be tolerated in Free Maioria.'

Oracle Hykerry looked slapped. Issa considered the woman, realising now that she was the famous Oracle. Cirosa was right about something—she was completely mad. The Oracle cackled madly at Naksu then all humour was lost from her face as she glared in utter hatred back at Issa. Issa took a step back, her hand dropping to her sword that wasn't there.

'She makes pacts with demons,' the Oracle hissed. Issa's eyes widened. How could this woman know? 'We all know what happens to those who make pacts with demons, don't we, Veren?'

Everyone looked at her.

'Get her, the charlatan, the one who'll destroy us all. Chain the demon-speaker!' the Oracle screamed. The guard started towards Issa, followed by her confused assistants.

Issa backed away. A loud crack from the seer's staff smacking the floor made them stop.

'Enough,' commanded the seer. 'No one will be chained. There's been enough madness today for a whole year!

'Oracle Hykerry, I will immediately report back to the Seers of Myrn what I've seen here today. They won't be pleased. I'll ask them to send one of their finest healers to assist you in your troubles, but until then, it will be in your best interests to refrain from ever using magic until the madness has left you.

'Mark my words, Oracle Hykerry, if ever the Under Flow is felt here again, the Temple will be closed by the King, the seers, the wizards and the people until future notice. Do I make myself clear?'

Oracle Hykerry went white as a sheet, making her seem like a wraith in her swathes of white robes. She began to giggle like a little girl.

The seer turned to her assistants. 'Get her some rest but don't forget what I've said. Using the Under Flow is a grave thing indeed.'

The assistants paled and nodded. Carefully they crunched over the broken glass to assist the giggling Oracle.

'Well, I never. I search for weeks and you turn up here?' Edarna beamed and stepped towards Issa.

'Edarna.' Issa smiled and hugged the old witch, Mr Dubbins purring between them. 'How did you get here?'

'Hah. Now there's a tale. One for later, I think. I'd like to leave this disturbing place.' She looked around and shivered.

'Me too.' Issa nodded. She noted the black-petalled flower decorating the floor and remembered the Mother's Chamber on Celene. Maybe this place too was corrupt, just as the Oracle certainly was. Perhaps the entire Order of the Goddess was infected by Baelthrom.

'What do you reckon, Naksu? A nice cup of tea or something stronger at home? I feel as old as my wand!' Edarna turned towards the door.

'I think so,' Naksu agreed.

They didn't speak as they left the glass-covered parlour until they emerged outside the golden gates.

'Who were those nasty people?' Hykerry asked, struggling to remember their names.

'No one to worry about, Oracle. They've gone now, thankfully,' said Veren. 'But they did advise you, for health reasons, not to use any more magic. You know how it tires you and makes you sick. I think you should do what they say.'

'All right, Jen.' She yawned. 'I never got on too well with it anyway. Oh look over there—a shining white feather!'

Hykerry found some energy and trotted over to pick the feather from the shattered glass. 'Oh it's beautiful.' She giggled and tucked it into her pocket.

Outside the temple there was a commotion and lots of shouting coming from beyond the golden gates. Issa glimpsed two older men mounted and surrounded by temple guards. A large crowd of people were gathering too. They hurried to see what was going on.

'Freydel,' Issa said in surprise as they neared. The wizard was riding a palomino horse and holding his staff menacingly towards two guards. 'Coronos,' she added, seeing the old Draxian atop his horse, Socks. More guards came running from the temple and pushed past them towards the men.

'In the name of all that is holy, let us through!' Freydel shouted. 'The enemy is amongst us. The Under Flow is here.'

'No one is going through these gates, not even the king himself,' said a guard reaching for his sword.

'Sacrilege,' the wizard retorted. 'Who do you think you are? Who do you think runs this kingdom? The king will hear of this. The Temple has clearly become too powerful if it thinks it can override a king's wishes!'

'It's all right, Freydel,' Issa raised her voice. He blinked and squinted through the golden bars at her. 'It's gone, whatever it was,' she added.

He lowered his staff and took in the women beside her. Surprise danced across his features.

'Naksu,' he bowed slightly from his saddle. 'What a pleasure it is to see you after so long.'

She smiled. 'Master Wizard Freydel.'

'A witch anywhere always causes trouble,' a guard growled at Edarna.

She scowled at him and reached into her pocket for her wand.

'Not now,' the seer said, grabbing Edarna's arm. 'Freydel's right. Let the king sort this out in his own manner. Our work is done here and we need never return.'

Edarna relaxed but never took her eyes off the guard.

'Let us pass,' Issa commanded when they didn't open the gates. 'How dare you talk to wise women like that.'

' 'Ew let you in?' said another guard, shock on his face.

'The goddess herself,' Issa retorted. 'Now let us out.'

One gate creaked open and she stalked through, scowling. The others followed. The crowd of people were sniggering at the spectacle. Clearly they were not too enamoured with the guards either.

'If any of you return here again, there'll be serious consequences,' a guard menaced.

'The only person who'll be returning here will be the king,' Freydel glared, 'and the consequences will be upon you.'

The crowd cheered and Issa suppressed a giggle.

Without rushing but without dallying, they walked away. When the temple was lost from view, the wizards dismounted and greeted the women properly. They all began to chatter at once.

'What happened?'

'Who do they think they are?'

'The king needs to be informed at once.'

'Seer Naksu, it's good to see you again.' Coronos smiled.

'And you, Coronos Dragon Rider,' she replied. 'How does your son fare?'

'He's fit and well but bored and getting into trouble, it seems. I try to keep him out of street brawls and mischief but I think he needs more. He needs a Dragon Lord's training and there is none to help him.'

Issa frowned. Asaph in street brawls? It couldn't be true. She remembered Cirosa's white legs wrapped around his body and shivered. Every time she thought of him she remembered that awful time in the Storm Holt.

'He needs his home; he needs his kingdom back,' Naksu said. 'The dragon blood that moves in his veins won't let him rest. At least he has the Dragon Dream.'

'Indeed,' Coronos replied. 'I wish I were younger. I could help him more then.'

'The dragons are not all gone,' Naksu said. 'And us seers feel them closer than most would think.'

Coronos looked surprised. 'Yes, he must seek them out. It's all he can do.'

'What happened back there,' Freydel blurted. 'I felt Baelthrom's hand and the sickening movement of the Under Flow. I couldn't reach the Flow to get there quicker.'

'The Oracle is truly mad,' Edarna replied. She eyed the wizards suspiciously, reminding Issa that she didn't fully trust men with magic. 'It seems she may be infected by one of *'em*.'

'But how? How did it get in?' Freydel said.

'We don't know; maybe we never will, but that place isn't safe,' Naksu said, creasing her forehead.

'Why don't you both accompany us to the castle where we can talk at length?' Coronos said. 'King Navarr would no doubt love to have a seer as a guest. And a witch,' he added hastily when Edarna glowered at him. Issa hid a smile. 'I haven't seen a wise witch for a long time,' he mused.

'The name's Edarna Higglesworth, Witch of the Western Isles,' she said proudly. Mr Dubbins meowed his introduction.

'Indeed. Nice to meet you Edarna,' Coronos smiled. Freydel gave her a bemused nod, and frowned at the blue cat.

King Navarr welcomed the women graciously and had his servants and kitchen set out a fine meal. He couldn't stay, however, having pressing business with the mayor.

Despite talking at length over everything that had happened, no one was the wiser as to how Baelthrom's hand had reached into the heart of

Carvon, creating a worried atmosphere. Coronos went to see if he could find Asaph and Freydel went to check on Arla, leaving the women to chat amongst themselves.

Naksu sipped her steaming mug of tea, one of Freydel's cinnamon blends, her eyes lightly resting on Issa who was chatting with Edarna. She noted the young woman's white tunic dress and pale blue cardigan. *She even dresses like a seer.* Her aura was indigo blue flecked with violet, and it radiated out in waves far beyond anyone else's.

Yes, she held magic, powerful magic, and it neither had the signature of a witch's, a wizard's or a seer's. Naksu was intrigued; the girl was a mystery. Though she was far older than any of their beginners, a seer's training would go very far indeed with her, to the Trinity level, no doubt.

Naksu had the ability to either dominate a room, or blend in so well that no one knew she was there. She was blending in with the energies now, but even so, Issa obviously felt her watchful eyes and turned to look at her. The young woman smiled.

'My mother, Fraya—well she was my adopted mother—wrote to the seers,' Issa said. 'She wanted me to become a healer but was worried when you never came. She told me my blood mother was a seer, though I don't remember her or even know her name. I have some ability with healing, only animals though.'

Edarna stood up whilst they chatted and snuck around, clearly taking the opportunity to explore every nook and cranny and ornament in the dining room.

'If letters ever reach us, and not many do, we reply in person when can, when the time is right,' Naksu said. 'With power such as yours, it doesn't surprise me that you have a healer's hand, but I don't think that's where your true power lies. How indeed could you use the Flow when it had been sucked away from us?'

'I don't know, exactly, but I drew it from the talisman,' Issa said and placed the sparkling raven talisman on the table. 'It works like an orb in that it's a key to drawing power from somewhere else, somewhere—'

'From the dark moon,' Naksu said and smiled at the shock on Issa's face.

Edarna paused her in-depth exploration behind the books in the bookcase and waited for more to be said.

'Yes. How did you know?' said Issa.

'Simply from the feel of it. It's the same feel I get when the dark moon rises,' Naksu said.

'Do you know any more about this talisman?' Issa asked.

Naksu looked at it and projected her mind onto it. The energy was different, not of this planet, and yet somehow connected to it and everything.

'It's not from Maioria,' she said, still focusing her attention, 'so it's hard to read. But its power comes from the dark moon. That's why it can be used when the Flow is compromised; its power is from beyond here. Look there—it has a hole, as if it fits on to something. It's very ancient. Hmm, that cannot be. It could be older even than Maioria herself. There's so much more about it that I cannot read... How did you come by it?'

'Arla found it. A little girl from the Temple of Celene. I'd love to learn how to read objects like that,' Issa asked.

'I can teach you, but you must come to Myrn and learn like all the other seers,' said Naksu. 'There's much you could learn there.'

'Yes, Arla,' Freydel said, overhearing them as he came back into the room. There was a worried look on his face. 'Naksu, can you help her?'

Naksu looked down at the small child under swathes of blankets. Her breath came weakly and she was so pale she was almost like herself—a White One.

Freydel explained everything that had happened to her—from his knowledge of her in the Temple of Celene, to her finding him in the astral planes.

Naksu pushed the blankets aside and laid a hand on the child's forehead.

'This isn't a fever; the child is cold,' she said.

There was something more too. She frowned and closed her eyes. The child was not quite right. She couldn't explain it. It was almost as if the child's soul was separated. She could see a long, thin white trail of the girl's aura leading up and out into the astral. Naksu stood up, shaking her head.

'She needs a Traveller. One who can travel beyond these planes easily and is adept in the art. Keteth was one such Traveller, of sorts.'

'I think Arla *is* a Traveller,' said Freydel. 'That's how she reached me.'

'Then she'll definitely need another traveller to bring her back. We have one or two on Myrn but it could take weeks for them to get here.'

Issa chewed her finger. Time was slipping by and nothing had been done; no one seemed to be able to help Arla. The girl couldn't last much longer.

Edarna pushed open a window, letting in a gust of cool air.

'Ah that's better.' She sighed. 'Poor child must be suffocating in here. Now then…' She bustled close, pushing the others out of the way, and laid a hand on Arla's forehead.

Mr Dubbins jumped onto the bed and sniffed the girl, his whiskers twitching.

'Hmm,' said the witch. 'Her soul is split. Part here, part…somewhere else I cannot reach. She needs to be rejoined, somehow. Either by taking her body there or bringing her soul here.'

'I did manage to rouse her,' Issa said. 'She asked me to take her to the boatman, but I'm not sure how.'

Naksu looked at her. 'The Ancient cursed to travel between places and to exist in none? Of course!'

'How do you know so much?' Issa marvelled.

Naksu smiled. 'Seers are Keepers of Knowledge. Whilst we are not Keepers of Orbs, ancient knowledge is our power.' She winked at Freydel, who gave a bemused smile.

'There's a lot I need to learn.' Issa sighed.

'There's a lot I still don't know,' Naksu said. 'But if you really want to learn, then you know where to come.'

Edarna stood up. 'I think you'd better do what she asked, missy. Take her to this boatman, and soon.'

'I was waiting for Asaph to return because he's called the boatman before.' Issa shrugged.

With nothing more they could do, they left Arla to rest. Everyone looked defeated. Outside in the courtyard, Edarna turned to Issa.

'Now then,' she said, taking out a yard of thread. 'I have a gift for you. It's a surprise so don't go asking what it is.' She busied herself measuring Issa with the yarn.

Naksu watched, intrigued. Did this have anything to do with what the witch was working on in her little room?

'A present? It better be some fine purple Atalanphian silk.' Issa grinned, lifting up her arms.

'Hah. It's better than that. Come by tomorrow, and it should be ready,' said Edarna. We live at number 48 North Street, above the red painted cobblers. She patted Issa's cheek.

'If you need us, we are here,' Naksu said, laying a hand on Issa's arm. Then she dropped her voice so only Issa could hear. 'We must find time alone to talk about these demons. The Oracle might be mad, but she does not lie and demon speakers are still hanged.'

Issa paled at her words. 'They mean me no harm. They want my help. They talk about a white spear and tell me the greater demons are coming to destroy them and then us.'

'I know a little about the white spear, but let's not talk about it here. There's danger afoot in Carvon,' Naksu said, no longer hushed. 'Hykerry was more than just mad. And that white owl is not what it seemed.'

'I had forgotten about the owl,' said Issa.

Naksu pursed her lips. 'From the little I can see, there's turbulent energy abounding. We all felt it in The Flow. Let's pray that the Oracle has not been spouting off about you and demons to everyone.'

Edarna nodded. 'They still flay and hang demon speakers. No idea what nonsense that nutter has been saying. Anyway, it's getting dark and I need to do my work.' The witch fidgeted.

'Looking at me, do you know who my blood mother might be? If she's alive?' Issa blurted. 'Apparently we have the same eyes and hair, though hers was lighter.'

Naksu looked at her then shook her head. Issa's face fell. 'I won't say that I do. Not all the women who train as seers stay on Myrn. But when we have some time alone, why don't we try to find her?'

Issa smiled, making Naksu feel better.

'I barely know you, but I mean it when I say you should come to Myrn. You know a bit of the ways of witches, more of the ways of wizards, but so little of the ways of seers. There is power you can learn that will help you. Come to Myrn, and soon.'

CHAPTER 14

Ancient Lovers

THAT evening after dinner, Issa went to find Freydel.

Apparently Asaph had returned, but she'd not seen him at all, not even at dinner. He hadn't come to seek her out either, and that left her with mixed feelings. She wanted to see him, even though she couldn't get the raw memory of him and Cirosa making love out of her head.

But it wasn't him and it wasn't real, she reminded herself. It had been demon tricks in a demonic world. Perhaps it was better they avoided each other for now, until she could get her feelings in order.

She knocked on Freydel's door and went in when he called.

'Wow, it's just like your old one,' she marvelled at his large, round room complete with a plush four-poster bed, tall windows and a desk covered with books and scrolls. 'And it's already a mess.'

Freydel snorted. 'Yes, it's in perfect order. Navarr is generous, but nothing can replace my stargazing windows. Now then, look.'

He placed the orb on its metal pedestal and carried straight on from the conversation they had been having at the stables, as if he'd been thinking about it all day. Within the orb, images formed. Huge crystal pyramids higher than any castle rose into the sky. Issa peered closer, staring in awe. It was surely the same place Zanufey had shown her—the same world. Could it be true?

As the images moved silently across the orb's surface, Freydel began to explain the images, telling her everything that had happened to him in the astral planes.

'This place is not Maioria. It was another time and planet entirely. The beings there were human-like, but they were so totally different and so totally advanced. The magic they could wield…' he trailed off and stared in wonder at the images. She gasped as tall, beautiful beings, swathed in glimmering robes, walked the crystal paths between the pyramids.

'They are the same I saw in a vision given to me by Zanufey,' she whispered.

'Incredible,' Freydel said. 'Tell me what you saw.' His eyes were bright with intrigue. She told him everything Zanufey had shown her of the planet that was destroyed. It wasn't easy to articulate what she'd witnessed, but Freydel didn't disbelieve a word.

'It's my gut feeling that the Ancients and these beings are related,' he said.

Issa started at the thought. Surely it was impossible? But now she looked at the beings, she could see the similarities: the six-fingered hands and toes, the power they held, the shape of their eyes and faces.

'But how can they come from there if this is a different planet and time entirely?' The thought suddenly scared her. She felt truth in Freydel's words but everything seemed too big and important for her to grasp.

'Look.' Freydel indicated towards the orb.

Her eyes rested on a being dressed differently from the rest, in dark robes rather than light. Cold gripped her heart and her throat. She knew that being. He might not look the same, but his essence felt horribly familiar.

'No, it can't be.' She stepped back, her chest constricting.

'Be calm,' Freydel commanded. 'He can't see us here. Tell me what you see. What do you feel?'

'It's him. It's…him. I don't know why or how but… I don't understand.' She stared at the being, the darkness of his aura, the way he moved, the power he exuded. It was as she had felt in the Storm Holt; Baelthrom's form so perfectly mirrored by demonic forces.

'I can *feel* it's him,' she breathed. Freydel nodded. 'The same dark power he holds, the look in his black eyes, the amulet on his chest—it's so alike the ones Dromoorai wear. I feel like I've known him before this life, known him for a long time.'

The thought sent her into a wild panic and she fell back. She shook her head. How could she know Baelthrom or this being? They couldn't be one and the same. Yet a part of her knew him beyond all those things. She didn't understand, didn't want to understand. She was afraid.

'Issa,' Freydel barked.

At his command the image dimmed, the being turned to swirling black and his hold on her released.

'Yes, it's him,' Freydel said quietly. 'I recognised him, too. He has the power to enthral even through the orb. I don't know why it took me there when I asked it to take me far away from Baelthrom.

'Perhaps it took me to where the Baelthrom we know now did not yet exist and couldn't reach us. Maybe it wanted me to do something, to prevent the reality we currently live. To undo what Baelthrom might become—it's the Orb of Undoing after all.

'The being you saw is called Ayeth, and he's the being who will become Baelthrom.'

Issa slumped into a chair. 'I don't understand; how is it possible?'

'I know. I don't understand it fully yet either. But Ayeth wanted the orb like no other, just as Baelthrom wants it now. He had some dark power back then, even though he hadn't fallen. He followed me as I struggled to return. It was the Ancient, Yisufalni, who reached me, and it was through her that Arla managed to bring me back. Without them I wouldn't be here. Somehow reaching me trapped Arla beyond our mortal plane. That's why I must try to return there and help her.'

'It's too dangerous. What if you get trapped too?' said Issa.

'It's the only way I—' The wizard stopped abruptly, frowning.

'There's more, isn't there?' she said. Freydel was holding something back. Was he afraid to speak about it? What was he hiding?

He nodded slowly. 'I've pondered long and late into the night on this. I wonder if I can return to Ayeth to stop the being he will become, to stop him becoming Baelthrom. His intentions are still good; I'm sure of it.'

'That's madness. You'll get trapped and die. Who knows what will happen—just look at Arla,' Issa blurted.

'Think about it,' he said sharply. 'What better way to stop Baelthrom ever coming here than by stopping him becoming what he is now?'

Issa looked to the floor, her mind whirring. Freydel had a point. If they stopped Ayeth, what would happen to Baelthrom here?

'I don't know, it sounds so…complicated.' Her head hurt with it all. 'But we must try to reach Arla if it's all we do. After that, maybe we'll know what to do next.'

'There's a reason the orb took me where it did,' Freydel began slowly. 'I really do think the Ancients are descendants of these pre-ancient beings, and I think they came to Maioria long ago, possibly even fleeing this Ayeth. The one Ancient myth we have left speaks about how they escaped from an all-consuming darkness… Of course, my thoughts are all theory. I've no proof they are related and may never have, but I'm determined to find out.'

She wanted to think him mad, but all she could do was wonder if it were true and what it might mean.

'You're right, though.' He smiled at her, looking suddenly drained. 'We must help Arla first. Tonight when the world is still, we'll call the boatman—with or without Asaph—and I'll try to reach her in the astral planes. Perhaps it will work, perhaps it won't, but it's worth a shot.

'Let's meet near the small lake—you know the one north-west of the city walls, barely a hundred yards away? I'll tell Coronos and we'll go together.'

A scratching at the window awoke Asaph with a start. He sat upright and wiped the sweat from his forehead. Someone had left a jug of water, two peeled oranges and a sandwich on the chair by his bed, though he'd not heard anyone come in. The bread had gone hard but he wasn't hungry anyway.

He flung the covers away and pulled off his drenched nightshirt. He used to have nightmares back with the Kuapoh and out of habit still kept a spare nightshirt under the bed. Now his nightmares were no longer about Issa but of a white owl chasing him and a beautiful woman making him go crazy with desire.

The scratching came again. He got up on shaky legs and pushed the heavy curtains aside. The room was stuffy and he opened the window. Cool night air rushed in and he stood there letting it blow over his sweaty chest.

Movement on the city wall caught his attention. It wasn't a guard but something small and white. He strained to see and leaned out of the window. The white thing shimmered and became the beautiful white woman sitting precariously upon the city wall, dangling her legs over the side. She beckoned to him. He felt something move; was it magic? It slithered thickly about him, befuddling his thoughts, twisting his reason.

He tore his eyes away and tried to focus on the magic, but only his dragon-self could feel and read magic properly. Why would she be using black enchantments upon him? Only witches and necromancers did that, and she was clearly none of those. If she'd wanted to hurt him, she would have done it by now. Unable to fight it, slowly his eyes were drawn—forced—back to the woman. He saw her lovely smile and full lips he wanted to kiss again and all he knew was that he had to go to her. If he wasn't quick, she might disappear again, like before. He would control himself this time and demand she tell him who she was and why she was following him.

As fast as his hands could work, he pulled on his clothes and boots, and ran as silently as possible out of the castle. The guards at the side door eyed him curiously when he burst through.

'Hi, er… I left something in my saddle bag,' he said, smoothing back his unbrushed hair.

They nodded. It seemed a good enough excuse not to cause any gossip. He hurried towards the stables but took a left, at the last minute, towards the gate. The lady was gone from the wall, but a shimmering bird he couldn't quite identify flew away from the city in the direction of the forest. He stepped outside the gate and again the guards there gave him questioning looks.

'I have to find some herbs; I forget what they're called, but they only flower at night,' he said, knowing it was weak. This caused a few raised eyebrows but before they could say anything, he hurried away. In the Old World collecting flowers was usually left to the women, but alchemists and wizards also went foraging. With the Kuapoh, it was the men who collected herbs. He didn't need to excuse himself to the guards, but he didn't want them gossiping either. With his sword in his belt, he still felt manly despite whatever the guards may have thought.

At the edge of the forest he stopped and looked around—his breath making clouds in the soft light cast from distant city lanterns. Where was the white woman? *What am I doing out here, chasing after her like an idiot?* The time it had taken to get here had lessened her power on him. His head began to ache dully now and he was cross with himself. Something wasn't right—the way she so easily affected him. His anger turned to concern with his own mental state and he started to walk back to the castle.

Just as he did he glimpsed white, slender legs moving through the trees.

'Hey,' he called out. 'Why are you following me? I demand answers.' His hand dropped to his sword and stalked towards the white legs. There came a long sigh and something tightened around his throat. He lifted a hand but could feel nothing there. His headache was gone and he felt good and able to think clearly. Her face appeared above a blackberry bush and she gave a comely smile that melted his anger.

'I just want to talk to you,' he said, his voice gentler. How could he ever fear this woman? All she wanted was company, whoever she was. He could see that clearly now. At last, a woman who wasn't afraid to be with him. He let go of his sword hilt and found his feet walking towards her of their own accord as if made to do so. She turned and, quick as a deer, bounded deeper into the forest. His feet dutifully followed and he tried to get a clearer glimpse of her, wanting to see her face and the curve of her body.

The trees closed in and the only sound came from the nearby gushing river. The light of Doon was particularly bright here, away from the city lights, and lined everything in silver.

She paused in the trees and waited for him, a soft smile curling her lips. His breath caught in his throat at her beauty. She reached up a hand and let the top of her dress fall down to her hips. He gasped, feeling raw need making his body tremble. Reaching out, he touched the cool smooth flesh of her arms and pulled her close, feeling his heart pound with intoxication. He pressed his lips on to her parted ones.

Issa awoke to the sound of someone knocking on her door. Freydel's hushed voice called from outside.

'Coming.' She jumped out of bed and pulled on her clothes.

Outside, Coronos held Arla in his arms. She was pale and still sleeping. Both the men's faces mirrored the worry she felt.

'Where's Asaph?' she whispered, realising she'd been looking forward to seeing him.

'We couldn't find him; his bed is empty,' Coronos said, his brow furrowing. 'I think he's sick again. He was burning up when I last checked on him.'

'Oh,' she said, feeling disappointed and also worried. He seemed to be sick a lot lately. It was odd that even Coronos didn't know where he was. Something was up and she resolved to talk to him as soon as she saw him.

'We'll try to call the boatman without him,' said Freydel.

Issa nodded, relieved to finally be doing something for Arla as they walked towards the gate.

'Good night for herb collecting?' said a guard as they passed through the gate.

'Indeed it is,' Freydel said with a beaming smile.

'And to ask for Doon's blessing for this sick child,' Coronos added.

'Right you are, sirs and madams.' The guards bowed. 'If you don't return before dawn, we'll send out a search party in case something's happened.'

'Thank you. That would be most kind,' Freydel said.

They hurried along the path leading towards the forest. The lake wasn't far and, after a left turn through ancient yew trees, they emerged at the water's edge.

It was a still, cloudless night and the lake perfectly reflected Doon's light and the Blaze of Eight trailing beneath it. Had worry for Arla not marred her mood, she would have revelled in the still beauty of the scene.

'Who'll call the boatman?' she asked.

'She asked you to take her to him; why don't you try?' Coronos said. 'Keep your reason clear in your mind and your need strong and urgent.'

She looked at Arla's expressionless face and a sense of hopeless urgency filled her. The boatman would come; he had to. It was a matter of life and death. She quieted her mind and held the image of Arla firm. When stillness came she spoke.

'Murlonius.'

She said it quietly but the word seemed to echo around them. Nothing happened.

'Murlonius,' she repeated, a little louder. The stillness deepened. Did she need to repeat it again? She was about to when dense mist formed above the centre of the lake until they could no longer see the other side. An orange lantern light appeared and then the beautiful carved prow of a boat materialised.

She stared at the bent-over old man rowing towards them—feeling again the waves of relief she had felt in the Shadowlands, knowing that she was saved. He had come, as easily as that.

'I can hold her.' She reached to take Arla from Coronos. The girl was horribly light and didn't even move. It was as if she was dead already. She stepped closer to the water, her feet crunching on the stones and then cool water slapping her sandals.

The boatman's eyes were upon her; she could feel his heavy gaze even though his face was hidden in his hood. This was what Arla had asked for. She only hoped he could help her.

The boat touched the shore and the man pulled back his hood just enough to reveal his incredibly wrinkled face and watery eyes. He said nothing as he looked at the child in her arms, then tears began to streak down his flaccid cheeks. She found tears filling her own eyes. Did he know this child?

'She's sick. Very sick,' Issa rasped. 'She asked to be taken to you. We don't know why.'

'Oh my…*allethi ama fiy,*' the man spoke in a language Issa had never heard before. It sounded elven but far more complicated, commanding and yet utterly musical. He reached out skeletal arms to take the child. Issa hoped he was strong enough to hold her.

Arla moaned and roused at his touch.

Murlonius knew it was her. Her body was different, but it was the one he had been waiting and longing for, for thousands of years. He could not be mistaken.

'Oh my Yisufalni.' He stroked the child's cheek and she began to glow a soft white light.

The humans clustering around him murmured. Slowly she blinked up at him, her pale eyes filled with unfathomable wisdom in a face that expressed only childish innocence.

'Murlonius,' she breathed in a voice that was half-childlike and half the one he remembered.

'I heard your voice calling to me all my long years adrift in emptiness,'

Murlonius whispered. 'It was all I clung to—the only thing that kept me going.'

'Murlonius,' she breathed and smiled. 'I'm dying. This body is unable to return to the ethereal planes where my spirit lives. I wanted to see you…before I go.'

'No,' Murlonius snapped, making everyone jump. 'I won't let you go. Not now, not after so long.'

'Murlonius, you know he'll come; you know he'll find us. Two together, the last of our kind united once more upon Maioria's sweet earth. Our essence together will be too strong for him to ignore.'

'I don't care,' he rasped. 'We shall die together. Let him kill us and end this sorry existence. Our time is done here and I'm tired, so very tired…'

'We cannot both leave,' she said, barely a whisper and even that seemed to pain her. 'One must remain for the Orb of Life. We must free it for the people of Maioria. She can recombine them. She has the power to make whole what was once broken.' She lifted a finger towards Issa.

His eyes rested on Issa for a moment. The Raven Queen seemed so young, so unaware of the power she held and the destiny that rested on her shoulders. She looked frightened too. Could she do what had to be done? Could she push back the darkness covering Maioria and filling their hearts?

He looked at the child in his arms. How long had he spent cursed to reside on his self-named Sea of Opportunity, the empty nothing place between places? Unable to live, unable to die, nothing but a glimmer of hope that he might one day see Yisufalni again, that he might one day be free—free to die. Now she was here; nothing could make him let go of her, not even Baelthrom himself.

'I cannot go on any longer without you, Yisufalni. I will not.'

'It's not for you to decide, my love.'

'But it *is* up to the Night Goddess,' Murlonius said. He glared at Issa. She was a disciple of Zanufey and Zanufey threatened to take away the only one he loved. 'Make Her stop. Tell Her she cannot have this one.'

Issa stepped back from Murlonius' glare. 'It's nothing to do with me. I cannot command a goddess. I have no power over life and death. I can only enter the realm of the dead and return—no more.'

He dropped his gaze and closed his eyes. Tears ran down his wrinkled cheeks. His pain was so raw. Did he think this was her fault? She didn't want Arla to die either, but she couldn't know Zanufey's intentions. That he thought she might have that power left her feeling strange.

Was Arla really his love? And not Arla at all but Yisufalni the Ancient who had helped Freydel in the astral planes? Was it the same Yisufalni who had come to her in the store rooms of Little Kammy? How could it be true, but how could it be a lie? The child was always odd, but to think she might be an Ancient, the last of her kind, was too much to believe— and yet it must be true.

'Let me stand. Let me hold you,' Arla said to the boatman.

Murlonius set her feet down but she was unable to stand unaided and slumped against him. For a long moment the last of the Ancients held each other: one trapped in an old man's body and the other in a child's. The Flow moved around them—a sea of pink shot through with silver. Issa thought her heart would break.

'I might be able to help,' Freydel said, his voice gruff with emotion. 'Maybe with the orb I can reach her, as she reached me. I don't know how to—'

'Do it,' the boatman said, his eyes wild. 'Do it now. You must. If she dies…'

Freydel glanced at Coronos then took out his orb. Coronos did the same and passed Issa the Orb of Water. Three orbs of power—black, blue and white—pulsed and hummed together. The Flow tripled in its pull; she could feel herself standing in it without even trying to enter it. The air was charged with power and Arla and Murlonius were glowing, an aura of light surrounding them both.

'With three orbs, we are mighty,' Freydel said, 'but also very vulnerable. Protect me, and more importantly protect the orbs at all cost.'

Issa entered the Flow, her consciousness switching from the world of matter to the world of magic. It was incredible. Lights like stars danced before her upon a sea of indigo and the sound was like nothing heard upon Maioria. Waves of the purest harmony moved through her. Before her stood the Ancients: two beautiful beings made of white light. Both were equal in height as they embraced and love emanated from them. She struggled to concentrate under the pure, exhilarating joy of it. She felt

Freydel and Coronos enter the Flow and the orbs appeared much larger—big swirling balls of pearl, sparkling black and turquoise magic.

The talisman in her belt grew hot but instead she focused her attention on the Orb of Water, asking it to protect them. She imagined a shield of water over them and when she opened her eyes a giant, aqua orb of magic surrounded them.

She felt Freydel do something with his orb but couldn't tell what. His body became less distinct in the real world but more distinct in the Flow. He moved farther away until he was no longer physically present amongst them.

She felt something strange move in the distance, something not right—a stain, a discordant sound within the Flow. Her concentration wavered again. She tried to see into the forest through the Flow. There was something familiar close by, and also something very wrong. She immediately thought of the white owl and the Oracle. She tried to dismiss her worries and focus on the Flow but the wrongness remained.

Murlonius did not appear to notice. He looked only at Arla in his arms, stroking her hair gently.

She swallowed. They were horribly vulnerable with three orbs between them, two Ancients, two wizards and herself all in the Flow, and the most powerful wizard upon Maioria entering the astral planes. Sweat clammed her back. Baelthrom was always watching, but he was far away from here. Still, it would be foolish to ignore danger she felt.

'Coronos, can you take my orb and hold the shield?' said Issa.

'I think so,' he said. 'You've created the shield, all I need to do is hold it. Why?'

'Something's not right. I need to be sure. It'll be fine,' she added, seeing his concern and showing him her sword and raven talisman.

He nodded but seemed unconvinced. 'Better check it's safe, I guess. Don't go far or your connection to the orb will weaken and I won't be able to hold it for long.'

Issa ran through the trees towards where the wrongness had come from. In the Flow it was a stain of black, deep in the forest. She slowed her pace to a walk. Gripping her talisman, she held her breath and listened. There was nothing, not even animal noises, just the sound of the gentle breeze in the leaves. She frowned; she *had* felt something and she'd learned to trust her feelings.

There came a faint laugh. She crouched low and moved forwards, treading silently like the Karalanths had taught her so that not even a leaf rustled. It came again—just the softest female voice and sigh. It didn't sound dangerous but she pulled her sword free anyway.

Something moved in the clearing ahead, platinum hair catching the light of Doon. Her head began to pound and she felt strangely sick.

There came a male voice, so low it was almost a whisper. Young lovers sneaking off into the forest for intimacy was not unusual or a crime. Feeling embarrassed she turned away. But the wrongness intensified.

The male voice came again. She straightened with a frown. *Asaph?* Her heart thudded.

She pushed through the bushes, not bothering to be quiet and trying to ignore the hammers pounding in her head. She saw figures embraced between the trees, both naked to the waist. A glowing red amulet dangled on a branch above them.

Her breath came fast as memory of the Storm Holt swamped her mind. Her whole body trembled but her feet dragged her forwards. The amulet flared, blinding. She raised her talisman and froze as Asaph kissed Cirosa hungrily, her legs entwined around his waist. She blinked and for one horrid moment believed she was still in the Abyss and everything that had happened since had been a great lie. She'd never really escaped the Storm Holt.

Cirosa was changed and yet it was she. Her skin was pale as a ghost and the Under Flow exuded from her, wrapping around Asaph in thick chains that he didn't seem to see. Something flared in Asaph's pocket making him yelp. He grasped at it and a broken amulet fell out.

She couldn't breathe and the world began to dance. Asaph was with Cirosa *and* in league with Baelthrom.

'Get away from him!' she heard herself scream, barely aware that she had pooled a vast quantum of the Flow.

'Fire,' she whispered. Indigo flames burst from her talisman, sending Cirosa flying and knocking Asaph to the ground.

Asaph rolled and clutched his temples. The Under Flow surged and the Flow turned sluggish. Issa dragged it to her and ran forwards. Her fist filled with magic, she punched down upon Asaph's broken amulet. Red energy exploded from it, flinging her on her back and knocking the wind from her lungs.

She rolled and staggered to her feet, searching for Cirosa and the other amulet. Both were gone and instead a white owl flew at her, talon's scraping her forehead. She stabbed her sword up, clipping tail feathers but no more. The white owl screeched and whirled into the air. Asaph was still struggling to his feet. The man's face was drained and he seemed weak as a child. Was he really in league with Baelthrom? Could he do that to her?

She ran at him, furious, sword raised. He didn't see her and instead clutched at his head. He seemed like a little boy cowering and in pain. Something had been done to him to make him this way. She lowered her sword; she couldn't hurt him no matter how angry she was.

The white owl struck her from behind, talons raking her shoulders. She slashed back at it with a roar, sheering off feathers. A dark shadow blotted out the light. Fear gripped her, draining her fury. It knifed into the pit of her stomach and radiated out in waves of pain, rooting her to the ground. She trembled all over, dropping the raven talisman and her sword.

The Dread Dragon screamed, driving all sense from her mind.

CHAPTER 15

Night of Terror

YELLING and screaming dragged Issa to her senses.

The Dread Dragon hadn't seen her and Asaph through the trees but the others were easy prey, exposed on the edge of the lake.

'Freydel!' Issa yelled.

She grabbed her sword and talisman, and tore back towards the lake. Leaping over bushes, she burst through the trees.

A spout of flame lit up the sky and flared against the aqua shield she had raised. The fire mirrored off the lake, making it seem as if they were surrounded in flames above and below. Murlonius and Arla clung to each other and everyone was trembling in dragon fear.

Without pausing her stride, she drew the Flow into the talisman, and sent it forth. Indigo magic smothered Dread Dragon fire in a wave. The dragon wheeled up and around, readying for another attack. She fell into the orb's protective shield.

'Coronos, give me my orb.' She gasped.

He gritted his teeth as he struggled to hold the shield and keep the path open for Freydel. His hand shook with the strain as he passed her the orb.

She closed her eyes, entered the Flow and strengthened the aqua shield around them. Dragon fire engulfed the orb, but could not penetrate the shield. The dragon screamed in frustration.

Asaph staggered out of the forest, sword in hand, and leaned against a tree. He felt as weak as a newborn lamb, all his muscles turned to jelly and his heart labouring.

For a moment he was away from the blonde woman and could think clearly. His sword arm trembled alarmingly and he doubted if he could raise it at all. But when he glanced up at the Dread Dragon, anger coursed through him. He harnessed the anger, turned it to rage and willed his dragon self to awaken. Nothing happened. The dragon within remained sleeping and felt far away.

The Dread Dragon circled low above the lake. He knew it was looking for a big enough space to land. Growling, he ran towards the others huddling under a shield of magic, only to smack into the shield as if it were made of solid glass. He shook his head, stunned. How had Issa walked through so easily?

'Let me in!' he yelled, panicking.

Issa looked at him astonished. 'It should let you in; it keeps only harm out!'

He frowned. 'How can I mean any harm?'

'Why were you with that woman, Asaph? What's going on? Are you in league with him? Damn you if you are!'

The pain and confusion in her face hurt Asaph more deeply than a sword could. She was afraid and he had hurt her, and now he couldn't even change into his dragon form to protect her. He bit back the bitterness and the rage.

He shook his head. 'I'm not with her. I love you,' but his voice wavered and he was afraid. 'I don't know; something's not right. I keep seeing her and a fog comes over me; I can't think straight. But I'll never hurt you or anyone! Please, let me in.'

'That woman was Cirosa. I don't know what she is now. She's in league with him, with Baelthrom. Don't you know that?' Issa shouted, her eyes darting from him back to the Dread Dragon circling. It landed in a clearing halfway round the other side of the lake and Dromoorai was dismounting.

He shook his head, disbelieving. His head pounded and he winced. Was Issa right? What had he done? How could he undo it? He felt sick.

'Do something, Asaph!' Issa shouted, her face full of fear.

'I cannot reach the dragon within,' he said it quietly, feeling utterly helpless. 'Something's been done to me. I'm sick.' He felt awful and couldn't even trust himself.

There came a surge of magic—dark light flooding from the Dromoorai walking towards them. Another source of black light grew on the other side of the lake. It flared across the water, combined with the Dromoorai's light, and surged towards their shield.

Asaph ducked and rolled behind it. Black magic surged, the ground shuddered and a sonic boom deafened him. He looked up. The aqua shield was utterly destroyed.

Freydel struggled through thick mist that dragged at his body and soul. His physical body hated being back in the astral planes; fatigue seeped through every muscle; even his bones ached. He gripped the Orb of Death, drawing from it every ounce of power and strength.

All the time he moved, he listened to the rise and fall of Murlonius' voice as he half spoke, half sang in the Ancient's language.

'Yisufalni…' Murlonius turned the name into a note. Love and power filled his words and the Flow moved to his song, like a bard skilled in magic was able to do. Freydel blinked back tears from the heartfelt beauty of the sound.

'Yisufalni, come to us,' his own voice was crude and hoarse.

'Where are you?' a faint voice called from far away.

Freydel moved forwards. A figure formed in the haze.

'Yisufalni? Is that you? It's Freydel. Come to my voice. Come to Murlonius'. Just like you told me to reach for your voice,' he said.

There came a jolt in the Flow. Blackness seeped into the mist between them. The orb in his hand grew hot and flared. The Flow began to drain from it.

'The Under Flow.' Freydel gasped, his strength failing. 'Baelthrom, oh no… Yisufalni, you must come quickly!'

'Reach for her, Freydel. Don't let her go,' Murlonius' voice commanded. 'Keep the connection or she's lost forever.'

He sang harder, louder, and Freydel found it gave him strength.

'We've been discovered,' Freydel rasped.

He gritted his teeth, wishing he had his staff. The Flow slipped in his grasp. He forced it back to him, groaning with the strain. It moved sluggishly as if it were cloying. The blackness was seeping upwards beneath him and he tried to rise higher in the sea of mist, away from it.

The shape of a woman lying down formed ahead. A voice, that was sound of the wind blowing down a chimney, spoke. It wrapped around Freydel's heart and made him shiver.

'Three orbs of power. Two Ancients. Two wizards. The Dragon Lord and the Raven Queen—all mine.'

Between Freydel and Yisufalni, the red eyes of Baelthrom formed. The Under Flow surrounded them. Freydel screamed and ran forwards through the eyes before they could take solid form.

Yisufalni seemed to be struggling, unable to sit up.

'Yisufalni, listen to Murlonius. He'll give you strength. Murlonius, sing harder!'

The melodic voice of the boatman came louder, rising and falling around him as he reached Yisufalni.

She lay in the mist, her body indistinct as if she were part mist herself. He expected his hands to pass right through her and was surprised when he felt soft skin. He pulled her up and draped her arm over his shoulders. She flopped weak and limp.

Turning, he was faced with a billowing wall of black.

'Murlonius, the Under Flow is all around us. It blocks our path.'

Issa gripped her sword, noticing Asaph do the same as the Dromoorai approached them fearlessly. They bunched close in front of Coronos who held the Orb of Air aloft. His eyes were closed and his face was twisted in immense concentration.

Murlonius hugged Arla and sang his strange love song, also with his eyes closed. Arla sagged in his arms. The Dromoorai turned and motioned to the Dread Dragon. It launched into the air, its black mass blotting out the light of Doon, then it disappeared over the treetops flying fast.

'It's going to get others,' Asaph said.

Issa looked at him then dropped her gaze. How long had they been together making love behind her back? She felt sick at the thought. The worst thing was she still loved him. Swallowing her pain, she clenched her sword.

'The orbs must be protected at all costs and we must bring Freydel back,' she said, her voice trembling.

Coming towards them from the other side of the lake was a white figure.

'Cirosa,' Issa hissed. 'She never had magic before, but look at her now. I don't think she's even human anymore.'

Cirosa's full red lips twisted into a smile. Asaph swallowed audibly and wrenched his eyes from the woman. Issa wanted to kill her where she stood.

'I'll take the Dromoorai,' he said in a strangled tone and backed away.

Issa nodded, both their faces were slick with sweat.

'You murdered Rance,' Cirosa said, stopping twenty feet away. A shimmer of dark magic surrounded her. The comment took Issa by surprise. In the corner of her eyes she saw Asaph raise his sword as the Dromoorai raised its.

'I did not—'

'Liar! In return I shall take *your* man.' Cirosa snarled.

Issa shifted. The woman was very different to how she remembered. Now completely animalistic and utterly dangerous.

'The last Dragon Lord will be a great gift to my lord.'

'What did you do to him, you bitch?' Issa growled, trying to control her anger and doing everything she could not to run recklessly at the woman and strike her down where she stood.

'Nothing on the goddess's pure earth would ever willingly be yours. It didn't take much for you to sell out to the other side, did it, High Priestess Cirosa?' Issa spat, raising her sword.

Cirosa hesitated and mouthed her own name as if she had forgotten it.

'Yes, that was me. The weak, pathetic priestess is gone. Now I am so much more. I have more power than you can imagine.' She raised her hand and erratic energy flared.

Issa jumped in the Flow only to see it drain towards the woman. She looked harder. The Flow was being sucked away and reversed into something else. A reversed, corrupt magic she could not use. It came at her as a sizzling mass of black destruction.

There was no time to respond. Issa raised the talisman and struck the black magic physically. It exploded, flinging her backwards. She rolled to her feet and ran at the woman, swinging her sword and dropping to a knee, but Cirosa moved so fast, her figure was a blur. Her sword tip tore something and dark blood splattered. Issa whirled around, sword and talisman raised.

Cirosa smiled at her a few steps away, a slight tear on the shoulder of her dress under which a line of dark blood welled.

'Maphraxie,' Issa spat.

The woman moved so fast Issa never saw the pommel of the knife that punched her in the face. She staggered and swiped with her talisman, finding contact in a flare of her own magic. She blinked, trying to get her bearings but the woman was gone. Her cheek was painful to touch, bruised and bloody.

A yell came from behind. She saw Asaph fall, the Dromoorai towering over him.

Forgetting Cirosa, she ran to him. Swinging her sword at the Dromoorai's shoulder, it glanced off black-iron and jolted her arm painfully. Its gauntleted fist lashed out, and she had to throw herself on the ground to avoid it.

Asaph booted it in the chest with both feet, shunting it back. She grabbed his arm and pulled him up, shocked at how he teetered.

'I'm too weak.' Asaph gasped. Sweat covered his body and matted his hair. He trembled all over and was white as a ghost.

Issa swallowed. 'I don't think I can kill a Dromoorai alone.'

'Murlonius, reach for us. Pull us back! Coronos, Issa, use your orbs to connect with mine.' Freydel screamed continuously as he struggled through the blackness that was trying to swallow him.

Yisufalni clung to him. She was trying with her mind to reach Murlonius; he could almost see her thought forms in the energy of the astral planes. They had made it this far. But the voice of Baelthrom echoed all around. He was closing all around them and time was short.

'Freydel,' Coronos' distorted voice echoed around them. 'I can't hold the gateway open for long. We're under attack!'

'Where's Issa? Tell her to use her power, use her orb!' Freydel screamed.

Coronos spoke, but Freydel couldn't make out his distorted words. He closed his eyes, focused on Murlonius' song and tried to shut out everything else.

The Dromoorai swiped its claymore at Issa. She jumped to the left. Asaph lunged but his sword sparked harmlessly off its breastplate. She ran forwards, stabbing at where she thought there was a gap in the armour but there was none.

The Dromoorai backhanded her, sprawling her five yards away into the lake. The Orb of Water pulsed in her pocket, maybe sensing its contact with liquid. She splashed to her feet and screamed as Asaph took a blow and fell. Sheathing her sword, she pulled out the orb.

'Water, be at my command.'

She sensed the water around her respond with eagerness and felt it fill the Flow with its essence—a swirling mass of blue. Directed by her will, water surged upwards out of the lake and then forwards straight into the Dromoorai. The Dromoorai was plunged off its feet into the trees. She looked around for Cirosa, hoping to blast her with water too, but couldn't see the woman anywhere. Not knowing where she was would have worried her more had she time to think.

Asaph staggered up, blood trickling down his sword arm. He took his blade in his left hand and ran towards the splayed Dromoorai. She jumped through the water to join him. Sword raised, he struck hard but red magic surged from its amulet, flinging them both backwards.

Issa rolled, gasping breath back into her lungs, her body trembling with fatigue. The Dromoorai was already up and coming towards them. It was invincible. She closed her eyes and tried to still her mind, despite the terror approaching.

Zanufey, help me reach the dark moon. I know it's coming closer. Help me feel its power. She could feel the dark moon out there but it was so far away it was hard to reach even a little of its power.

'The Dread Dragon is coming back.' Asaph gasped. 'I can feel it. I don't think it's alone.'

'Then we must kill its rider before it gets here.' Issa scowled. She held the orb up. 'I don't know how to use you but you must help us or we'll die. Protect us!'

The orb flared aqua blue. Water rose from the lake, pulling together into the shape of a figure: human-like and as big as a Dromoorai. It even had a nose and eyes made only of water. It stepped towards them, walking easily on the lake's surface, pulling from its waist a glittering blue whip made of water.

The water elemental lashed the whip. It snaked out and struck the Dromoorai as it got to its feet, sending it back to its knees. The Dromoorai swung its claymore, severing the tip of the whip. It splashed on the ground. The elemental flicked it back, ready to attack again.

Issa turned to Asaph. 'I've an idea. I don't know if it'll work, but I must try. I'll fight it from another plane. They are undead, right?'

Asaph nodded. 'I think so. But their souls are gone.'

'All right, pray it works. Stay close to the water elemental.' Seeing the terrible weariness and worry in his face, she dropped her anger, cupped his cheek and smiled. 'We can do this.'

Holding the talisman to her raven mark, she spoke the elven words.

'A'farion, A'farion, A'farion.'

Cold fire burst upon her chest and spread throughout her body. She fell forwards into silver.

A shadowy replica of the lake scene formed. Everything was in dreadful shades of grey, reminding her of the Shadowlands. Breathing hard, she wiped her forehead and calmed herself.

Her eyes travelled over the ghost-forest and settled on a dark shape. The Dromoorai was the same as in real life: armoured and tall and full of darkness. And it was fighting something she could not see—its sword driving left and right. *Asaph and the water warrior.*

She ran forwards, a hundred thoughts flitting through her mind. Could she kill it here? Was it more dangerous? What if her sword passed right through, just as it would through a wraith?

'Fight me,' she yelled, her voice oddly loud and eerie in this place.

Her sword slammed into its armour, taking her by surprise. It didn't pass through or shatter on impact, but her blow sent it to one knee. How did she have the strength to knock it down?

Afraid, she stepped back as the Dromoorai rose and looked around.

For a moment she wondered if it could see her at all but then its eyes, all black in this colourless realm, found her. It lunged its claymore frighteningly fast. She gripped her sword in both hands and swung with all her weight. It clanged against a shoulder plate, sheering a piece off. In shock she fell back, but it came on, not giving her time to pause.

Again and again she dodged and struck, and each time armour flew off but nothing halted its steps. In the realm of the dead, her sword could cut through its impenetrable armour. Black iron had no strength here.

The claymore arced towards her. She dropped to the ground, feeling it brush past her hair. She rolled, jumped up and fell back but couldn't seem to create enough distance between. She stumbled; the flat of the claymore's tip smacked her hip, followed by bruising pain.

She entered the Flow. It felt different. It seemed airy and light and harder to grasp, but it still came to her and there was no Under Flow to taint it. She formed her will, but the Flow seemed only half willing or half able to do her bidding.

Realisation struck. *I'm not dead. I shouldn't be here. I cannot fully command the elements of a place in which I do not belong.*

'Strength,' she commanded, pooling magic in her fist and holding it there. Screaming, she ran forward and punched the Dromoorai's helmeted face. A whole chunk of its head came off, leaving only one eye and two prongs of its helmet remaining. Black gas billowed from its hideous wound.

It lashed out. Its hand death-gripping her throat before she could escape. Her breath stopped and blood no longer flowed to her brain. Her heart pounded harder and harder. It lifted her by her neck into the air, forcing her to stare down at it. Black gas still flowed from its wounded head. She wanted to be sick, felt herself passing out. She desperately needed air. Her struggles weakened.

'She's mine. Bring her to me,' a voice rasped. It was coming from the Dromoorai's amulet, black in this realm.

She sagged in terror. Her struggles became horribly weak. For a moment the real world of colour and chaos came into focus as the Dromoorai aided by Baelthrom's power tried to drag her back into it. If she went back there, she would be captured.

In a glimpse she saw Asaph sprawled on the ground. The water elemental was gone. Beyond them, Murlonius held up a hand glowing with white light. He held a limp Arla in the other. Coronos was on his knees with Cirosa's arm tight around his neck. She too had her arm raised and black light poured from it. In the sky, dark things descended with terrifying speed.

The Dromoorai seemed to be weakening and its grip on her neck loosened. She sucked air into her ragged throat. Closing her eyes, she gripped the talisman and forced herself back into the realm of the dead. It took an age to raise her sword, her body was so weak. She stabbed at its head, plunging through the smoking wound and grinding into what felt like solid rock.

The grip released her throat and together they fell. She gasped and rolled off the thrashing Dromoorai, clamping her hands over ears as it screamed and roared. Then it lay still and crumpled to dust. She had to get back to the living though she had barely caught her breath. Holding the talisman against her chest, she willed herself back into the world of the living.

A vivid scene of chaos and magic materialised. Cirosa's magic slammed into her before she gained her balance and she slid in the mud to the water's edge.

'Wind,' she commanded, still lying.

Wind whirled around her, forcing back the suffocating black magic. She glimpsed Asaph using his sword to haul himself onto his knees. The horror on his blood-stained face moved her to action and she dragged herself up.

Cirosa still gripped Coronos' neck. He was on his knees, restrained by black cords of magic. The Orb of Air lay before him and was flaring wildly against the smothering black.

Asaph ran in lurches towards them as Cirosa drew a knife, white and glinting. Black magic like fog moved and wrapped around Asaph's legs, tripping him to the ground.

Issa frantically reached for the Flow but all she found was the Under Flow surging, a visible black mist that slowed everything. The blackness was spreading everywhere and now reached her, making it hard to move forwards. Where the hell was Freydel?

She squinted through the mist to find Murlonius. Tears were streaming down his face and Arla lay still and grey at his feet. The black magic cloyed thicker around her, making her choke and scattering her thoughts. Baelthrom's voice whispered to her, but she tried to ignore the words.

Cirosa reached down to Coronos' orb. Lightning snaked out from it as if it were angry. Issa struggled towards her, willing the talisman to give her strength. The blackness thickened. Inch by inch she moved forwards. Black magic, orb magic and talisman magic battled, and the world became darkness, lightning flares, and screaming wind.

Cirosa raised her blade. Baelthrom's voice howled. Cirosa's blade fell. The world fell silent. Her heart skipped two beats. Bright red spurted. Coronos fell. The world turned mad. There came a terrible screaming; Issa realised it was her own. It was joined by a man screaming. Asaph.

She thought she might faint, struggled to remain standing. Something black exploded out of the trees, slamming into Cirosa. The horse reared and neighed as the blackness surrounded it. Duskar. How was he here? Magic pulsed, flinging the horse back as if he were a toy.

Dread Dragons screamed above—not just one. She fell to her knees, dropping her sword. Fire filled the sky. She gripped her orb and talisman, her will working faster than her commands, faster than her thoughts. Water sprayed upwards from the lake, extinguishing the flames, and her indigo magic flowed against the cloying black mist.

Two figures ran into the clearing, one dressed in a blue robe, the other in green. They seemed familiar through the billowing fog of black. The Flow surged against the Under Flow, light against dark. A shield was raised and Issa added magic to it with her orb. The wind dropped. The blackness cleared, and the madness lulled. Cirosa was gone and the Dread Dragons were silent.

Issa staggered up, ran, and fell besides Coronos and Asaph. Bright blood pumped from the wound in Coronos' chest. His face was grey and his eyes were closed.

She slammed the talisman to her chest, not caring for the rules or the consequences should she enter the realm of the dead twice in a day. The ghost world appeared and her living body screamed in agony. She felt her soul detaching itself. Ahead she saw a robed man running.

'Coronos,' she screamed. He turned.

'I can reach them.' He smiled, unhurt and lively. He seemed younger and his face was light-filled. 'Freydel and Yisufalni need me. They are so close.'

'How? How far are they?' It took all of her will to move towards him, her body barely responding.

Ghosts flittered close—dark shapes looming left and right. She tried to ignore them.

'So close, but Baelthrom stops them. Stay here,' Coronos said.

'But what about you?' she asked. 'I can save you.'

'I'll be all right. I understand now. This is what I have to do; this is the last,' he said and reached to stroke her face. 'Help the others, help Asaph.'

'I don't understand,' she said, tears filling her eyes. It felt like goodbye but she didn't quite comprehend why. Coronos became white light so bright he blinded her.

'Don't worry. Don't fear—not for any of us. Feygriene is with me,' his voice echoed, then she felt him go.

CHAPTER 16

The Scattering

SILENCE and bright light bathed them, blotting out the world beyond.

Issa was on her knees, completely numb as she looked upon the two figures lying still.

One was a woman with six fingers and toes, and skin like silk. An old man sat on his knees, stroking her shining hair. She looked like a fairy, though she was taller than most men.

The other prone figure was old and grey and lifeless. Great pools of blood soaked his long white beard and the ground on which he lay. Beside him Freydel stared dumbfounded, his face a mask of horror. Issa trembled. Coronos couldn't be dead; he just couldn't.

Asaph pulled the grey man to his chest and silent sobs shook his whole body.

Only two women and Duskar remained standing. The horse was sniffing the white space that enveloped them. Issa blinked at the women. Edarna—how was she here? Her face was drained of colour and she looked in shock. Naksu trembled visibly as she gripped her raised white staff.

She realised the seer was creating the protection around them, the strain of it adding to the burden of her sorrow.

'What happened? Where are we?' Her voice didn't sound like her own and seemed to float around her.

'The Orb of Air is gone.' Naksu gasped. 'Baelthrom has taken it. Coronos is…gone. How can it be?'

The words didn't seem to mean much to Issa in her numb state. She clung to that state, knowing when it broke so would she.

'Where are we?' she repeated, looking around at the white space. It seemed like a domed cave but the walls were all smooth and glowing white. Several arched doors surrounded the walls.

'We are in the sacred mound. I had to protect us and the rest of the orbs, but I can't hold us all here for long,' Naksu said. Her voice gave out and she staggered to a knee. Edarna reached to help her.

She'd taken them to the sacred mound just like that? How was it possible?

'Hurry, we must leave here. Tell us what to do, Naksu,' said Edarna.

'Baelthrom has found us. We must scatter; our very lives depend upon it. All of us and so much power in one place drew Baelthrom right to us. We must separate and flee. Choose now where you will go, but let it not be the same place we were in. Better still, choose far from Carvon for the safety of the people there. It's better that we don't know where each other has gone for now. The power of the orbs scattered the Dromoorai, but they will return swiftly, hunting for concentrated pockets of power.'

Issa nodded and her eyes fell upon Coronos. His once life-filled face was now grey, grey like his daughter Ely. Both gone forever from Maioria. Grief welled up beneath her numbness; her heart began to break. She went to Asaph and touched his shoulder. He looked up at her, his face horrific. She dropped down to hug him and Coronos both.

'I saw him. I tried to stop him,' she breathed into his ear, felt his hand stroke her hair. 'He wanted to go. He knew only he could help them. And he did; he saved them. He said Feygriene was with him and it was the last thing he had to do.'

'It's all my fault. I led her here,' Asaph rasped. 'I caused all of this.'

'No, she tricked you. I see it now and I know what it's like,' Issa said. 'I was tricked in the Storm Holt. They would have found us all anyway.'

'Please hurry,' Naksu's strained voice came from behind.

'We must go,' said Asaph. 'We're a danger to each other right now. I'm a danger to everyone'

Tears filled her eyes. 'I know you hurt terribly, but don't leave me. I don't want to be alone.'

She was more afraid of being without him than she had ever been in the Storm Holt. He looked surprised and for a moment she saw the old Asaph there beyond the pain and self-loathing.

She hugged him again. 'I love you. I'm sorry if I've been withdrawn. I'm afraid of losing you, of losing everyone.'

He kissed her lips gently, then looked into her eyes.

'If you don't want me to, then I shall never leave you. There *can* be time for us. Right now my duty is to my father. I'll take his body north, to his resting place in the land of the Lords of Dragons. But I'll return. I *will* find you.'

Issa nodded but she trembled all over.

'I can't hold us.' Naksu gasped. Her face was flushed and her eyes closed. The walls began to shake and dissipate.

Issa ran to Duskar and gripped his mane; he wouldn't know what Naksu asked. Naksu's staff pulsed. She stared at Asaph as the light engulfed him; his blue eyes seemed to shine in that light. She closed her eyes and tried to think where to go. All she saw in her mind was Ehka. *Take me to him,* she held the intention in her mind.

Rushing, roaring air and light scoured her body and ears.

All was still and dark. Duskar snuffled the air. To Issa it smelt fresh and full of the forest. Bats squeaked above and the wind rustled the leaves in the trees, but otherwise it was quiet and she could sense no danger. The night was calm.

'Faint light,' she whispered, quietly pulling the talisman from her belt, not trusting they were safe yet.

The talisman glowed faint indigo that barely illuminated the old chestnut trees around them. Duskar was already nose to ground chomping on grass. They were in a forest, probably somewhere on Frayon, given the western direction Ehka had flown in, but it was too dark to see much. She had no reason to distrust Naksu's spell, so Ehka had to be somewhere around here.

'Ehka?' she called softly, reaching out with her mind to find the bird.

She took a step forwards and staggered to one knee. Her leg was sore and suddenly throbbing. She reached a hand down to mid-thigh. It was hot and wet and there was a dark patch on her leggings. It hurt like hell. She'd been injured, probably by the Dromoorai's sword, but so much had been happening she hadn't even noticed. Now she knew about it, the pain filled her head. She checked herself for other wounds but found none. If that's all she'd got, she'd come off lightly. It didn't bare thinking about Coronos.

A Dromoorai's blade would be poisoned or enchanted, probably both. She fumbled in her belt pockets for a strip of cloth she used to tie back her hair. It made a poor bandage, but it helped put pressure on the wound. She reached for the barest bit of magic. It was hard to control and very exhausting. The magic helped ease the pain a little bit. She sorely needed rest.

She stood up, putting all her weight on her good leg, took a step forwards and nearly fell again. The blade hadn't gone deep enough to reach bone, but it was painful enough to cause trouble walking. Perhaps she could find a stream to bathe it and bind it better. Ahead and to the right she was sure she could hear the faintest tinkling sound.

'Come Duskar, let's get to the river,' she said and hobbled in that direction.

'Ehka,' she called softly as she limped. The bird had to be somewhere near.

She tried to move quietly, but it was impossible with her leg. Twice she stumbled, cracking twigs and cursing under her breath.

Something moved ahead—a black shape disappearing behind a thick tree trunk, too big to be a bird. She froze, hand on hilt, all her senses alert. It was probably just a deer, though it was really too tall to be any animal. Should she call out? Should she enter the Flow? What if they used magic?

A shape moved again. The same being or another? What if there were several? The last thing she needed was another fight in her exhausted and wounded state.

She dimmed the talisman, cursing herself for shining like a beacon in the dark. But now it was pitch black and she couldn't see anything. Duskar snorted and she shushed him. There was nothing for it; anything could pounce on her right now. She pulled her sword free, making sure the unsheathing ringing noise could be heard. Let them know she was armed. She entered the Flow.

There were several auras—six or more people. Something, or someone, exploded into her back, flooring her face-down into the dirt. Her wound hit the ground and she gasped as exquisite pain exploded from it, followed by hot blood.

The Flow slipped away. Something heavy lay on top of her, making it hard to breathe. Her sword arm was lifted and twisted painfully. She yelped, dropped her sword and heard it clatter to the ground. The raven talisman was yanked from her other hand. There came a surprised cry of pain as it was taken and something heavy dropped, probably the talisman. Her hands were tied behind her back at the same time as her legs were before she had the thought to use them.

Duskar whinnied once then soothing voices speaking in Elven calmed him. The heavy weight got off her, and she gasped in air. She reached for the Flow but for the first time in her life she felt something blocking her. Rage exploded in her belly. How dare anybody block her from the Flow? Not even she knew how to do that.

She began to shout curses and spells. Strong hands lifted her off her front. Everything was still dark. She struggled madly despite her poisoned wound and tied hands and feet. Her tunic ripped as she thrashed—which made her even madder since she'd only just bought it—and she fell hard on the ground, winded. Blinking, there was nothing to see but blacker shapes moving in the dark.

'Who the hell are you? Get off me, you bastards. You'll wish you were never born!' she screamed.

A blow to her stomach winded her again, hurting old wounds and knocking the curses from her mouth. A gag was tied, preventing any words or swearing she might have spoken. Her belts were yanked off and she panicked, remembering the Orb of Water. If they tried to take it they would die—the thought pleased her. Unless they killed her, that was.

She choked against the gag, blinking dirt from her eyes, trying to see who she was up against. A lantern flared, held by the one who had a hand on Duskar, but everything was too blurry to see clearly. The pain from her leg was getting worse, the poison working its way through her body.

A face pushed close to hers, all blurred. It seemed human, but strange. It had one normal, albeit violet eye and one huge black eye. He was speaking to her, but his words seemed all moulded together and oddly deep. Pain throbbed in her leg, in her head. The more she tried to focus, the more everything went blurry. She heard a raven squawk, a yelp and scuffle, and then the world just slid sideways.

The white light faded. Asaph found himself under a sky filling with the orange light of dawn. He stood at the mouth of a shallow cave looking out across a vast expanse of sea. The wind tugged at his hair and clothes. Below, maybe five hundred yards away, was a town. Houses, painted yellow and pink, sprinkled ambling cobbled streets. As pretty as they were, the houses seemed worn and in need of fresh paint. Many roofs had holes and every one with thatch had not seen a thatcher for decades.

His eyes were drawn to a much bigger building dominating the town in the port. This building was dark grey, towering and square—lacking anything that could have made it ornate. It was ugly. Around its scaffolding, black shapes moved. Maphraxies. There were no people.

So this was what had become of Avernayis, the only place he could think to go, the place where Coronos had been born. Avernayis. He had brought his father's body home to Drax, but never did he think he would visit the home of his birth in this manner. For all the long years he'd yearned to come here, he'd always intended it to be joyous return. It was the exact opposite.

He moved to the back of the cave to keep the wind from clawing at Coronos' body. Bending his head, he gave in to the sobs. He tried to blame that witch-woman Cirosa, he tried to blame himself, but what difference did it make? Nothing would bring Coronos back. Nothing he could do, think or feel would numb the pain that consumed him.

He sat down, trying to ignore the desperate thirst overcoming him. Coronos had a waterskin tied to his waist. It seemed wrong to take his water; he would have preferred to die. In the end he slipped it free and drank half. Hunched beside his father, his eyes raw from tears, he watched the entrance of the cave as the day moved on.

Thinking it right, he pulled the hood of Coronos' cloak over his grey face, concealing it forever. He took off his belt and its attached pouches and folded his robes neatly and meticulously around his body.

'I need you, father,' he whispered in a trembling voice. 'I wanted to tell you about that woman, but I couldn't. She cast a terrible spell on me. I can still feel her hold on me now, even here. I've been tainted and even the dragon door won't open to me. I'm an outcast, and now I have nothing, not even you.'

He bowed his head, willing himself to be strong but failing. There was nothing to be strong for and no strength to be found within him.

He watched the day turn into night, listening to his growling stomach. The thought of food made him feel ill. It was cold, colder than he had ever known it. He would have lit a fire, Coronos would have liked that, but the Maphraxies down there in the deserted town would see it. Though he cared nothing for himself, he would not let them touch his father's body.

Instead, he pulled his cloak around him and curled up, drifting in twisted thoughts upon the cold stone floor of the cave. He should burn Coronos' body and set his spirit free to go to the Fire in the Sky. That was the Draxian custom, and it was also Kuapoh custom. He should call the Fire Sight, Draxian custom again for the death of a loved one, but it didn't seem right here with the Maphraxies close. And his father wouldn't want to be in the remains of his village whilst it was occupied by them.

A part of him worried that she would find him again. He couldn't let that happen. Her hold on him was overpowering; it terrified him. But where could he go to be free of her chains?

I'll go north, as far north as one can go. To the frigid lands no human goes, to the lands they said the dragons had fled to. There, far away from the dominion of Baelthrom and his bastards, he would burn his father's body to ashes for the wind to carry and set his spirit free.

He must have drifted to sleep then, though when he awoke it was still dark. He should go now. Fly to the north in his dragon form, using the night to cloak his presence.

Looking down at the town—the only light came from the ugly Maphraxie building at the port entrance. Two massive braziers burned on turrets, illuminating the black shapes of the enemy who never slept. The light reaching the cave was too faint for them to see a dragon. He had to take his chances.

He closed his eyes and remembered Faelsun's tuition, allowing himself the barest feeling of relief as the dragon came easily, painlessly and fast. Cirosa had been blocking him from reaching his dragon-self, he was certain.

In his dragon form, the sorrow that had consumed him diminished. Instead a cold determination stole over him, and a terrible desire for bloody vengeance. Holding his father's body in his claws, he launched into the air. Cold wind blowing strong off the ocean lifted him high, fast. Instinct told him which way was north, and into the cold blackness he flew.

Murlonius held Yisufalni tightly as the serpent-prowed boat drifted upon the Sea of Opportunity. She was weak but blessedly conscious. He could feel the light flutter of her pulse in her wrist under the tips of his fingers. All that mattered in all the worlds was that she was here with him now and they were together once more, after thousands of years alone and apart.

'I've been so endlessly lonely,' he whispered.

'As have I,' she said. 'Are we free of our curse?' Hope inflected her voice and made him hope too.

Could his curse have been lifted now? He was with her after all—the only other Ancient in all Maioria, and whom he'd been cursed to be apart from forever. Did he dare to hope after so long? He sighed and shook his head.

'I don't think so… Maybe for you, but not I. Otherwise how am I still here? On this cursed ocean? Only when Baelthrom is sent back into the Dark Rift will it end. He'll never let us be free. Even here I fear we aren't safe.'

'Then I don't think our time together will be for long,' she said. He knew she spoke only with reason. 'Outside the ethereal planes this body feels weak, even if I hold my true form and a child's body no longer. I don't think I can reach those planes easily anymore.'

She looked up at him, her beautiful violet eyes so full of the life he once remembered. He bent to kiss her and she parted her lips in return. The softness of her touch melted his heart, and for the first time in millennia he felt the blossoming of desire—a wondrous, beautiful thing.

'I love you,' he breathed.

'I love you too,' she said. 'I spoke to you, in the ethereal planes. I could see your boat and you rowing it, but never could I see your face or reach you.'

'Sometimes I heard a voice whispering, barely audible on the wind. It gave me hope, soothed my heart,' he said, blinking back tears. 'I prayed it was you.'

She held a hand to his cheek. 'Now we're together, I would happily die.'

'As would I, but they still need us,' he said. She nodded and looked away.

'The Orb of Air is gone,' she said, staring out across the glittering ocean. 'All the time I curse the day our elders split the magic of the world, and I pray for the day when the orbs will be united, and the magic made whole once more. Where do we go now? What will become of us?'

'I'm more lost now than ever I have been,' he said. 'You have to return to the mortal planes, but I cannot bear the thought of spending another hour without you. I'm sick of being alone, out here.'

She hugged his arms tighter around her.

'This place used to frighten me,' he said, a hint of bitterness in his voice. 'I call it the Sea of Opportunity, for nothing ever happens here except what one can imagine in one's head. I've never seen a fish or bird, not even seaweed. I've been doomed forever to exist between worlds.'

'But I've broken free. There's hope,' Yisufalni said. 'Now we know one of us can break the curse, we must try to break the curse that binds you. Until then, my beloved Murlonius, let's drift on this sea together. Hold me and touch me like once you did when the world was free and we were young.'

'Drat and blast it,' Edarna shouted. Naksu slumped onto the grass. 'I thought Carvon. Carvon! Not bleedin' wherever the hell this is.'

'What?' Naksu's weak voice caught Edarna's attention. She hurried over to the collapsed seer and turned her over onto her back. Her face was pale, if that was possible for an albino, and her skin a sheen of sweat. She blinked and looked around with luminous eyes. A smile spread across her face.

'We made it.' She laughed, then frowned and shut her eyes again.

'Made it? Made it where?' Edarna looked around. 'This is nowhere.'

They were on a small hill surrounded by deciduous trees and circled by twelve amethyst crystals, each about a foot high and arranged in a six-yard-wide diameter. In the distance beyond the trees, the sea sparkled. There were lots of trees—actually there were only trees and no buildings or villages to be seen. It looked very like nowhere at all.

'Thank the goddess. We made it to the Isles of Tirry,' Naksu said and sat up. 'This is the Western Isle. I held so many people in the shield, I was worried I wouldn't have the strength to make it here.'

'Isles of Tirry?' Edarna squeaked. 'What use is that? I thought Carvon, not Tirry. What about my stuff? My potions and my chest of things? What about my cat? Never mind the cat…'

'Well,' Naksu began. 'You must have wanted to come here more, otherwise you wouldn't be here.' She was scowling now.

'I… Hmmm. Well I did wonder how I would get to Myrn at the last moment. But most of the time I was thinking Carvon.'

Naksu blew through her lips. 'Well, you're here now, and that's it.'

'That's it?' Edarna shrilled. She sat down. What about all her dragon scales? Her clothes? She hadn't even sent out flyers or checked the posters yet.

'I have to go back and get my things; it's too important.' The seriousness in her voice must have roused the seer.

'Well, it'll be all right there. Our room has been rented for a whole year and the landlady doesn't bother us. We put a protection on the place too. Remember?'

'Yes, but… But… Anyway, Mr Dubbins won't like it at all,' Edarna said.

'Hmm, well, with Mr Dubbins there, a living creature and all, maybe we can form a connection and bring him here. And maybe with some belongings, *maybe*,' Naksu said. 'But I can't do that until I've had a good rest.'

Edarna nodded and set about polishing her glasses with her shawl. 'I suppose it's nice here. Sunny n' green n' all. At least it's away from *him*. I guess you did well.'

'Goodness,' the seer said, ignoring the witch's reluctant praise.

Edarna followed her gaze to the gnarly staff lying on the grass. Using her own staff to heave herself up, the seer went over to it. Edarna stood beside her, a lump forming in her throat.

'Poor, poor Coronos,' Edarna said. The sight of the blood-covered old man was horribly vivid in her mind. She didn't really know him, but he seemed kindly and gentle and not too *wizardy*. A part of her vaguely remembered him as a younger man, an advisor to the King and Queen of Drax. She'd only ever seen him once from a distance at a Midsummer's Celebration on the Isle of Celene a long time ago.

'A life lost and so is another orb.' Naksu shook her head. 'This is terrible. Terrible.'

'Baelthrom just grows in power.' Edarna sighed, struggling to fathom what it meant now the Immortal Lord had another orb.

'Come,' Naksu said, grabbing the wizard's staff and standing up. 'We must tell the Trinity immediately and scry for the others. Pray they are safe. We haven't a moment to lose.'

She whirled away and trotted down the hill.

Edarna hurried after her. She didn't dare to admit it, barely even to herself, but she already missed Mr Dubbins running by her side.

Freydel slumped onto his bed. His head spun and his body shook. He barely made it to the bed pan before he heaved up the contents of his stomach. Whatever he did, he never ever wanted to travel into the ethereal planes again. Every time he went he felt his body fragmenting more.

Glugging down a glass of water, he crawled into bed and pulled the covers up, still fully clothed. Arla had been saved but she was not what he had thought. He could barely believe she was an Ancient. All was overshadowed by the terribleness of what had happened. Baelthrom had the orb and Coronos had been murdered. He couldn't believe it, couldn't believe anything. He felt hot and threw the covers off. Was he in some awful nightmare?

Naksu and the witch had come, thank the goddess she had. She'd held them all in a safe place somewhere, and the only place he could think to return was here, his room in Carvon—there was nowhere left in the world he could think to go.

Baelthrom had to be stopped—perhaps he knew a way to do it. When he was well again he would visit Ayeth and do whatever he could to turn him from his dark future.

CHAPTER 17

Dark Memories

CIROSA cowered before Baelthrom.

He had brought her to the chamber of the iron ring, after the humans had escaped in a flash of seer magic that had left her reeling.

'You are lucky, my priestess, that you bring to me an orb in place of the Dragon Lord,' her lord's voice rumbled around the chamber. His hand stroked the surface of the white orb as it lay nestled in the pedestal next to the Orb of Life.

'Thank you, Lord Baelthrom,' she whispered, dropping her gaze to scowl at the dark dwarf beside him. His horrid yellow eyes never stopped staring at her. She imagined pulling them out slowly and smiled. With lowered lids, she looked through her eyelashes at the imposing form of Baelthrom.

'I had him. I still have chains upon—'

'But you lost him,' Baelthrom bellowed. Vibrations shuddered her body and the iron ring crackled. She hung her head.

'He won't get far, and he won't be strong enough to break my chains,' she said. 'I didn't know the others—seers and powerful wizards with their orbs—would be there.'

He became absorbed in the orbs, holding his hand over them, either forgetting she was there or ignoring her presence. Losing his attention was a relief. She wiped her forehead with a shaking hand.

'I alone hold two orbs now,' he said, his eyes smouldering dark orange. 'Twice the power I had before. No other on this planet holds as much. Now it's time to take the rest.'

'It's as you deserve, my lord,' she said, stepping closer, eager to please.

But he ignored her still and turned to the ring.

'Our tactics have worked, thanks to Hameka,' he said. She grimaced at his name. 'And our army is vast.'

The iron ring flickered into life and she looked upon endless rows of Maphraxie soldiers stretching as far as the eye could see to the red horizon of Maphrax. Dromoorai filled the eternally smouldering sky and Dread Dragon screams echoed through the chamber.

'The Feylint Halanoi are spread out and weak,' said Baelthrom. 'They cannot hold the whole coast of Frayon. Soon Vornus will devastate the weakened north, and Hameka will assault the west.

'And there's no army to stop us ploughing into the Uncharted Lands. It seems the last will fall quickly to me, and the more I take, the closer the Dark Rift draws, the closer to home we will be.'

Kilkarn snivelled laughter beside him. Even Cirosa smiled at the thought of victory, of revenge, and of the powers she would be given.

'We have a formidable new addition to our ranks.' Baelthrom's chuckle rumbled as the image in the iron ring changed.

Cirosa looked on in awe. Mounted atop massive horse-like beasts were four horsemen encased in black iron armour and holding long swords and black shields. They were as big as Dromoorai and wore the same tripartite helmets, but their eyes did not glow and instead black holes were there. Holes that sucked the life out of things. Cirosa had to tear her eyes away, her heart pounding in her chest.

'Four cursed knights whose souls were already damned,' Baelthrom whispered, the rare sound of joy in his voice. 'Now their souls are within the Dark Rift, and to fuel their bodies they must consume the life-force of the living. Do not look into their eyes.'

Cirosa marvelled. The horsemen seemed to fade now and then, as if they were part-real, part-ghost. The horses' eyes were also black and their skin scaly and metallic like Dread Dragon scales. Their manes were black horns and their tails were weapons all covered in gleaming spikes.

'An amazing creation, my Lord Baelthrom,' said Kilkarn.

Cirosa murmured agreement.

'These Knights of Maphrax are adepts in the Under Flow,' Baelthrom said. 'They are more powerful than my necromancers and their horses are faster than the wind. There are eight more I want to capture, and you, Cirosa, will bring them to me.'

Baelthrom turned from the iron ring to look at her, his eyes glowering. She dropped her gaze and tried to still the tremble in her shoulders.

'Yes, Lord Baelthrom.' She nodded.

'I've lost a Dromoorai, but I still have its Dread Dragon. You'll be joined with it and your minds linked. Take my wondrous gift and bring the last Dragon Lord to me,' he said. 'If your chains upon him are so strong, where is he now?'

'He went north, my lord.' Her voice was low, but thankfully not quivering. 'I'll find him.'

'Good. And what of the Order of the Goddess?'

'The seeds are sown, as my lord requested,' Cirosa said. 'The Oracle's mind is weak, half given to madness. It wasn't difficult to invade and control. It'll be easy to destroy the Order from within, rotten as it is already.'

Baelthrom's eyes turned pale yellow, perhaps with pleasure. 'In every county there's a Temple. There we shall attack the spirit of the people of Maioria. When the time is right, you'll take control of the entire Order, and turn their worship to me.'

'Nothing pleases me more than to hear that, my lord.' Cirosa nodded, grinning.

'If you find that wizard, or the Ancients and the seers he was with, bring them to me. I want them alive. You'll be my High Priestess and my huntress. Go now and bring me the Dragon Lord. Don't fail me this time.'

Baelthrom barely heard the high priestess leave, his mind already caught up in thoughts of the dark-haired one. Every time he almost had her, she evaded his grasp. He was beginning to see her in a new light. She had come into her power, and even then it was still young, still untrained.

It came from the dark moon, and soon it would rise again. He would have to move before it did. He would have to invade Frayon quickly. If the moon was full, would she have the power to thwart his attack? He wasn't sure, and that disturbed him. One day he would have the power to destroy that moon utterly.

'The moon,' he rumbled. An image of the blue moon formed in the iron ring. 'It must be destroyed.'

'Yes, Lord Baelthrom,' Kilkarn said. 'But why? We fear nothing.'

'It's the cause of our...problems, and the source of the Raven Queen's power. The goddess moves in her. Every time that moon rises, its light cleanses the land of Under Flow and the power of Maphrax weakens.

'She has a talisman of power that comes from the dark moon. It holds the same essence and it's shaped into a raven. The raven is native to this world, but it came from the dark moon. I want all ravens destroyed. Tell the Maphraxies to destroy them wherever they see them.'

'With pleasure, my lord,' said Kilkarn.

'My mind has been hazy since my consciousness was scattered and I was remade, but still I remembered that moon from long ago. I've seen it in my slumber and in the brief moments when my mind is clear and memory returns. Back then, it wasn't a moon but a planet and much larger than it looks now. I know its power, I *feel* its power.

'It came from the Dark Rift, Kilkarn. It escaped. Maybe it followed me to haunt me. The Ancients had records, until I destroyed them all and they forgot their own history. Their ancestors came from the dark moon long ago. They were escaping the devastation that was wreaked there.

'I have memories...strange dreams... They tell me of the past, before I came here. They tell me that I came from that dark moon too, that I hunted the Ancients' ancestors and followed them here. I still feel the...rage. Yes, rage.' He could feel it now, a wonderful fury that burned within him, giving him immense strength.

'They took from me. They destroyed me in some irreversible way that I cannot remember. So I destroyed them in turn, and hunted down their kin. That's why I came here, Kilkarn. But the blue moon plagues me. Wherever I go, it follows. Now that I have two orbs, my power is growing. Soon I'll have the power to destroy it utterly. Until then...'

Until then, how would he stop the Raven Queen in her growing power? He had failed to capture her after all this time, now he had to change his tactics. Perhaps he could lure her to him, perhaps he could seduce her to his powers. Could she even be seduced? He knew too little about her, and that angered him. He clenched his fists.

'My lord? "Until then" what?' Kilkarn asked.

'Until then we must destroy those close to the Raven Queen. Maybe they're easier to target. We'll work on them instead, and rot them from within. That wizard she's with is strange… I know him from long before, and yet I can't quite grasp it…' In response to his thoughts, a wavering image of the purple-robed wizard formed in the iron ring.

'You took his staff, Great One. He'll be easier to target than the others,' said Kilkarn.

Baelthrom glanced at the staff leaning against the pedestal. The dwarf was right—taking something that belonged to another created a strong link. There was something else—a hazy memory from long ago. He cursed the time he had come to Maioria, when his being, his consciousness had been scattered so much he could barely remember himself.

'I know him from before the time I took the staff. Long ago, when the blue planet was whole and the Dark Rift unformed… Yes. A spark of memory came to him. 'There were pyramids, great crystal pyramids. Within them were huge azure crystal caverns. The planet, my planet, was formed of blue rock. That is why the moon is blue.'

His head throbbed as he struggled to retrieve the scattering memories. They were there but all jumbled nonsensically. He'd met an alien-looking man with an orb of power long ago. Those amber eyes, short neat beard speckled with grey, the feel of his magic…

He'd had the orb when he'd recently caught him in the astral—the Orb of Death, the sister orb to the Orb of Life. The one he needed most of all. He felt the desire for it now as he'd felt it then. Memories flickered. If he could just reach them… He saw the crystal caverns in his mind.

'Yes, I… We created the Dark Rift. There was another; I can't quite remember.' Deep pain clenched his core. Images, weak and confused, moved in the iron ring. A planet in the darkness of space. Giant crystal pyramids and temples. The iron ring flickered as if struggling to reveal the images in his mind as he struggled to remember them.

He'd had power—terrible, awesome power, coursing through him. Scouring the land, obliterating it to dust. Blue sand… His people fleeing into the pyramids and from there to other worlds. Yes, the pyramids were gateways to other worlds.

Rage, all-consuming fury flooded through him now as it had then. Something had happened, but what? A word came to him, and with it memory. With memory came power. He breathed the name aloud, feeling it fill his whole being.

'Lonaaa.'

Cirosa trembled, her eyes travelling endlessly over the enormous bulk of the riderless Dread Dragon before her. The fear she felt angered her. It should tremble in *her* presence. It was lying still and its great snout came up to her waist. Its horn-covered back rose like a mountain and its massive tail, ending in black spikes, was curled around its legs.

It appeared to be sleeping and looked uncannily placid, despite the fear that trembled her organs. Chains thicker than her body were roped around its legs, neck and tail, but still she imagined them breaking and crumbling like cheese if this beast awoke in a rage.

'It misses its rider,' the necromancer beside her hissed. She looked at the repulsive being, once male or female, she could not tell. They all seemed to look the same: tall, thin and gaunt, bald-headed and deathly grey skin. Its hands were clasped in front—long fingers and fingernails twitching. This one had eyes that were all white and deeply disturbing.

'I'll be its master now,' Cirosa said.

'Everything is ready for the linking of minds. There must be a blood exchange.' The necromancer nodded with a smile that revealed long yellow teeth. 'This hasn't been done before—the linking of a non-dragon mind to a dragon. It's very exciting.'

'Just make sure that when it dies, my mind is safe.' Cirosa scowled.

Twenty or so necromancers clustered around the dragon. They were on a great platform high up on the edge of the Mountains of Maphrax. The sky was dark—it always was here—and magenta-tinged clouds rolled endlessly across it.

The Dread Dragon moved, and opened a massive black eye, its nictitating membrane sliding back moments after its eyelid opened. Cirosa stepped back, as did the necromancers. Just because she would do whatever Baelthrom told her did not mean she liked it. She thought she had no need for a dragon, that it would hinder her, but looking at the magnificent creature she began to reconsider.

She sidled over to the beast, daring to lay a hand on its cold, bony snout. It snorted—a gust of putrid rottenness engulfed her—and jerked its head away. A half smile turned her lips. So, it feared her, or at least disliked her. Soon it would learn to obey her.

'We're ready, High Priestess.' The necromancer bowed slightly.

They motioned her to lie down upon the blanketed pallet beside the dragon. She frowned when they strapped her arms and legs down.

'For your own protection, high priestess,' the necromancer explained. 'You wouldn't want the blood tubes ripped from your body, would you?'

She gave a tight nod. If she needed to get free, she could easily break the fabric straps and kill them. Her powers were stronger than any necromancer.

A needle was sharply pressed into each arm and bound there. She looked at the long tubes they were attached to, following them up until they disappeared into the foreleg of the dragon. What did the blood of a dragon feel like? The Under Flow moved around her and the dragon.

'Let's begin,' the necromancer said.

Her dark blood began to flow out of her into the tube and up towards the dragon. A woozy feeling settled upon her, lucid and dream-like. The dragon's black blood seeped down the other tube into her other arm. It was cold and watery, not thick and viscous like she'd expected.

Burning pain filled her arm. She arched her back and screamed. The dragon reared and roared, a sound that shook the entire mountain. The chains rattled and clanged but held.

The wooziness thickened, and vision-like dreams consumed her, stamping down the pain. She saw dragons and Dromoorai, dark corridors and necromancers, Maphraxies and battles. Rage and hunger. Then she was flying with mountains and rivers far below. Then she was fighting with claws and fire. Not dreams, memories. She was experiencing the dragon's memories.

Memory of the black drink loomed. Pain flared as the rending of her body into two was relived again. Even her mind was split apart.

She screamed and struggled. The experiment had failed. It was killing her. Why didn't the necromancers end it? Blackness swallowed her.

Power bloomed in the nothingness and a hunger for more of it consumed her. She swam in darkness, thick and water-like, but she could breathe it, sucking it into her lungs and filling her. The darkness swirled with magenta like blood, or like the sky above Maphrax. It thickened and she sank, suffocating.

Light came and more memories, older, hazier. Who was she? She was dragon. Random thoughts flowed through her. She looked down; her scales weren't black, but light green. Then she was standing up, like a human. Boots, trousers, and long reddish-blond hair braided neatly.

Light flashed. Before her a door with a dragon on it, then nothing. Silence.

This was important, something she should know. The door. She tried to bring it back; it seemed to take an age. There it was. A wooden door with a great, carved dragon head. A secret, a powerful secret. She smiled. Dark nothingness came again.

Cirosa opened her eyes—her eyes or the dragons? She looked down upon puny humans. She blinked, the world shifted and she looked up at the dragon. It looked at her; for moment she saw herself lying there through its eyes. They blinked in time.

Necromancers huddled close and removed the needles and restraints, keen smiles on their pallid faces. She stood up, feeling stronger than she ever had. She walked towards the dragon; it watched her.

'We are one,' she said.

'We are one,' the dragon repeated in her mind.

She threw back her head and laughed. The necromancers joined her, wheezing in glee.

'The dragon and I are joined. In our making I saw something of importance. I saw a dragon door, and where it leads to...a secret held amongst Dragon Lords,' Cirosa said.

Baelthrom paced the floor. Initially irritated that she was still here, but now thoughtful.

'The dragon door was uttered by some Dragon Lords in their agony of immortal change—as if they were reaching for it in their metamorphosis. We could not unlock its meaning,' Baelthrom said.

'I've felt a powerful dragon place that is inaccessible to me, just as the Elven Land of Mists is inaccessible,' he said, pausing to stroke the Orb of Air. It swirled grey at his touch. 'Perhaps this place is reachable now that I have the orb of the Dragon Lords. All these places are reachable, in time. Somewhere on Maioria there is a door—a gateway that leads there. A physical place. Find it, high priestess.'

'Yes, my lord.' She smiled. 'I'll find it when I capture the last Dragon Lord.'

CHAPTER 18

The Man with Many Names

ISSA growled against the gag.

They'd blindfolded her now too, making her even more furious. She breathed hard through her nose, fighting down waves of nausea. Her wounded leg burned with pain. Wherever she sought the Flow, all she could find were solid walls, as if she were in a lead box blocking her from magic.

Something was being done to her leg and it throbbed. She tried to kick them off, but all she managed was an awkward wiggle.

'The poison's gone,' a woman's melodic voice said.

'Is that what the Maphraxies use?' A man replied, his voice similar in melody.

His voice reminded her of Daranarta. Had she been ambushed by elves?

'Yes. Their blades are poisoned and enchanted. But good healers can heal the wounds,' another man's voice was courser and human sounding.

'With the power and magical objects this one has, we were lucky to attack first,' another male human voice said.

'Aye, she be a right fighter, this one.' This voice was gravelly and accented strangely. How many people had ambushed her?

'Looks like she'd still fight now, despite losing all that blood,' said the first human voice. 'She could be in league with them; I can't be sure. Better seal the wound and find out more about her.'

A searing pain made her scream and sent her back into darkness.

When she came round she was propped up and something was draped over her. She felt stronger and her wound no longer burned but throbbed dully. She was still bound and blindfolded, but her gag was looser and more humanely wrapped around her face.

A warm bundle nestled by her leg and the only thing that did that was Mr Dubbins or Ehka. She still couldn't reach the Flow, but now her rage had calmed, she wondered how she had been blocked from using magic. She was desperately thirsty and tried to swallow.

'She wakes,' said the elven male voice.

Footsteps came over; somebody knelt close. These people weren't Maphraxies and they didn't appear to be in league with Baelthrom, but who were they? Did they mean her harm? Why hadn't they killed her? Rather than angry, she should be terribly afraid of them. She laughed at the thought. Anger first, fear later. She wished Asaph was here.

'Are you in league with that immortal bastard?' the first human male asked.

Why would they think that? Maybe they were as afraid of her as she should be of them. The thought surprised her—had she really become so powerful and fearsome? Her, just a farm girl from Little Kammy?

She shook her head.

They removed her blindfold, followed by her gag. She swallowed reflexively but her mouth was so dry. She blinked but her vision was all blurry.

'Water,' said the man.

A canister was held to her lips and she glugged the delicious water down, not caring if it splashed over her face and tunic.

Her vision was clearing. A rich-smelling bowl was pressed to her lips, and she swallowed the broth, salty and spicy. Warmth and strength returned, and with it, anger.

She blinked up at the man. He didn't have a huge black eye like she'd thought, but an eyepatch and a scar that must have taken his eye. She stared and stared at him, then at the others crowding around. Two elves— tall and regal, dwarves she had only ever seen from a distance, and other humans—all dressed as knights in shining armour. Only the black Atalanph with the shining blue eyes she didn't recognise and he wasn't dressed in shining armour. Her eyes rested on the dark-haired man with the eyepatch.

Zanufey had shown her these knights. A distinctive-looking, tall man with dark hair and beard. A patch over his left eye…

'I know you,' she rasped in shock.

A good king but also brings disaster. Was he really a king? What Zanufey had shown her had been confusing. Was this the one the demons searched for? *Yes.* The thought was a whisper in her mind, and she wondered if it had come from the demons. She remembered their pact—a weight upon her shoulders.

'The Cursed King and his Banished Legion,' she breathed.

Shock spread across their faces, apart from the man with the eyepatch. Recognition passed across his. He knew her too, she thought.

There was something odd about him, something not right, but it was too hard to put her finger on. It was like a curse—something he had that was not his and shouldn't be there. It made her afraid of him. As she looked into his good eye, she sensed immense sorrow. She blinked and looked away from the sorrow deeper and greater than her own. As deep as Murlonius' pain.

Marakon stared back at the young woman bound before him. He had seen her before in a dream, fighting against Dread Dragons. He had seen her face in the blue moon that rose. Who was she, and why did this heavy feeling settle upon him?

She had magic, powerful magic and powerful magical relics. His half-elven blood could feel that much. She also had skill with a sword, and would have been dangerous were she not carrying a Maphraxie wound. His white eye began to throb and he rubbed it in irritation.

He could see the mark on her chest beneath her torn tunic—a shimmering blue raven. It was important. He and his knights had pledged themselves to Zanufey, had called themselves Knights of the Raven in her honour, and now here was one carrying a raven mark. The raven that had come to him only yesterday nestled against her leg, and was clearly her pet.

He got the feeling that he should give this woman respect, rather than keep her bound. She looked pretty angry though. He would make sure his knights and Bokaard were safe before he untied her and released the elven block on her magic.

His half-elven senses detected something more beneath the anger in her eyes. Was it sorrow? She carried a burden as did he, and in that way they were alike. Warriors filled with sorrow and revenge and walking a dark, lonely path.

'Who are you and what are you doing in the middle of the forest with a wound made by a Dromoorai blade?' The man with the eyepatch ignored what she had said, his face becoming guarded.

'What's that mark on your chest? It's magical.' He pointed to it.

She hesitated. Should she tell him anything? Was there any point lying? She had nothing to hide.

'I'm Issa, from Little Kammy. Though that was a long time ago… We were attacked by a Dromoorai. Then a seer saved us… It's complicated. The mark is none of your business. And I'll say no more until you untie me. How dare you block me from the Flow.' She scowled at him.

'It's for our own safety.' The man gave a wry smile.

Was he wondering whether he could trust her? He was probably right; she felt furious. But these people, though armoured and armed, were not her enemies, and from the looks of it they had done an expert job at tending the wound in her leg. It hurt less and less beneath smooth, white bandages of a shimmering material she'd not seen before. It looked and felt Elven.

'It's taking two of us to block you,' the female elf said, sounding strained. 'We are protecting ourselves.'

'Who are you?' Issa demanded. She wasn't ready to set them at ease.

'We are Knights of the Raven, called upon by Zanufey. And I am Marakon Si Hara, commander of the second fleet of the Feylint Halanoi.'

Her anger dissipated into surprise. So her feelings were true. This *was* the man, the Cursed King. Ehka had found him.

'We'll untie you only if you promise not to attack us. We won't hurt you. As for removing the block, that's up to those who can command the Flow.'

'When did the raven come to you?' she asked, barely a whisper, her eyes never leaving his face.

'Yesterday. Why? A raven came to me before…' He said no more.

'I sent him—the raven. His name is Ehka.' She didn't know why she told him his name. 'I sent him to find a man, a king.'

Marakon's eye narrowed. 'What king, and why?'

She shook her head and looked at her bindings.

'All right, untie her.' He sighed. A tall man and a woman with a braid bent to undo the ropes.

'Careful,' murmured an elf man coming to stand behind Marakon. 'See how luminous her eyes are? She's a wizard.'

Issa kept her face blank and rubbed her wrists when the bindings came off. They had not dropped the block on the Flow yet though. How much could she tell this man? He would think her mad if she spoke of Zanufey and that she had shown her a vision of him and his knights, and of the demons. How would he take it if she told him the demons wanted him?

She realised she was staring at him and he at her. She took a deep breath.

'Months ago, my home, Little Kammy, was destroyed when the Maphraxies came. I escaped with the aid of this raven sent by Zanufey. I met a witch who told me that the raven searched for the Cursed King and his Banished Legion.'

As she spoke, Marakon and his knights gathered round and knelt or sat beside her. Their faces were at first sceptical, but when she continued to speak in detail about things she could not have made up, their faces turned to wonder.

'I don't know why the demons contacted me. I wanted nothing to do with them and I'm not in league with them. But please believe when I say they saved my life in the Storm Holt, and they are in desperate need of one who can wield this white spear—Velistor,' she finished. There was more she could have said, much more, but tiredness made her stop.

'Velistor,' Marakon repeated, his eyes wide in wonder. 'I have memories of a shining white spear such as you described. Is it the key to our freedom?'

'I've shared everything with you. Now who is this Cursed King and his Banished Legion? What is the white spear? Why do the demons need you?'

Marakon took a big sigh and looked far away into nothing. 'I was once known as King Marakazian, in a lifetime thousands of years ago. I created an honourable order of knights—Knights of the Shining Star—to fight against the demons that plagued our land. A land called Unafay, now destroyed and gone from the world. All that's left of it is in the memories of the dead who walked the ghostlands.

'Great evil befell us and terrible deeds were done. For that we were cursed, and I've returned lifetime after lifetime to right this wrong and set us free. This is my story, our story.'

Hard-faced, Marakon told her about him and his knights and the trickery of Karhlusus. To Issa it seemed so awful, sorrowful and unjust, that she couldn't stop tears filling her eyes. What if a spell were cast on her and she killed her friends, killed Asaph? She would spend her life seeking revenge, would spend many lives, just as Marakon had.

When he came to an end there was one question that still burned in her.

'Do you know anything more about the spear? Where it came from? Who made it?' Issa asked.

Marakon shook his head. 'Not all of my memories are open to me, and for that I'm grateful.'

Issa sighed. 'I agreed to help the Shadow Demons and find you. Otherwise the greater demons will invade here.'

'To make a pact with demons is a double-edged sword,' tutted the dwarf with a greying beard and a face full of scars, echoing what Coronos had said.

'I know… I didn't have much choice,' she said. 'It is my plan to turn it to my advantage, our advantage, and ask them to fight with us against the Maphraxies when the time comes.'

Marakon laughed, short and bitter. 'I'll never fight alongside demons… But from what you've told me, they're right. If Maioria is attacked now by greater demons, when she's weak and tired from war, we'll all be slaughtered and the Maphraxies and demons will be left to fight over the spoils. The Feylint Halanoi can't survive another enemy invading; we are exhausted enough as it is.'

'Which is why we need more fighters,' said Issa, clenching her jaw. 'Like for like. If the greater demons destroy the Murk, then they will come to Maioria. If the Maphraxies destroy Maioria, they'll take the Murk next. That's why the lesser demons and us must stick together.'

Marakon pursed his lips. He didn't like it, she could tell, but neither did he deny that she spoke the truth.

She spoke more gently. 'I don't want to fight alongside demons, either. But from what I've seen of them, the lesser demons aren't our enemy. Some of them have…qualities I didn't expect.' She thought of Maggot, and her heart softened.

Marakon snorted, then looked at his knights. 'If we must go to the Murk to destroy Karhlusus and remove our curse, then I'll go gladly and die trying. How do we get there?'

Issa looked at them all. There were a lot to take to the Murk. Was it even possible? The symbol could take her there, but a whole legion?

'I'll find a way,' she said.

'Coronos!' Issa screamed.

He was ahead and everything was soaked in brilliant light.

'I can reach them,' he said and smiled back at her.

'You're wounded, hurt terribly. You must come back or we'll lose you too!' But he carried on. She followed after him.

A shape appeared in the distance, bathed in light so bright it was hard to look upon. Shielding her eyes, she caught up with Coronos. Something stopped her going forwards, as if an invisible barrier blocked her path. If she went beyond that barrier, a part of her knew she would not be able to return. The shape turned into two people.

'Freydel? Arla? Yisufalni?'

The Master Wizard was supporting a tall woman who appeared to be swathed in gossamer, her slender arm draped over his shoulder. Freydel's eyes were wide and he kept looking behind. All around came the soft singing of a man's beautiful voice. Murlonius' song, she realised.

Coronos carried on; the barrier did not stop him.

'Coronos, wait. You won't be able to get back,' she cried. Did he know there was no return?

'I'll be all right. This is what I have to do, this is the last,' he said and reached a hand back to stroke her cheek. 'Look after Asaph for me.'

'No, don't.' She gasped, but he moved fast. Taking Freydel's arm, he pulled them to him then went behind them. Light came from his whole body as if he was trying to block anything that had been following them.

Everything became drenched in light.

'Feygriene is with me,' she heard Coronos whisper.

'Coronos, come back!' she cried, tears seeping from behind closed lids. Something was holding her back. She struggled against strong hands, gasping for breath.

'Issa, wake up,' a man's voice commanded.

She blinked open her eyes. Tears covered her face and blurred her vision. She swallowed back a sob and took a deep breath. Marakon's forehead creased into a frown. The panic loosened its grip but aching sorrow filled her heart. She was immediately aware of the Flow again. They had unblocked her.

'What is it? What happened? You were fighting and screaming in your sleep,' he explained. He must have seen the confusion on her face.

'I… Coronos.' She clenched her eyes shut, shaking her head, still unable to believe it was true. 'A friend was murdered when I got this wound.'

She couldn't think of anything else to say but the understanding look on his face and hint of pain in his eye told her he knew exactly what she felt. He didn't say anything and instead helped her to sit. The others were up and pulling on armour or tending their horses. It was barely dawn and the brightening sky was still filled with stars. Her belt, sword, orb and raven talisman were by her side.

All her being ached with sorrow and she had to force down the bread and dried fruit the knights kindly shared with her for breakfast.

Why did you take him, Zanufey? Why? Why wouldn't you let me save him? I could have reached him, I was right there.

Asaph needed her. She worried for him. He could die returning Coronos' body home to Drax. The thought of him not returning made her feel faint. She should have gone with him but Baelthrom had been so close. Naksu was right to make them scatter. They were all safer apart for now, even if it meant they were alone.

They ate breakfast mostly in silence, the knights keenly alert for the sign of enemies. Ehka's presence beside her was comforting. She gave him a chunk of bread to peck at and stroked his back.

Duskar was happily munching on grass nearby. As usual, she hadn't needed to hobble him, he always stayed close to her. She noticed that the white horses were also free-roaming, and yet they stayed close to their humans. How peculiar. It was also odd that Duskar stood close to them, when usually he kept his distance. Now that the Flow was unblocked she noticed the knight's horses all had white auras. The knights also had perfectly white auras.

'What is it?' the elven woman asked, seeing her stare. Her name was Ghenath, if she remembered rightly.

'It's your auras, and the horses'—they're all white,' Issa said.

The elf-woman smiled. 'We had wondered about that, for Marakon's and Bokaard's are not.'

Issa nodded. The commander had an aura of blue and pale orange at the moment, and Bokaard's was yellow.

'We have died and returned,' Hylion replied. 'Perhaps our souls have been cleansed in death and they await to return to the One Source.

'How are ye feeling, girl,' asked the dwarf. Cormak?

'Stronger, much,' she smiled. Her leg didn't even throb now. 'Thank you for helping me. I apologise for my outbursts. I'd come from battle and didn't know who you were.'

The knights chuckled.

'Let's get moving,' Marakon said, eyeing the forest to the west. He seemed pensive as he pulled on his armour.

'Where are we? Where are you all headed?' Issa said.

'We're a day from Wenderon on the coast, and we're headed to Carvon,' the big Atalanph warrior said. He had bandages on his arms and around his waist.

She noticed many of the knights had bandages on legs and arms, and bruises or cuts to the face.

'We were attacked,' Marakon said before she had a chance to ask. 'Maphraxies on ships, too many to fight.'

Issa nodded. 'Were many killed? Taken?'

The look of grief on Marakon's face was beyond words. He turned away.

'My wife and children,' he said, his voice quiet. 'Four knights taken.'

Issa dropped her eyes. 'I'm sorry,' she mumbled. 'It seems we all suffer and grieve. I came from Carvon. We were attacked there too, but not by an army. The king already knows about the attacks on Celene and he sent an army marching west—'

'It won't be enough,' Marakon interrupted her. 'They returned. To

Wenderon, to the whole north-west coast. They numbered in the thousands. They mean to settle there. Wenderon is lost and soon too the entire west coast of Frayon.'

'That many? It can't be,' Issa said, unable to contemplate the thought of losing Frayon.

'Then that's why there were so few Maphraxies north and Haralan was empty,' said Bokaard.

Marakon nodded. 'We don't know how far east they're raiding. Which is why we must keep moving.'

She breathed a heavy sigh. Things were moving fast now, too fast.

Marakon mounted his horse.

'No armour?' Marakon asked, looking down at her.

She realised she wore her tunic dress, leggings and sandals. At least she had her blacksmith's belt and sword. With an embarrassed shrug she shook her head. 'No saddle or reins either.'

Duskar nuzzled her leg and she stroked his nose. 'He got out, somehow, and followed me. He's not supposed to be here.'

How indeed had he broken out of his stable to find her? She imagined a smashed door and terrified stable boy with a sigh. 'I can ride him bareback, though not fast.'

'We can't go fast through these trees anyway,' Marakon said, motioning to the dense thicket of brambles, trees and ferns.

With help from the big knight Lan, she heaved herself up onto Duskar's back. Nobody said anything as they walked, and despite the pleasant company of the knights, and the intriguing dwarves and elves, she found herself sinking into sorrowful thoughts.

The orb was gone. Whether the seer or Freydel had managed to retrieve it was an unknown. It didn't seem likely. The Ancients had returned and they would be as hunted by Baelthrom as she was. She should have fought Cirosa harder, but the woman had disappeared somewhere. She should never have left Coronos' side, either. There came a heavy pressure in her head and suddenly she was not alone.

'Remember our agreement, Raven Queen. Time is short.' The words whispered in her mind, breaking her thoughts so that she looked up, thinking someone had spoken aloud.

Demon Slayer, that's what they'd called him. Marakon, the man with many names. The thought of returning to the demons filled her with dread. No matter that they were lesser demons, they still made her afraid. And how was she going to take him and all his knights to them?

'*Use the mark of the Murk,*' the demonic voice came again, startling her. Could they read her thoughts wherever she went? She tried to communicate back.

'*We have problems here. Our enemy is invading.*'

'*So will the greater demons be, and soon,*' came the reply.

The heavy feeling in her head went and she was alone. This wasn't going to stop, she thought. The whole world was at war and she would always be fighting. She looked at the knights. They always fought too: for good, for freedom, for all the things the fables said great knights did. That gave her comfort.

When they next stopped she would honour her pact with the demons. She would draw the mark of the Murk in blood and go to them.

CHAPTER 19

Demon Fear

MAGGOT watched the half-moon of Zorock dipping into the greeb trees with a heart full of reverence.

His tail wrapped around a branch, anchoring him to his favourite tree—a perch that gave him an awesome view over the forest to the Bone Mountains in the north-east. The moon tinged the orange clouds with green and tendrils of mist swathed the treetops. A hot breeze brought the rich smells of the swamp up the hill.

He'd discovered this secret place when fleeing the torments from his older, bigger brother Grub. Grub had been dug out of the rock by their father a week before Maggot was found, but they looked nothing alike and Maggot wondered if someone else had really found his brother. Grub did nothing but tease him whenever he was near—playing tricks that hurt, and always pulling his ears and tail.

Once he managed to slip away from his tormentor into the shadows and discovered the tiniest tunnel. To his delight, the tunnel wound on and on through the rock, always going upwards slightly. It brought him here, to a greeb tree high upon the hill.

He'd been here for a while thinking on everything but, despite the view, today it could not lift his spirit. He scraped his protruding tooth with a claw and wiped the grime onto a branch.

'You saved her, great Zorock,' he said to the moon. 'You saved her from…them.'

He shuddered, remembering the terrible feeling he'd felt when he saw her in their clutches. Shadow Demons weren't supposed to feel fear—fear was punished harshly with pain—but he couldn't help it; it had trembled through him and made him feel sick.

He wasn't the only one to feel fear. Grub had been shaking when the wursel hunter had shouted at him. And at the last meeting, there was fear on the faces of the Shadow Demons when the King roared.

Them. What were they who existed beyond the Pit? They weren't greater demons. He didn't have a name for them. They had no form, but moved in the air. They seemed mad, like they would devour anything without cause or reason. They fed on energy, negative energy at that. Even when he watched from the safety of the crystal shard, he could feel them drawing close to him because he was afraid. His fear fed them and they hungered for it.

She, a human and not even a demon, had been amongst them...and survived. She was so brave, he couldn't think about her without a sense of awe. And his Lord Zorock had saved her. All demons would happily feed on human flesh, but their lord hadn't. Why? Maybe she was the one, then, who could help them. He shook his head and took a big sigh. Maybe she wouldn't reach them in time.

King said the greater demons were coming and that they would attack at any moment. In the crystal shard he'd seen them amassing outside Karhlusus Keep, whilst Issy hadn't even found the Demon Slayer yet. What hope was there for his kind? King had refused his advisor's advice to flee and find another home. They were to remain here in their home and fight to the death. That was why Maggot was sad.

Even if she came here right now with the Demon Slayer, how would they find the spear they needed to kill Karhlusus and stop the greater demons for good? It was hidden deep within Karhlusus Keep; not even a Shadow Demon could find it, so how could a human? But thinking of her *did* lift his spirits. She had been braver than him. Unlike him, she hadn't even hesitated to enter the Storm Holt. Maybe if he was brave, Zorock would reward him too.

A glimmer of an idea rolled around his brain. Could he find the spear? He shook his head so hard his vision blurred. Stupid thought. No demon could look at the spear without being hurt, let alone touch it. Even if he found it, he wouldn't be able to lift it. The thought of entering Karhlusus Keep sent his heart hammering. He wasn't *that* brave. But it seemed that Zorock rewarded bravery, and he imagined what would happen if he *did* find the spear.

There would be endless tables of wursels and jugs of wursel blood. There would be great fires and chanting. The greater demons would be gone, pushed back into the Pit forever, and he would give back to his king their home in Carmedrak Rock. All the demons would be in awe of him and his bravery, and his stupid brother would apologise and be his servant. He would be surrounded by the smelliest she-demons, and he would never know fear or hunger ever again. He snivelled in glee.

He was so deep in thoughts of glory that it took him a while to notice the tree was shaking. He looked at the branch. It shuddered a little, and beneath his clutching hands and feet there was a tremor. One-two, one-two—the tremors went like a beat. A shiver went down his back.

A high-pitched horn screeched, making him jump. Another one sounded farther away, and then another. Was there a fourth too? Heart in his throat, he leapt from the branch and dived into the secret tunnel.

The Shadow Demons' lair was a roaring mass of anger, terror and confusion. Demons screamed orders at each other as they ran backwards and forwards in the dim light of the caverns. Red eyes flared and teeth snapped as weapons and armour was tossed between them.

Despite King Gedrock's plans, drills and preparations, Karhlusus' horde massed on the border lands. The enemy would tear their home apart and they, the Shadow Demons, would be slaughtered and eaten or worse—enslaved. Even the most powerful protective magics they had woven around their stronghold would be no match against the power the greater demons could wield. The enemy was bigger, stronger, more resilient and powerful in every way.

Maggot scowled at the unfairness of it all. Surely Zorock and Almighty Carmedrak would protect them? He refused to believe what the most fearless Shadow Demons said—that Carmedrak himself was a slave to the greater demons.

Well, *he* would not be a slave, and neither was he going to be killed and his body eaten, he thought as he half ran, half flew with the others towards the main exit. Twice he was kicked by demons nine feet taller than him as they ran, not that they noticed. He launched himself high to fly above their heads.

King had ordered all his warriors to face the enemy outside. They had the advantage against any attacker, so he'd said. Their lair had been chosen for its defensibility long ago. A narrow path led through cliffs and hills densely packed with trees. Their tunnels led to elevated points along the cliffs where the enemy could be attacked from above. King said they had a chance at defending their home and winning, if they were clever. Maggot trusted his king.

Following the loping bigger demons below him, they emerged outside onto a wide plateau. Maggot landed on a jutting rock just above the demons' heads so he could see. His mouth dropped open. Below them wound a crawling mass of brown Grazen and black greater demons. Above them, on wings of shadow, circled the biggest demons he'd ever seen. A whimper escaped his mouth. A Shadow Demon scowled and snarled up at him. Maggot clamped a hand over his face and swallowed.

He pulled out his weapon and practised scowling. He could pretend to be fearless and fearsome, even if he didn't feel it. He looked at Jabber, his foot-long spike. It was half his body length and the only weapon he'd ever managed to master. It was thin and very sharp and he'd crafted his very own enchantment upon it. He was not good with magic, but he'd spent a long time learning certain enchantments in Master Crawl's lessons.

The enchantment made the spear fly farther and strike harder than he could ever have thrown or thrust it himself. He could also call it to return to his hand. A grin spread across his face as he stroked the dull grey metal. He'd never successfully used it but he was incredibly proud of Jabber.

'Maggot!' the howl cut through his thoughts and froze his heart. All demons looked at him, frowning. His eyes travelled over them and settled on King's face.

'Yes, King,' he thought he'd mouthed, but all that came out was an airy moan.

'Get back inside and get the Raven Queen. You'll not be out here today.'

Unable to speak, Maggot snapped his teeth—another way demons said "yes"—and found his wings carrying him back inside the lair.

King had told him yesterday that he was to stay by the crystal in case she returned or tried to communicate. But he didn't think that meant right now. What if King was killed and their lair invaded? He wouldn't be able to escape down there. He gripped Jabber and prayed to Carmedrak.

The great hall was frighteningly empty and quiet. The crystal shard slowly pulsed green, like a great heart sleeping. He slumped down beside it and dropped his head. The whole place was deserted. He would die down here, alone. If he listened hard, he could just about make out the howls and clangs of weapons as the battle above unfolded.

King wouldn't even let him fight. How could he sit here and wait? The Raven Queen wouldn't come. Humans were liars, especially in the things they said to demons. But she had been brave and promised to help them. He struggled with conflicting emotions. He didn't like humans. Who did? But she was different to what he'd been told.

That thought came again, about being brave and finding the spear. Another thought swiftly followed: if their enemy was attacking them here, how many would remain in Karhlusus Keep? Maggot trembled at his own thoughts.

Issa looked down from above, seeing through Ehka's eyes. Whilst they rested, he'd gone to the Murk, and she was seeing what he saw. Everything was cast in the dim green light of the half-moon Zorock, the squat trees, the black rocks and the great mass of demons lumbering below her.

Screeching filled the air and she glanced up at black shapes moving in the sky. Cold filled her. Greater demons, like the ones she had escaped in the Storm Holt. Red eyes burned into her. She dropped down into the trees.

Demons screamed—a sound no normal beast could make. Mayhem unfolded; it was hard to see what happened in the gloom, especially when demons moved so fast and many were only partially solid. Shadow Demons flew or ran and every so often they dissolved into shadows. The flying greater demons had no solidness at all. They melted and flew as black patches or sometimes with bat-like or dragon-like forms.

Only the brown demons were solid. Grazen, the word came to her. Metal scoured against metal. Murk magic oozed—a sickening feeling. The sky blazed with blood-red fire.

She cowered close to the tree trunk as a Grazen was speared then beheaded below her, its body turning to molten rock then exploding. A Shadow Demon materialised in its place, hissing and roaring, its muscles bunching and bulging all over its shiny, hairless body.

Another Grazen jumped forwards, fangs bared, tail lashing. Its sword was a blur as it stabbed into the Shadow Demon's neck. Both demons melted into shadow; the look of horror on the Grazen's face, as it disappeared, made her heart shudder. The Shadow Demon materialised, alone. What had happened to the Grazen? Where had it gone? She didn't understand this battle and Murk magic swamped her mind.

Green fire flared. The flow of Murk magic rushed around her then receded, doing things she couldn't see with her physical eyes, but could feel with every cell of her body. Her head pounded. She had to get away.

Ehka, come back. She called to him as she pulled her mind away. But if anything the battle around her grew louder: the sound of shouting, the sound of swords being drawn, the whinny of horses.

Issa blinked and jumped up, pulling her sword free as the sound of shouting came to her. Her leg wound throbbed from the sudden movement. Her muscles were taut and ready, as if the battle she'd witnessed had prepared her body. She tried to get her bearings in the dark barely illuminated by the remains of their smouldering campfire.

Marakon was already up and partially dressed in armour—breastplate but no helmet, boots or greaves. He was in a fighting stance, half squatting, sword raised, and a dangerous look on his face. The shadows before him danced and she realised they were foltoy. Two of them shied back from his flashing sword.

Snarling came from behind. She whirled around. The elves were also up and facing black shapes she couldn't quite make out for the trees, either foltoy or death hounds. A dwarf jumped up—she couldn't tell who—only saw his wide, thick stature and swinging axe. He moved towards something in the shadows beyond the hearth. The others were springing up and grabbing their weapons.

A shape came at her—the size of a wolf but smaller than a foltoy.

There was no time to be afraid. She swung her sword, it ducked and lunged up. She jumped back and fell over a saddlebag. The death hound followed. She rolled and stabbed, her sword sinking into flesh more by luck than anything else.

Cold, black blood oozed over her hand. She gagged and kicked the jerking death hound off her sword. Another attacked before she was standing, and she rolled evasively. Marakon's sword sliced an inch above her head and decapitated the hound. She glanced up, caught the battle fury in his eye, nodded her thanks and screamed as knife-like claws swiped towards his turned head.

He ducked. She pulled on the Flow and lifted her hand. Blue fire surged into claws. The death hound howled and was incinerated. Marakon had no time to thank her as another leapt upon him. She rolled up and together they stabbed it.

More came. She marvelled at the skill and speed with which his sword moved. He seemed to dance, and his sword was an extension of himself. It would have been graceful if it weren't so deadly. Only the elves moved with similar speed, reminding her of his heritage. She hoped she'd never have to fight him. He was a veteran, an ancient king, an ancient warrior. She could not match his skill, but perhaps she could learn from him. She hoped he would agree to teach her.

'Bunch up,' Marakon yelled.

Issa obeyed along with the others, and they clustered together—a tight knot of warriors, a ball of prickling swords. Before her advanced a wall of fury, snapping fangs and dripping drool. Her sword rose, stabbing forwards and back, left and right, finding a target every time. Blood sprayed.

She found herself being inched backwards behind the better-skilled, better-armoured knights. She realised then they were trying to protect her—perhaps because she wore no armour and held only a short sword that had little reach compared to their longer weapons.

She fought harder, frustrated. She *could* fight and she wanted to use her sword. The frustration ended when she entered the Flow. Perhaps magic was the best way she could fight this battle. But all she could see was the blue moon huge before her, instead of the fields of energy that should be there. She blinked and tried to refocus. Again, only the blue moon was before her, massive and powerful.

Small dark shapes appeared between her and the moon, moving close. They had no auras and the Flow did not move through them. Their energy was dead. Were they the foltoy and Death Hounds?

She drew upon the Flow, but it wavered. She was still drained from the battle against the Dromoorai. Then it came to her fully, and for a moment she was lost in a sea of beautiful indigo, filling her with glory. Was the dark moon giving her its power?

Screams came from the material world. The knights! Her gaze remaining in the Flow, she focused hard until she saw their bright auras huddling around her.

'Fire. Blades,' she commanded. The Flow moved and she looked upon the material world.

Weapons burst into indigo flames and the enemy fell back. Overcoming their shock, the knights wielded their flaming blades. The stench of searing flesh and howls of pain filled the air. The death hounds yelped and turned tail.

'Let none escape!' barked Marakon lunging after them.

Issa focused on the dark shapes in the Flow.

'Fire. Death hounds.'

Those nearest bust into indigo flames. There came yelps and howls then silence. The others were hunted down by the knights whilst she remained in the Flow, ready for any more attacks. Both Marakon's and Bokaard's auras were red and flaming. Battle fury, she thought. The auras of those with magical abilities—the elves—were still white but they crackled with energy.

She gently exited the Flow. Calm and the darkness of night closed in. The forest seemed so dark and boring compared to the fields of magic light she had just been witnessing.

'You fight well. Fearless, but also recklessly,' Marakon said, cleaning black blood off his sword.

She bristled, then softened when he grinned at her.

'A Karalanth taught me for a time, the rest is…just experience. And not enough of it either,' she said.

'A Karalanth? Now that's a formidable teacher. I didn't know they spoke to humans. Usually they just kill them,' Marakon said.

'They nearly killed my friends. Both Draxians. They were wounded already and so they spared them. Can you teach me?' she asked hopefully.

A strange look passed over his face. 'I've taught many, in my time. Only to see them die. Perhaps I taught them wrong. I don't think I want to do it anymore.'

'You taught all of us,' barked Cormak.

The knights laughed.

'You know it's right,' Cormak continued. 'We talked about it; you starting the Knights again. The Knights of the Raven—and you'll need a darn sight more than us lot.' He chuckled.

Issa wondered at the name. Knights of the Raven. An order of elite knights. She liked it.

'It was a long time ago, Cormak. And I have bad memories.' Marakon sighed.

'You had good memories before though. You know you'll start it in the end. This world needs knights of honour now more than ever before,' Cormak pressed.

'I'd be first to join,' Bokaard said. He was smoking on what looked like a soft, thick twig. The smell was nice, like burning pinecones, but heavy. He was busy blotting a shallow wound on his forearm.

'Me too,' Issa piped up at the thought and imagined learning Marakon's sword skill. Bokaard laughed and Cormak winked at her.

'All right.' Marakon lifted his arm. 'I'll think about it. But you have magic and powerful…relics. You don't need a sword so much.'

'I need to know how to fight. Magic is not always there, as you so recently taught me. You're part elven, aren't you?' she added, unable to contain her curiosity.

The question caught him off guard and he spluttered on the water he'd just swallowed.

'That obvious?' he didn't sound pleased, which confused her. Had she offended him?

'Well, the way you moved your sword, like dancing, the same as the elves did. The way you move body, more elf-like than human. Your eye, I guess…' She felt embarrassed mentioning only one of his eyes. But then he had a thick beard and black hair, which was not elven at all, and his ears weren't very pointed.

'My mother was elven,' he said. 'One of the good elves, the courageous ones who stayed here. Unlike the cowards who fled.' He scowled.

So he was ashamed to be part elf. She found that strange. She would love to have their speed, grace and beauty, if only a little.

'It might be difficult for you to believe, but remember I told you about Karshur yesterday?' she said. 'Well, it made me return it to the elves. It took me to the Land of Mists.'

Everyone's ears pricked up. The elves watched her without blinking. They had already told her how hard it was to accept that their kin had withdrawn from the world, leaving it to its fate in Baelthrom's hands.

'I couldn't stay long. I was only there by invitation and the power of Karshur. But the raven mark on my chest, well, that happened there. A gift from Karshur before he departed. There I met with the leader, a man called Daranarta.' The blank looks on their faces told her that no one knew him.

'I asked them to return to Maioria, to help fight against the darkness smothering us. I told them that Baelthrom would find them eventually anyway. But they wouldn't listen and I got angry. I suppose I wasn't very diplomatic. I failed to get them to even consider returning.' She remembered the futility, felt the anger now as she had then. The elves faces were pinched and anger was bright in Marakon's.

'It seems they would rather die alone than join with humans and dwarves. Maybe demons will make better allies.' Marakon winked. She smiled though knew he was only joking.

Ehka cawed and landed on a branch above her. The horses appeared and clustered below him.

'You brought the horses back,' Issa said and laughed.

She had forgotten about them in the chaos. Had Ehka led them to safety? Duskar seemed quite calm as she patted his nose.

'Let's get going. I don't want to stay another moment here,' Marakon said. Everyone agreed to travel in lantern light and rest at dawn if they needed. They packed away their things and buried the fire.

Issa felt someone enter the Flow and instinctively entered it too. She jumped up and looked around. The two elves were in the distance looking down at the body of a foltoy. The foltoy began to glow.

'Relax,' Marakon said. 'They're burning the bodies, silently, and without harming anything else around them. They want to remove the infection from the forest.'

She watched, fascinated as the body burned with a low white flame and then was gone. They repeated the process for each of the twenty or so undead beasts. They worked fast and it didn't take long. Soon they were moving through the forest.

She was exhausted, as if she'd fought two battles today and not just one, and let her eyes close as she sat on Duskar. But as soon as she did, her mind relived the battle she had witnessed between the demons.

CHAPTER 20

Sleeping Dragon

ASAPH flew north, where the wind blew frigid and the sea froze.

Mountains encased in ice and snow rose up, and between them ice fields stretched—long planes of flat, glistening white, unmarred by the footprints of any living thing. This place was empty, eternally frozen. He flew deeper into it.

His hide was thick and the sun strong, but whenever a cloud passed across it he felt the cold sap his strength away. He could freeze to death here, he realised. This was a dangerous place for dragons and their cold reptilian blood. Icicles formed on his wing tips and tails. His nostrils crusted with ice as he inhaled and melted as he exhaled. Coronos' body was frozen in his grasp.

In dragon form his sorrow was dampened, and in this extreme place thoughts of survival and warmth were closest to his mind. It was a blessed relief from the emptiness that threatened to consume him. He reached with his mind, searching for the sleeping dragons he knew existed out there, somewhere.

He could feel them, barely, and not just one but several. They seemed everywhere like ghosts, felt but not seen. He thought about finding them. He thought about staying in his dragon form forever so sorrow could not reach him, but his thoughts turned to Issa. Even as a dragon he cared for her and he would not leave her for long.

He crested a towering ridge and beyond it a massive plateau of white expanded. The mountains bordering the plateau to his left and right steadily rose until, in the far distance they were at their highest. There, in the lee of the tallest peak, he would rest his aching wings.

As he neared his destination, something on the mountainside gleamed golden in the sun. He bristled, expecting trouble, and looked through the Flow. A blazing swirling sea of white greeted his vision. Ahead was the slower-moving energy forms of rock and something else—a gleam of pastel, the barest hint of magic. *An old, old enchantment,* he thought. The magic he felt was too ancient to read clearly and seemed more about preservation than anything else.

He drew closer. There was a small building, a temple of sorts, nestled on a naturally flattened-out section of mountain. Smaller peaks surrounded it, protecting it from the wind and yet allowing in as much sunlight as possible. A cleverly chosen place in this inhospitable land. Rough-hewn steps led down to the plateau below it. There were more steps leading around and down the other side of the peak.

Asaph landed in what seemed like courtyard. Large flat stones were visible under the layers of ice. The temple was built of stone and covered in some kind of liquid gold. He stared closer, mesmerised by the beauty of it. He could smell that it was indeed gold, as if it had been melted and poured over the temple. The gold seemed to stop any snow from covering it.

The temple was perfectly round, its walls flaring out from the base to create a bulge before narrowing majestically until it formed a beautiful needle-thin spire a hundred feet high. He wondered who had built it, sensing that it had been here for a very long time. He searched in the Recollection, but nothing came to mind.

He looked down at his father's frozen body—his own talons were frozen around him. His heart felt heavy in his chest. His father would have been fascinated by this place, and now he would never share a moment like this with him again. As sorrow seeped in, the dragon form slipped away and he knelt beside his father's body. His face, partially visible through his hood, was perfectly preserved in ice.

'I must let you go,' he whispered, feeling the tears freeze on his cheeks. 'I've brought you this far, away from the enemy and closest to the dragons I can feel sleeping somewhere near, and now I must let you go.'

He stood and went to the temple, carefully walking up the steps that were sheets of ice and snow. The arched wooden door had a gold handle about a foot long. He expected it to be frozen solid, but when he pushed, the handle turned easily with the heavy sound of a lock being released.

Opening it was another matter because it opened outwards and snow blocked it. He scraped the snow and chipped the ice away with his boot and managed to open it a foot or so, just enough to squeeze his body through. He was met with another door, of the same size and wood, but covered in golden whorls and scrolls. This too had a handle, and when he pushed down it opened easily, inwards. The temple wasn't locked, so perhaps it was meant as a resting point for cold, weary travellers.

Inside it wasn't dark, as he had expected, but filled with daylight. Looking up, the gold-painted stones were now clear like glass and he could see the sky and mountain above. The paint was amazingly see-through from this angle. He found himself wondering and staring up for a long time.

The floor was made of smooth, pale pink marble. From the floor to head height, the walls were covered in dark wooden panels, carved perfectly to fit against the rounded side of the temple and in keeping with its domed shape. There was a large, raised fireplace in the centre of the room, blackened from ancient use. Beside the hearth was an iron crate, half filled with what he sought. Logs.

He investigated the temple further, but couldn't find anything more than he had already seen. It may not have even been a temple, apart from its beautiful design. Perhaps it was simply a resting place for the weary from the bitter elements. He began to gather logs and take them outside to build a pyre.

It was hard work and his back soon ached, but at least the workout kept him warm. When he had finished, he lifted Coronos up and tenderly laid him upon it. He leaned his head against the pyre, panting to catch his breath. The altitude was taking its toll. His muscles trembled from fatigue and his belly rumbled with hunger. He ignored it. Food was far away, and he didn't care so much if he never ate again.

The hairs on his neck prickled. He froze, all senses alerted. Had she found him already? His heart pounded. He wanted to kill her, but the thought made him mad with confusion. Could she reach him even here? No, it felt different. It wasn't her; it was something else. Then he saw a huge furry head peering from the craggy cave entrance in the mountainside beyond the temple.

The grimcat was massive, three times the size of those he'd seen in Kuapoh lands, and all white too. Huge canines hung down below its jaw, brown eyes gleamed and narrowed into slits, and its pointed ears lay flat. The great cat sniffed the air, scenting him and probably his father's body. His heart pounded.

He had a connection with beasts—part of his dragon blood—and he tried to reach out to it. He felt nothing but hunger and anger. This was the grimcat's lair, and food had arrived. He reached for his sword; it was frozen stiff in its scabbard. The grimcat leapt out of its cave and stopped. Its white fur glistened in the sun. It was skinny and its giant ribs were visible under its thick coat. Its eyes were full of hunger and devoid of reason as it watched him—his prey. *Food must be hard to find in this frozen desert,* he thought.

Once more he tried to reach the grimcat, but again all he found was hunger—ravenous, maddening hunger. Pursing his lips, he wrenched at his sword but it was stuck solid. There was a knife in his boot, but it would barely penetrate the thick hide of this beast.

The grimcat padded forwards and stopped. Asaph stood between it and his father. He would not let his father's body be eaten. The thought gave him courage, but what could he do without his sword? He didn't want to kill the magnificent beast, but he would not be eaten by it either.

'Go away. We're not for you,' he shouted.

It roared in response, a gusty sound that echoed. Its breath was thick in the air, and its brown teeth frighteningly large. The grimcat lunged. Asaph braced himself, refusing to give up his father's body. He meant to punch the grimcat full in the face, but the grimcat was too fast. A paw knocked him sideways; claws raked across his arm, tearing his clothes. He smashed into the ground, dazed and wounded.

The grimcat was half on the pyre, Coronos' foot engulfed in its mouth.

'No!' Asaph screamed.

The fury made the dragon come. In a heartbeat he was looking down at grimcat. It had slipped off the pyre and was now frozen in terror, brown eyes wide and unblinking, tail tip twitching.

The anger surged. He took in a great breath and spewed fire. The grimcat exploded into flames, bellowed a horrible sound then rolled onto its side.

Asaph roared his rage until his lungs were empty. The noise filled mountains and echoed back and forth.

Looking down at the blackened carcass ignited his ravenous hunger, driving away his own reason. He did something he'd never done before—he ate as a dragon. With relish, he ripped into the grimcat, tearing out chunks of flesh and swallowing them whole until there was nothing left of the beast. He even licked the blood-covered snow until no red remained.

Clouds had gathered whilst he ate, but the frigid wind had dropped and all was still. It should be night by now, but the days were long here, ancient memory told him. Snow began to fall, delicate and floating. He was glad for the meal in his belly.

There was something he had to do. He looked down at the body on the pyre. Before sorrow could touch his dragon heart and steal his dragon form, he breathed in and blew gentle flames upon it. The centuries-old wood caught quickly and soon the pyre was roaring.

Releasing his dragon form, he huddled close to the flames. He felt ashamed, even disgusted, for killing and eating a majestic grimcat, especially in the presence of his resting father. If he had not killed it, it would have killed him. He closed his eyes and brought to memory the words of the Fire Sight. He had only ever spoken them once or twice before. Staring into the flames, he spoke them aloud.

Fire is the sun, the light, the life-giver,

Fire is the dragon, the passion, the flame within my heart,
Fire fills my soul, fire stirs my spirit, fire lights my way,
When the darkness comes and all seems lost,
Feygriene lead me home to the One Flame.
The flame that burns with truth,
The flame that burns with love,
The flame that burns eternal, the light that never dies.

'Go to the Fire in the Sky, Coronos Avernayis Dragon Rider, my beloved father. I will always miss you.'

The fire blurred in his vision and his whole world was filled with flames. Memories of their happy times together played out in his mind: when he was a boy, growing up with the Kuapoh. His father who was always there for him, never far from his side. His father who had shared the same room with him for twenty-five years.

Now his father was gone, the last of his family gone forever; he wondered why he was left here. An orphan, an exiled prince, the last Dragon Lord. The loneliness consumed him.

'Take me with you, father. Don't leave me alone,' he whispered.

A face formed in the flames—a female face he'd seen before. Her hair was fire and her skin gold. Her eyes knew him intimately: every good deed, every bad word. Feelings of love and reverence rolled over him, filling the pit of despair he felt, though he didn't want it filled. He was humbled.

'Young Asaph,' Feygriene's voice was deep and soft, meddling with the roaring of the flames. 'Coronos chose his time to leave. He gave himself in the greatest honour so that others might live. Your time has only just begun. Strong heart. Strong mind. So many need you, call to you. Help them, Asaph.'

The face disappeared and he felt keen loneliness again. Curled up beside the pyre, he must have fallen asleep, for when he awoke, all that was left of his father was ash and smouldering logs. His clothes were soaked through in melted snow. The sky was clear above, but the sunlight frigid. He couldn't stop shaking with cold and it was that which drove him inside the temple.

He shut the doors with clumsy, frozen hands. It was still freezing inside but at least the wind didn't blow here. He threw logs into the fireplace and struggled with the flint and tinder. Fire was easy for a dragon, but sometimes impossible for a human. After many sparks, one ignited and a flame grew.

When the fire was roaring he pulled off all his clothes and hung them to dry. The shivers left his body but the grief remained. He tried to hold on to the words that Feygriene had whispered, but without her presence here, the words felt empty.

He felt broken—utterly. He might have sought solace, but even the Dragon Dream was closed to him. He was tainted by the white woman's hold upon him. Cast out by everything and everyone. He had betrayed Issa. He was weak, useless. What good was he to anyone? He'd brought the danger. It was because of him that his father had died.

He could not return to Issa and risk her, or anyone else's life again. Would she even forgive him for what he had done? She would be better off without him in every way. He would hide away forever, eking out his existence here where no one could be harmed. But the white woman would find him eventually.

He could not be captured and turned into Dromoorai—not because he cared about himself, but because the thought of turning against his people was sickening. If she didn't find him, eventually Baelthrom would. It was obvious, then, what he had to do.

WHEN he stepped outside, it was dawn, though the night had never fully come. The sky was tinged orange and pink, and the wind whipped and hugged his naked body. He forced himself to stop shivering and walked to the ridge where the steps led down the other side of the mountain.

The scenery was as before: endless snow fields and ice mountains. He walked away from the steps onto a ridge, his feet turning blue as agonising cold seeped up his legs. He ignored that too.

It wouldn't be hard, he thought—just one step over the edge and into darkness. A sense of relief, a feeling of release came with his decision.

He clenched his fists and roared, his human voice weak and feeble compared to his dragon roar. His echo came back and he roared again and again until his voice broke.

He lifted a leg to step forwards but as he did so the ice-ledge beneath him suddenly cracked and gave way. With a yell he fell with it several feet before slamming onto another ledge. That too broke.

Again he was falling. Then he was sliding through snow. Rocks of ice cracked against his ribs and jarred his back; pain flooded his mind. The world tumbled as he rolled, then he was falling through air again. He slammed into something hard, ending his tumble.

Something shook him moments later, or perhaps it was hours; he had no sense. He spat blood from his mouth. His body was so cold it was beyond shivering.

He felt again what had roused him.

The earth trembled. Huge cracks snaked through the snow. He tried to roll away but only managed to move a foot, his body half frozen and his mind delirious. He blinked, only half believing what he was seeing as the ground in front of him began to rise. It seemed that the mountain he'd just rolled down was moving like a living thing. It rose up and up and up. Rocks, snow and ice cracked and fell from it.

Beneath the falling snow appeared bluish-white ground, the same aqua blue colour as glaciers, but carved into dragon scales. What he thought were spiky rocks turned out to be horns. What he thought was a crack, opened. A golden eye stared at him, but was so big it probably stared at a hundred things. Swathes of snow fell away and a long neck revealed itself from its icy enclave. What he had taken to be a snow-covered mountain, was a snow-covered dragon, and he was lying on its giant paw.

He gawped up into the huge eye as a wave of dragon fear shuddered through his body. The dragon shook, sending avalanches of snow from its body. Ice-blue scales gleamed in the sunlight. It opened its great mouth and yawned; its giant paws with glacier-coloured talons stretched. The dragon skin beneath him began to warm his body.

Asaph's eyes travelled along the dragon's great length. It was easily as big as he was in his dragon form; the only difference was that this dragon had no wings. Instead, two angry red scars ran along its body where the wings should have been. The dragon's wings had been ripped off. He felt sick at the horror of it.

In a voice as deep and thundering as the boulders of ice that tumbled around him, the dragon spoke.

'Who brings the tainted into my domain?'

Asaph's mind was a whir. Could the dragon feel Cirosa's chains?

'I-I came here only to rest,' Asaph stammered. He could change into a dragon, but would that cause a fight? His dragon form would be weak too.

The dragon dropped its head and brought its eye just a foot from Asaph, blinking and peering. Vertical slit widening.

'Ugh, you're one of them, a half-thing.' The dragon sounded disgusted and lifted its head away in disdain. 'And you're tainted with black enchantments. You are as close to death as any I've seen. If it weren't for your taint, I would already have eaten you.'

'Who are you?' Asaph's curiosity barely overcame his fear.

'Who am I?' the dragon roared—making Asaph flinch—and brought its eye back to stare at him. 'Don't you know? Are you a fool? I am the great Morhork, King of Dragons.' The dragon closed its eyes and nodded, as if pleased with himself.

'I'm sorry, great Morhork, but I've been away from the Known World most of my life, and I've never heard of a king of dragons before. Faelsun never mentioned—'

'Faelsun!' the dragon roared. Asaph cowered, suddenly realising he lay naked on top of the dragon's trembling paw. 'My brother can rot in the Abyss.'

The dragon raked the ground back and forth with the paw Asaph lay on, scouring deep grooves in the snow and ice.

Asaph sucked in a breath, his sore ribs complaining. Faelsun had a brother? A brother who was king? A brother who hated him? Could Faelsun be hated? He had shown Asaph nothing but courtesy and kindness.

'So, you're a real dragon,' Asaph spoke his thought aloud.

'There are only real dragons. You Dragon Lord scum are not even half-breeds,' Morhork said, glaring. 'Tell me who you are and why you have ruined my sleep before I eat you?'

'I am Asaph Dragon Lord.' His voice shook. There was nothing more he had to lose, and so he was honest despite the tears stinging his eyes. 'I was heir to the throne of Drax until the Maphraxies invaded. My family were killed. My adopted father was just murdered by those who killed my family. And I came here to…to burn his body and set his soul free to Feygriene. And I-I came here to die.'

'Drax was ours until Faelsun decided it was his to give to you pathetic humans,' Morhork growled and began raking the ground again. His skin was almost hot underneath Asaph, and he was grateful for the life-giving warmth.

'It may have been dragon-owned, but Drax has fallen to the immortals, the Maphraxies. Maioria herself and everything that has life will fall to them if they are not stopped.' Asaph chose his words very carefully. This dragon hated humans. 'Everything in my life has also been lost. If you wanted to eat me, it would be a welcome release from this world.'

'What are Maph-raxies?' asked Morhork.

Asaph blinked. Did this dragon not know? Surely he knew about the fall of Drax?

'The taint you see upon me, one of theirs did that. They're enemies of all living things, of all Maioria, and they want to take and enslave our souls. Their master is Baelthrom, and he came from the Dark Rift in the sky.'

'How interesting. I saw this in my slumber. Let me look,' the dragon said, and pushed his massive head close to Asaph.

He felt the strangest thing then; the ancient dragon opened the Recollection within him and together they looked at its contents. Images moved back and forth. Asaph watched, amazed. He saw how Morhork worked it, like a reference book but using feelings and thoughts to search, rather than words like he had tried to do.

'So that's how it works,' he breathed.

Morhork blinked at him. 'Have you had no education? I would have thought Faelsun fawned all over you.'

Asaph looked away. 'I've been taught nothing.'

The dragon blinked at him, as if seeing him in a different light, but said nothing and instead focused on the fall of Drax.

For the hundredth time, Asaph watched his home burn, and his brethren and sistren murdered or enslaved. Afterwards he felt utterly exhausted.

'My brothers and sisters…murdered.' Morhork's voice was low and airy and filled with uncertainty. 'I had horrible dreams. Their screams in the dark… Where are those who survived?'

It was unsettling to Asaph that something so big and ancient should be given to uncertainty.

'I don't know. I've been trying to find them. I'm not your enemy. It might please you to know that all the "Dragon Lord scum" are gone. I'm the last.'

The dragon gave an unreadable expression. He seemed confused. Morhork looked at him intensely and he felt the dragon's mind enter his own, much like Keteth had done. He couldn't resist. An image of Cirosa holding a bloody knife above Coronos forced its way into his mind.

'No,' Asaph gasped, shaking his head.

'Hmm,' the dragon said, tendrils of smoke coming out of his nostrils. 'That one had you bound with powerful chains. Why don't you remove them?'

'I don't know how.' Asaph shrugged.

'Stupid human. Even I could break them. Why don't you ask Faelsun? He loves humans. I'm tired now. Go and die somewhere else.'

He barely twitched his paw, but Asaph went rolling head first into the snow. He gasped against the cold and struggled to get his face out of it. He felt utterly pathetic. This was not how he envisaged meeting his first dragon.

Morhork had laid his head down on a mountain ledge and closed his eyes.

'I cannot enter the Dragon Dream, if that's what you mean. The way is barred to me, because of this "taint." Faelsun does not want me there ruining the dream.' Initially he spoke in despair, but now he was angry.

'And besides, what kind of stupid dragon lies up here sleeping for thousands of years? What happened to your wings? I can see the scars where they would have been. Why has Faelsun cast you out?'

The dragon whipped his head up and glared at Asaph. 'None but the "pure" may enter the Dragon Dream,' he spat. 'That's how *he* wanted it, and that's why we never got on. My *brother* ripped my wings from my back. An unforgivable crime for which he has never answered. Do you know how long it took for me to *walk* here?

'It took me centuries to learn to harness enough of the Flow that would enable me to fly again, but always I returned here. The world holds nothing of interest to dragons whilst it's run by humans. It may seem like I'm sleeping but my mind is most certainly working…on other things. Whilst my true form sleeps, a part of me moves in the world of men, undetected.' He paused then chuckled, a deep rumbling sound.

'What are you talking about,' Asaph huffed, standing on one frozen foot, then the other, not bothering to hide his nudity.

But the dragon didn't expand upon what he remembered, leaving him confused. How could Faelsun do something so awful as to cut his brother's wings off? It didn't make sense; Faelsun would never do that.

A dragon screamed from far away, or was it in his mind? His thoughts scrambled and Cirosa's invisible chains tightened—pain, everywhere, and a choking sensation, as if he had a collar about his neck. He gasped and fell, writhing in the snow. She was hunting for him.

'What's wrong with you?' he heard Morhork ask, but pain gripped his mind and all he could do was shake and gasp.

CHAPTER 21

Isle of Myrn

'AN honoured member of the Wizards' Circle has been taken from us, and the Orb of Air has been lost to Baelthrom,' Freydel finished in barely a whisper.

All eyes were upon him in the Wizards' Circle as he finished explaining everything that had happened. His heart was so heavy, he could barely speak. The grief on the wizards' faces was tangible.

'For these reasons, we shouldn't hold this meeting for long. Baelthrom is hunting for the others and now he's far more powerful.

'Coronos' staff is safely in the hands of the seers and on Myrn. They will return it to the circle when it's safe to do so. There's nothing more I can say.'

Silence descended upon the Circle. Freydel worried his beard. The joy of saving Arla and discovering she was an Ancient was marred by the loss of a dear friend, the orb and his own staff.

'There is nothing we can do about the orb, except count our blessings that we still have the other three,' Averen said in a soft voice. 'How long has this High Priestess been in league with Baelthrom? I query how tainted the Temple has become. It's been diverging from the old ways for a long time now.'

Freydel frowned. 'For the past year or so I barely spent any time in Celene. Cirosa had merely been prickly at best, but nothing had prepared me to realise she had become a murderer. I would like to think better of the Temple, but after what we witnessed at the Temple of Carvon, I think Baelthrom's hand has indeed shadowed it.'

Averen nodded. King Navarr's face had remained dark since the meeting began. He clearly had not slept and looked as exhausted as Freydel felt. Navarr had told him before the meeting that there had been an incredible light display over the forest next to Carvon that night. Even those who could not see magic saw the dragon fire and magical flares.

It ended with a flash of bright light followed by a flare of red, and everything went calm. Soldiers found nothing of the Dread Dragons nor any people. Everyone had vanished and all that remained was a blackened, flattened forest and a pool of blood. Navarr spoke now.

'The Temple has made itself powerful. I cannot simply chuck them out and close their doors without fear of an uprising and riots. At this point the people need to come together, not fight amongst themselves. I will, however, warn them of danger within Carvon's walls and place soldiers around them. They will think it's for their own security.'

'How can the enemy be at our gates so soon?' He shook his head, clenching the pommel of his sword. 'I've since requested half of the Feylint Halanoi to move to West Frayon, and a quarter of that number to come and guard Carvon itself. It will take them weeks to arrive, unless we're very lucky.'

'We can do no more except pray,' Freydel said. 'We, all of us, must be ready to assist Navarr whenever he has need and we must warn the other countries, ask them for aid if they have any to spare.'

'Atalanph can send warriors, though many are already north with the Feylint Halanoi,' Haelgon said.

'Aye and dwarven warriors can also be sent,' Drumblodd seconded.

'I'll travel to Lans Himay,' said Averen. 'As dangerous as the place may be, there are warriors there aplenty and every man and woman has a sword.'

'Domenon?' Freydel asked the brooding man; he seemed to be involved in his own thoughts. 'Can Queen Thora send any aid?'

'Yes, I'm sure Davono will be willing.' He waved his hand dismissively.

Freydel frowned. Domenon was acting more oddly than usual. Coronos' death had shaken them all, or more likely he was missing the Orb of Air.

'Good. That's something. I'll travel to the Isles of Tirry to see what wisdom the seers can offer, and to retrieve Coronos' staff. The enemies' noose is tightening—'

'This should never have happened,' Domenon blurted, his face pinched. 'If we had left the orbs here, like I'd suggested, this couldn't have happened. It's no secret that Coronos was the weakest wizard amongst us; he even said so himself many a time.'

'Coronos was more than able,' Freydel said, stiffening. 'No one could have foreseen what would happen. How can you blame him? You weren't even there. And besides, as I've explained, Arla and I would not have returned if he hadn't saved us.' He was too tired to be angry, and he certainly didn't have the energy to fight with the other Master Wizard.

'And how many more orbs will we let go?' Domenon's voice rose to shouting. 'Issa is not trained to handle an orb at all. How long before that one is lost too?'

'None of us were trained,' Freydel reminded him.

His head was beginning to ache. The Flow was moving very strangely—sluggish—but all in one direction—towards Domenon. But when he looked, the dark-haired man was not actually in the Flow and he certainly wasn't pooling it. Freydel wondered if he was even aware of the magic moving around him as he vented his anger. The wizards looked at each other, clearly feeling and seeing it too as Domenon ranted on.

The Flow shuddered and ceased moving. Everything was still and quiet, as if a continuous, monotonous noise had suddenly stopped.

'How long—?' Domenon paused mid-sentence, a look of utter confusion spreading over his face.

'Domenon?' Averen was concerned.

Domenon shook his head, as if trying to remember what he was saying, then all the colour drained from his face.

'What is it?' Freydel asked, fully entering the Flow and feeling others do the same.

Domenon was still not in the Flow. The dark-haired man stood up. He seemed weak and shaking.

'I feel unwell, I-I must rest…' With a motion of his hand he exited the Circle fast. He seemed to fall forwards as he dematerialised.

Freydel looked at the others. They shared the same worried and baffled expressions.

Back in his room in Castle Carvon, Freydel was still deeply concerned by

Domenon's disturbing behaviour. He'd considered scrying to reach the man but, given that they had never talked that way and didn't exactly get on, he dismissed the idea just as quickly. Domenon was secretive and never discussed his health problems with anyone. He was probably just sick with a stomach bug or something. Freydel decided to settle for the weak conclusion.

With a sigh, he prepared himself for translocating to Myrn. Being weak and tired, he would never normally translocate physically given how demanding the process was. But this was an emergency—dire things had happened.

He had rarely visited the largest isle within the Isles of Tirry, and the last time was over twenty years ago. Normally he loved travelling, but after all that had happened, he just wanted sleep.

'He didn't know Seer Naksu well, but he did know a member of the Trinity.

'Iyena,' he said her name aloud as he trimmed his beard. She had already been a seer for ten years when he'd first met her. Back then, he hadn't really thought much about a seer's ability to command the Flow, more through ignorance than judgment, he admitted to himself, but after witnessing Naksu hold the force field around all of them and thwarting Baelthrom, he conceded they were far more powerful than he had thought.

He leaned against the alcove, staring out of the window over the sun-drenched forest. Beyond the city walls in the forest, where the Dread Dragon had attacked, there was a great indent of broken and blackened trees marring the perfect carpet of green. He gave a silent prayer to Feygriene for Coronos.

For a moment he imagined the whole forest broken and burning, and beyond it a wasteland of grey and a sky of black and red. He shivered. That was how Maphrax looked. He had seen it often in the orb and on his own mind journeys. They could not let that happen to Frayon. With all his power and knowledge, there had to be something he could do.

As much as he tried to avoid thinking about him, his thoughts drifted, as they often did, to Ayeth. If he could bring himself to travel back in time again, could he change the course of history and prevent Ayeth from ever becoming Baelthrom? Had he been shown these things so that he might try? As the most powerful Master Wizard in the Known World, was he duty bound to try to help Maioria in whatever way he could?

Ayeth was so powerful… Could he teach Freydel some magic or skill that could help them all? The thoughts plagued him. He should tell the Circle about Ayeth, but something always stopped him. He even wished he'd never told Issa, and prayed she wouldn't tell anyone else.

With a sigh he moved away from the window and pulled out the orb. It was time to visit the seers.

He started the spell, intoning the words faster and louder to build the magic. His world became a mass of spinning white and violet light and his body was lifted from the floor. He directed his thoughts out to Myrn and in response felt magical energy return. Magic from the seers. They were ready. The two magic streams touched and flashed. The connection forged and from that he built a tunnel of energy.

With a word he entered the tunnel. He lurched forwards, his physical body becoming pure energy. The translocation was fast.

Freydel stood blinking and his stomach churning as the waves of magic dissipated and calmed. His legs turned to water and he sank rather gracefully on to the grass. Taking a tissue from his pocket, he wiped his sweaty forehead.

Looking around, he sat in the centre of twelve amethyst crystals arranged in a circle several yards wide. He was on a hill and below swept a forest down to a blue sea. The land curved into a near-perfect crescent shape and, across a short channel, there was a much bigger island; round and just as green. Over there were low, dome-shaped, white buildings amongst the trees.

He took a few shuddering breaths and looked up at the albino seer who came to stand before him. Her companion, the plump elderly witch he'd briefly met in Carvon, was standing proud. The seer was smiling, the witch scowling.

'Greetings, Master Wizard Freydel.' The seer held out her hand.

'Greetings, Seer Naksu, and, er—'

'Edarna, Witch of the Western Isles.' The witch stood taller.

'Yes, indeed. I remember now.' Freydel nodded, feeling awkward. 'I, er, feel more than a little unwell after that journey.'

'Take this,' the witch said promptly and stuffed a small, blue vial into his hands. 'Cures all travel sickness, but the sooner you take it the better.'

He peered at the murky liquid inside. Just looking at it made him feel sick.

'I, er, drink it?'

The witch nodded and gave a look that made him feel like a schoolboy. He hated medicine but the look on the witch's face made him think twice about disobeying.

He opened the vial and swallowed the liquid in one, hoping it wouldn't touch the sides. His stomach somersaulted and he thought he would faint. Then everything cleared. The weakness in his body left, the brain fog went, and the sickness disappeared.

He stood up and smiled at the witch. 'It really does work. Fast.'

'Of course.' She sniffed.

He took a deep breath and admired the view.

'Yes, this is where I arrived years ago. That's the main island—Myrn—across the channel and this is the West Isle.'

'Yes, you remember correctly,' Naksu said. 'None can enter Myrn directly because of the protective shield. Come, let's go to Myrn where we can eat, talk and rest.' She began walking down the hill.

'What's on the other islands?' Freydel found his inquisitiveness sparking as they walked.

'They each hold a circle of crystals, but only this one is amethyst.' Naksu spoke freely which surprised him. He'd expected such knowledge to be withheld from outsiders.

'Each type of crystal holds a particular type of property. Aside from crystal circles, we grow food and collect water. This island, for example, grows oranges and other citrus fruits, vegetables and herbs and nuts that all enjoy lots of warm sunshine. Look to your left—the round, shorter trees are orange trees.'

Freydel nodded, looking at the green, unripe oranges on the trees.

'The crystals help maintain the climate of each island. So we can, for example, keep the southern island tropical and grow bananas and mangos. Don't ask me how.' Naksu held up her hands when Freydel began to speak. 'I'm not versed in Crystal Lore, nor Climate Science. There are far better minds than mine for that.'

Freydel was disappointed. He longed to know more about it. Why, after all his hard years of study, did he not know everything yet?

'We can't excel at everything.' Naksu smiled at him. 'We're given particular gifts to use and use well.'

'What are your areas of expertise?' Freydel asked.

'I have lesser talents than Crystal Lore, but more than one. Herbal Lore is one of them. I'm very good with plants—growing and nurturing them. Which is why I come to the Outer Islands, to tend the plants. I'm also a skilled tracker. I can see that surprises you. I grew up in a poor house in the middle of a forest. I learned to track every animal and, I'm sorry to say, eat them. Though now I'm a seer, I'm forbidden to kill anything that's not directly attacking me.

'Language Lore is another gift, albeit a nurtured one. I can commune with almost anything—which is why I'm a Wayfarer.

'The Trinity deem it wise that I use my gifts to aid Maioria outside the Isles of Tirry. So, unlike most seers, I'm rarely on Myrn. That was how I came to know of Asaph Dragon Lord, and his poor father, Coronos Avernayis Dragon Rider. They were staying with Karalanths that I'd befriended. My gifts with plants and language allow healing to come naturally and easily.'

'But the magic you used was none of those things,' Freydel said. The woman was full of surprises.

Edarna walked silently beside them, seemingly also engrossed in what the seer was saying.

Naksu smiled. 'That's my final gift—magical ability. Though it's a gift, I've spent years mastering it and don't find it easy. I had magic ability from birth. I was average, as female wizards go, but years of hard work have given me the powers I now possess.

'Though I'm not old, in my travels I've been to many places and seen many things, and collected gifts of power along the way. I've also passed the Trial of Fear, and have mastered all things that would make me afraid. Although dragon fear still touches me.

'I don't say these things to brag, but only because you asked, and I would like you to know a little of our ways and abilities. We're not as secretive as everyone thinks. We just keep ourselves away from the world, out of necessity to protect our knowledge from Baelthrom who sits on our doorstep.'

'That can't be easy,' Freydel said.

'It isn't. That's why many of us try to master fear. Our home is in the shadow of the enemy, and we keenly feel his threat. If we knew everything, we would have found a way to end that threat long ago.' She gave a wry smile.

Freydel considered her words. Had they been too hasty to disallow women on the Wizards' Circle? The decision had been made by others hundreds of years before his birth, but he couldn't help but question it.

'We're all devastated by the loss of the Orb of Air,' Naksu said, changing the subject. 'And I'm broken by the loss of Coronos. I wish I could have done more. I got there too late.' She blinked back tears.

'We're all devastated.' Freydel sighed.

They came to a pebbled shore and simple wooden jetty, at the end of which was moored a white boat. When they got in, Freydel noticed it wasn't painted, but made of white birch. He stroked the smooth wood.

'The White Trees grow on the northern isle,' Naksu explained. She picked up the oars and began to row. She seemed rather small for the job though she rowed strongly. Edarna took the tiller.

'Would you like me to do that?' Freydel offered.

'How about a little push?' Naksu grinned, making her seem like a child.

Freydel laughed and, with a motion of his hand magic, moved the boat faster towards the other shore. While they moved, he looked up at the sky. It was blue with no hint of the force field except when he entered the Flow.

The magical field felt exactly the same as that covering the Wizards' Circle, only much bigger and possibly stronger. He could see purple waves stretching overhead and mingling with other colours. The amethyst crystal circle, he realised, helped to create the force field.

The jetty they arrived at was made of the same beautiful white wood as the boat. To the north was a much bigger jetty, but a large ship was docked alongside it. The ship looked to be of Atalanph design.

'We receive cloth, food and spices from Atalanph, once every two months,' Naksu explained, seeing him looking.

'Lots of fit young men too, by the looks of it,' the witch spoke for the first time. She had her eye glass on.

'I'm convinced you can see far more in that eye glass than you let on, Edarna,' Naksu said. The witch popped the glass into her pocket and winked.

'We witches have our own fancy things,' she explained.

'And not for the faint of heart,' Naksu muttered. Edarna tutted. Freydel hid a grin.

They walked up a white, stoned path through old oak, chestnut and yew trees. A few were young and carefully pruned, suggesting someone meticulously managed the forest. The place exuded calm and serenity, much like he had felt when he'd been invited to an Elven Grove long ago. They passed a clearing within which a simple white dome-shaped house stood.

'Because of the merchants, the main town, sanctuaries and courtyards are very busy today. But for our purposes, the southern dwellings have been vacated and I brought Coronos' staff there,' Naksu said.

Freydel was disappointed. He had wanted to explore the whole of Myrn, particularly wherever the seers spent most of their time. He felt it rude to ask, however, and decided he probably didn't have enough time anyway. He'd have to return and stay longer when their situation wasn't as dire.

They reached a larger domed building just as the sun was turning orange. The setting was beautiful, beside a twelve-foot-high waterfall and surrounded by chestnuts whose leaves were turning golden. It was on an elevated position so it gave a stunning view of the sea stretching out to the south-east. He could just see the tip of the West Isle beyond the trees.

Inside, Freydel stared at the pale blue crystal floor. It seemed to flicker in the light that came through the glass ceiling—which immediately reminded him of his study on Celene.

'Yes,' Naksu grinned, 'we also watch the stars.'

Freydel nodded approvingly. The place was bright, airy and a small. A neat fire already burned in the central hearth.

'If it's all right with you, we shall dine here tonight and sleep.' She motioned to the six recessed rooms within which were single beds. The curtains that covered each entrance were drawn back. 'Food and wine will be brought to us, and anything else we require. After which you're welcome to join me and the others at the Lower Spring.'

'I'd be delighted,' said Freydel.

Within the hour, two young seers arrived, bringing local wine and tropical fruit—some of which Freydel had never tasted—sweet and delicious. A boy accompanying the girls brought rice and yellow sauces, fried mushrooms and golden bread.

'That's from Atalanph,' Naksu said as she dipped her round bread into the sauce.

The food was truly delicious. While they ate, Freydel considered Edarna. The witch had remained quiet, though from her earlier quips and her actions at the Temple of Carvon, Freydel suspected this was not her usual manner. She seemed nervous. Perhaps all witches were nervous in the company of wizards—probably because other wizards were always treating them with disdain.

But now Freydel was older he realised the loss of witches to each village and the world as a whole. No pregnant woman ever really wanted a male wizard in their birthing chamber—and most wizards balked at the thought of it. He wanted to break the ice but could think of nothing easy to say to her.

'Are you planning to stay here?' he chanced.

'Hmph, no,' she said. 'This is a seer's place and I have my own plans and work to get back to. I'm planning on rekindling the coven.'

Freydel spluttered on his rice.

Edarna gave a wicked grin.

CHAPTER 22

Mission from God

THE others were sleeping, with Cormak keeping watch at the edge of the forest.

Issa had settled herself away from the others to scry for her friends, but kept within sight of the fire. It was well past midnight, but she couldn't sleep for worry of Asaph and memories of Coronos beneath Cirosa's blood-dripping blade.

Turning her attention to the smooth, shiny surface of the raven talisman, she brought Asaph's face to mind.

'Asaph,' she whispered. 'Can you hear me?'

The surface of the talisman seemed to bend and swirl. Nothing appeared at first, and then the high peaks and valleys of a snow-covered place came into view. His face did not appear. She closed her eyes. She could feel him, somewhere far to the north. The flame ring on her finger grew warm, but still she could not seem to reach him. It was a long way to scry and her mind grew tired. She let go with a sigh.

Knowing he was alive was a relief. His face before he left had been so utterly filled with grief, she worried for his state of mind. She longed to see him, to know he was safe.

Perhaps she should try to reach Edarna. She focused on the talisman again. It was harder the second time, her mind weary from the first.

'Edarna,' she whispered. The witch was easy to find, and her round face and rosy cheeks soon appeared in the talisman.

'Is that you, dear?' Edarna said, her voice faint.

'Yes. Where are you? Are you safe?'

'I'm with Naksu, on Myrn. Where are you?'

'I'm safe, somewhere in the forests far west of Carvon. I could think of nowhere safe to go, so I went to Ehka. I've found him, Edarna, the one you mentioned. The Cursed King,' she spoke fast with excitement.

Edarna's face became serious and she nodded. 'The time is coming then…' The witch faded.

'Edarna? Are you there?'

'Yes, dear.' Her image came back again. 'Naksu says scrying through the protective field will be tiring and difficult. She says you need to come to Myrn, that there are important things you must learn… Hang on.'

There came muffled sounds of people talking, then Naksu's white face came into view.

'Seer Naksu, thank you for saving us back then,' Issa said.

'I couldn't save us all… I wish we'd come sooner.' Naksu smiled sadly.

'We all wish we'd done something different,' said Issa. 'Asaph is…in pain. He's gone to bury his father. I can't reach him by scrying; he's too far north.'

'I would like to offer words of comfort, but given the gravity of the situation, there is little I can say except please come to us in Myrn where we can talk in person,' Naksu said, her face earnest.

'I will. There's much I still need to talk to you and Edarna about. It's the demons; I agreed to help them. They saved my life.' Edarna's face appeared beside Naksu's as she spoke. 'I see them in my dreams. They're fighting. They keep warning me that the greater demons are coming.'

'A pact with demons is a dangerous thing,' Naksu's face was grave, 'but for them to help a human is…unheard of. We've talked about King Marakazian at length, but I know nothing of his purpose, other than he's cursed by the demon wizard Karhlusus. Sometimes only eliminating the curser can end a curse. I know something of the white spear but we cannot talk about it like this, and…'

Naksu's face faded as a wave of exhaustion flowed over Issa.

'What about Freydel and Arla? I mean, Yisufalni.' Issa brought the talisman close to her face.

'Freydel is with us. He came to collect Coronos' staff. Regarding Yisufalni, trust she's safe with Murlonius. If they have survived this long, they'll survive a while longer. Much has been lost, but at least two Ancients still exist upon Maioria to keep their presence and power alive.'

Naksu smiled, but Issa was sure she could see tears in her eyes.

Issa breathed a sigh of relief. The image wavered again.

'Come back to Carvon too.' Edarna pushed her face into full view. 'By the time you reach the city, the heat will be off. You never came for your gift.'

'I will, I—'

The image went. She rubbed her temples and stood up. She desperately needed advice on what to do about the demons, but no one seemed to have any.

She sank down beside the fire onto a cloak the knights had given her, wrapped it around her, and fell asleep.

The blue moon filled her dreams. She sat on a shore, looking out across a calm ocean, and the great indigo moon broke over the horizon. Its blue light flowed over and through her, filling her with omnipotence, love and sanctity. She wanted to drift in that holy bliss forever.

Something cold was pressing on her arm. She tried to nudge it away but it came back and squeezed harder. She turned over, and the serenity of her moon dream shattered.

'Hey, what?' she mumbled, really needing a few more hours sleep. She blinked, but there was no one there.

The big man Lan was keeping watch, his eyes drooping as he sat just beyond the fire, sword on his knees. The sky was barely brightening with dawn. The shadows around her moved and became one. She reached for her sword when a familiar face materialised.

'Issy? Shhh. Don't let them know I'm here.' Maggot's voice trembled and his eyes darted over the sleeping knights. His blood-red tongue licked his protruding fang.

'Maggot? What are you doing here? How did you get here?' Issa whispered.

'You're not going to help us, are you?' His bottom lip trembled and his yellow eyes were huge.

'Maggot, I made a promise. You saved my life—'

'But there's no time.' He wrung his tiny hands that materialised out of the shadows. 'The greater demons are attacking. We might hold them off this time, but not for long, so King says. You have to help us. King knows you've found the Demon Slayer.'

'Yes, but what can we do? How can we get the spear?' Issa asked. Despite her oath, the last thing she wanted was to fight demons in the Murk. 'Humans can't just arrive into the Murk, walk into Karhlusus Keep and pick it up.'

Maggot blinked at her. 'I know, I-I've been thinking.'

Lan coughed and looked around, hand resting on the hilt. Maggot gulped and faded into the shadows.

'Maggot, I *will* come.'

'Please come now.' His voice came clearly from the shadows. 'Remember the symbol. That's how you get to the Murk.' His voice faded away and then he was no longer there and the shadows were normal.

Maggot melted away from the watchful eyes of the hated knight, and returned through the green crystal shard. The demon hall seemed emptier than before. There came muffled demon screams from the battle above ground. It would only be a matter of time before they came here. He huddled down beside the pedestal and hugged his knees.

'Maggot,' a deep voice whispered, so low it rumbled through his body.

He yelped and hid behind the pedestal. The greater demons were here; they had come to enslave him.

'Maggot,' the voice came again, and he realised it came from not one place, but all around, even inside his own head.

He couldn't call out; they'd find him. But they already knew he was here if they were calling his name and inside his own head. He trembled and belched, hoping they wouldn't hear that. He began praying to Almighty Carmedrak, whispering in demonic, begging for courage.

'I'm already here, Maggot,' the voice rumbled through him, shaking the floor. Maggot detected exasperation in its tone.

'Who…who is it?' His voice quivered, a squeak compared to that mighty voice.

'You know who it is.' The voice rolled around the cavern.

'King?'

'No, Maggot. The other one.'

Maggot's black heart nearly stopped. 'Lord Carmedrak?'

'Yes. I've given you enough signs. You know what you have to do, Maggot, so go and do it before it's too late.'

Maggot trembled all over and could barely breathe. His *Lord*? Was it possible? His teeth began to chatter and he flapped his wings madly. They lifted him fast off the floor, straight into the ceiling.

'Ouch!'

He spun back to the floor and rubbed his head. But what did he have to do that he knew he had to do? Get the Raven Queen? He'd already tried that.

'The spear, Maggot,' the voice whispered in his mind.

'Yes, my Great Awesome Lord,' Maggot spluttered out the words.

He would do that, right away. If Lord Almighty Carmedrak told him to get the spear, then Gedrock wouldn't be angry. He stood up and swallowed. On shaking legs he slipped around the pedestal and headed across the hall then paused.

'How?' he squeaked.

'Don't make me explain everything,' said Carmedrak.

Maggot nodded then pulled on his ears.

'Go!'

The voice made him jump and he ran to do his task. He had a mission, a mission from god. He would be praised by his kin, he was going to save them. He *would* be as brave as she was. Carmedrak had spoken to him, to *him!*

Just as he reached the great doors of the demon hall, a spark of green exploded out of the crystal. He yelped and ducked as the spark squealed past him, the squeal like the sound of a mouse screaming. It crashed into the doors, whirred dazed to the floor, then darted through a gap at the bottom.

'Ugh, swamp fairies.' Maggot immediately felt sick. He hated swamp fairies. Gedrock would be furious that it had got into their lair. Maybe it had broken free from one of the lanterns and hit the crystal shard.

Swamp fairies were only good for lighting, but they weren't easy to capture and contain. Strong glass and magic was needed to ensnare and trap them. They made good lamps but they didn't last long and they tasted horrible.

Maggot melted into shadow, slipped under the door, and followed the swamp fairy. Unfortunately it was going in the same direction he was headed.

He growled when it disappeared straight up his special secret tunnel. How dare it know about his secrets? Swamp fairies always knew how to ruin things, and it was ruining his divine mission from Carmedrak. He slipped in after it, and flowed in the shadows around the winding tunnel.

When he emerged, Zorock had set and instead the orange light of their small sun, Zorock's Eye, spread across the greeb trees.

He paused at the exit of the tunnel, listening to the distant sound of war. Screams and howls reached even here. He gulped, pulled his ears down under his chin and let them flick back up. Dark thoughts whittled through his mind. If he went, would there be anything left of his home to return to? Would he even return? He shivered.

She'd been brave and I'm far stronger than a human.

Though he had made up his mind, it was with a lot of effort that he eased himself off that ledge and onto the ground. He became aware, then, of how desperately long the journey to Karhlusus Keep really was. It could take days to reach just the Black Sands, and then the worst part would begin. He could fly, then run when his wings got tired. Melting through shadows was the fastest way to travel, but tiring.

A flying grub buzzed near—a fat one too—and he jumped to catch it in his mouth, gulping it down with relish. At least he would have plenty of fresh insects to eat. Might even catch a bat or two.

A little reassured, he hopped through the trees, half flying, half jumping. What if Issy came and he wasn't there? He couldn't do anything about that; Carmedrak had sent him on a mission. He would have to be as quick as he could be, though. But what if she arrived and needed him? She was vulnerable down here. King would look after her.

A thick swarm of flies rose up from a muddy puddle. He jumped to gulp them down and carried on. Burping loudly, he realised eating and hopping didn't mix. There could be greater demons near.

He froze with his hands clamped over his mouth, but there came no sound other than toads croaking in the bushes. He had a mind to hunt for them, but his mission drove him on. He resolved himself to flying and not catching any more food for fear of burping.

Twice Zorock's Eye rose and set by the time Maggot arrived at the Black Sands. He'd seen greater demons flying high in the sky but nothing else. They hadn't seen him amongst the trees, or in his passage through the shadows as he scaled mountainsides. A Shadow Demon could travel in any possible direction as long as there were shadows to meld with.

He stuck his head out from behind a gnarly tree at the edge of the woods, and stared out at the expanse of black sand. The flat wastelands were bordered on the left by jagged, black cliffs. It was night, and the soft light of Zorock flooded the desert valley below. Maggot shivered. He was closer to the Grazen and the greater demons than ever he had been. If he was caught, he would be killed or enslaved—he preferred the former.

For several long moments he crouched there, staring until he felt his eyes bulging out of his head. He pulled his ears down and let them flick back up, daring to scan for enemies. He could just make out horrible black specks in the sky.

This was not a good idea at all. He looked back the way he had come through the trees and the mountains beyond. It was a long way home.

He looked at the black spire. Karhlusus Keep was much closer. *Carmedrak Rock*, he reminded himself. It wouldn't do to be on a mission from his lord whilst calling that place the name of his enemy.

There came a squeak, a thump on the back of his head, and then a green light flashed past him.

'Hey,' he howled, then clamped a hand over his mouth.

Stupid swamp fairies. They were everywhere lately. What was going on? Why were they always going in the same direction he was? He scowled. It couldn't be the same one stuck in the demon hall. He wished he was that small so he could dart about unseen by things above, but he wasn't and he was stuck here whilst Zorock's bright light illuminated everything and drove away shadows.

He waited. As Zorock moved, the cliffs began to throw shadows on the ground until a continuous line of dark was drawn around their base, enough for him to melt into and move. Always watching behind, ahead and above, he moved in the shadows until he was as close to Carmedrak Rock as he could get. It was still a long way away.

The Black Sands stretched out before him, illuminated unforgivingly by Zorock, and Carmedrak Rock towered into the sky like a giant dagger. The moonlight now cast the shadow of the rock for miles in front of it.

If he waited for the shadow to grow longer, it would reach him and he would be able to move in it.

He stared up at the spire. Dark caves dotted from its thick base to its jagged tip. They were entrances. Looking at its peak made him dizzy. He dropped his eyes and clutched his spinning head.

In his mind was embedded the memory of his race's ancient home. There were enormous wondrous halls that put their own great hall to shame. Maggot had never seen the halls of his true home but he remembered them in his ancestral memory. The knowledge of his ancient roots was held deep within in his black demon blood. For demons were made, not born, and instilled with the same essence as all their kind were. In those dark caves only the Grazen and greater demons now dwelt. Thousands of them, mostly enslaved.

Looking at his ancient home, he longed to see inside it. Karhlusus Keep—pah—what a slight upon their god. No demon resided in a keep. Maggot realised he was growling. He swallowed. Somewhere in there he would find Velistor.

There was an old rumour that Karhlusus himself had freed the spear and used it to defeat and bind their Lord Carmedrak, but Maggot could never bring himself to believe this. Carmedrak had spoken to him, and he hadn't mentioned needing help.

All knew that the spear would destroy Karhlusus, as it would any of them. So Karhlusus had sought a thousand ways to destroy it first, but not even the strongest and oldest demon magic so much as dented the spear's surface. Unable to break it, Karhlusus bound it deep within Carmedrak Rock.

The moon had moved again, and now the shadow of the rock was close to where he hid. As soon as it reached him, he took a big breath and flowed into the shadow, moving fast across the barren Black Sands.

Halfway across, he looked up and froze. More greater demons circled the spire, seeming bigger now he was closer. A shiver trickled through him. A shadow headed straight for him, screaming. He was shaking so much his body partially materialised. Black leathery wings, easily fifteen feet across, sliced the air above him as it hurtled past. He closed his eyes, unable to move and wishing with all his heart he had never left the great hall.

But the killing blow never came. He forced open one eye. The demon had flown straight past him and was circling higher up the rock. He let out a long breath and opened his other eye. Sudden relief made his guts wobbly.

His eyes wandered upwards, and for a heart-stopping moment he thought it was Karhlusus himself glaring down at him—a pale white thing looking over a balcony halfway up. A glimpse was enough to send his heart racing. Was it Karhlusus himself in Demon King Kull's form? It slunk away, back into the rock.

Maggot tried to melt back into the shadows but he was shaking too much. Mind-numbing fear made it impossible to de-materialise the body. This divine mission was turning out to be much harder than he'd imagined.

A green light sparked somewhere between him and the rock. It made him angry, angry enough to forget his fear. A swamp fairy did not belong in this sacred place. He melded with the shadows, and flowed forwards once more.

He reached the base of the rock and re-materialised, panting, hugging the stone and thanking Carmedrak for protecting him. He stayed there long enough to feel sleepy. He had never been able to fend off sleep, not even in King's awesome presence.

The moon was setting behind the mountains; soon it would be completely dark. He couldn't sleep here though, amongst his enemies. They would find him for certain.

He yawned and slumped.

CHAPTER 23

Dragon Pity

ISSA'S face formed in Asaph's mind.

She was smiling at him, her blue-green eyes full of light. She called his name, then faded away. He reached out to her, but she was gone.

He jerked awake, coughing, finding himself sprawled face down on the warm floor of the temple. The fire burned in the hearth, but it was low and smouldering. It was dim but not dark. How had he gotten here? Had Morhork picked him up and thrown him in here? It seemed like the only reasonable explanation. The dragon hated humans, so why had he bothered to save him?

Dragging himself up, he pulled on his dry and warm clothes, and set about looking for a cup or something he could melt snow in and drink from. There was nothing.

He went outside, called the dragon within, and glided down to the lake. With the sun so low on the horizon beyond the mountains, it was very cold.

At the lake's edge, he breathed in and flamed the ice. The ice was several feet thick, but he eventually melted a hole big enough to stick his snout in. He gulped the frigid water down, feeling the cold slow his reptilian body but slake his thirst.

As he stared down into the black depths, something shiny glinted far below, like a gold coin but much bigger, being so deep. He stared at it but couldn't make anything out other than gold shining, like the gold paint of the temple.

He entered the Flow, and felt the same kind of old magic that encased the temple coming from it. It filled the bottom of the lake. Perhaps there once was more than one temple here, and they had since crumbled into the lake.

Back in the temple he stoked the fire. Meeting Morhork had helped push back the sorrow for Coronos and reminded him of his mission to find the other dragons. He almost felt ashamed for wanting to kill himself.

He closed his eyes and searched for the dragon door. It appeared easily enough in his mind, but still would not open. After several tries he gave up. How could he remove Cirosa's chains? She would hunt him down eventually and he wasn't sure if he could fight her, given her hold upon him.

He should find Morhork again and try a different tack. The dragon hadn't killed him, so surely he would eventually help him. No one else could.

Asaph left the temple when the sun was high and peered over the mountainside to where he'd fallen. There was a great hole where Morhork had been. Asaph's heart fell. There were several massive paw prints leading away, and then nothing. Had the dragon vanished? He sighed and slumped onto his knees. He'd imagined his meeting the other dragons to be a wondrous celebration, not this indifference, or worse, hatred.

His eyes travelled across the desert of snow to where an avalanche revealed a great cave. He stood up. It wasn't an avalanche—something had been digging in the snow, something big. Could it be a dragon? His heart leapt in his chest.

Changing into his dragon form, he launched into the air and glided to the cave. He stared into the darkness. Snow became ice, became rock, until there was just darkness—a natural cave big enough and deep enough to fit a dragon.

'Hello?' he called.

A hot gust of dragon breath exploded out, but nothing answered. He could faintly hear a deep-throated snore. He peered farther into the dark. Was it rude to walk into a dragon's lair when it was sleeping? Dragons did a lot of sleeping, it seemed.

'Hello?' he tried again, a little louder.

Nothing.

Deciding to remain in his dragon form, he shuffled farther in. The cavern went deeper then wound around to the left. He followed it and snaked his head around the corner. There at the end, curled up with tail resting on snout, was Morhork sleeping. Every now and then the tip of his tail would lift off his nose, pause in mid-air, then rest back down.

Asaph swallowed. The dragon hadn't been happy to see him before; he was unlikely to be happy if he woke him up again. But if he didn't wake him up and get answers, what had he achieved? His life was hopeless anyway.

If he really was Faelsun's brother, and dragons weren't known for lying, maybe he could help get him into the Dragon Dream. Once there he could explain to Faelsun what had happened and beg him to help break Cirosa's bonds and remove the taint.

Otherwise he'd have to return home, wherever that was, or die alone out here. Both options left a sour taste in his mouth. He decided to wake Morhork up and braced himself against the dragon's rage. He bunched up his muscles and shouted.

'Morhork!'

A great golden eye snapped open, the Flow crackled in the air, and the dragon whipped its head up.

'Piss off!' Morhork roared.

Asaph leapt backwards as a wave of flame exploded towards him. Bursting through the flames came a ferocious ice-blue dragon. Morhork slammed into him, sending them both rolling backwards. Talons ripped into his shoulders and teeth clamped onto the underside of his jaw. They rolled out of the cave and fell down the mountainside.

Morhork managed to keep on top of him as they slid down in the snow. Asaph was too shocked to move, and the ancient, more experienced dragon had him in a perfect grip. He could not move a limb; all were pinned down and his head twisted in the dragon's jaws. Even the Flow was not his to command, but slipped around him as if avoiding him. He realised Morhork could easily rip out his throat. Asaph froze.

Morhork kept him pinned there for a long moment, making it clear who was in charge, who was more powerful. He felt like a young dragon whelp. Morhork's teeth tightened on his jaw. Asaph gasped and snorted in pain. Then the jaws released him.

He gasped and shook his head.

'I'll kill you if that's what you want,' Morhork said. 'I'm hungry.'

'Do dragons eat their own?' The thought filled Asaph with revulsion.

'You're not our own,' Morhork roared.

He felt ashamed. 'I can't help what I am.'

'Obviously.' Morhork snorted in pity.

'I need to get to the Dragon Dream. I need to remove the "taint" you mentioned, but the dragon door won't open. Faelsun won't let me in. Can you talk to your brother?'

The dragon laughed, not a nice laugh. 'You think he'll let *me* in? I've been denied entry from the beginning, and I don't even carry the stain of abomination on me. Even the physical door is guarded against me.'

Asaph blinked. 'The physical door? You can walk in physically?'

'Are you a special kind of idiot?' Morhork growled, his golden eyes narrowing.

'I-I've been taught nothing.' Asaph stumbled on his words, feeling like a complete ignorant fool. 'You're the first dragon I've ever seen. Apart from Dread Dragons.'

'Dread Dragons?' Morhork said.

Asaph felt the Recollection open again and they looked at it together. Memories of Dread Dragons came—those he had seen destroying Drax, and then his own battles against them. The Recollection snapped shut.

'I've been asleep a long time,' Morhork said, as if to himself. 'They were in my dreams. I thought them nightmares.'

'So, I'm not the only who's ignorant,' Asaph said.

Morhork growled.

'If I'm so stupid and ignorant of the ways and powers of dragons, why don't you teach me?' he chanced.

'I don't teach human scum.' Morhork snarled and pushed his face close to Asaph's. 'I'm still deciding whether or not to have you for lunch, but I don't like eating tainted things.'

'Then maybe we can get rid of the "taint" and then you can eat me.' Asaph growled back. He was getting stiff and cold from being pinned down, not to mention his lost dignity and growing anger.

'Ask your guardian, Faelsun. He'll do anything a human asks.' Morhork released one of his limbs and Asaph stretched it. Could he take on Morhork if it came to it? He doubted it.

'The dragon door—is it really a physical place?'

'Of course it is. You humans don't understand anything, never did. Everything you see in your mind is real, somewhere. Especially the thing you see frequently. Faelsun created the door from this world to the Dream.'

There was bitterness in Morhork's voice that made Asaph wonder. Did the dragon secretly wish he was invited there?

'Dreams are for humans,' Morhork scoffed and released him.

Asaph struggled up and shook himself, feeling the blood flow back into his aching limbs. Morhork had turned and was walking away.

'Wait,' Asaph called. 'Tell me how to break the chains. Tell me how to get to the dragon door. How did you fly to the cave when you have no wings? And what's in the lake?'

Morhork paused.

Asaph moved to catch up with him. 'I saw gold in the depths.'

Morhork scowled at him, but he seemed tired not angry, even though he had been sleeping for hundreds of years.

'Go away. I have nothing for you. Find the other dragons, if you must. I'm busy elsewhere... And I must sleep.' He turned away again. 'Go ask Faelsun about the lake.'

'But how can I do any of those things? You can't sleep. Baelthrom's coming. He'll destroy us all.'

'That's not my concern.'

Asaph paused, stumped. 'Not your concern? How can it not be? Don't you care if you die? It's obvious Faelsun cares far more about everything than you do.'

The dragon was a blur of blue. The wind was knocked from Asaph again as he was thrown to the ground. This time the dragon's teeth clamped onto his neck, not breaking skin yet, but hard enough to cut off his breathing and blood flow. He squirmed, helpless.

A terrible screeching echoed around the mountains. Cirosa's chains tightened. The dragon cry came again, but there was something odd about it. Fear shivered over him. It was the scream of a Dread Dragon calling for him.

Cold entered his heart and he convulsed. His mind scrambled and he felt a desperate need to find the pale woman. Morhork's grip on his throat released, and a strange airy whimper escaped Asaph's mouth.

A black speck wheeled in the sky. Terror shook him, beyond dragon fear. His strength vanished and he felt himself shrinking into his human form. Above him loomed Morhork who was looking to the sky at the Dread Dragon. Asaph could only shake.

'Ah, the one who binds you hunts you.' Morhork's voice rumbled through him. 'The chains that snare you are long and deep. To break them may very well break you anyway. It seems to me you will not have long to wait until you have your wish and death finds you.'

Morhork picked him up and the Flow moved around them, lifting them into the air. There came a great whoosh and then the sky was a blur. He was moving faster than he had ever gone before, so fast he could not see anything but a wash of a pink sky.

In his mind Cirosa's beautiful face formed; her cruel smile and red lips he longed to kiss, beckoned to him. The chains tightened.

The air became so light and the speed so fast he felt himself passing out.

Morhork lunged into the Flow, drawing great swathes of magic to him, wrapping the energy around and around his body at great speed. His brother may have taken his wings, but he could never take his magic. And over millennia he had learned how to use it to fly with far greater skill than any dragon before him.

It took much longer to launch into the air using magic instead of wings, but once he was airborne, he could fly infinitely faster. It was immensely draining on his magic reserves, however, which is why he slept a lot.

The abomination was coming closer and all he knew is what his ancestors screamed at him. *Get away from it.*

At his command, the magic lifted him up and thrust him forwards, faster than an arrow. The clouds above and the snow below became a blur and all he could see was a world of white and winds so fierce his lips flapped open.

In the Recollection he saw the deaths of his brethren as he had seen them in his dreams. Groggy and stiff from sleep, he was certainly not ready to fight, but he had magic reserves aplenty and could outfly anything on Maioria. And he needed time to think. He found himself relaxing into the speed.

He'd intended to kill the Dragon Lord, more from being bored of his tireless questions than hatred of the half-breed. When the human abruptly disturbed his sleep, his consciousness had been ripped painfully away from its alternative focus, sending him reeling in confusion upon awakening. Being asleep so long did something funny to your real-life memories and he pieced them together now and grinned.

A very clever thing he'd done all those years ago before he went to sleep: he'd found a man with magic and taken him to the brink of death and slowly beyond. When the man's soul and consciousness departed, he'd poured part of his own mind and spirit into the frail human form, keeping the physical body alive. The man's body was his to command: fully functional, and to his delight, incredibly long-lived. He discovered that, as long as he was alive, so was this human part of him.

The only problem was, this dual existence was very tiring and he wasn't able to function in two bodies at once for long. Either he slept whilst his human body was awake, or vice versa. He was tired of his great lumbering dragon body without its wings, and in the body of a man he had a better chance of thwarting the world of humans to fit his design. His grand plan was to have dragons rule Maioria again, with humans either destroyed or their serfs.

But having been asleep so long, he was having trouble re-forging the link with his human self running around out there. The longer he was awake, the stronger the connection became. The fog of eons spent asleep slowly washed away, and more and more memories returned.

He could feel his human body sleeping at this moment. It was lamentable that he couldn't be in two places at the same time, but consciousness just didn't seem to work that way. It had taught him a lot. Whilst many things could be thought of at once, only one thing could hold the focus of attention for any length of time.

He remembered it being hard at first, pretending to be one of them—the humans he detested so much. He looked normal to everyone else; only his mind and soul were not human but fully dragon. No one ever suspected that a dragon could inhabit the body of a human. Not even Faelsun knew of what he had done, what he had created. That made him smile.

He remembered the plans he'd forged long ago. Wait for the immortal bastard to take everything, and when he eventually screwed it up, as he was bound to do, Morhork would return to take the spoils. But Baelthrom was still here thousands of years later. He'd proven more formidable and powerful than ever Morhork had suspected.

Spending so many years as a human had changed him. And now he had...feelings. He didn't like them. They were confusing and made him hesitate.

He should crush the fool, who had awoken him, in his grip but he couldn't do it. He felt...*pity*. He hoped he never felt remorse.

Asaph, he'd said his name was. And he'd been cast out by Morhork's brother, just as he had. No Dragon Lord had ever been denied entry to the Dragon Dream until now. His brother's actions never ceased to make him furious.

"I cannot help what I am." The man had said.

"Yes, Faelsun made you what you are—a half-breed, and when you don't meet his expectations, he casts you out, like he cast me out."

Those thoughts had twice made him stay the killing blow. The half-breed in his grasp was poisoned by black magic and utterly helpless, and then his brother cast him out. Who was the one who really cared? Morhork was the only one who cared enough about his own species to fight back—and for that he'd been driven out and his wings ripped off. Maimed forever. That's what caring got you.

He tried to be angry, wanted to roar and shout and fight his brother all over again. But he just felt tired. There was human doubt and weariness in his heart. He began to wonder if keeping a part of him in a human body had done him permanent damage.

Yes, he hated Dragon Lord half-breeds, but what had he actually done to himself? He'd turned himself into a half-human too—a human body with a dragon consciousness and soul. The thoughts disturbed him.

He slowed when he reached the familiar ridge of rocks, unchanged in a thousand years, and hunted for the hidden tunnel.

At the northern most part of Maioria there was a natural dip in the magnetic and electrical energy of the planet. Approached at just the right height and angle, a narrow entrance to a large tunnel in the interleaving mountainside would appear. Approached wrong, then the entrance was invisible. At the end of that long tunnel was the dragon door, created long ago by his brother. Through that door one could walk into the Dragon Dream if one carried dragon blood, or was accompanied by a dragon.

He wondered if Dread Dragons could enter. But it was far behind now and would never find the secret entrance. He grinned, imagining the look on his brother's face if Dread Dragons flooded through the dragon door.

He swooped through the narrow entrance and slowed inside the giant cavern. He flew through darkness until a red glow came into view. Magma chambers. The frigid wind of the North Pole dropped and was replaced with warm gusts from below. These soon became hot and his dragon body revelled in the fiery heat. He'd been frozen for far too long.

The dragon door was ahead, as huge as a dragon and nestled on a slab of rock surrounded by oozing lava. Thousands of years had not changed it either—it looked as pristine now as it had been when he'd flown out of it in a rage all those years ago.

Now he looked at it not with anger, but with weariness. Human weariness. Had he become weak over the years? Did he not hunger for revenge quite so much as he had? Dragons don't change.

He landed before it, the rock hot beneath his feet. The man stirred, overcoming the side-effects of his lightning fast flight. The half-breed *had* been fearless of him—desperate, yes, but fearless nonetheless. That made Morhork respect him just a little.

'You turned your back on me, Faelsun; don't turn your back on your own creations.'

With a great sigh, he walked towards the door and entered into bright light.

CHAPTER 24

Iyena

'FREYDEL,' a woman called, catching his attention over the laughing throng of seers gathered at the sacred Doon Pool.

It was midnight, and he'd been invited to attend Doon Rites which consisted of a small celebratory gathering held when the moon Doon was at its fullest. The pool was roughly two yards in diameter and fed by a small waterfall. Naksu had told him there were many such waterfalls and pools on Myrn and her sister islands. All were sacred and held some special property or other, mostly for healing.

He searched for the person who had called his name and spotted a woman's face in the crowd, more wrinkled with age than he remembered but still familiar. She was dressed as everyone else, in blue robes over a white gown. The only difference was she held a slender, white wooden staff. She smiled, creating more wrinkles on her face.

'Iyena?' he said and laughed, embracing the older woman.

She was tall, almost as tall as Freydel, though age had shrunk her a little. At least she still stood straight and strong. Her long white hair was brushed but loose, falling to her waist. She'd always had long hair, he remembered.

'Your hair was red last time I saw you,' he said.

'And I was taller than you back then too.' She grinned, her grey eyes still bright and youthful.

'You look well, Iyena. Thank you for inviting me here.'

She nodded but the smile left her face and her eyes clouded with worry. 'I was well, until I learned of the attack. What do the wizards propose to do now? We've strengthened the shields covering these isles, but all of us are deeply concerned.'

'What we did was necessary to save Arla, yet also foolish—having so much power concentrated in one place. Baelthrom was sure to detect the orbs, wizards and magic—we just never thought he would be so brazen to attack like that. It cost us a precious life.' A lump rose in his throat and he blinked back tears. 'But what can we do? King Navarr is strengthening his defences as we speak, and all us wizards are on high alert.'

'As are we seers,' Iyena said. 'For decades we knew at least one Ancient was still with us. We could see it in our sacred pools. I will endeavour to reach this Yisufalni I've been told about. If you see her, tell her about me; tell her I need to speak with her about a great many things.'

He nodded. 'I will. She is safer with Murlonius than on Maioria. A part of me wishes we'd never brought her back from the Ethereal Planes.'

'Shh, don't say that,' Iyena said. 'She would have died had you not saved her. Listen, if ever you need our help, you have but to ask. For now, I hope you can find a little peace whilst you are with us. We're blessed to have a male wizard here on the Night of Doon. We do have some male seers, as you can see.' She gestured to the younger people. Freydel's eyes rested on a few young men.

'Yes, I'd noticed. I didn't realise men were allowed.'

'Hah. What on earth does the world know of seers, hmm? It seems only rumours abound. Men just prefer the hype of wizards.' She winked.

'Well, you do keep yourselves very secretive,' Freydel reminded her.

'Safe, not secretive. Indeed, the gift of becoming a seer is not for women alone. We're not priestesses and priests, or kings and queens, or, dare I say it, the Wizards' Circle, no. We're not elitist. All are welcome here to learn our ways and our art. But few men come. They prefer swords or wizardry.' She smiled, despite her words.

Freydel sighed. He appreciated Iyena's direct manner, even if it was uncomfortable. In the past they'd argued bitterly over the apparent elitism of the Wizards' Circle. Keeping their differences, they had seldom spoken to each other after that. He was, after all, Master Wizard and leader of the Wizards' Circle, and she the eldest member of the Trinity.

'Don't worry, Freydel, I'm playing with you. I have no time or energy for grudges these days.' Her face turned serious and she touched his hand. 'You look tired. And we're all devastated by the terrible news of Coronos, and the orb. He was a dear man, and a friend I saw too little of.'

Freydel knew nothing of their friendship, but Coronos had made friends wherever he went.

'We'll pray for him tonight. But we of the Trinity are deeply concerned for his adopted son, Asaph Dragon Lord. In our visions we knew a last Dragon Lord lived and we have seen him in terrible danger. In the Pools of the Sun Goddess, there are two clear timelines for him: one in the clutches of the Immortal Lord, and the other in the skies with dragons. We pray for the latter.'

Freydel barely hid his surprise. They knew of and could see different timelines? Was the future no longer dark? She seemed to interpret his frown and spoke.

'We haven't always been able to see anything in the future, as well you know. But for Asaph, we can sometimes see these futures. For Issa the Raven Queen, there are more timelines, most of them…terrible. We cannot help but worry.' She looked into the distance, frowning.

'We all worry for Issa, but what she needs most is our strength and support,' Freydel said.

He glanced over the crowd of young seers. His eyes passed over Naksu who was chatting to Dar, a middle-aged woman with a mass of greying-brown, curly hair. Beyond them, Edarna was bending down to stare at herself in the pool. He hid a smile when he saw she was trying to discreetly fill up a glass vial partially hidden in her sleeve. Iyena's eyes rested on the witch too.

'She only has to ask.' Iyena sighed. Freydel chuckled.

'Well, witches are very proud. I can't blame their secretive actions after what the Order did to them,' Freydel said.

Iyena nodded. 'The Temple has long strayed from its original teachings, and now we have proof that it's tainted by Baelthrom's hand. Navarr must do all he can to contain the Oracle. But that's a matter to be discussed another time.

'Edarna is friends with Issa, and, from her, we've learned much about the Raven Queen. But she's so young and so ill-prepared for…' Iyena bit her lip.

'She's very powerful. In the little time I've spent with her, I taught her the basics of magic and she excelled at it,' said Freydel.

'Yes, magic is good, but that's not what I meant.' Iyena sighed.

'You want her to be a seer,' Freydel smiled, 'and that's understandable. Her mother was a seer.'

'She should already be a seer. She would have knowledge and understanding of the ancient wisdom. Regarding her mother, we still aren't sure who she might have been. It could be someone who ran away, either out of disgrace or in order to protect Myrn. That's my strongest hunch, anyway. We only hope that she'll heed Naksu's advice and come here to learn what she can.

'Edarna thinks she should be trained as warrior and a witch.' Iyena laughed, but there was no malice in her eyes.

'I, too, wanted her to be one of us—a wizard—the first female to sit on the Wizards' Circle after so long,' Freydel said. 'But she also has a warrior's spirit. You should see her with a sword, and a novice still.'

'Perhaps, then, her path lies with all of us. Perhaps that's the Night Goddess' way,' said Iyena.

'My thoughts exactly. She'll need many skills if she is to face the Immortal Lord.'

Another woman began speaking, not loudly, but her voice spread calm across everyone and the voices fell to silence. They turned to look at Dar.

An old woman stood at her side whom Freydel didn't know. She must be the third member of the Trinity, though she seemed frail and weak, hunched over as she was, and her head was a shock of white hair. Her watery blue eyes surveyed the crowd.

'Greetings fellow seers, witches and wizards.' Dar inclined her head towards Freydel and Edarna. 'We are honoured to have guests amongst us today. We gather tonight to receive and give blessing to Doon, Father of the Forest, protector of children.'

Dar stepped into the pool, fully clothed. The white-haired woman and Iyena followed. They stood knee-deep, facing each other, and held hands with their eyes shut. Their lips were moving but they spoke too softly for anyone to hear.

Freydel could see nothing with his physical eyes, but when he observed the Flow, bright white light drifted down from the moon Doon, casting the seers in a pillar of light. They began to glow.

Dropping hands, they turned to face those gathered and held hands again, murmuring softly. Again Freydel could see nothing with his physical eyes, but in the Flow, white light flowed from the seers, spreading across the crowd.

'If you wish, accept the blessing of Doon,' Iyena said.

Those who silently accepted began to glow white like the seers. Freydel hesitated for a moment, noticed that he was not glowing, then accepted the blessing. He began to glow like the others and chuckled. He wasn't one for religion—it was a passing thing for him—but he didn't disbelieve. His interests just lay in magic, within which he was fully absorbed.

Peace and calm settled upon him, as if he'd just had a relaxing nap. He had not expected to feel anything, much less see anything, and it left him with a sense of wonderment.

Doon, if you can hear me, bless the spirit of my dear friend Coronos who will pass through your splendid forest on the way to the light.

He offered his prayer silently to the Forest Lord, and a sense of release settled in his belly.

The next morning, after a breakfast of orange juice and sugared oats, Naksu gave Freydel Coronos' staff. He took it with a heavy heart. It felt cold and lifeless in his hands. In a subdued silence they walked to the jetty and took the boat to the West Isle.

'You're welcome to stay longer and may visit us any time,' Naksu said, taking his hands as they stood in the amethyst circle once more.

'I would stay longer but I can't; not right now. I must help King Navarr and the Wizards' Circle. I would be honoured to return, however.' He smiled. 'Edarna, are you ready?'

The witch had insisted it was better for her to return to Carvon with Freydel to her cat and "stuffages" rather than bring everything here to Myrn. Naksu agreed, in case Issa needed her there.

Edarna paled, but nodded stiffly. 'Wizard magic is no good for witches.'

'A long time ago, we all shared the same power and knowledge,' Naksu said. 'Perhaps that time will come again. Take care of yourself, and scry often.' She hugged the witch.

'Now then,' Naksu held up her staff, 'the crystals hold protective magic, and I'll stabilise the Flow. All you need to do is think on where you want to return to, and direct your bodies there.'

Freydel took Edarna's hand, noticed a tremble, and started the translocation spell. The amethysts began to glow and a purple dome spread over their heads. Wind and light swirled. He saw only Naksu's face in the spinning light. In a flash and a squeal—which he assumed came from Edarna—everything was gone.

The light and wind disappeared. He swayed, alone in his room in Castle Carvon, and reached in his robes for Edarna's potion before he vomited.

Edarna arrived in her room, standing on top of her bed. A blue fur ball flung itself into her arms, sending her flat onto cushions. A sandpaper tongue scraped her face, making her want to vomit all the more. She was home, thank the goddess.

Hand on Mr Dubbins' head, she fell straight asleep.

CHAPTER 25

Lord of the Forest

JARLAIN had no idea how long she'd been lying at the bottom of the ravine, but it felt like days.

She had dreams, vivid dreams in which she could see with her eyes. Now awake and blind again, she missed those dreams bitterly.

She tried to move, but every inch of her body screamed in pain. Her left arm was the worst. Her right arm was above her head and she couldn't feel it at all.

It seemed to take an age to drag it, inch by inch, to her side. Only then did the blood begin to flow back into it properly, and with it came exquisite pain. She was barely aware of moaning, and wishing for all the world that she wasn't alive at all.

She reached over to her left arm and gasped. It was bent where it shouldn't be and hot wetness told her it was bloody. She moved and screamed again. Her ribs were severely bruised, maybe even broken.

Pain seemed to flood every part of her body. More blood trickled down her arm as she moved away from the rock that had been stemming the flow. She held her left arm in her right, and breathed. Curse Hai, she couldn't even see to fix her own wound and now she would die of it. She managed to sit up. She was desperately thirsty, and beyond hunger.

With one hand she grappled with the sackcloth she was wearing and tore a long strip off. She wrapped it around her arm. Without a healer or bone setter, this wound was probably going to kill her.

From what she could see in her red vision, steep cliffs rose up on all sides, and she was in a gully some thirty yards wide and dotted with stunted trees. If this had been a river bed, it had long since dried up.

She stood up, her head pounded with thirst and she swayed in delirium. Feeling her way with her stick she walked around the wall of rock. There was no path back up. Had she two good arms, she might have been able to climb up.

She searched for twine, or rope vine, but there was nothing, just twigs, stunted trees, and fallen leaves. How could she find anything useful, much less make anything worthy, without eyes?

Had Hai deliberately sent her to her death? She slumped down onto a large, flat rock. Did he hate her that much? Bitter tears welled up, and she sobbed.

'I'm sorry, Marakon, my love,' she whispered, and lay down with difficulty.

This place would soon be her grave. Her whole body throbbed and already blood had worked its way through the bandage. Running a tongue over her parched lips, she imagined a stream running close by, its deliciously cool water slipping down her throat.

Hai stood at the Centre surrounded by those from the seven tribes who had made it here alive. The fifteen-foot-high, great rock was perfectly round—which is why they called it the Centre. Its light grey surface was smooth and cold under Hai's touch.

No one knew why the stone was here or how it got here, or even if it had been created by human hands. There were no other rocks around the stone, and none had ever reported seeing another like it. No ivy or moss dared cover its surface.

The elders of every tribe were taught to memorise the location of the Centre, and here they would come to meet each other once a year as they had done ever since their ancestors first set foot on this land.

The sky was darkening. Trees crowded around them: familiar palms amongst broadleaf trees that did not grow in Gurlanka lands. It was colder here and he shivered. Sharnu draped a blanket over his shoulders, and he smiled in thanks.

He looked from the pale faces of the northern tribes, to the darker faces of the southern tribes. Thousands of people gathered, all stricken in pain and grief. There were some babes, few children, and very few elderly. Only the fastest and fittest adults had survived. Many carried wounds and wore bandages. Some lay prone, carried there by their relatives. Many would not make the night, he knew.

There were some elders besides him and Sharnu, but he was the only High Elder. He struggled to not let that bother him. He was the High Elder of all the tribes tonight. More people would be coming—the slower ones who had survived the assault of the immortals. He could not wait for them; he must begin the Gathering Rites immediately.

'Destruction has come to our shores, as the Hidden Ones have warned us. We're not surprised, but we're filled with sorrow for those who have left us in the darkness while they fly free to the One Light. Pray that they bless us for the darkness we must now endure without them. This is the end of our days, and we gather here for one last time, to reunite the tribes of Unafay.

'Evil has come to our shores and the Hidden Ones are falling silent. We're no longer a people of peace; that time has passed. Now we, the peoples of Unafay, have come full circle and a new age dawns. As in the past we were called to war, so too today will we return to war. This isn't a battle for our beloved lost land, but for the whole of our beloved Maioria.

'The Dark Rift in the sky draws close, but the dark moon of Zanu holds us in her light. If we do nothing, we shall fall into the oblivion of the rift. This the Hidden Ones told me before their silence.'

He settled himself down before the Centre and placed his staff upon his knees.

'The Gathering Rites must begin at once. Place before me the staves of the High Elders,' he said.

Staves were passed between the people and placed before him. If the people spoke, he didn't hear them with his inner ears. The time for talking had passed. He looked at the seven staves. They would have been given to a runner by the High Elders of each tribe before they died, and each would hold the history of that tribe. There were no other High Elders to sit with him and work the rites. He blinked back tears; there could be no sorrow.

He started to hum the tune of the ancient rite and began to speak the words. He couldn't hear what he was saying outwardly, but he could feel the vibration of his words and his inner sound was alive with music.

The staves began to glow yellow. The crowd inched closer. He took his time, going slowly to get it right and find the momentum, then gradually intoning faster. He began to speak the words louder, in the pure runic tongue of the elders—the sacred language they'd once used on their lost land, Unafay.

Each word had a corresponding symbol, and this symbol he traced with his fingers into the wood of his staff. Around his staff he moved tracing symbols all the way down until he reached the bottom. Then he worked his way back up without pause. The air stilled as he worked, heavy with the weight of ages and the words of enchanting.

His trance deepened until he was no longer aware of the others. Time seemed to pass in a strange manner—fast—and yet everything he did was slow as he worked his memories and the story of his people into his staff.

He became aware of the full moon Doonis rising, the light adding its own power to the staff he worked upon, and those before him. He also knew when a raven landed near, but none of these things paused his work, and soon time faded away too.

Hai didn't realise he'd stopped humming until the silence and stillness roused him. Everything was covered in soft mist—the great round stone behind him and the glowing staves before him. The mist moved and the trees took shape once more. He'd arrived in the realm of the Hidden Ones—something he'd only done once over fifty years ago. It was only possible to physically travel here when beside the Centre.

Figures of light moved in the mist, so faint he could barely make them out. They were twice as tall as he was and incredibly thin and long-limbed. They had told him the first time that he would only be able to see them as beings of light because they existed in a higher dimension.

Hai felt wisdom and understanding flow from the light beings as they reached down and held their palms towards the seven staves. The staves rose, moved towards each other and became one—a smooth, straight rod of yellow light that rested down before him. *Seven tribes made one,* he thought. They beckoned to him and turned away.

Hai picked up the staff; it was warm and pulsating in his hands, and followed them into the swirling light.

Through the trees another being moved forwards, blinding light coming from behind. It seemed to be a giant stag with great antlers rising above its head. Hai blinked and squinted and saw the outline of a man's face beneath the antlers. He was bigger than the beings of light and seemed more real, more solid. His torso was that of a human's but his legs were tree trunks—all thick, rough bark—and his feet were roots that disappeared into the earth.

Not a man, Hai realised, but a god. Hai dropped to his knees before Doonis.

'That is a gesture created by misguided people.' The Forest Lord's voice was deep and rumbling.

Hai blinked; he could hear him clearly despite his broken ears. The Forest Lord lifted his hand and raised Hai up without touching him.

Hai stared into the changing face of Doonis. Sometimes he seemed an animal and had the face of a stag, a rabbit, a bear or something else Hai wasn't quite sure of, and then he would have the face of a man, bearded and hazel-eyed.

'Yes, my Lord,' Hai found himself saying.

'I am no lord, no matter what humans would call me. I am simply what I am, and I am here. Creation does not kneel to creation, Elder Hai.' He shook his head and his long brown hair flowed around his muscular shoulders.

'I'm a guardian, Hai, as are you. Only I am guardian of much more than just my tribe. One day, Hai, in your journey back to the One Light, you will be a guardian of much more than I am now. We are all equal in value—a mouse, a tree or a man—but we are all different in being and at different stages in the journey.'

'Yes, Doonis. I remember,' Hai said. The Forest Lord's words unlocked memories of ancient truths.

'You've made a great sacrifice by coming here physically,' Doonis said, his eyes changing from dark green to earthen brown as he spoke. 'It's taken so much from you to reach here, that your physical body will not be able to return. I think you knew it would be this way.'

'Yes, but if I hadn't done this, then greater pain will come,' Hai said.

'You see truth very well, High Elder Hai. Darkness covers Maioria, and even now we cannot tell whether it will fall into the Dark Rift or not.'

'The days of my people are over,' Hai said. 'War has found us once more. But we thank you for giving us refuge in your forest for all this time.'

'You seek the answer to your people's future. The way forward is dark for you and you don't know which way to turn.'

Doonis spoke what was in Hai's heart. He nodded.

'Zanu's light touches Maioria, whilst Feygriene's light wanes, but all the guardians of Maioria work together, and beyond this realm we are all one. Beyond here in the higher realms, the darkness also plagues us. The darkness *is* us. It's this darkness within us that we seek to heal.'

Hai struggled to understand of what Doonis spoke.

'Great Doonis, I seek only to pass the staff of my people to one of my daughters. I've seen a path for us and it lies with her. That's why I've come here. I seek to awaken my people to what they once were, to the memory I've seen in the past.'

Doonis smiled as if something Hai said had moved him.

'Indeed Hai,' Doonis said and placed his huge hand upon the staff Hai held. 'Are you ready, courageous one?'

Hai nodded and smiled. The staff burst into light.

The face of an old man formed in her delirium. Jarlain blinked. Was she seeing him with her physical eyes? She blinked again. All about was white mist and a man stood before her. Dark skin heavily wrinkled, long white hair, and a dyed-red beard. She reached a hand up to her face. The blindfold was gone.

'Hai?' she croaked.

Tears of relief and anger fell down her cheeks. She closed her eyes, not wanting to see him, but he was behind her lids too. She opened her eyes. Hai was there, his mouth moving, but she couldn't hear what he was saying and didn't want to hear.

'Damn you, Hai,' she rasped. Why was he haunting her mind? To mock her that she was not as strong as he was? How many thousands of miles lay between them, and yet still he had the power to reach her? Couldn't he just let her die?

'My daughter, do not hate,' Hai whispered. His voice became stronger. 'I was wrong to curse you and cast you out, but had I not, we would all be doomed.'

She felt tears fall down her cheeks. Knowing Hai did not hate her and wanted forgiveness lifted a weight from her shoulders. She felt like a little girl, and he her father.

'Our time is at an end, and great things must come to pass. Remember our people, Jarlain, and lead all of us into the new age.'

For a moment she thought she saw hundreds of people crowding around him, people from her tribe amongst the lighter-skinned tribes to the north.

'Elder Hai, I don't understand,' she began.

But he was looking beyond her at something she couldn't see, and a smile spread across his face.

'Help me understand, Hai.'

'I see us now. What we once were long, long ago. That time will come again. The darkness came, Jarlain, the immortals Marakon warned us of, and our people are no more. Those who survived are gathered at the Centre.'

'Our people are gone?' Could it be true? Was this vision a trick of her dying mind?

'My daughter, do not be sad for what has come to pass. You have come to use your gifts more powerfully than ever I did when they cast me out. I've seen you, what you might become, and your true name is Little Bear. Look.'

The name resonated through her as he spoke. The air swirled between them, more mist in a mist-filled place. She saw people mounted atop great bears. The bears were tame and the people could commune with them.

'Little Bear,' Hai continued. 'A long time ago, our people, the ancient people of Unafay, were called the Navadin, Riders of the Bear. We've forgotten much but now we must remember. We must find the old strength within us to fight the darkness swallowing this world. You will reignite our peoples' ancient memory. Call the bears, Jarlain, call them.'

Jarlain frowned. Had that been why the bear had spared her earlier? She had a thousand questions, but the mist was thickening and Hai's face fading.

'Wait,' she croaked. She didn't want to die here alone. Hai had got it all wrong. She wouldn't be able to do what he asked of her. Her body was at the bottom of a ravine, broken and bloody.

'Hai, come back. I'm dying; don't leave me.'

But the mist went and silence settled on her. The familiar itch of her blindfold returned and the dark told her it was night. Desperate thirst maddened her mind, and her arm throbbed in agony. She was too weak to move and lay there panting, praying for sleep or death to come.

Light roused her. She thought it was dawn but the light held no heat like the sun would. The light spread and seemed to come into her eyes through the blindfold and her closed lids. It spread through her body, bringing with it calm and easing the pain. Was this what dying felt like? She wondered if Marakon could remember dying; the thought seemed funny in her mind.

She sensed someone beside her, a presence, and she would have been frightened were it not for the calming light.

'Jarlain,' the voice whispered, a deep male voice that soothed her mind. It seemed filled with knowledge and wisdom.

A large, warm hand laid across her blindfold and it disappeared. She blinked in the light that surrounded them. It came from the being before her. He was very big, maybe twelve feet tall, and great antlers spread out from his head.

He was naked, something that would have embarrassed her or made her afraid had she not been so close to death, and had his presence not spread calm and peace. His legs were the trunks of trees and his feet were roots. As she looked at him, his face seemed to change like leaves moving in the trees. His eyes were brown and green and golden and filled with peace and ancient knowledge. She could hide nothing from those eyes; he seemed to know her intimately.

Jarlain lowered her gaze at the sight of the god; it was all she could move.

'Doonis, Lord of the Forest.'

He shook his great head and his long brown hair floated around his shoulders. 'Guardian, protector. I do not rule above other living things.'

He laid a huge hand on her broken arm. There was no pain, only intense heat and a sickening snapping sound as the bone cracked back into place. Then he placed his huge hands on her chest, engulfing her broken ribcage. Her sackcloth melted away and she trembled under his touch, a strange mix of awe, fear and desire moving through her. The heat came again and she felt an intense itch as her fractured ribs mended.

With the pain gone, her mind cleared. They were in a forest. Pale light spread around them and she could hear the sound of running water. He moved his arms under her body and lifted her easily. The beat of his great heart shuddered her body as he carried her. She stared up into his impossibly handsome face, wondering why a god would come to her.

He took her to a waterfall and waded into the pool at its base. A myriad of rainbows gleamed all around where the light caught the mist. The water shone bright aqua, and felt so light on her skin it could almost have been air. It was slightly cool and her skin tingled all over.

'Go ahead, drink,' he said, lowering her so the water came up to her shoulders and neck.

She dipped her head and drank until she thought her stomach would burst. It was sacred and purer than any water she had ever tasted. It slipped down her throat, bringing purity and life with it. She began to cry, feeling the desperation of thirst and fear of death that had consumed her, begin to leave her.

As her mind relaxed it began to expand and release, as if it had been unnaturally chained to the mortal world all her life. She felt connected to all things: the earth, the water, the air—they were a part of her like her own hands.

He stepped deeper into the pool, still holding her, until they were both submerged. She felt him looking at her and opened her eyes under water. The water didn't sting and it was not as heavy as normal water. Aqua blue surrounded them, and his golden eyes saw through to her soul.

Gently he lifted her out of the water. It dripped and evaporated from her skin, leaving her dry and clean in moments. On the grass beside the pool, he set her down on her feet. She looked at her arm made whole again, felt strength in her limbs and vigour in her body that she had not felt before. She was alive, aware and utterly free.

'The darkness that spreads across this world also fills the plants and animals,' his voice moved through her, filling her. 'They don't want this. You are not Daluni, and to understand how they think and feel, your mind must be opened. Zanufey has returned to help us. Will you stand with the Raven Queen and help fight this darkness?'

'It would be an honour,' she said. She understood the essence of his words without knowing who this Raven Queen was. 'I was born to serve the light in whatever way I can.'

'You are descended from the Navadin. Do you wish to be reminded of your ancient past? Do you wish for the gift that will open your mind so that you may call the bears once more?'

So what Hai had said was true and she felt now that this was her true path.

'I don't understand what is required of me, but I accept this divine gift,' she breathed.

He smiled at her with reassurance, warmth, and a sense of deep pure love that she had never felt before. It was the purer love of spirit. He bent to kiss her forehead. Light burst there then coolness. The world and he filled her senses: the thunder of his heart, the depths of his beautiful eyes that were all the colours of the forest, the heat of his naked chest. And then they were melting into each other. They were themselves completely, but a part of them was shared.

Things that were beyond normal understanding became very clear to her. She understood deeply the nature of the earth and how it moved, the desires of the air and the memory of clouds. She saw as trees do and how ants think. She even knew where the sun and moons were, and the terrible Dark Rift rent at her soul and hurt as physical pain.

She saw those people again—the ones mounted atop bears, only she was one of them and the bear she rode she understood intimately. She could hear his thoughts as her own and could speak his language.

The deluge of information slowed and calm awareness followed.

The Guardian of the Forest looked down at her and she smiled, tears of wonder falling down her cheeks. He was moving away now and his body fading into the light. She didn't want him to leave her but when he was gone she languished in the calm light for a long time.

CHAPTER 26

Fighting for Demons

TO find time alone, Issa went foraging for berries when they stopped for
lunch and ate the last of their rations.

Nobody knew for sure how far it was back to Carvon, but Ehka
seemed to think it wasn't far.

Now it was autumn, the forest was filled with blackberries, and it
didn't take long until her sack was full. She found a bare patch of earth
and set the berries down next to a tree. Ehka landed beside her.

'You know I don't want to go, don't you?'

She remembered what the demons had said: *"When you step upon the
symbol of the Murk, speak your intention and spill your blood. It will bring you here."*

She grabbed a stick and drew the symbol of the Murk in the earth—
two crescent moons joined by a line. She stood up and took a deep
breath, casting a glance at Ehka.

'You'd better be coming. I don't want to go alone this time,' she said.

He croaked. She took it as a yes.

Standing tall, she drew her sword and held her hand up. The thought
of cutting herself was scary, taking more courage to do than facing a
foltoy. It couldn't need much blood, could it? Just a drop was enough,
surely? She nicked the side of her hand, smarting at the sting. Bright red
welled up, but not much. She held her hand over the symbol and let the
drops fall. As they hit, the symbol glowed a fascinating green.

'All right.' She held her breath and motioned to Ehka. He flew to her
shoulder, and she stepped upon the symbol.

'Take us to the Murk.'

The green glow engulfed her, and a blast of air flowed from beneath her feet. Her stomach rolled, and she felt sick and dizzy even though her body did not appear to be moving.

The gushing air stopped and a cloying heat hugged her. The green glow dissipated. There was a moment of black and silence, and then noise erupted around her.

Un-human screams and howls, the sound of flames and explosions, the clash of metal against metal. Ehka leapt from her shoulder, squawking. She gripped her sword before her, struggling to gain her senses and willing the sickness in her stomach to go.

Her eyes adjusted to the growing green light. Things moved all around her in a cavernous room. Fire flared over her head, lighting up everything and she ducked down beside the green crystal shard.

Another flare burst. The great hall and crystal she remembered was momentarily illuminated, and what she saw made her legs shake. Brown and grey demons were locked hand-to-hand in battle. There were other horrors. Black shadows of scowling faces with red eyes and tongues and teeth. Terrible magic that made her want to scream.

Demons from the Pit—she'd prayed she'd never have to see them again. Her soul shook and her legs trembled. She clenched her eyes shut.

A voice bellowed something in Demonic somewhere to her right. Gedrock? She tried to get a grip on her terror, pulled her sword free, and stood up.

A Pit Demon came for her, huge and insubstantial. She sliced at it with her sword, but the blade passed through its face, halting the demon a little but doing no damage that she could see. She reached for the Flow, but the magic of Maioria was far from this place. She was helpless.

She thought about the raven talisman. It wasn't from Maioria, so did it have power here? She pulled it out. The Pit Demon hesitated. Was it afraid of it? The demon came on. She backed up until her shoulders hit the great stone throne beside the crystal. There was nowhere else to go. Smelling her blood and living life-force, other Pit Demons turned in her direction, red eyes in black shadowy faces, hungry for her flesh and soul.

Gedrock roared. She glimpsed his great head and gnashing fangs in the dark ahead. The battle seemed to lull, then Shadow Demons flowed over the floor, straight into the Pit Demons coming towards her. Were they protecting her?

Despite the Shadow Demons smashing into them, Pit Demons seemed to be everywhere. She slashed as some reached her, watching her sword pass uselessly through their immaterial bodies, barely slowing their approach.

Memories of the Storm Holt flashed through her mind and she saw Pit Demons chasing her in Karhlusus Keep, draining the life force of her soul. The black nothingness and feeling she would never get out. The madness of the red world and the emptiness of the Abyss.

She would die here and now, rather than go back there. She screamed and slammed the talisman against her chest. The raven mark burned and she fell forwards into silver light.

The realm of the dead was alive with movement. Dark figures bulged around her and beyond them was a world drained of colour. She looked down at her body; it was grey and white, and ghost-like. Ehka was already beside her, his head darting left and right.

She stepped back as Pit Demons loomed close. They looked the same as in the living world but were more solid here, and their eyes were not red but a lighter shade of grey. They looked about as if hunting for something they couldn't quite see. Every now and then a lesser demon would appear, weapons and fangs bared, screaming a maddening sound. They lunged at the greater demons and then mysteriously disappeared, as if they were dipping into and out of this realm.

A Pit Demon rose ten feet into the air and lashed down upon something she could not see. A Shadow Demon appeared at its feet— dead—and then it was gone.

Issa lunged towards the demon. It turned to face her. Its long snout twitched and foul mouth opened. It howled, a sound her soul seemed to hear more than her physical ears. She jabbed her sword into its face. It felt like thrusting through thick mud. The demon screamed. She gasped, pulled her sword free and fell back. It collapsed into a writhing fit and then just dissipated into black specks.

Another came at her. Its long, dagger-claws swiped, leaving her no time to move. The claws moved through her. It felt as if her body was made of water, and its claws had passed through, leaving a sickly feeling. Realising she was unharmed, she struck back, grinning. They couldn't hurt her here.

The demon fell, writhing. She moved forwards, on the attack, hacking at every greater demon. For every one she felled, two more seemed to materialise.

A bellow came from somewhere and Gedrock appeared, his head nothing more than a grey shadow. A look of surprise passed across his face and then he was gone.

Greater demons swamped her vision. Everywhere she struck and sliced there was a black mass, an endless sea of demons. Their claws racked through her body, draining her even though they didn't hurt. Exhaustion stole over her, eating at her soul.

She fell back. The mass of greater demons came on—hundreds of eyes watching her. They were wary. The weariness rose and her mind became fuzzy and confused. She had to get away from them, but how? She couldn't return to the demon hall; they could kill her easily there. The demons rushed at her.

A howl cut through everything, followed by a blaze of green light that sent her staggering. She glanced behind, saw Gedrock with his hand upon the crystal which looked grey in this world. Her head pounded, a voice whispered, but it wasn't Gedrock's.

'Touch,' it said, echoing. A disembodied green hand with black claws reached and touched the crystal.

'Touch.'

She remembered the green beast with black horns and eyes. *Zorock.* She slashed her sword, driving the demons back, and fell towards the crystal. Talisman in one hand she reached to touch the crystal with her other. The talisman shuddered, its power filling her. Indigo light blazed from it to mingle with the grey light flooding from the crystal. Screams shrieked through the air and began to fade. Unholy energy receded. There was silence and darkness.

The rock was solid and cold beneath her. A brazier flared into life, then two more. Issa looked up and started. Demon faces crowded around her, ugly and flat. Shadow Demons. Gedrock's face pushed past the others, a hint of surprise in his eyes as he glared at her.

The green crystal beyond them was dim, its magic drained. The talisman was heavy and cold, also drained. She sat up and the demons moved away. Cautious. The room was empty, the Grazen and greater demons that had filled it were gone.

Gripping the crystal pedestal, she pulled herself up, trembling with exhaustion. Ehka flapped down to land at her feet.

'I came to tell you,' she said, smoothing back her hair with a shaking hand, 'that I've found the Cursed King and his knights and we're ready to come here. But I think I picked the wrong time.'

'We know,' Gedrock said, unsmiling as ever. 'Bring him now. Immediately.'

'But how?'

'Just as you came here, it works for one or hundred, but all must give blood.' Gedrock climbed the steps and slumped into the throne. He looked exhausted and his pointed ears were sagging.

'What happened? Where did they go?' Issa asked, looking around.

Shadow Demons had begun to clear up the carnage. Mangled demon parts, horrific to look upon, littered the floor. Black blood sprayed the walls, and pooled in cloying lumps. Issa looked away, trying not to gag.

'The crystal drove away the greater demons and then the Grazen fled.' Gedrock's voice was monotone. 'A great risk, using the crystal. It will take weeks to recharge. They won't go far and soon they'll be back.'

Issa nodded, the sombre mood dampening her excitement. 'I agreed to help you, and I meant it. I just don't know how. How will we get the spear, Velistor? Humans can no more easily walk into Karhlusus Keep than you can.'

Gedrock shrugged and rubbed his snout. 'Great Carmedrak will make it possible. "The Raven Queen will find a way", the crystal told me.'

Issa blinked. Were even demon gods talking about her now too? She didn't have the answers.

'So I'll just bring them?'

'Yes,' Gedrock said. 'How did you do that?'

'Do what?' she frowned.

'None but demons may command the crystal, and only the demon king at that.' Gedrock scowled. 'To touch it without invite is punishable by death.'

'I was asked, compelled, I guess. I didn't know not to touch it. I heard a voice and saw a...a being I'd seen before—all green with black horns and eyes. He told me to touch the crystal.' Issa shrugged.

The demons were all looking at her again, their ugly faces a mix of awe, fear and distrust.

'Zorock,' Gedrock breathed.

'Yes, if that's what you call him. It was the same one. And then my raven talisman flared indigo as the crystal flared. I didn't *do* anything, but felt the power flow from it. Then the demons were gone.' She struggled to explain what she had witnessed.

'How did you fight them? One moment you were here and then you were gone, into there, into the shadow realm.' Gedrock leaned forwards.

'Like the raven, I can enter the realm of the dead. It's one of my gifts, as befits the Raven Queen.' It was the best explanation she could offer. It seemed to satisfy him and he sat back, his yellow eyes not leaving her face.

'Your power comes from the dark moon, the moon of your goddess. The talisman comes from that moon. The crystal and its power comes from Zorock, the moon of the Murk,' Gedrock said.

'The dark moon rises here?' Issa stepped forwards, her turn to be eager. How could he know if he hadn't seen it?

'We don't speak of it.' Gedrock scowled.

'Please, I must know. If it rises here, I have power that might help.' The wizards didn't know everything, and if she was filled with its power, maybe she'd have the strength to walk into Karhlusus Keep.

'That's why we don't speak of it. Only Zorock rules here, through Carmedrak's power, and no other.' His voice rose at the last and echoed around the hall. The demons shuffled nervously. Issa was not fazed.

'You've seen it, haven't you?' Her voice was quiet.

The skinny demon she'd met before came to Gedrock's side and whispered in his ear. Wekurd, that was his name. Gedrock's scowl deepened.

'We have seen the moon, yes. That's when we first learned of the Raven Queen.' Gedrock shifted in his seat, clearly uncomfortable admitting it. 'But it's far away, a third of the size of Zorock, if that. Its power will be weak.'

Issa gasped. In her mind's eye, she felt it out there, far away, but there nonetheless.

'It will rise on Maioria soon. I can't be sure when, but when it does I'll return with the knights,' Issa said.

'We can't wait a week,' Gedrock said.

'Only days, I'm sure of it,' Issa said. 'Please, if you can, hold until then. How far is it to Karhlusus Keep?'

'Carmedrak Rock,' Gedrock growled. 'Two days, maybe three.'

'Let's meet there and face Karhlusus at the rock. But how will I reach you?' said Issa.

Gedrock took a while to answer. 'Wherever the crystal is, is the entrance to the Murk.' He seemed to be holding back.

'Then bring the crystal,' she said.

'It hasn't left here since we made our home.'

'If you don't bring it, you won't *have* a home,' said Issa. 'You've seen what the crystal can do; we may need it again. It's no use stuck here whilst we're all fighting hundreds of miles away.'

'Enough,' he said, but she could tell he was thinking on it. 'Just bring the Demon Slayer. And wherever we are, you will be.'

'I need your word on our protection.' Issa licked her lips. 'The knights are concerned. They hate you as much as you hate them. To fight this king demon wizard, we need to work together, as one.'

'They've killed more of us than we ever took of them,' Wekurd spat out.

'The greater demons and Karhlusus have always used us for their wars.' Gedrock's eyes slid from hers to stare into the crystal. 'If it weren't for them, we would have nothing to do with your world. I can promise them protection from Shadow Demons, but from us alone. The Grazen and greater demons are nothing to do with us. You'd better make sure they can tell the difference, otherwise Shadow Demons will attack back.'

Issa nodded. 'They already know the difference. We've spoken at length on this. Shadow Demons won't be harmed. I promise.'

'So be it, Raven Queen,' he said, and gestured to the crystal.

She stepped up to it, and was about to place her hand on it when a thought came to her.

'Where's Maggot?'

'Maggot? He's gone. Dead or captured, we don't know.' Gedrock's face was guarded.

Her stomach lurched.

'I'm sorry,' she said, her eyes misting over. 'He came to me not long ago. He was afraid. That's why I came…'

Gedrock said nothing and she wondered if demons felt grief. She knew they felt anger. Ehka flew to her shoulder and with a heaviness in her heart, she placed her hand upon the crystal.

Green light and rushing wind came from above this time.

She gripped the dirt forming beneath her hands and feet, closing her eyes against the dizziness. Breathing in the forest air deeply, she heard someone call her name. She looked up.

'Issa,' the shout came from afar.

'I'm here.' She got up and grabbed her sack of berries. It was past midday and clouds half-covered the sky.

'She's here,' Ghenath shouted as she arrived back at the camp.

The fire was out and the horses saddled. Everyone was ready to go. The elf-woman slapped her shoulder.

'You disappeared for over an hour. We thought a foltoy had snatched you. What happened? You look exhausted.' Ghenath looked down at the dirt and fresh tears on Issa's tunic dress that had already been dirty and torn.

'Great goddess, I need some new clothes again.' Issa sighed. 'It's a long story.'

When they were mounted and on the road leading east to Carvon, Issa told them what had happened. She always felt uncomfortable mentioning the demons. Thoughts of the oracle accusing her of making pacts with demons filled her mind. Did they really still hang demon-speakers?

'When will Zanufey's moon rise?' Nemeron asked.

She'd spoken to him the least. He was quiet by nature anyway, and seemed shy around her. He'd already lent her his rapier, and taught her a few tricks with it. It was a strange weapon, long and thin and so very light, she was worried it would snap. She couldn't see how useful it would be against a heavily armoured Maphraxie, but the young knight was confident.

'I don't know for sure,' she said. 'A couple of days?'

She felt pensive and restless, despite her fatigue. Was the anxious excitement coming from Zanufey's moon? It must be. The latent power was building in her.

'What is this power that comes from the moon? Is it magical power?' he asked. The other knights walked their horses closer so they could hear her.

'Yes, it's magical power,' she said. 'It's not like the magic of Maioria, but it's good, not like the Under Flow. It works in harmony with Maioria's energy. I'm not a learned wizard, so I struggle to explain it.'

'I suppose it's a bit like us.' He smiled, his brown hair tousled and unbrushed. 'We don't understand the power that brought us back. But I long to end this curse. It's like a darkness that never leaves the mind. Like waking up from a nightmare and having your day troubled after. You have walked the world as a ghost in the Shadowlands. Imagine what it's like to be fully that and filled with sorrow and anger, for thousands of years.'

'I would rather face oblivion than that.' She shivered.

'So would we,' he said and the others murmured agreement. 'When the light of the goddess surrounded me, I heard my king's voice.' He looked dotingly back at Marakon, who shifted self-consciously. 'I knew the nightmare had ended, or had at least released me.

'My lady.' He turned to look fully at her, and she blushed at the address. 'I would go to the Murk this moment if it meant we could drive away the black cloud that hovers over us. Only when the demon wizard is dead will the light of the goddess fall upon us.'

The passion in his voice moved Issa and she swallowed down a lump. 'I will do all that I can to help you, Nemeron. Zanufey guides me, and I must await her call. Besides, as much as I love my horse, I'm sick and sore from riding him without a saddle, and I'd rather face demons than ride another day.'

The knights laughed.

Unfortunately she had to ride another day without a saddle, but to keep her mind from thinking about her sore groin, she thought about the dark moon. Nemeron's questions were ones she had rolled around her mind for a long time. They often led to thoughts about her origins and her parents. If her father was dead, as Fraya had said, could her mother still be alive? She dared not let herself believe it.

Come to Myrn, Naksu had said. Would her answers lie there? The war was here though. Surely Zanufey needed her here, not half the world away learning ancient Seer Lore. The dark moon was rising, and the world needed her power. When it rose she'd have her chance to take revenge. Coronos' death would not be for nothing.

Cirosa's face flashed in her mind, making her angry. She imagined killing her, the way the woman had killed Coronos. The thought was disturbing, but at the same time satisfying. So many had died; she would avenge them all.

'Is everything all right?' It was Marakon. He was looking at her strangely. The other knights were talking amongst themselves as they walked uphill through forests. She released her scowl.

'Yes, I…was thinking of those who have died. I want revenge,' she said.

She suddenly felt uneasy, as if being watched or that danger was near. Was it Marakon's presence that made her feel that way? Now that she thought of it, she always felt uncomfortable when he was near. She knew he was a good, honest, even courageous man, so why did she feel this way? *It was his curse,* she thought, but then why didn't she feel the same way around the other knights? They carried the same curse. She wanted to trust this man, but something stopped her. She worried that something awful was going to happen. She tried to push the feelings aside as he spoke.

'Revenge is a sickness I've suffered from for many lives.' He gave a wry smile. 'It goes nowhere but down a dark hole where it will eat you alive.'

'I can't help it.' She shrugged. 'I keep seeing the faces of my friends who were murdered. I want to murder back. How can I fight anything without the desire for revenge?'

'That's what being a knight teaches you,' he said. 'You fight for honour, for what's right, and to help those who can't fight. But I understand exactly how you feel. You remind me of me. I still fight with revenge, when hope seems lost. Especially now, now my wife…'

The raw pain in his eyes ignited her own. Her mother's blackened face and Ely's tortured body flittered through her mind. They rode in silence.

There was truth in his words—to fight for honour not revenge. What did she fight for? All she thought about when fighting was to stay alive. It seemed there was far more to being a warrior, an honourable one, than she'd thought.

'I guess I've got a lot to learn,' she said. 'Would you make me a knight?'

Marakon laughed.

'I can use a sword to protect myself, and magic. What's so funny about that?' she said, feeling embarrassed.

'I was surprised you asked because I've been thinking about it a lot. I've been a leader many times, even in this lifetime, but I don't think I want to be one anymore. I think you should lead the Knights of the Raven. You are, after all, the Raven Queen.'

She pulled Duskar up short. 'Me? Lead the knights? Are you mad? They'd laugh at me. I can only just wield a sword—'

'I've seen you fight. If you're a novice, well, you're already better than some of my experienced fighters. You have a natural ability. And people fear magic wielders. Fear creates respect.'

They continued walking.

'The Raven Queen,' Issa tutted, 'whatever that is. She's like another self. I can't work out if I like her or loathe her. I either want to be me, just Issa, or her, a cold-hearted warrior.'

'Who do you think I am when I fight?' Marakon said. 'Do you think I'm the same man when I'm in bed with my wife?'

Issa coloured at the thought. 'No, that's not what I meant.' She shook her head. She didn't know what she meant.

'We all have different sides to us,' Marakon said. 'I have a side I struggle with, always.'

She wondered what that side was, but he said no more. 'It's just, I don't know,' she said. 'I just hate all these prophecies. It's like I am being told who I am, what I am, and what I have to do. It's like I don't have a life at all.'

She felt like a brooding teenager. But talking to Marakon about it seemed far easier than talking to Asaph, Freydel, or Coronos. Maybe it was because he was more of a stranger to her.

'Why don't you think about it? We'll teach you everything we know, as we always have done,' Marakon said, bringing the conversations back around to his knights. 'I think you'd make a good leader. I'd be your advisor, your trainer, if you wish. But me being a leader again, after losing so many? I don't think I want that. No, I definitely don't want that. Think about it. This world needs an elite group of warrior knights more than it ever has.'

It seemed like a huge responsibility but Issa found herself saying, 'I'll think about it.'

CHAPTER 27

The First Code

ASAPH lay blinking in the bright light of two suns.

The Dragon Dream—he'd made it. But why did the suns seem faded and their strength weak? Morhork had been carrying him, and they'd flown so fast he'd passed out. He'd never experienced such speed before. How could anything fly at that speed without wings? Then he remembered seeing sparks of magic all around the dragon's body. *He flew with magic?*

He'd glimpsed a great hot chamber, and then the dragon door. How had they come through the dragon door? Wasn't he barred? He looked up at the ice-blue dragon towering above him. Morhork angled his head down and regarded him with one eye, his face unreadable.

'He shouldn't be here,' Faelsun's voice boomed.

Asaph sat up. They were on one of the wide landing platforms surrounding the magnificent Tower of Flame. Its red-brick turrets and great arched doorways loomed around them. But looking at it now, the fortress lacked its former lustre. The turrets were old and crumbling and the landing platform was covered in cracked stones and sprouted weeds. There were no longer dragons guarding the entrance and when he reached out with his mind he could barely feel any at all.

Had the dragons left, or were his own abilities failing because of Cirosa's chains? It seemed unfair that he was to blame for those chains— the 'taint.' Had he been weak somehow? How could he have stopped Cirosa's poison? It seemed everything he did was wrong.

He looked up at Faelsun. The white dragon ignored him and glared at his brother. Now they were together, Asaph could see the likeness. They were identical in form, had the same elegant head, majestic horns and long snout, and they were the same size. The only difference was Faelsun was white whilst Morhork was ice-blue.

Morhork's jagged red scars, where his wings had been, made Asaph shiver. He looked at Faelsun and realised how little he knew the Guardian of the Dragon Dream.

'Greetings, brother.' Morhork's voice was sweet. 'I can tell you've missed me after all these thousands of years.'

'Get him out of here. He's corrupted with Baelthrom's black magic. You'll bring this place to its knees.' Faelsun moved closer to his brother.

Asaph felt intimidated. He had never heard Faelsun talk in this manner before.

'I, too, am corrupted. So once you said.' Morhork sneered. 'Do you turn your back on all things that don't pass your mark? Even those abominations of your wilful and stupid creation? What care have I for a Dragon Lord? And yet here I stand doing more for him than you are. Break the bonds the immortals have placed on him and remove his taint. You know how.'

'Why, indeed, do you care, Morhork?'

'I know the mark of Feygriene when I see it.' The flame mark on Asaph's chest tingled as Morhork spoke. 'This fool disturbed my sleep, and now undead dragons hunt him. You'd better hope they haven't followed us here, brother.' He grinned when Faelsun's eyes went wide.

'You haven't led them here, have you?' Faelsun's voice was dangerous.

'I've done nothing but return to you your own creation. Better remove those bonds before Baelthrom and his horde start hunting dragons again.' Morhork yawned a row of pristine white fangs, seemingly uncaring.

'Have the years not made you see reason, or perhaps the barest understanding of the peace I helped create between man and dragon?'

Morhork growled, a low rumbling sound. 'Look at my deformed body. You think I'll ever forgive you for tearing the wings from my back? Joining man and dragon was an abomination. And now look at what they are: Dromoorai ravaging Maioria.'

'That was Baelthrom's doing, not mine,' Faelsun said.

'And what are you doing to stop that immortal bastard? Hiding away in your ridiculous Dragon Dream?'

Faelsun said nothing, but his tail tip whipped back and forth. The tension in the air was palpable. Asaph moved away so he was no longer between the two dragons. They didn't seem to notice.

'Look at this place. What happened? Where are all the dragons circling the skies of freedom? Bah, it's deserted and crumbling,' Morhork spat out.

Asaph agreed. The fort was turning into a ruin and the whole place, even the suns, seemed dimmed of their splendour. He braced himself for Faelsun's retort, but the white dragon seemed more sad than angry.

'Time moves faster here than in Maioria. You know that well, brother. But the Orb of Air was taken, and since then this place began to fade. Even my strength is waning, and I struggle to keep the dream alive,' he said quietly, as if ashamed.

'Nothing made by men can ever last. They shouldn't be ruling Maioria. We should.' Morhork narrowed his eyes, but there was weariness in his voice.

So that was the truth of it, Asaph thought. Morhork obviously hated humans, but why? It couldn't just be jealousy. After all, when dragons were more numerous, they had ruled the north.

'The cunning of dragon and man is well-matched, Morhork.' Faelsun sighed as if it were an old argument. 'It was foreseen that we would destroy each other until nothing remained of either—just as Slevina and Qurenn destroyed each other. 'Peace between our races was instigated by a human, Morhork. One braver than you or I. Have you forgotten Ralan Afisius in your millennia of slumber? Not all dragons are like you and hate humans, and not all humans hate dragons. Many of us longed for peace.'

At Faelsun's words, the Recollection opened in Asaph's mind. Ralan Afisius. He knew that name. The Recollection moved back in time, so far back the images became hazy. The images slowed, and stopped.

His eyes rested upon a tall, slender woman with blond hair and brown eyes. She wore a long, silken red cape over riding clothes and boots. Her features were sharp and angular, but her face had a quirky half smile. She held an air of extreme intelligence. Though he'd never personally met her, he knew her name was Ralan Afisius, one of the greatest wizards.

Before her loomed a dragon whose scales were such dark red they were almost black. The dragon's name was Ark. They were talking, but he couldn't hear what was said. They seemed amicable, even friendly, and she patted the dragon's claw and he bowed his massive head. They were surrounded by mountains and stood beside a gold building partially hidden behind the bulk of Ark. A gold building with curved walls and a spire…just like the one he had sheltered in in the north.

Asaph blinked and the image was gone. He looked into the faces of Faelsun and Morhork. He was still getting used to the fact that, when in the company of other dragons, they could see what he was seeing in the Recollection.

'The First Code,' Faelsun said to him. Morhork scowled. 'After they fought and failed to destroy each other, Ralan Afisius and Ark saw that they were equally matched in magic, skill and intellect. They did something wise; they decided to talk. Between them they formed the First Code, Feygriene's Accord, and for the first time dragon and human communed with reason and in peace.

'The wars between dragons and humans continued, but the seed had been sown. Ark was slain by humans, and soon after, mad with grief, Ralan took her own life. It would be hundreds of years later that Qurenn slew Slevina, but Ark and Ralan were never forgotten.'

Realisation dawned on him. 'The lake, that was what was in the lake. The gold building…'

Faelsun blinked. Morhork brought his head closer.

'Yes, fool. I destroyed it after my wings were ripped away,' he growled. Asaph felt a tremor of fear and forced it down. 'Peace may have formed between human and dragon, but all it did was divide dragons against each other.'

'You divided dragons against each other,' Faelsun growled.

'Not I, brother. You.' Morhork raised his head, his eyes glinting dangerously. 'Don't think because I have no wings that I cannot fight. You crippled me, but I've become far stronger in magic than you ever will be.'

The argument could not be won, Asaph realised, wondering how he could diffuse the tension between the two dragons.

'It was Feygriene's desire to——' Faelsun was cut short.

'Pah. How dare you speak of the goddess' desires? No good can ever come of aligning human with dragon, and not this disgusting abomination.' Morhork sneered at Asaph. 'Humans made us weak and turned us into their lap dogs. In return for trying to bring us back to our glory and might, you destroyed my dragons and banished me. You turned your dragons upon me, your own brother. Your desire for peace with humans was stronger than your desire for peace with your own kin. There's no sin greater, brother.' Morhork snorted smoke.

The ice-blue dragon's anger was short-lived, and the scowl on his face softened as he stared into the distance.

'What point is there looking into the past for old arguments, when new arguments can be found?' Asaph said, not quite sure where he was going with this. 'Shouldn't we look to fighting Baelthrom and his horde instead of each other? He'll destroy all of us anyway if we do nothing.'

'Not if I can help it,' Morhork said.

Asaph wondered what he meant. Did he think he could stand against Baelthrom alone?

'We've failed, you fool,' Faelsun said to Morhork. 'Can't you see it? Look around you. This place is a reflection of the energies of Maioria. If this is dying then Maioria is far worse. There's no hope. Our time is over, for human *and* dragon.'

The hopelessness in Faelsun's voice shocked Asaph. Had losing the orb meant that much? He couldn't believe it was hopeless; he was too young to believe it.

'The boy has failed.' Faelsun looked at him.

Asaph frowned. A sinking feeling settled in his stomach.

'Failed?' Morhork snorted. 'Failed at what, brother? How can you fail when there is nothing to win or lose?'

Asaph frowned. He just couldn't work out if Morhork was on his side or against him. Morhork was likely on nobody's side except his own.

'Failed at becoming the Dragon Lord I was supposed to be.' Asaph sighed. The dragons looked at him. 'I've failed at everything—' He bit back his own self-pity and tried not to think about how he'd failed Issa by falling to Cirosa's bewitching. He tried to grow a backbone despite his exhaustion.

'Failed to find the dragons in time. Failed to keep the Dragon Dream alive. I've failed in this too. The time of dragons has come to an end.' Faelsun sighed. 'You've been sleeping, Morhork, whilst everything rots and fades away.'

Morhork laughed. 'You think because you exiled me, because I chose sleep rather than existence in a world of fools, that I didn't see what was happening? Dear brother, I saw more in my slumber than ever you saw with your eyes, and it has made me wise and powerful.

'I saw him come out of the Dark Rift. Now I see Zanufey's moon rising and a change in the ages of Maioria. I didn't believe in the ancient scriptures of humans, but when I saw the Raven Queen come, I realised I was wrong.

'Nothing's determined. That's what I've learned in all these years. It's not over until it's over and you never know what is around the next corner. The Raven Queen brings hope, but no more. Even she might fail. As far as I can see, she is...' Morhork trailed off, as if trying to find the right words, '...in doubt,' he finished.

'Bah, this place. You, him,' Morhork nodded to Asaph then Faelsun, 'all bore me. Heal him, or not, it's nothing to do with me. I have my own plans.'

Before any more could be said, the blue dragon whirled around and leapt back through the dragon door.

Morhork couldn't stand the place anymore. The Dragon Dream, where he wasn't allowed. Their dream should be lived on Maioria, not outside of it. The dragon door closed behind him, and he again enjoyed the heat of the lava chamber.

What did he care about the Dragon Lord anyway? Cursed abominations. Seeing the shock on his brother's face when he walked through the dragon door had been worth it though. It had been so long; even the dragon guards watching for him had been removed from that door. Had Faelsun thought him dead?

Yes, he'd been sleeping, but a part of his consciousness had remained very active in the body of a human. He yawned and spied a near horizontal crack in the cavern some hundred feet up in the rock close to the ceiling.

He gathered the Flow and launched into the air. The crack was just big enough to fit his body in and he crawled inside. He would rest in the warmth until his magic reserves had recovered. With a yawn he snapped his jaws and curled up.

He'd barely drifted off when screams howled through the cavern.

Feeling safe and uncaring on his ledge he ignored it and curled up tighter. The sound came again, louder and closer. A feeling of dread came over him and the Flow turned sluggish. He jerked awake and peered over the ledge.

Black dragons flew down the tunnel towards the door, their undead screeches echoing off the walls. Even Morhork's fearless warrior heart beat faster. These dragons were big, as big as he, and insane. He reached for their minds but they were empty of living thought and filled only with a ravenous hunger for more than just blood and flesh. They wanted the life of living things.

A strange, sickly-sweet smell followed them. The Recollection opened and he saw endless bottles of Sirin Derenax, the Black Drink of Immortality. Memories from the part of him located in his human form confirmed the look and smell of the deadly drink.

They neared and he saw that their eyes were black or glowing red and atop each of them was a rider, armoured in black metal and carrying a claymore. Red amulets blazed on the chest of each of them and hurt his eyes. The Dromoorai had cunning minds, but were also soulless and lacking autonomy. They were utterly controlled and dictated to by their master, Baelthrom. Morhork found them fascinating.

One rider, flying in their midst, caught his eye. She was small, unarmoured, dressed in white, and had pale hair and skin. A red amulet also swung on her chest. She was human and yet not. She was not dead like the others; her mind was alive with cunning and cruelty, and she was linked in some detestable way to the Dread Dragon she flew. Behind her was a man whose face he couldn't see because he was hooded and cloaked. His mind seemed familiar and he was about to open the Recollection as he probed further but detected a shield. Morhork stopped probing, fearing detection.

The female was the one who'd bound the Dragon Lord. In the Flow he could see the black tendrils of her leash leading to him through the dragon door. So that was how she'd found him so easily. The Dragon Lord was going to have a hard time breaking those chains. Morhork did not envy the man. The woman even made him uneasy—something he was not inclined to feel. Unsettled, he lowered his head and hid his presence with the barest magic.

Morhork thought hard but still didn't know what to do. How could he warn Faelsun? Should he even bother? They had severed their connection long ago. Perhaps those thousands of years spent sleeping and moving part of his consciousness around in human form had changed him. Weakened him, no doubt, as all contact with humans seemed to weaken dragons.

He peaked over the edge again. No way could he fight them. There were ten Dread Dragons now, hovering before the dragon door. Were there even ten dragons left in the entirety of the Dragon Dream? Faelsun would know what to do to keep his realm safe. He would have prepared long ago.

Morhork relaxed. Let Faelsun fight his own battles; this was nothing to do with him. He sank back into his hole and closed his eyes.

CHAPTER 28

Broken Dreams

FAELSUN watched his brother leave, but his heart wasn't as hard as once it had been.

He'd thought his brother long dead and hadn't mourned him. Seeing him again was a shock. They'd talked more then than they had the last time a thousand years ago.

How had Asaph wound up with his brother? The last living Dragon Lord finding the one dragon who hated them most in all the world? He smiled at the irony.

Without his brother there, the place suddenly felt empty. Few dragons came here anymore and the realm was passing into obscurity. The dream was fading. Most of the spirits of those who had stayed had decided it was time to leave for the Fire in the Sky. No man or dragon came here to share the dream, despite all the sleeping dragons upon Maioria. Maybe they had all forgotten this place existed.

The only Dragon Lord left was falling to Baelthrom, and the only other dragon awake hated this place.

Perhaps he, Faelsun, should fade along with the dream. Losing the Orb of Air had been the death blow. No magic of his could stop the fort crumbling. Now, with the orb in his grasp, Baelthrom could leech away the life energy of the Dragon Dream, unstopped. Even though he was a dragon, he began to feel there was no forever anymore.

'I'll do anything I can to remove the chains around me and destroy whatever infects me.' Asaph's voice roused Faelsun from his thoughts. 'It was done against my will. I had no way to protect myself against it.

If I failed in some way, I'm sorry. You can't turn your back on me now.'

Faelsun looked at the man. 'We've all failed. Look around. Even the dream is failing.' He sighed. He entered the Flow and saw the black chains embedded in Asaph, all evil and wrong. They moved and squirmed like snakes. The chains, invisible to the naked eye, wound away back through the dragon door, still linking him to whoever held those chains.

'If I remove those chains, you'll be very weak. You could die,' Faelsun said.

'I don't care. Death is better than this.' Asaph's face was pinched, full of desperation. 'If you don't remove them, I'll be enslaved and turned into a Dromoorai. Death is better.'

Faelsun nodded and focused on the chains. All at once they tightened. Asaph yelped and fell to his knees.

'I haven't touched them yet.' He gathered the Flow and reached for the chains. They were slippery and squirmed in his grasp. He gripped one and snapped it. Asaph groaned. The broken chain slithered back through the dragon door, but there was still part of it embedded in Asaph. To remove them fully he had to unhook them.

Grasping the chain in the Flow, he found it embedded deep in the heart chakra. It was fiddly, tiring work. The one who had placed these snares was clever.

Finally it came loose, Asaph gasped, and the chain disintegrated to nothing. There were six more chains, each embedded into the man's seven chakras. He worked on the base chakra next, the chain slithering and slipping away from him. Now he knew what he was doing, it came away easier.

Asaph groaned and was now prone on the ground, drenched in sweat. The man's energy was draining away, but if these chains were not broken, the man was dead one way or another.

He worked next on the seventh and sixth chakras, hoping to at least free the man's mind and spirit sooner. It might help him find strength whilst he removed the others. One by one they came away and he struggled with the last two.

There came a surge in the Flow. It came from beneath, like a current of filth pushing up. Black pooled beneath the swirling fields of energy and Asaph's remaining chains tightened. He screamed.

Faelsun swooned and grappled for control of the Flow as the Under Flow made him reel. The Dragon Dream jerked and shuddered. Thunder tore across the sky and back again though there was no storm. The dragon door exploded open and disintegrated, destroying itself in the process. Waves of corruption rolled through the gaping hole and in the Flow, the Under Flow surged, black and smothering. Asaph screamed again and writhed, deathly pale and drenched in sweat.

A Dread Dragon clawed its way through the door, an abomination Faelsun hoped he would never see here in his beloved Dragon Dream. It was followed by another, then another—Dromoorai riders sitting atop each of them. A scourge upon the land, a dirty stain upon the purity of the realm.

The Tower of the Flame trembled, cracked and splintered. One of the towers crumbled into the sea. The Dragon Dream could not tolerate evil; it was crumbling before his eyes.

Dread Dragons continued to pour through but they did not attack. They were waiting for the command from their master.

Faelsun didn't need to wait for that. He picked Asaph up and launched into the air, watching below as the platform he had stood on cracked and crumbled. The sea around the tower frothed and raged.

He lifted higher into the air until the storm shield engulfed him. Wind and rain tore at him, but no storm could protect the Tower of the Flame anymore; it was over.

'Brothers and sisters who remain, leave this place. It's over,' he called with his mind to the dragons within the tower and elsewhere in the dream. He felt sadness return, a keen desire to fight, and then nothing.

Lightning flashed and rain ran down his scales. Beneath him black dragons appeared through the clouds. Perhaps Morhork was right. He should not abandon the Dragon Lord, not when they all had failed and there was nothing left.

He turned and flew deeper into the storm. Though dragon doors could be opened in the mind of all dragons and Dragon Lords, there were still two physical doors that could be opened and walked through. The destroyed one was invaded beneath him, and another was hidden in a cave in the mountains.

Only those who had entry into the Dragon Dream knew about it. Morhork did not. This door Asaph should have known about, but did

not. Now it led directly into enemy lands, but it was the only chance
Asaph had of returning to Maioria, or dying with him here in the dream.
And Faelsun knew he was soon to die.

He emerged out of the storm over a surging sea. Land appeared; that
too was quaking. The green pastures buckled and shook and huge cracks
snaked over the beautiful plains. Ahead, white-tipped mountains loomed.
Behind, a black cloud of Dread Dragons pursued them.

Faelsun found the cave easily, despite not having been here for
centuries. He angled his wings down, feeling the cool mountain air flow
over his wings, and landed on the ledge before the entrance. The ground
trembled under his feet, and snow and rock rolled down the mountainside.
He prayed the dream would hold together just a little longer.

He laid Asaph down in the cave, entered the Flow, and grappled with
the next chain. It took time like the others, but finally it broke free. Asaph
didn't even move.

A scream scoured his ears. He turned to face the enemy at the cave
entrance. They clustered, hovering in the air before him, still waiting for
their next command. Looking at what a man and dragon had become
filled him with sorrow and revulsion.

A Dread Dragon pushed through the others and he saw two humans
on its back—not Dromoorai, but still changed with the Black Drink. The
smell of it made him gag. The one mind-linked with the dragon was
female and all-white as if the colour had been leached out of her when
her soul was enslaved. In the Recollection he knew her. Cirosa, once High
Priestess of the goddess, now traitor.

The other was male, dark hair showing beneath his hood, and as
white-skinned as the woman behind which he rode. His eyes were wide
and seemed to glow like the Dromoorai's. He had the look of one insane,
and yet dangerously powerful. He recognised Vornus instantly and his
scales crawled. How could he forget the face of the man who had
betrayed and destroyed Drax, and murdered so many of his kin?

'Greetings, Vornus. I see that immortal bastard has bestowed upon
you great gifts you never had in life,' Faelsun said.

The man growled and his eyes flashed.

The Under Flow surged around Faelsun, but he was ready and pushed
it back with the Flow. He would not be able to hold it back for long. The
Under Flow was rapidly gaining strength as it leeched away the living

energy of the Dragon Dream, but the Flow was still stronger for now.

The woman laughed making a sound like a tinkling bell, but cold and heartless. It made the fires in his belly go out. She was the one to be feared. He prepared himself for anything.

'Come now, boys,' she said, her voice smooth and melodious and laced with venom. 'Give to me the one who is mine, and then you can fight over this pathetic place.'

Faelsun said nothing and shifted his body to hide Asaph.

'Baelthrom sends his emissaries instead of facing me himself? Is he so afraid?' Faelsun spoke in ancient dragon tongue.

The priestess looked blank and then broke into a smile. Her human voice struggled over the words, but to his astonishment she replied in dragon speak.

'Baelthrom could not be bothered. He instead watches through our Shadow Stones.' She smiled and came closer.

'Your unholy mind link to your Dread Dragon will be your undoing, traitor,' Faelsun said in Frayonesse.

'I will be your undoing,' she replied.

'Baelthrom's a fool to trust two traitors, don't you think?' said Faelsun, buying time. 'You suck the life out of this world and revel in your pitiful immortality. You'll walk a world that's dead, yet still won't ask yourself if it was worth it as all around you becomes a wasteland. You make me regret the day man and dragon became one,' he spat out. The fires in his belly reignited and rumbled, and tendrils of smoke came from his nostrils.

'Your time is over, old lizard,' Cirosa said. The old insult stung. 'Your beloved Feygriene is dying and her power waning, if she ever really was there at all.'

'You could never hear the goddess' voice for the clamouring of your own vicious, greedy thoughts, Cirosa. You betrayed your own race.' She looked surprised. 'Do you really think I don't know who you are, High Priestess? I've watched Maioria and the scourge upon it since that abomination first came here.'

He nodded towards the man. 'Did you bring that bastard Vornus here to gloat? The heir of Drax escaped your clutches. I'd be afraid, Vornus. Your death lies in his hands.'

'I came to take him in chains,' Vornus replied, his eyes glaring. Faelsun breathed in slowly as the man spoke. 'I knew the bastard son somehow got away. It was all just a matter of time until we found him. You think I'm afraid of him? Hah. What a disappointment he is.'

Faelsun sprayed fire at them, but Cirosa was ready and, with a flick of her wrists, it went out before it reached them.

'Enough.' Cirosa held up a hand. 'Give us the fool. Baelthrom requires him as bait for the Raven Queen. He's not much interested in this pitiful place or you. You'll simply feed our dragons.'

She moved closer, almost close enough to land on the jutting ledge. Faelsun shuffled backwards and drew on what he could of the Flow. He had to release the last chain binding Asaph before the end. He breathed and spewed flames again. Distracting them with fire, he focused on the Flow and grappled with the last chain.

'Is that the best you can do?' Cirosa laughed from behind the wall of fire.

The chain broke. Asaph screamed. Cirosa fell silent. The flames dissipated and Faelsun looked into the face of fury. The priestess raised her hands and the Under Flow surged into him. It penetrated his chest and shook his pounding heart. His mind scattered and his body convulsed. The cave vibrated and lightning flared.

He lost his grip on the Flow and fought to regain it. He roared under the assault, his heart hammering in his chest. The Flow surged around him, breaking the assault. His whole body twitched and buzzed. His mind stopped rolling. Everything became still.

Cirosa raised her arms again. The Dromoorai brought their mounts closer. Vornus grinned. The Dread Dragons hung motionless as their wings beat steadily. The Dromoorai's eyes glowed red, then green, then black—all changing colour together as if they were one being chained to one master.

Faelsun stared, almost mesmerised. The Flow stuttered in his grasp, failing as the Under Flow overpowered it. For the first time in thousands of years he wished that he were not alone, and that Morhork was here. His brother was far away in the mortal realm, but he sent his last call into the ether.

With a roar of flames, Faelsun lunged at the closest Dromoorai whose mount was setting foot on the ledge beside Cirosa. He sank his talons into the Dread Dragon's flesh and snapped at a Dromoorai on its back. Armour crumpled and softened in his flame-filled jaws and the

Dromoorai screamed.

Watery blood flooded into his mouth, a bitter poison making him gag. He snapped again and wrenched off the Dromoorai's head, ignoring its thrusting claymore that ripped into his jaw. He spat its head and blood out.

Pain seared up his front leg as the Dread Dragon clamped onto it. The other Dread Dragons closed in and the Under Flow smothered him in waves of agony that rippled through his scales.

Fury became him and he released the Flow; it was useless to him now. Madly he clawed and struck, finding flesh or armour everywhere he fought. He fought with everything he had, not needing to keep any energy back. This would be his last fight.

He breathed in and flamed everything in front of him turning all to chaos and fire. The world was teeth, magic, claws and flames. His own hot blood poured down his back and legs, mingling with the cold blood of the immortals he fought. Dromoorai swords lacerated his wings, their poison flowing in his veins. He could no longer fly.

Swords flickered in firelight, smoke choked the cave. The wounds he dealt and received he lost count of and pain became a dull ache in his entire body. He was mortally wounded, in his chest, his throat, his mind, but he could still fight.

A surge of the Under Flow pushed him back into the cave. Asaph's prone body nudged against his foot. The dragon door was behind, not far. He had to get him through it and destroy it. He shuffled backwards. Dread Dragons filled the tunnel in front of him, red eyes and amulets lighting the darkness, the smell of blood and Sirin Derenax cloying the air.

Between the snaking heads and helmets, he glimpsed Cirosa's pale face smiling. She was gathering the Under Flow.

He picked Asaph up with a hind leg. With all the chains broken, the man tried to rouse himself. Soon he would see it all in the Recollection. Let him see dragon power, and glory, and fearless rage. Faelsun sprayed flames, snapped and tore with his teeth, lashed with his talons.

The Under Flow reigned. His strength was draining fast; he didn't have much fight left. All he needed was a small amount of magic to complete the task.

He flamed the cave once more and turned around, exposing his back, readying himself for the final blows. He lunged towards the dragon door set in the rock at the cave end, ensuring that his bulk filled the tunnel between him and the dragon door.

Asaph opened his eyes but was too weak to do much else. Faelsun looked at him as dark magic swamped them. It filled the cave, blotting out all except the face of the man he held. The Under Flow sucked all the strength from his body. His back legs shook violently then collapsed. Jaws clamped onto his tail and wrenched. He howled as the end was ripped off.

Dragons clamped onto his spine. The pain was immense. His blood flowed down his body and pooled around his feet, making the floor slippery as he hauled himself towards the door, clinging to what he could of the Flow. One last thing was all he had to do to save his soul from being enslaved by Baelthrom, and showing Asaph how to do the same should he ever have need.

Asaph's face was a mask of pain, for himself or Faelsun, he couldn't be sure. The man tried to speak but only croaked. The dragon door was before him. Jaws—three pairs of them—clamped on his back legs and tail, wrenching and dragging him back. He groaned in pain and clawed forwards, his body shaking.

Despite the black magic that filled the chamber, another light was beginning to glow, this one gold and ethereal. It soothed his shuddering heart. He wondered if anyone else could see it. The life was draining from him, but Feygriene's light was filling him. It gave him clarity and he pooled the last of his magic.

Golden light burst from him, blasting open the dragon door. He shoved Asaph through. The man struggled to sit up, eyes wide in horror. Faelsun wondered what he must look like, his body destroyed and blood dripping everywhere.

'Remember the Dream.' Faelsun gasped, never dropping the man's gaze.

The blackness was trying to swallow him, and he had to stay with the light. He filled his belly with fire and the Flow, mingling them together. Then he let them both out. White fire engulfed him. The dragon door exploded and crumbled, destroyed forever.

The flames filled Faelsun within and without, consuming his body and all the Dromoorai surrounding him. He roared in pain but reached for the light. He felt his soul shaking free. There was black all around him, but above there was light coming from a white-gold sun. He had to go to it. Reaching higher, closer to the light, the pain began to fade. He touched it and the light became him.

CHAPTER 29

Demon Spear

MAGGOT awoke when Zorock was gone and Zorock's Eye was rising over the mountain ridge.

His body was only half in the shadow of Karhlusus Keep. He scrambled out of the sun and melted into shadow, heart pounding. Greater demons wheeled high above, around the tip of the rock. He was lucky they hadn't come down and spotted him.

He closed his eyes, trying to find the courage to go on, but all he found was a reason—it was simply a long way back. Not even Carmedrak himself, or being brave like Issa, could instil the courage in him right now, and so he stayed there melded in shadow, trembling.

A beetle zapped past. Quick as a demon he materialised, snapped at it and gulped it down. Food helped. He wished he had his favourite bowl of maggots. That's where he got his name from. He loved the things, bowls and bowls of them all wiggling and juicy in his mouth. He felt better thinking about his favourite food.

He couldn't stay out here, he decided, and preferred to hide inside, away from the flying greater demons. Looking up the rock, there were numerous crags and maybe holes that led inside. He couldn't risk using one of the main tunnels, so he'd have to explore the crannies. He liked exploring.

About four feet up was a crack. He flowed in the shadows up to it. It was shallow and went nowhere. A little farther up was another crack, but that too was shallow. Higher he moved until he was a third of the way up. There he found a hole out of which air flowed. It was no bigger than a rat hole, but if it was shadowed all the way in, he could get through.

He peered inside, took a deep breath, and flowed into the tunnel. Sometimes it became so narrow it was less than half an inch wide. It went up and up, then down and right. Then he wasn't sure if he moved up or down or in any direction. He even went through a pool of water. He'd never dragged his shadow body through water before. He didn't like it. It was slow and cold and he came out the other end shivering.

The exit came abruptly and he almost fell out into the main hallway. Voices came. Grazen voices. Maggot froze and peered out. The hallway curved around a corner and a brazier cast an orange glow. Shadows moved on the walls and then two Grazen appeared, about seven feet tall. Maggot stared at them. They looked just like Shadow Demons, but brown and not grey.

'…because Master said. We must pace the halls in case of attack, Bog,' one said.

'Yer, I know, but I'm sick of it. No one would miss just one wursel. C'mon, Kulk, it's so close,' said the other. 'There's no one gonna attack 'ere. No Shadow Demon 'as the brains or guts to come. And Master is busy. He won't even know. I'm so 'ungry.'

The other sighed. 'I dunno…'

They disappeared around the corner. Maggot sat still for awhile, afraid of going into the hallway, yet angry with his cousins. Shadow Demons were brainy and gutty. Why did they think otherwise? Stupid Grazen. He looked down.

The hallway was empty and there was enough shadow beyond the light for him to move. But where would he go? All he knew was the spear was down, deep down in the dungeons. He could get lost forever in the cracks of Karhlusus Keep and never ever get out.

Much to his fury, a swamp fairy darted by, making a squealing sound that only small demons could hear. It flashed around the corner. That was all he needed. He slipped out of the hole and flowed through the shadows on the floor, following the green light. Swamp fairies were everywhere lately; he couldn't get away from them.

The buzzing swamp fairy found a hole in the floor and tried to squeeze into it. Maggot was almost upon it, mouth open and tongue at the ready, when it popped through the other side. He growled and peered through the hole. When its light faded and it was dark again, he melted into the shadows and flowed into the hole.

This hole went straight down and he moved fast. It started to narrow but soon opened up to a foot wide. The fairy had gone, much to his annoyance, but he carried on, hoping this way would lead to the spear.

The hole widened again to over two feet and he decided to move in solid form for a little bit. The shadow form was making him tired. It was much slower going as he clambered down, though when space permitted, he was able to open his wings and glide. He yawned, found a ledge to rest on and a jutting rock to scratch that difficult spot between his wings.

Maggot jerked awake. How long had he been asleep? He took a while to get his bearings. It was strange being in the place that should be his home. It felt natural to be here and yet very dangerous. If this were his home, he'd spend all day exploring every crack and hole. He yawned and sat up. Only then did he notice the barest white light coming from below. It was unsettling.

He clambered down the ledge and made his way towards the light. He didn't like the feel of it on his skin, all crawly and tingly. He scrambled over another rock and a blaze of light struck up through a crack. Sweat trickled down his back and he tugged on his ears.

Could it be the spear?

It was so bright, like that horrid place Maioria. It made him feel sick. A belch clawed its way out of his mouth and echoed around him. He stood there frozen, hands clamped over his mouth. There was no sound, nothing at all. It was horribly silent. He couldn't look into the light, he just couldn't. But if it was the spear, he'd found it.

It took all of his willpower to force his legs forwards towards that awful light. He longed to be back in the shadows in the lovely dark where he belonged, but a nagging feeling forced him to the hole. Blinking, he stuck his eye to the ground and peered down.

The light was so bright he fell back gasping, covering his burning eye as his head throbbed. He lay there a long while, waiting for the pain to go, and then he tried again. It didn't hurt as much this time and he could almost see clearly.

He stared in awe at the glowing white spear suspended in the air above a crude octagonal pedestal. It was deadly and beautiful and filled him with dread. Even greater demons feared it. It was set in the centre of a small, rough-hewn room. It looked as if anyone could simply pick up the spear, but then he felt the magic that bound it—greater demon magic and extremely powerful.

'Velistor. A spear made to kill demons,' he whispered. He couldn't stop trembling.

An awful realisation came over him, something that could very well ruin his expedition. He stood still as his thoughts connected to each other to make one very coherent problem. Despite all his efforts to get here, he hadn't thought about how he would get the spear out, then make it all the way back home in one piece. From where he was, he couldn't see any door into the room, but surely there must be one, for how did they get the spear in there in the first place?

Frowning, he sat down, forcing his brain to think, but thinking was boring and he fell asleep.

What awoke him, he wasn't sure, but the light that spilled through the hole was no longer white but green. He stuck his face to the hole and glared down.

A bloody swamp fairy! The ball of green light bobbed around the spear, coming close as if looking at it, then darting away from it, afraid. Without realising quite what he was doing or being able to stop himself, he cried out.

'Hey, that's my spear!'

The green light darted into the darkest corner of the room and went out. Frightening himself, Maggot fell back from the hole, his heart thumping in his throat.

There came a terrifying crunching sound, and a portion of the chamber slid aside to reveal a well-concealed door. A short, stocky Grazen with a spike-studded club and dented helmet came stalking into the room. Another similar looking Grazen stood in the doorway.

Too frightened to drag his eye away from the hole, Maggot stared terror-stricken. Instead he flattened himself against the rock, hand over mouth, quietening the sobs, wishing desperately that his heart didn't beat quite so loudly.

The scowling Grazen shielded his eyes against the light, looked up and down the chamber, then grunted and left, the door sliding shut behind him. Maggot slowly let go of his breath and tried to see where the swamp fairy had gone. Could it be the same swamp fairy following him here all this way? He shook his head. How could it be? But it shouldn't be here.

Thinking about it made him angry. He'd travelled a long hard journey to get here, and he wasn't about to see his prize taken from him by a swamp fairy. Why else would it be here if not to steal the spear?

'Who are you? What do you think you're doing?' he rasped through the hole.

Long moments passed then the green light appeared and darted up to Maggot's spyhole so fast, he fell back against the wall.

'Hey,' he cried, then froze. The swamp fairy froze. But the guards didn't come in. The swamp fairy buzzed and flickered in front of the hole, and he scrambled onto his feet again.

'Bugger off.' He scowled.

A high-pitched whirring sound emanated from it, sounding like laughter.

'What do you mean "bugger off"?' a high-pitched voice demanded. It sounded angry. 'I was here first. The spear is mine. What are you doing here, Shadow Demon?'

'I've come for the spear. Lord God Carmedrak wants it. And the Raven Queen sent me,' he lied. 'Besides, why should I tell you what I'm doing, you stupid...*thing*.'

The light burst through the hole and became a solid, green-skinned *thing*, smaller and much skinnier than he. Despite its small size, it pushed him to the floor and pinned him there.

'What do you mean "stupid"?' said a green face. It seemed female, sounded female, but looked too ugly to be sure. 'You're the stupid one. How do you think you're going to even get the spear?'

Maggot squirmed in disgust, heaved himself up and pushed the swamp fairy off.

'Ugh,' he spat out. 'A fairy touched me.'

He brushed his skin, wrinkling his nose in revulsion.

'I haven't got that far yet,' he growled. He wasn't about to explain any of his plans to this disgusting fairy that belonged in a jar lamp, even if he didn't have any plans. 'And you still haven't said why you're here.' He glared at her.

'Why should I?' she said.

Maggot opened and closed his mouth, looking for words but finding none. 'Stupid fairy. I should eat you.' He bared his fangs. It really annoyed him was that she was totally unafraid of him.

The fairy glared. 'Well, I don't see how you're going to get in there or undo the magic that binds it.'

'Well, even though you can get in there, how do you think *you* will get it out?' Maggot said. 'Even if you manage to undo the strongest of demon magic.'

It was the fairy's turn to open and close her mouth.

With an exasperated sigh, Maggot sank back against the wall, realising he could not actually find a way to get the spear out, and the fairy was just wasting his time. The sound of stone grinding against stone came again and they both dropped to the floor to look through the spyhole. The fairy got there first, its head right in his way. He shoved her back, and stuck his eye there instead. She scurried away, looking for another hole. Maggot's heart almost stopped in his chest.

Karhlusus himself walked into the room and stared. He was human-shaped, but his head had become sort of longer and grey and completely bald. His nose had lengthened and sunk, so it looked halfway between a demon's and a human's. His eyes were not human at all. They seemed black and copper with elongated demon slits for pupils. He was very tall and thin, and long claws came from his bony fingers rather than nails. Horrible magic exuded from him: Murk magic, human magic and something far more terrible. Pit magic. Despite everything he had seen, nothing frightened Maggot so much as this being.

The demon wizard stared at the spear, a mix of horror and obsession on his face. He reached out. The spear glowed orange as his fingers neared.

'Come now, Velistor. I feel you're restless today. I'm still part human. You yielded to me once, remember?' His voice was low and airy, not quite human. 'Soon the Murk will be ours. You'll be used against the one who crafted you—we needn't fear him. And after that, Baelthrom requires your services, but not before I've finished with you.' He took a breath, let his hand drop and turned from the spear. He said something to the guards on his way out as the entrance slid shut.

Maggot waited a few moments, then picked up the argument with his unwanted companion.

'The spear has got nothing to do with you,' he said.

'The Raven Queen didn't send you. What would a demon know of her?' The fairy scowled.

How dare she accuse him of lying?

'She showed us Velistor, and I've come to get it for her so she can give it to the Cursed King Demon Slayer,' he said, folding his arms over his belly in triumph.

'Wrong. *I* came to get it so she can give it to the Cursed King and free him and his knights of their curse,' the fairy retorted, shaking her head from side to side, straggly green hair flailing over her face.

'What?' Maggot was taken aback. How did a swamp fairy even know anything? 'Who sent you?'

'A seer did. So I came. Because I'm brave and powerful. Because I can move through Fairy Pockets best.'

The fairy was grinning at him in the most annoying way. What was a seer? Sounded human, and certainly didn't belong down here. A sly, clever thought came to him. He smiled deviously.

'Well, how do you propose to get it out then?'

The fairy stared back at him.

'Hmph,' she said, turned into green light, and darted back into the chamber.

Maggot dashed after her, pressing his eye against the hole.

'Wait,' he whispered. 'Maybe we can help each other.' He hated the thought. He alone wanted Issa's praise and Carmedrak's glory, but there was little time and he couldn't think how he would get into that chamber.

'I can't get in, and you can't undo the magic, or get it out, even if you could,' he said.

The swamp fairy darted back to the hole, flashing violent flickers of green so fast that he fell away, startled.

'And you think *you* can? You ugly demon,' she squeaked.

He swallowed his frustration. Was she just going to waste time arguing?

'Look, we don't have much time, and we can help each other,' he said grudgingly.

The swamp fairy hummed, the green flashes softening as she pondered his words.

'If I agree, you must promise not to eat me or trap me,' she said.

'I promise,' Maggot said, and placed a hand over his heart. He didn't mean it at all. Already he was thinking how to trap it. It would look nice in his room, glowing on the wall.

'Well?' squeaked the fairy, making him jump. 'What now?'

'Er...' Maggot racked his brains. 'Go next to it, and tell me what you feel when you touch it. From here I'll try to undo the bindings and the trap.'

She floated down beside the spear, materialised and fearfully stretched out a tiny hand towards it. Maggot pursed his lips and held his breath.

'The air feels hot and cold at the same time, and it feels as if it's trying to work me out,' she said.

She stretched a little closer and nearly touched it when there came a crackle and a flash of electricity that flung her backwards into the darkness. Was she still alive? The minutes passed but no one came in. She crept out. Maggot let go of his breath.

He closed his eyes, feeling the magic surrounding the spear—Pit Demon magic involving light. Shadow Demons used shadow magic.

'I think I know how it's bound,' he whispered. 'Velistor wants to be free,' he said in wonder. Could spears have feelings?

'Or maybe it wants to be free to spear me,' he added and swallowed. Well, he wouldn't let it. He told the spear mentally he was here to set it free. He wondered if the spear was listening.

'Hurry up.' The fairy huffed.

'Where there's Light, there's Shadow,' Maggot murmured, recalling Master Grouch's magic lessons.

Master Grouch never liked anything or anyone, but Maggot was sure he liked him the least and made him work harder than the others. He sighed, recalling the gruelling teachings and harsh penalties for the slightest mistakes. But those lessons were useful now, and slowly he wove his shadow magic, feeling the darkness hug him close as he drew it to him.

Slowly he formed tendrils of moveable shadow, and these he let drift through the hole as feathers to land upon the bindings of light he could see in his mind. The shadow bindings replaced, or negated the light bindings, and bit by bit they loosened. There were still piles and piles of chains of light on the spear. It would take him a while.

'Swamp fairy,' he said, his voice strained with effort. 'When I say, you must take the spear, if you can.'

'Of course I can,' she retorted. 'We fairies have our own magic, you know. Much purer than your disgusting demon magic.'

He chose to ignore her; he was too busy concentrating to argue anyway.

Bit by bit the bindings faded. Still he wove his shadows, feeling more and more tired and hungry as he worked. One of the main bindings faded and the rest suddenly followed.

'Now.' He gasped and slumped to the ground.

The swamp fairy reached for the spear once more, her hand trembling visibly. Her fingers touched the spear. Its surface moved and shimmered as if she had touched the surface of a pond. Maggot stared at it, mesmerised. She gripped it with both hands, and with all her might tried to lift it, but it dwarfed her and was impossibly heavy. She sagged after a second try.

The bindings were trying to reform under his shadow magic. His head throbbed and his vision blurred with the strain.

'Quickly,' he said. 'I can't hold it for long. Try again.'

He felt a strange magic then, like a smell he'd never smelt before—not unpleasant, but different. He stared in amazement as the swamp fairy grew and grew until she was as big as a human. Fairy magic, Maggot thought distastefully. Her green light grew too and soon the chamber was filled with it. He worried that the guards would see it. She reached forwards and picked up the spear. It was still heavy and she had to use both hands.

Maggot let go of his magic, and lay shaking, the relief threatening to make him pass out. The swamp fairy stared at the spear open-mouthed.

'Hurry, bring it here. We must go quickly,' he said.

She stared up and began poking the spear through the hole. Maggot fell back, both from her huge face looming at the hole and the horrid spear coming through. The spear flared orange in his presence. He heard voices growing louder outside. Panic flooded his body.

'Hurry, quick,' he rasped.

The fairy shook so violently, she had trouble pushing the spear into the hole. It stuck on a rock and was too long to get in all the way. She began to whimper and Maggot belched. There was no hope. He clenched his fist and punched the spear, knocking it away from the rock blocking it. Intense pain seared up his hand and shook his body. He was barely aware of the spear slipping past the rock and shooting in, followed by a ball of green light that smacked against the same rock and flopped to the ground.

He clutched his blackened hand, in too much pain to make any noise. His vision turned muddy as black demon tears filled his eyes and streamed down his cheeks.

'You fool,' the fairy said. 'No demon can touch that and live.'

Agony prevented him from retorting. The sound of a door grinding open came from below.

'Let's go.' Maggot gasped.

'But how do we carry it?'

The pain began to subside, but his hand was useless and stuck in a claw shape. He dissipated his damaged hand into the shadow; it would heal better that way. It gave him an idea. The spear hated demons, but did it hate shadows? He reached for the spear with his shadow hand. It felt horrible but there was no pain.

'Let's drag it,' he gasped.

Together they dragged the spear, inch by inch, back the way he had come. Below them a howl cut through the air. They stopped and cowered. What if they used magic to find them? Maggot hurried forwards, dragging the spear with his shadow hand, the fairy trembling as she pushed it from behind. From the look on her face, she wanted nothing more than to eat maggots and sleep, just like he did.

CHAPTER 30

Crystal Staff

'YOU'VE returned. Why?' Ayeth's beautiful voice was made even more musical in the blue crystal cavern.

Freydel considered his words. He thought he had prepared himself for returning to this place, but now he was here, in the power of Ayeth's presence, his thoughts scattered and everything he had planned to say seemed silly. He felt like a child.

'I came to warn you,' Freydel said honestly. Ayeth laughed, but he went on.

'There's something you'll do, a path you'll choose, that will cause the destruction of millions, maybe even whole planets. In the end it will destroy you too.'

Amusement flickered across Ayeth's face. Freydel tried to read his large oval eyes, hunting within for the being he would become. He could detect no real malice, only disturbance, or unsettlement, as if something ate away at Ayeth. Perhaps it was the beginnings of what he would become. But what was going to happen to him that would turn him into Baelthrom? Ayeth spoke his thoughts aloud.

'What is it I'll do? As much as I'd like it, I don't have that much power. No one does.' Ayeth stepped closer. This time he was alone, without the black-eyed female, and he didn't seek to intimidate or even approach Freydel this time. Though he was still unnerving.

'I wish I knew,' Freydel said.

A smile broke across Ayeth's mouth.

'I see. So you're in danger. You and your…loved ones? Maybe even your whole planet, from actions that I've undertaken.'

It wasn't a question, but Freydel found himself nodding. He found the whole conversation to be very dangerous for some reason and he was sweating.

'Yes, something like that,' said Freydel. 'But the being you will become... Even you won't remember who you are or what happened. Your body was destroyed and your essence scattered when it came out of the Dark Rift.'

'The Dark Rift?'

'Yes. It's a scar, a tear in the fabric of our galaxy created long ago. It's where darkness and death came from and entered our world.'

'Death? What is this word?' Ayeth frowned. 'I can read the essence of it, but I don't understand.' He seemed disturbed.

Freydel blinked in shock. Did they have no death? How old, then, were Ayeth and all the beings here?

'Death, it's... Our bodies grow old and die. They can't go on and so they wither and shut down. We have been dying younger and younger since the Dark Rift came.'

From Ayeth's face, Freydel could tell he was having a hard time comprehending this.

'Did I create this...Dark Rift?' Ayeth said.

'Perhaps. We don't know. The being you will become destroyed all our records. For this reason, we suspect that you might have,' Freydel said.

Ayeth turned and began to pace before the crystals, his robes shimmering.

'I do that? Millions destroyed? How can it be? What does it mean?' Ayeth spoke to himself. Despite his features being different to a human's, and therefore harder to read, it was obvious Ayeth was anguished. This moved Freydel.

'It doesn't have to be that way. That's why I have come. Perhaps there is something we can do,' Freydel said. He was already beginning to feel weak. Though it had been relatively easy to get here now that he had visited before, it was still incredibly taxing on his body. He gasped and leaned against a wall.

Ayeth lifted a hand. Powerful magic moved and Freydel felt strength return to his body. He nodded his thanks, wondering how Ayeth had done that. That he chose to help warmed him to the being.

'Tell me about the future. Tell me everything. Show me the orb of power you carry, and I promise not to take it.' Ayeth came close, his eyes wide and sparkling.

Freydel's hand instinctively brushed the orb in his pocket, but Ayeth seemed different this time. Almost innocent. Perhaps it was the female's influence on him that changed him, made him greedy. Was it she who led to his downfall?

'I'll tell you about the past, about everything, if you teach me your power,' Freydel said. His heart beat faster. It was all he wanted, to learn some of this being's power. He held great magic, and there was nothing in all the world that Freydel wanted more. His desire must have shown in his eyes, for Ayeth hesitated.

'I would teach you what you can learn. But why? Don't you have powers of your own? We're all given powers from the One, as to our need.'

'Yes, but I can learn more.' Freydel stepped forwards this time.

'What is it you think I can teach you? What is it you want to know?' Ayeth frowned.

'Anything, everything. I will learn what you value most,' Freydel said, then had a thought. 'You have something of mine. Not here, but where I'm from. You took my staff. It has power, magical power.'

'If I took it, then I'm sorry. Why don't we create another one here? That would be a start. While we work you will teach me of the future and your planet. What did your object of magic look like?'

Freydel smiled and pulled out the orb. If Ayeth desired it, he didn't show it this time. Instead he stood looking coolly at it as Freydel brought an image of the staff into it.

'It was made of oak wood, and one hundred and twenty-four spells of magic cast upon it. Unfortunately, I cannot remember them all,' Freydel said.

'You won't need to.' Ayeth smiled, his eyes alight with the task at hand. 'The crystal you hold remembers all.'

'You can see that?' Freydel asked. Could Ayeth actually *read* the encryption of his staff within the crystal?

'I can feel it,' he said. 'It's like reading words, but more feeling them. But one thing, we cannot use wood. We do not kill trees; that's barbaric.'

'How will you make it then?' Freydel frowned.

'We will ask the crystals,' Ayeth said. Freydel's frown deepened. 'Come, bring the orb closer to them.' He beckoned Freydel to the wall of blue crystal.

'Can the crystals see me?' Freydel asked, holding the orb close.

'Of course. They see and memorise everything, just as your eyes and brain do. Their structure is very similar to ours, though they look different. I see you don't understand, and that is hard for me to understand. Perhaps if you show me in your orb some of your world, I would understand better.'

Freydel considered. Perhaps he could show him Celene and his tower. Maybe some of the recent Midsummer Celebration events. He held up the orb and images formed. Ayeth came close, his eyes wide and intrigued.

'Your structures are...small. I see you destroy trees, and cut rock,' Ayeth said. His face was troubled, and it seemed he struggled to look. 'You put things in your mouth to swallow?'

Freydel was stunned. 'Yes, it's called eating. Don't you eat?'

'To consume another is darkness,' Ayeth said. 'That's what they do on other systems that are falling. But it's clear you are not falling, not yet. There is light within you and the grace of the One Source. I don't understand. No, we don't eat. The sun's light fills us. It's everything we need.'

'Like plants?' Freydel blurted.

'Like everything here. The plants and animals. Nothing *eats* anything else; that is violence,' Ayeth said, pain in his eyes. 'I try to stop Lona *eating*, but she gets sick.'

Freydel felt dizzy; he wanted to sit down and think. These beings were vastly different, or were they? There was a time on Maioria when life was eternal. Could you have eternal life at the expense of another? No, that couldn't be fair and that was how immortals survived. Could there really have been a time on Maioria when nothing ate anything else?

'It seems we are falling, Ayeth,' he said quietly. 'We're not the great beings we once were. But you are right, the One Source is still with us, in us. That's why I'm here, to stop the darkness engulfing us utterly.'

Ayeth smiled. A smile that filled Freydel with warmth and joy, making him wonder if he ever would become Baelthrom at all.

'Maybe you should understand something about me, Master Wizard

Freydel,' he said formally. 'Through the grace of the goddess, I've been tasked with a great healing mission—to help the Yurgha and stop them from falling. My powers are greater than any of my kin, and because of this I hold a great responsibility. It makes me tired sometimes—this responsibility and this power—but I'm strong and I must help them. I can see a future where they are healed, and my beloved Lona is what she once was.'

'Is that why they anger you? The other people of your race?' Freydel asked.

A flash of irritation passed across Ayeth's face and he looked into the middle distance.

'They don't understand as I do. They don't see the things I see. They don't have the power to do so. It is challenging to convince them.' Ayeth nodded.

'Is she your…lover?' Freydel wondered how to phrase it. The look in Ayeth's face said it all. His eyes turned bright.

'She's my light,' he said, then frowned, pain vivid. 'But she has become…sick. It's not her fault. Her race made…bad choices. But I know how to help them. With the crystal pyramids that the Anukon have given us, we have great power.'

'Anukon?' Freydel asked.

'Another race from a planet in the adjacent eveca,' Ayeth said.

Freydel frowned, wondering if he meant "galaxy", but he didn't ask. Simply knowing they spoke to and interacted with races from different planets was enough to make him faint.

'Soon, when the alignments are right, we'll fix everything that went wrong.' Ayeth smiled and nodded to himself.

'What do you call your own race?' Freydel asked.

'We? We call ourselves Aralans.'

Freydel was taken aback. So the Ancients remembered something of their past, even if they didn't understand it fully. Were these people really the ancestors to the Ancients? Had they come from a different planet to Maioria? Freydel's mind boggled.

'And the planet is Aralanastias?'

'Close. You're clever.' Ayeth smiled, impressed. 'Aralansia. Now. This staff.'

Freydel took a deep breath to calm himself.

'So, let us create this staff you have shown me,' Ayeth said.

'Wait. Won't a better substance be better? Surely rock will shatter and crack?' Freydel said.

'No, it's unbreakable except by tremendous force.' Ayeth laughed, as if what he'd said was silly and turned his attention to the blue crystal. Laying a six-fingered hand upon it, he began to speak in low simple words Freydel didn't understand.

'Loweth. Ahhri. Pelanya.'

Ayeth repeated the three words over and over as he stroked the crystal walls. He walked forwards, still touching the wall and stopped halfway around the chamber. Here he repeated the same words and moved his hands back and forth.

Freydel felt wondrous, pure magic move coming from both Ayeth and the crystal wall he touched. Under Ayeth's hands the crystal shimmered aqua, then a long shard of it came out and floated in mid-air.

'This crystal wills to become your staff.' Ayeth smiled. 'I was concerned no crystal would want to leave its home planet, but crystals have vast wisdom. Now for the shape.'

Ayeth closed his eyes and began moving hands back and forth as he murmured new words. The crystal began to lengthen and straighten.

'Bring your crystal orb close and show the crystal your staff,' Ayeth said, his voice strained a little in concentration. Freydel did as he asked.

The blue crystal reached the length of his old staff and straightened. Then its edges became smooth and round until it was perfect.

'Take your staff,' Ayeth said, his eyes wide and smiling.

Freydel gripped the staff and felt it bind to him, just as his old staff had done. It had all of the old spells upon it, and more. Spells he had forgotten, spells he had yet to learn. To hold his staff again brought tears to his eyes. Ayeth must have seen for he spoke in a humble voice.

'I'm sorry if I took something of yours wrongly. I only know who I am now, not who I'll be in the future. That's where you have far more power than I do. There are many futures and perhaps I'll never be this thing of which you speak.'

'Thank you,' Freydel breathed, marvelling at the glittering blue staff. 'It feels so powerful.'

'The crystal will teach you things better than I can,' Ayeth said. 'Now, tell me more of your world. Tell me about your orb.'

Freydel nodded, and began with the Ancients and the splitting of Maioria's magic. But all the while he spoke, he wanted only to learn more of Ayeth's power and do half the things he could. There was so much he didn't know, so much he could become. After all, it was his yearning for knowledge and power that had made him a powerful Master Wizard in the first place.

CHAPTER 31

Little Bear

JARLAIN awoke to a sore back from lying on the hard ground.

Cold dew covered everything and dampened her sack-clothing. The birds were singing so it was some time past dawn. She rubbed her sides then her arm. There was no pain or bruises; all her wounds were healed. She was just horribly stiff.

The Forest Lord had really come to her. No, the Forest Guardian he'd called himself. She wasn't thirsty or hungry. The sacred waters still filled her. She tried to remove the blindfold, but intense pain throbbed her head and her hands trembled. So, Hai's curse still remained.

She focused on her inner sight. In shades of red, walls of rock towered above her on both sides. She was still in the ravine. Though now her body was no longer broken, she had a chance to get out. Could she get out blindfolded? It would be dangerous.

She stood up. A strange lightness filled her body. She felt strong and pure and oddly otherworldly. She wished the Forest Guardian was still with her.

The foresight came upon her. She saw, in her mind, dark shapes moving through the trees. Great beasts with no life force that seemed like black holes in the forest. The vision went. Her heart pounded and a shiver ran down her back. The beasts were near.

She searched for somewhere to hide—a cave or crag that could conceal her, but there was nothing good. Feeling with her hands she found a stunted bush nestled between the two cliffs and inched herself behind it, wincing as thorns scraped her bare legs. Huddling her knees, she quietened her breathing.

A wave of silence descended upon the forest as the birds stopped tweeting and flitting between the branches. The hairs on her neck rose and fell. She hated not being able to see anything again and the choking vulnerability. She closed her eyes and focused on her hearing. Was that soft footfalls of padded feet?

Her inner vision flashed again. Above her were the same dark beasts: two of them. They were scenting the air and looking down into the ravine. She had no idea if they could see her or not. There wafted a sickly sweet smell that made her gag.

Footfalls sounded, high on her left. A twig moved, snouts sniffed. She trembled. Of course they could smell her, but could they get down into the ravine? One gave a strange growl. These beasts weren't normal. Perhaps they were one of the undead things Marakon had told her of.

Heavier footfalls came, no longer trying to be quiet. A rock tumbled into the ravine, then another. They were trying to get down. What could she do? Her groping hands found a pebble and a useless twig. She couldn't fight. She couldn't run. Had she been saved by Doonis only to die in the teeth of these beasts?

More rocks fell, closer. She began to pray and shake, feeling pitiful and wretched. Her only hope was that they wouldn't find her. A fool's hope.

Something growled straight ahead followed by more sniffing. One howled, filling the ravine with noise. Jarlain cowered.

It was answered from above by an almighty roar, making her heart pound in her head and her blood run cold. Bears had come too, to fight over her remains. But surely they wouldn't harm her? She was Navadin. Doonis had shown her the bear riders and Hai had said to call them. Now they were here, she was terrified. The beasts scuffled to and fro, but didn't come closer. The bear roared again, and the beasts howled back.

Rocks crashed down the cliff, followed by the pounding of heavy feet. She clung to the wall as the bear and beasts roared and howled at each other. There came the sound of teeth snapping, grunts and violent scuffling, then howls of pain.

Now and again her inner vision showed a mess of red and dark. Three beasts fighting, one bigger and heavier, the other two tall but slender, like wolves or cats. She smelt blood, she had never *smelt* blood before. Perhaps it was because of her heightened senses now her eyes were bound, or perhaps all her senses were heightened after Doonis came to her.

Blind and helpless, she flinched at every snarl and roar. The vicious struggle went on for a long time. She glimpsed one beast lying still and unmoving, but the other seemed fit and fast as ever. She pushed the visions away and covered her ears, but still the roaring came through. It seemed to go on forever.

The snarling and scuffling ceased. A sighing whine came, and something lumbered slowly towards her, sniffing the air. She stayed still, frozen. For the briefest moment the face of a bear appeared clear as day in her mind, as if the image had been put there by the bear. Her mind reeled in shock—the bear was the same one she'd seen before. The same scar lifted its lip slightly, the same huge and powerful body. She waited for it to attack, almost giving herself up to him.

'Come,' a voice said in her mind, though it sounded as clear as if someone had spoken it aloud. If she weren't so scared, she would have thought it came from the bear. She stayed still, silent, praying the bear would go away.

'Come, or die here,' the voice said again. It had to be the bear.

It stepped closer. She could feel its hot breath. Why wasn't it attacking her?

'Are you talking to me?' Her voice trembled. She readied herself for it to lunge at her.

'More will come. I must rest,' the bear said.

Had Doonis really done something to her so she could hear the beasts of the forest? She inched herself onto her feet.

'Why have you come to me?' she asked.

'You called me. Ood sent me.'

'I can't see,' she said.

'So you'll die. I'll carry you,' the bear said. His answers were abrupt and simple.

'Carry me? Ood is Doon? I don't remember calling anyone.'

'You are "she" sent to us. Navadin. Hurry, immortals swarm the forest.'

Navadin, riders of the bear. Little Bear. Hai had said those things. Wasn't that a dream? Or a vision...

She reached towards the bear, her hand trembling as she doubted whether it really was speaking to her and not just her crazed mind.

She found its snout and flinched from the size of it. Her head could fit in its jaws. The bear didn't move as she gently touched him. The soft, puffed skin of the scar lifting his lip. A hot wet patch dripping. Blood—its or the beasts she couldn't tell. She moved back over its huge head and neck. Hot blood dripped in several places.

'You're wounded,' she said.

'*I need rest,*' he repeated. '*You can't see. I'll carry you out of here.*'

'I ride you?' The thought terrified her and she worried for his wounds.

'*Hurry,*' was all he said, almost a growl this time. She felt him crouch low.

The bear was right, about everything, and she would die here. After a moment's hesitation, she inched her leg over his back, trying to avoid the bloody patches covering him.

He immediately set off. She clung to his thick fur and struggled at first to work with his lumbering gate. She couldn't sit up and instead wrapped her arms around his neck. The smell of him filled her nostrils— a wild animal smell.

In her red vision something white glared beyond the rocks where she had been lying.

'Wait. Hai's staff.'

The bear stopped and she slipped off his back. As soon as she touched the staff, she knew Hai was gone. Tears filled her eyes, despite the anger she felt for everything he had done to her and caused her to suffer. Her home was gone. Were her kin even alive anymore? There was nothing to return to. There was only forwards, and Marakon.

She pushed the staff behind her back under her sackcloth and mounted the bear again. She buried her face in his fur as he carried her out of the ravine, trying and failing to stop the tears. The world had changed and nothing would be the same again, but something was blooming within her—an ancient memory, a feeling of coming home after a very long journey.

It was hardest to hang on when the bear ran. All she could do was cling and bounce awkwardly. He seemed to run for a long time; she could hear his laboured breathing and worried when the wounds still dripped blood onto her leg.

He slowed beside a river and she got off his back to drink alongside him. She remounted and they carried on. Finally they stopped in a cold place. Her red vision revealed only darkness. The sound of a river came in the distance.

'Is this home?' she asked, slipping off his back.

'Yes, for now. The immortals are coming. We must leave soon.' His voice sounded strained in her mind and he flopped onto the ground with a sigh.

'I can help your wounds,' she said. He didn't reply. She wondered if he was asleep. 'But first they must be washed.'

She took the strip of sackcloth that she had bound her own wounds with and went to the river. Hai's staff gave her greater confidence when she walked. It seemed to read the ground and give information back to her through her grasp. She suspected the staff could do many more things, but that she would have to find out over time.

She washed the cloth and herself in the river and went back to the bear. Carefully, she found his bloody wounds by feeling over his body and wiped at them, trying to clean them as best she could. He lay still, breathing heavily.

Twice more she went back to the river to rinse the cloth, then sat down and laid her hands upon him. She focused her mind on the wounds and imagined them closing as the elders had taught her to do. She was not a great healer, but she had some ability, and she felt the wounds respond a little.

When she tired, she lay down beside him, listening to his slow rhythmic breathing.

When she awoke she was certain it was dark. The bear hadn't moved beside her, but he still breathed and his wounds were no longer wet and bleeding. She lay there thinking about Hai's staff, wondering who of her people still lived. In the staff, Hai would have inscribed the story of the Gurlanka.

'High Elder Hai, if you have written our story, please show it to me now,' she whispered, touching the staff and closing her eyes. Images came, like a vision, but clearer like memories and without the ambiguity of the future.

She saw the Maphraxies invade, as Marakon had said they would. Terrifying man-beasts without souls and great black lizards that could fly and breathe fire. They destroyed her village and her people fled. Her heart bled.

She saw Hai, and all that remained of the other tribes, gathering at the Centre. Hai went with the Hidden Ones and made the final journey to Doonis. She understood then why she had been given the gift. She was to be the first of the Navadin, and she would bring that skill and knowledge to the seven tribes.

But first she had to find Marakon. With everything that had happened, she had lost the thread of where he was, but she could still feel the bear stone he had, more now than ever.

When the dawn light poked through her blindfold, she made a fire. It took a long time to find and collect sticks and moss, then use the staff to strike sparks from a rock as she had seen Hai do. Twice the sparks hit her bare flesh making her yelp before the moss caught light.

By the time the fire was lit, the bear finally roused. She listened as he walked heavily to the river. *He must ache and be sore all over,* she thought. He splashed around in the river for a long while and she wondered what he was doing. When he dropped a cold, heavy, wet fish in her lap she almost jumped out of her skin.

So, he'd been fishing, and these fish were for her. Everything that this bear did surprised her. Settling down beside her, he snapped and sucked and tore at his own fish. She didn't like fish and never ate them at home, but there was nothing else and she'd learned to be grateful for anything until eternity. She put the whole thing on the fire and poked a stick into it to tell when it was done.

'What's your name?' she asked when the bear stopped eating and rested once more.

An image came into her mind: a cave, deep and long, and then danger striking out of the dark. An immortal like the beasts he had just killed. Formidable danger that was overcome.

'So that's how you got your scar? Hmm, I have no name for that description. How about Fenn? It means fearless in my language.'

The bear said nothing, but she felt acceptance. He yawned, sighed and lay still. In her red vision, she watched his huge, magnificent, sleeping body for a long time, thinking about how strange her life had become since Marakon had walked into it.. As long as she could feel him out there through the bear stone, she would spend her life searching for him.

Now she had a powerful companion, this harsh new world no longer seemed quite so scary. She just prayed she would reach Marakon before the distance between them lengthened.

CHAPTER 32

Demon Alliance

MARAKON stared at the bear stone Jarlain had given him and wondered if he would ever see her again.

She would become a High Elder and be a great leader of her people. He smiled. With all the trouble that seemed to follow him, she was far safer without him.

'It's ready,' Issa said.

He looked to where she'd finished drawing a huge symbol of the Murk in the dirt, big enough to fit them all in and their horses. He held her sea-green eyes for a moment. Her gaze was steady, hard even, and reminded him of how he used to be—a tough, bitter young soldier. Bitterness made you strong but reckless—it could get you killed. There was much she needed to learn and he could teach her, but at least for now she had courage and was willing.

Tucking the stone into his pocket, he stood up and gripped the pommel of his sword for reassurance. Going to the Murk was the last thing in the world he wanted to do. His breath caught in his throat at the thought of it.

His knights were watching him, waiting for his command, hands holding their horses' reins. The sky was darkening with dusk and it was turning cool.

'Knights, it seems today is the day we fight for our ultimate freedom. Whether or not we survive what's to come, I'll never forget you. To have known you and fought beside you is the greatest honour any man can wish for. If I should fall, know Zanufey is with me, as she is with all of you.

'But first, there are two who must be invited to join our order.' He grinned as Bokaard and Issa looked at him wide-eyed.

'Well, it's obvious, isn't it?' he said, dropping all ceremony and grinning. The knights nodded and laughed.

'Issa, Queen of Ravens—' He almost laughed when she grimaced. '— do you wish to take the honour of knighthood and join the order Knights of the Raven?'

She opened and closed her mouth for a moment, then nodded. 'I do.'

'Then, please, come here and kneel. There's no time for extended ceremony, as is often the case before or even during a battle. We can have a proper ceremony later.'

He gestured for her to come closer and she awkwardly kneeled before him. Drawing his sword, he tapped her on each shoulder with the blade as he spoke. Memories of knighting people came rushing back and he saw in his mind the faces of the knights he had long forgotten as he spoke.

'Issalena Kammy Raven Queen, do you swear allegiance to the Knights of the Raven? Do you accept the vows and take the oaths that such an allegiance demands? Will you face evil with courage and strength, protect the weak, never deal with enemies or traitors, never give evil counsel or aid evil? Will you always, to the best of your ability, seek and defend that which is just, true and pure?'

'I do and I will,' Issa said solemnly.

'Then rise, Knight Issalena Kammy. Welcome to the Knights of the Raven,' he said.

She stood up, looking incredibly nervous. Everyone cheered, making her colour.

Next was Bokaard. There was a gleam in his eyes and possibly tears as he knelt and looked up.

'I knew there was something more about you, you white belly. As if the gods had marked you,' he said.

Marakon grinned. He knighted him, then made him rise.

'And so, the first knights of our new order have been ordained.' He smiled. 'Let many more follow and our ranks swell.'

Cheering and clapping rang through the forest. He didn't want to ruin the moment by adding that this was the last time he would be knighting anyone, and his successor was already in mind.

'Is that it?' Issa asked, and he laughed. She'd clearly been expecting more—maybe a flash of light or knightly gift just as he had when he was knighted thousands of years ago.

'Yes. Did you want a bigger crowd and roses?' Marakon grinned.

'No.' She coloured. 'Well, maybe. I expected a longer ceremony, I guess. Maybe some divine spark of light or something. Will I get armour? A sword?'

'Yes, in time. And training, lots of it, with many different weapons. Your horse will be trained too,' he said.

Duskar pricked his ears and looked at them.

'I don't know if that'll go down too well.' She looked dubiously at the black horse. Could he be trained to be a war horse? Perhaps he was too free-spirited. 'Your armour looks a bit heavy, but I could do with training in plate. I guess all that'll have to wait. Are you ready to go to the Murk?'

He nodded. She knew he wasn't really ready; none of them were. No one could be prepared for what they were about to find down there.

'Expect to find hell. They're at war,' she said.

Marakon spoke loudly so all could hear. 'The time has come to meet our destiny and face that for which we have returned, by the grace of the goddess. The time has come for us to finish what was started millennia ago and for which we have suffered ever after. Let us make right our wrong and redeem ourselves in the eyes of the goddess and the world.'

He purposefully stepped first onto the symbol of the Murk, bringing his horse with him. The others followed, faces hard and keen.

'Remember the difference between the demons. Only the grey Shadow Demons are our…friends,' he said.

Issa gave a half smile of encouragement, took a deep breath, and stepped into the centre of the symbol. The knights and their horses clustered around her. Ehka was perched on the blanket on Duskar's back. They had already nicked the horses for a pinprick of blood, and now they held the knives to their own hands. She grimaced and let the bright drops fall upon the ground.

As soon as her blood touched it, it hissed and became puffs of smoke. The symbol burst into green light. The light engulfed them and air rushed from beneath as if they were falling down a hole.

Light and movement stopped. Then the sound of war filled her ears. They drew their swords in unison as the battle scene unfolded.

They stood at the base of a mountain range that ringed a vast plain. In the centre of the plain stood the huge black spire of Carmedrak Rock, striking up into the sky. Thousands of demons, brown and black, surged before them, and behind them was a mass of howling grey Shadow Demons.

The black, indistinct greater demons lunged towards them. The knights bristled forwards, blades shining. Marakon danced his sword in a stabbing motion that pushed the demons back most effectively. He sliced down then side to side in the shape of a cross, so rapidly his blade was barely visible, before plunging it into the partially immaterial demon. It fell back screaming, maybe not killed but badly wounded in some way.

She tried to copy him but lacked the speed to be as effective, and resorted to desperately stabbing as the knights pushed against her sides, forming a protective wall.

There was no time to mount their horses, so the prancing animals were pushed back behind the knights for protection. They were surrounded by demons, friend and foe, so they couldn't bolt even if they wanted to. Duskar's nostrils flared and he stamped his feet unhappily.

'Behead the brown ones and remember to duck when they explode,' Marakon shouted over the din of clashing metal.

A brown Grazen's head toppled off his sword. Its ugly demon features made her shiver. Marakon swiftly booted the body in the chest, kicking it away. The knights bunched backwards and ducked. She watched in awe as it turned to molten rock then exploded. She caught an equally shocked glance from Bokaard.

'They explode on death; be ready for it,' Marakon shouted.

The knights stayed in a tight knot until they'd managed to clear space around them. In the heaving mass of demons behind, she glimpsed King Gedrock immersed in battle, surrounded by enemies. It seemed as though he was retreating. She pointed to him and shouted at Marakon.

'The Shadow Demon king, the one I showed you.'

Marakon shoved a demon back and dared to glance to where her finger pointed.

'Knights, retreat. Fall back to the Shadow Demon king,' he yelled.

Following his lead, they moved backwards, swords never ceasing their blows. Everything was a chaotic mess of demon faces, explosions, blood and her swiping sword as she parried and struck again and again. Mostly she couldn't tell if she was causing damage and all the time she tried to ignore the demon screams and howls that rent her soul.

They manoeuvred beside Gedrock. He stepped back, moving his demons in front of him to hold the front line, and took a moment to look at her then Marakon. The vertical slits within his yellow eyes narrowed then widened and his frightening face was a mix of expressions she couldn't easily read.

'I came, as promised,' she said, standing tall.

'We won't win, unless we get the spear. More will come from the Pit until the gates are closed,' he said, his face grim.

She nodded and looked to Carmedrak Rock.

'I'll go get it, then,' she said and swallowed.

'How?' he asked.

'I don't know, but maybe I can fly, and maybe there's a chance in the Dead Realm.'

He nodded.

'The Demon Slayer comes to the Murk,' Gedrock addressed Marakon. Marakon gave a short nod, his lips pursed. She wondered what emotions were ploughing through the man who had spent all his lives fighting demons.

'My knights will not knowingly harm a Shadow Demon,' he said.

'Then let's fight together, human and demon, for the first time,' Gedrock roared and turned to engage the advancing enemy, raising his strange double sword.

Issa jumped beside Marakon as the Grazen followed by Pit Demons surged. Though the Grazen had solid form, she struggled to even cut their tough skin. A stabbing motion with her sword only kept them back. Breathless, she lunged and tried again, only nicking her enemy.

A claw swiped her cheek, knocking her sideways and dazing her. Blood trickled down her face from a shallow cut. She heard Gedrock howl and saw her attacker fall, beheaded. She ducked as it exploded, and showered them all in sparks and dust. Decapitating them was the only way to kill them, but there was no way her sword could hack through their tough necks. She wasn't being much use. Her sword arm ached already and her wounded leg throbbed.

She was doing nothing here and Gedrock was right—they needed the spear. The enemy was too numerous. She pulled back. The knights filled her place.

Hopefully Carmedrak Rock would be empty of demons, but it was a long way from here to there. Zorock was beginning to pass behind the mountains. How dark would it get? She tried to feel for Zanufey's moon, but couldn't still her mind in the midst of battle. It seemed far too late to start making her plans on the battlefield.

She squeezed through the press of demons towards Duskar who was stood pinned with the other horses by the rocks. The Shadow Demons partially materialised as she moved through their lines. They eyed her silently as she passed, but left her unhindered. Could she trust them? If they so much as touched Duskar...

A small, flying demon caught her eye, and she started towards it. But the name "Maggot" died on her lips when she saw its face. It didn't have a protruding tooth, and its eyes were different. The pain for the little demon took her by surprise. She didn't even know how he'd died. He'd saved her and now she'd never get the chance to repay the favour.

She looked at the vast enemy horde and her heart sank. Would there even be enough time to find the spear? She needed days, not minutes. Just getting to the rock would take a few hours walking. They couldn't possibly hold the fight for that long and were already falling back. But she had to try.

She sheathed her sword and gripped the raven talisman. She smiled. Who needed to walk when you could fly?

'Make me raven,' she commanded.

Her body shrank rapidly and became weightless. She ruffled her feathers delightfully and looked up at Ehka hovering above her, already waiting for her to follow. She laughed and cawing came out of her beak.

He cawed back.

She jumped into the air, beating her wings hard to rise fast above the demons and get out of sight of the Pit Demons as quickly as possible.

Far away in the distance the black obelisk loomed and the battlefield sped away below. Flying here, in this foreign, barren, demon land, held less of the glory of flying in Maioria and felt far more dangerous.

As she neared Carmedrak Rock, she angled her wings down and landed on its tip, scanning the skies for demons. Most of them were back by the battle. She couldn't see any demons below so she circled down to the ground, hugging the sides of the rock to avoid being spotted.

The entrance to the rock was a huge, dark, yawning maw. She shivered. She couldn't simply walk in the front door. She looked for another way in. There were smaller entrances halfway up, but then she would have to find her way down on the inside. Gedrock had said the spear was underground.

She looked up and froze, her heart pounding. Karhlusus, the Demon Wizard, stood on a balcony halfway up. He was dressed in white and his face as white as his clothes. She considered the demon man for a moment. His face was deformed, half human, half demon. If she looked hard she could see the massive dark shadow of the demon King Kull surrounding him. Just the sight of him made her shiver.

He looked down and she darted forwards into the entrance, her heart in her beak. After a several long moments, she turned and peered up. He was gone but he was in there somewhere. She'd hoped he would be on the battlefield. Had he seen her? Could he feel her presence? She didn't like it at all.

From the dark entrance, roars came. She darted up to a jutting edge and flattened herself against the rock, praying Ehka hid too.

Twenty or more greater demons emerged from the entrance, snarling and gnashing at each other as they ran on clawed feet. They spread their shadowy wings and launched into the air, screaming their gut-wrenching howls as they flew towards the battle.

Gedrock was right; more would come from the Pit so long as the gates were open. Not only would they have to kill Karhlusus, they'd have to close the gates as well. Marakon would know what to do; he had to or they were doomed.

CHAPTER 33

Stealing the Spear

MAGGOT ran, dragging the spear in his shadow hand, pulling the swamp fairy along behind him.

They'd covered it in a discarded sack to try and hide its glow.

'I can't run that fast,' the fairy wailed.

Maggot ignored her. They had to go fast; nothing else mattered. Every demon in the rock was hunting for the spear, and that terrified him. He prayed the Grazen didn't know which way the spear had gone, or who had stolen it.

Not stolen, saved, he reminded himself. The Murk was finally going to be theirs again. Carmedrak Rock would be freed. Lord Carmedrak would give him greatness and Issy would be impressed. That's if they ever got the spear out. He tried to go faster.

They no longer appeared to be going straight, but upwards. The growing dread that he'd eventually be forced to use the main hallways became a reality. The tunnel led out onto a ledge above the main hallway. Light spilled in from flaming braziers on the opposite wall.

The gruff rasping of demon voices came from beyond and they fell back into the darkness. His heart was pounding so loudly he could barely hear their words.

'Spear's gone,' said one.

'Praise Carmedrak it has. I hate that 'fing,' said another.

They sounded like the demons from earlier. There came a third voice but he couldn't make out what was said.

'We still have to find it. It can't have gone far,' said the first.

'Who'd steal it anyway? I hope we don't find 'em. I'd much rather be out there fightin'. We always get the shit jobs,' said the second.

Their voices and the clanking of their spears on stone faded away, but still Maggot remained pinned to the wall, afraid to make the slightest noise.

'Go on. They've gone,' the swamp fairy whispered impatiently.

Maggot licked his lips and nodded. His heart still beat too fast, but he was determined not to let the fairy know he was scared. He tried to move forwards into the light, but his feet wouldn't obey. He actually had to lift his leg with his hands and place it forward.

He edged farther into the light, closing his eyes and pressing so hard against the wall he thought he'd become part of it. The fairy followed him and gave an exasperated noise.

'Stupid fairy,' he muttered. 'No idea about anything.'

This whole thing was a bad idea. No, a terrible idea. He scanned the hallway for another hole to slip into, but there were none. It was very narrow on the ledge; only his claws digging into the rock and his flapping wings stopped him from slipping all the way down. If he fell there would be no way back up since he couldn't fly with the spear as well. Any Grazen passing would see them, and they would be lucky to see another hour of life. He kept his shadow hand low in the shadows. It had gone past aching. Now it was numb and he couldn't feel it at all.

There came a boom that shook the whole hallway. The walls shuddered from the blast and rocks dislodged themselves from the ceiling. Maggot struggled to cling to the wall as the rock under his feet crumbled.

He fell, the fairy squealing as she was dragged down with him. He scrambled to his feet, choking in the dust, and froze as voices came from somewhere.

'I can't lift the spear again,' she said, staring up at the ledge now high above them.

'Some use fairy magic is,' he growled.

She scowled at him, making her even uglier. The voices came louder.

'What do we do?' She was shaking.

'Run,' Maggot said, desperately looking around.

They struggled with the spear, turned and ran away from the approaching voices down the bright passage. Frequently the light would dissipate Maggot's shadow arm and the spear would drop. He had to pick it up five times, each time praying to Carmedrak to help them. The voices were gaining on them. He could hear what they were saying.

'What made all this mess?' said one, followed by, 'Look there. Footprints.'

Maggot found more strength in his legs and dragged fairy faster.

'We can't outrun them.' She gasped. 'We have to hide.'

'I know that,' he growled, but everywhere he looked there wasn't even a hole or cranny into which they could crawl. He stumbled on, the voices behind them, just around the corner.

'There, look.' The fairy pointed to the base of a door where a rat or some other creature had chewed the corner away.

'I can't get in that in this light, and who knows what's on the other side,' he said.

'Maybe we can hide the spear in there,' she said.

Looking at the hole, a lump in his throat formed. 'Go, I'll push the spear inside.'

'What about you?' she said, wide-eyed and shaking.

'I'll find another place,' he said, trying to convince himself. The voices were so close now.

'Go,' he pushed her towards the hole. She became a tiny ball of light and zipped inside.

He shoved the spear in after her, immediately glad to be rid of it, and looked around for somewhere else to hide. This was the last door before the hallway turned right. The next hallway was the same as this one with no place to hide. He sagged. What would Master Grouch do now?

Flow. He would shadow flow. Maggot ran back to the door, stuck his hand through the hole and out of the light. He melded it into shadow and imagined himself flowing into his hand. He scrunched his eyes and willed really hard.

His hand began to feel like it was swelling as the rest of him shrank. It was working, but slowly. He was not good at shadow flowing. The more of him he got into the shadow, the faster he flowed until shadow engulfed him fully. The cool dark was wonderfully soothing and he stayed there for a moment, a formless pool of unmoving dark.

Clawed footsteps clattered on the stone floor outside. He moved away from the door, holding his breath.

The footsteps passed.

He materialised, let go of his breath and looked at the fairy. The spear was lying where he'd shoved it. Neither spoke for a long time. The footsteps did not return.

They were in a room that was virtually pitch black save for a dull light that came from somewhere on the opposite side. A beetle scurried across the floor. He jumped on it and gobbled it up, all crunchy on the outside and squidgy in the middle. The fairy groaned in disgust.

Heavy chains dragging on stone came from the far side of the room, making them both jump. A jangling noise was followed by a gravelly sigh. Maggot froze. It may have been a good idea to hide in here, but until that brazier went out or the door miraculously opened, he was well and truly stuck in the room, a prison of his own making, and who knew what was in that corner.

Becoming curious, he inched his way over. A tug on his tail gave him a start, and he whirled around.

'What are you doing?' the fairy hissed.

'Well, how else are we going to get out of here if we don't look for a way?' he said.

'It's dangerous,' she moaned and shivered.

He pitied her weakness. 'Come, I don't think it's dangerous. I'd feel it.'

He turned, inched forwards, and paused when another rumbling sigh came. In the shadows a great mass moved. There were huge chains bolted to the floor. He crouched in the darkness, the fairy hovering behind, her green light muted.

'Hello?' he croaked. The fairy buzzed.

The great mass froze then roared, thrusting its head into the dim light, baring and snapping its fangs. One eye was missing and the brutal scar across it had barely healed. The other eye was a mixture of fear, madness and fury.

Maggot tore back to the other side of the room, too terrified to scream, the fairy tumbling after him. There he cowered and watched as the big demon slumped to the floor. When it didn't move for a long time, Maggot gathered his courage and stepped closer, ignoring the fairy's grasping hands and protests.

'Don't be scared,' Maggot said to the demon, his voice trembling. 'I'm a Shadow Demon too.' He held himself proudly.

The chained demon looked at him with one eye, the rage and

madness calming. The demon's silence was unnerving and Maggot dropped his proud stance.

'Um. What are you doing here?' he asked.

'Bound,' the demon said and pulled on his chains. 'Karhlusus enslaves, tortures, chains—sends us to Baelthrom.' The demon spoke in stutters, as if talking took considerable effort.

Maggot grimaced and noticed the scars littering the demon's body. As he came closer, he noticed that what he thought was a wall, were bars. The room was a prison and much larger than he had thought. Chains rattled farther away.

'There are others?' he asked.

The demon nodded. 'Many others. Many prisons. Many floors of prisons.'

The fairy pulsed brighter and he glimpsed more bars beyond these, separating each cell as far as the eye could see. Mounds huddled in the corner of each cell.

That's what would become of him if he was caught. He shivered.

'All Shadow Demons?' he whispered.

'Mostly,' the demon said. 'Some Grazen—those who fought him. Though he killed most.'

'What's your name?' Maggot asked.

The demon didn't look at him, but flopped onto his front. His arms were bent in odd positions, as if they had been broken and healed that way.

'Don't remember. These chains are magic. Make me forget. Stop me becoming shadow and escaping.'

Maggot's mind began to spin. He slumped onto the floor too, holding his head with both hands. Had the Grazen really fought against Karhlusus? That changed everything. Would they join the Shadow Demons to fight him again?

'No demon should be chained and afraid. No demon should forget their own name.' Maggot moaned loudly.

'Shhh,' said the swamp fairy. 'You'll bring trouble. We must go now. They'll check everywhere and we can't hide forever.'

'Where? We can't get out and we need to get them out too.' He jabbed a finger at the chained demon.

'I don't see how you're going to do that.' She straightened, hands on hips.

'Well, what do you think we should do? I can't get out of here, and you can't carry Velistor on your own.'

The other demon lifted his head. 'Velistor? Here?' He cowered away from them.

'We've rescued Velistor. Great Carmedrak told me to. And the Raven Queen has need of it.' Maggot stood tall as he spoke. 'We'll kill Karhlusus.'

A noise came from outside, sending them into a panic. Dragging Velistor into the farthest corner of the room, they hid in the dark as the bolt on the door ground open. Two guards carried something that smelled delicious and tossed it into the cell where it landed almost on the chained demon's head.

The door slammed shut and was bolted quickly. The door to the next prison cell opened and another carcass was tossed in. Maggot barely breathed until after the last door slammed shut.

The demon ripped into the rotting meat. Maggot inched closer, hoping to get a mouthful.

'If we free you, you can help us escape,' Maggot said.

A scrap fell and he darted his tongue out to snatch it up. It was all slimy and smelly and delicious. At least they got good food in here.

'How can we escape?' the bigger demon said.

'We can use the spear,' the fairy said. 'Use the spear to undo the chains.'

Maggot stared at her, grudgingly impressed. 'We can try, but then what?'

The fairy's lower lip quivered. 'I don't know, but we could try anyway and think of something whilst we do it.'

The big demon flinched as they struck the spear tip into his chains. Where the white metal hit, red sparks flew and a thin line of hot metal appeared. The demon yanked on his chain and it splintered.

Maggot stared in awe. 'The spear can break the strongest metal,' he said, recalling the myths surrounding Velistor.

The demon stood to his full ten-foot height and stretched himself with a groan. His back looked like it would be forever bent. Maggot didn't want to know how long he had been chained in here.

'I remember,' the demon said. Shaking his head as if to shake the fog from his mind. 'My name is...Grunt. I am Grunt.' He gave a short laugh.

Maggot grinned and jumped, flapping his wings.

'We must free the others,' he said, and showed Grunt how he had created his shadow hand to lift the spear.

With a trembling shadow hand, Grunt lifted the spear and struck it against the metal bars. They seared and snapped in a flash of light. Bending them back, he climbed into the next cell.

They didn't pause until all twenty demons were free of their chains.

Issa and Ehka found their way into Carmedrak Rock through the bars of a small window. Inside it was dark and silent. After a moment listening for danger, she shifted out of her raven form and pressed herself against the wall.

'We can't simply walk or fly around in here,' she whispered to Ehka, loosening the neck of her tunic.

Taking a deep breath, she lifted the talisman and closed her eyes. How she hated going to the Dead Realm. Why couldn't Keteth have given her any other gift but this? She spoke the entrance command. The raven talisman tingled and magic flared.

Rather than falling forwards into silver, indigo light engulfed her, filling her being. She was aware of Ehka cawing.

Instead of the shadow world, the blue moon rose before her, bigger than a sun and so close she could touch it. She breathed deeply as great power moved within her. When she opened her eyes, the moon had faded, and the familiar, foreboding ghost world materialised.

Ehka was by her feet. Indistinct grey things moved, both small and large. They seemed formless and malleable, and they had no faces that she could see. Were they dead demons or the souls demons had taken? Did demons even have souls? She wondered. As long as they left her alone, they weren't a threat.

She was keenly aware that she didn't have long in this realm before she would begin to become part of it. Being trapped forever in the Shadowlands of the Murk made her blood run cold.

She moved to the door and peered outside. A corridor stretched left and right. Voices came, echoey and indistinct. Shapes moved—large, ghost-like demons. She sank back against the wall, holding her breath, Ehka nestling behind her legs. So they did have ghosts then.

The ghost demons paused beside her, sniffed the air, and carried on. She looked down at Ehka.

'Can you find the spear? I've no idea where it is, other than down.'

Ehka looked around and shuffled, clearly unsure. He flew into the air anyway and headed down a grey tunnel leading right. She drew her sword and followed him, the talisman hot in her belt.

Magical energy suddenly flowed into her. She gasped and closed her eyes. She couldn't reach the Flow here in the Murk, but this magic was pure and all around her—not grey like it should be in the Dead Realm but vivid, living indigo. The dark moon called to her. Her pulse pounded and she could barely breathe for the excitement that overwhelmed her. It ebbed, leaving her shaking and confused. She tried to pool the Flow but it was absent.

Ehka was gone. She carried on and came to a fork; one led right and up, the other down and left. The spear had to be down so she went left. More voices came and she hunkered down in a dark corner. Ghost demons ran towards her, barking in guttural Demonic. Sweat soaked her back. Surely they could see her? She closed her eyes, but the ghosts ran straight past. She let out a breath, thanking Zanufey, and then more cautiously, Zorock.

Inching forwards, the tunnel wound round and down. Braziers, appearing grey-white, lit the way. The tunnel opened up into a huge cavern and she emerged onto a high ledge.

Screams echoed below, making her heart shake. She hunched down on her knees and peered over the edge. Immediately she remembered this place. She had fallen through here in the Storm Holt. The memories of the greater demons chasing her filled her mind and she shivered.

Cries came from all around and great black shapes flittered past. She clung to the wall, forcing herself to look. Greater demons were everywhere, clinging to the walls and ceiling like bats. More came up from the blackness. This had to be the gate to the Pit, the place where she had descended before.

The shadow world wavered and the yellow colours of the braziers in the living world fed through into the Dead Realm. The veil between the dead and living was thin here, and she struggled to remain in the realm of the dead. If the greater demons could see her in both worlds, perhaps it didn't matter which one she was in.

A pale figure moved in her vision. She looked down and saw two beings in one place: a tall, thin, white form and a huge hulking black form engulfing it. Karhlusus and demon King Kull. He started screaming in demonic and more demons howled out of the black gate in the ground, rising in great numbers. There were so many, they created a thick impenetrable cloud.

Heart in her mouth and trying not to cry out, she slid along the wall to a corner and flattened herself on the floor. Karhlusus continued intoning, sometimes screaming and sometimes his voice so deep and low, it vibrated the ground. His demonic words made her tremble and shake. They wrapped around her soul and tugged.

She closed her eyes and focused on her task. The spear wasn't here and neither was Ehka. She had to get away from the maddening noise of Karhlusus' summoning and the screams of demons.

Not daring to get up, she crawled. It seemed to take an age to inch herself away from the ledge. Once round the corner, she ran back all the way she had come.

She took another tunnel. Time was running out. There were more ghost demons but the Grazen ghosts didn't seem to be able to see her. She passed endless doors and rooms but nothing led downwards and she didn't see Ehka.

Again the Dead Realm faded and the real world materialised. The walls became solid and real, the braziers orange and bright. Panic filled her and she grabbed the talisman to her chest.

'Take me back to the Realm of the Dead,' she gasped but the raven talisman was cold. She tried again. Nothing happened. She shook the talisman and wiped sweat from her face, but nothing she did returned her. She was here, fully, in Karhlusus Keep, deep in the lair of the enemy.

The clash of metal and roaring made her stop and she darted into an empty room. The sound of fighting came closer, and then real Grazen guards appeared.

They were stepping backwards, fighting a losing battle against a menagerie of unarmed demons. Some were big and fat, others thin and small. Many wore metal collars around their necks and broken manacles around their wrists and ankles. Some were brown and others grey. They seemed to be a confusing mix of Grazen and Shadow Demons.

One guard crumpled under the mighty fist of a huge Shadow Demon. The other guard ran. Why were they turning on the Grazen guards? The demons looked at her and howled. She drew her sword, realising how useless it was as they charged.

Ehka darted over their heads and landed between her and the demons. A strange green light followed and buzzed around Ehka. The demons faltered. A small, pot-bellied demon half ran, half flew above their heads towards her, wailing. He stopped and stared at her, gulping back his wail.

'Maggot? What are you…? I thought you were dead,' she said. He flew towards her and wrapped himself around her leg.

Ehka hopped to her feet and the green light buzzed around her head, inspecting her. What was a swamp fairy doing here? How was Maggot here? And why was Ehka with them? She shook her head and stared at the little demon hugging her leg. She hesitantly scratched his bald head affectionately with a finger.

'Issy, you came,' he said, his voice muffled against her thigh. He looked up at her, eyes wide, face as ugly as ever. 'Help us get out.'

The green light buzzed in her face and she wafted at it irritably.

'I'm trying to get out myself. We must get the spear,' she said. 'We don't have long. Hundreds have come out of the Pit. King Gedrock can't fight them all.'

'We have the spear, but it's hard to carry,' he said.

'What? Tell your friends I mean no harm,' she said, eyeing the other demons who were snarling at her.

Maggot growled in demonic. They shuffled awkwardly and lowered their weapons, looks of confusion passing between them.

Behind her came deafening roars—lots of them. A Pit Demon hurtled towards her, a black ball of flapping wings, flashing eyes and bared fangs. She ran towards the odd medley of demons with Maggot still clinging to her leg.

The Shadow Demons melted into shadow and flowed past her towards the Pit Demon. Horrific screams ripped through her soul and she cowered.

'You, take,' said a big demon and dropped a rag-covered object with a clang.

Pulling the rags off, she marvelled at the spear's shining beauty. The demons fell back from it with a unified groan. She looked up at the demon who had given it to her. He scowled and disappeared into shadow.

Touching the spear, light flared in her mind. It spoke to her in a flash of pictures. It was an ancient thing created long ago by the races of Maioria. She saw not a spear but a simple shaft, as white now as it had been then. It could open tunnels of light or darkness. She didn't quite understand.

A man appeared. He looked uncannily like Marakon, only he had no injured eye and was wholly human, not half-elven. He was forging a red-hot weapon on an anvil—a beautiful, deadly, leaf-shaped spearhead. He plunged it hissing into water then slotted it upon the shaft, turning it into a weapon.

The vision ended. The spear hummed in her hand. More Pit Demons howled in the tunnels ahead.

'Get back,' she cried, hefting the spear, its light filling the tunnel.

The lesser demons groaned and shrank from her as she lunged past them at the closest Pit Demon. It screamed as the spear sank into its shoulder, thrashed wildly as black smoke gushed from its wound then disappeared. Again she stabbed, this time into a Grazen guard. It howled, turned black, and disintegrated. The spear's complete power over demons was shocking. There were more coming, howling and scraping towards them. The spear's power was immense but she couldn't fight them all.

'Fall back,' she yelled.

They fled through a maze of tunnels. Some Grazen, seeing their kin revolt, joined them, but most fled when they saw the spear. The Pit Demons always attacked.

They found the main entrance and hesitated. There was a huge open plane to get across, and the sky was filled with greater demons. In the darkness behind them, howls echoed. Maggot flapped nervously beside her, pulling on his ears. Ehka circled above.

'We have to get the spear to Marakon,' she said.

She tested its weight and wondered if she and Ehka could fly with it between them. But what about the others? They'd be killed. She'd have to leave them. If the spear didn't get to Marakon, everyone was dead.

'Maggot. Get to safety. Hide.' She crouched down and looked into the little demon's eyes. 'I still can't believe you're alive. I can't believe you found Velistor.'

He smiled. A kind of ugly smile that wrinkled his face. She stood and changed form.

As a raven, the spear was heavy, and she and Ehka struggled into the air with it grasped in their talons. The wind gusted, lifting them higher, but when it dropped they descended helplessly down. It would work if they managed to ride the wind.

It was slow going and the greater demons soon spotted them. They screamed as they lunged, trying to get the ravens to drop the spear without getting too close to it. She found that if she flew erratically, they could never get close enough without risking themselves. Darting up and down quickly became exhausting and they were only halfway across the plane.

In the distance she glimpsed white horses and knights surrounded by demons. It was a miracle they still lived. She angled her wings keener.

A dust cloud billowed on the ground below. She peered at the black beast galloping. Duskar. He was moving at breakneck speed away from the battle and towards Carmedrak Rock—towards where he knew she had gone. She swooped down towards him.

The greater demons attacking her now also lunged at him. He reared at a swooping demon then staggered. She cawed loudly, trying to catch his attention. He regained his footing and galloped on, the whites of his eyes vivid and sweat drenching his back. If he was wounded, he didn't show it.

She dropped lower and cawed again, greater demons following her descent. Duskar saw her and whinnied, slowing his pace. She flew erratically to avoid two gnashing demons, hoping Ehka would be able to keep up.

Lower she flew until she was merely feet from Duskar's back as he cantered. In one motion she changed form and slipped onto his back, spear in hand. Ehka landed on her shoulder.

She stabbed straight up at the demons. Light burst, a demon howled, fell and disappeared into black smoke. Another took its place. She struck again and again, felling another and driving back two more. Duskar pranced beneath her.

She urged him around with her legs, wishing she had a saddle and reins, and galloped him back towards the battle. Gripping his mane in one hand, she held the spear aloft. The demons followed but always avoided the spear.

As the battle neared, she screamed. The press of demons paused, turned to stare at her, then howled and fled away from her charge like two waves parting. The tide of battle changed.

The galloping of Duskar's hooves, the screams of demons, the clash of metal—dropped away, one by one, into silence. The moon would rise soon. Her heart calmed, her pulse dropped, and her breath came slow and steady and deep. Her mind stilled and everything slowed down as her hyper-awareness grew. Indigo light flowed around her, filling her mind, her body, and everything that she was.

Marakon was ahead, turning in her direction to see what the commotion was. He was still and calm too, and there was a look on his face she would never forget—determination and absolute knowing.

She pressed forwards, ploughing through demons that couldn't get away in time. She drew her hand back and hurled the spear at him. It flew, sure as an arrow, over the cowering demons. Marakon reached a hand up—casually it seemed—and caught it.

The sound of a great gong throbbed from the spear. She slowed Duskar and pirouetted him around, the silence and calm of her mind filling everything, the waves of indigo magic flowing around her.

Marakon jumped his horse forwards towards her, his knights trailing. The calm receded, noise returned, and everything became motion. The horses neighed, demons howled, knights cheered. As one, they galloped back across the black sands towards Carmedrak Rock, the demon army struggling to regroup and follow.

She glanced at Marakon and the knights galloping at her side. He smiled; they all did. The spear suited him. She grinned, feeling the thrill of the ride together and the promise of victory fill her. Magic was filling her again, pure and powerful. She breathed deeply. She must be ready for it all, ready to be the vessel for the power of Zanufey.

Ahead, a plague of Pit Demons swarmed from the entrance of the keep. The knights were vastly outnumbered, but in this strange space she knew no fear, only calm silence in the serenity of the indigo magic. The moon was rising, the magic building, and she had to ride the wave.

She looked ahead beyond the keep as the dark moon tipped the mountain peaks. The first rays shone across the planes to strike her. The moon's power filled her talisman first then spread throughout her body.

She gasped and let go of Duskar's mane, spreading her arms wide as the magic filled her.

Duskar slowed. A cloud of demons descended from the sky. Marakon dropped to a canter and turned to look back at her, but she could say nothing; the all-consuming power held her in stasis.

Her arms rose higher, and all she could think about was the indigo moon of Zanufey. Everything was unreal—a dream. Only the moon was real.

She was aware of light spreading upwards from her as she sat atop Duskar in the middle of the barren plane. The light was a dome, a shield pushing back the demons as it rose.

Marakon turned and pushed on with his knights, as she'd hoped he would. She could communicate nothing to anyone, she could only be the vessel for the power of the dark moon and all she knew was that she must hold that power until the moon set.

CHAPTER 34

Demon Slayer

FEARLESS, Marakon reached to catch the spear Issa threw at him.

It seemed to fly direct to his outstretched hand. As his fingers wrapped around it, light flared from the spear and memory exploded in his mind. His white eye burned, forcing him to lift his eyepatch. Touching it again ignited memory. He saw the far distant past.

He sat at a blacksmith's fire, nothing but the flames and burning embers lighting his task, and worked white metal from deep within the White Mountains of Unafay to forge the leaf-shaped spear tip he now held in his hands. He'd turned the powerful relic into a devastating weapon—a weapon to kill the demons plaguing Maioria.

He knew that the long white shard, filled with magical power, was crafted long before him during the birth of Maioria by the first beings upon her.

Velistor—Staff of the Gate, it was called, and its purpose was to open Maioria's portal gateways that led to specific points on the planet thousands of miles away. It was how the early peoples travelled across Maioria, covering many leagues in the blink of an eye.

Over millennia, all the portal gateways had been closed and deliberately lost and forgotten in countless ancient wars—but it did not mean they no longer existed. The Storm Holt was still remembered to this day.

The staff now made into a spear was the most effective weapon ever created to kill demons. It sent their demonic essence back to where they came from, and it was how, as King Marakazian, he had managed to defeat the demons and close the gates to the demon world so long ago.

Now he was being asked to do the same thing again. A divine task appointed to him by the goddess.

He looked ahead. His knights were smiling at him, hope for freedom and redemption bright in their eyes. They remembered as did he. He would not fail them or Maioria or Zanufey.

He slammed his visor down and kicked his horse into a gallop, following Issa's charge to the keep. The black spire struck up into the sky, refusing to be moulded by the wind and sand that scoured the plane. Freedom would be theirs.

He stared as the moon rose above the mountains, bathing the black sands in indigo. It seemed to concentrate its light on Issa, filling her from within, then bursting out brighter all around her, creating a shield that drove the greater demons back. They galloped unhindered beneath the safety of her shield towards their destiny.

They were almost at the keep when Issa dropped behind. He slowed and stopped, turning to look at her. Both she and her black horse stood still as a statue. Her arms were half spread, palms up, eyes seeing into another place. Indigo light flowed from her in great waves and no demon could even get close. Her light extended farther until it reached the edge of Karhlusus Keep. He stared in wonder. She was protecting them all so they could complete their task.

He tried to judge the arc of the moon. It was shallow. As soon as it dipped below the mountains, its power would wane, and so too would Issa's. She wouldn't be able to hold the demons back then. He had an hour, maybe two at most.

'Stay with her, Bokaard, and protect her. This one isn't for you,' Marakon said to the big Atalanphian. 'If we're not done when the moon sets, she'll need help. We'll all need help.'

Bokaard started to protest, then nodded. 'May Doon protect you,' he said, blue eyes sparkling.

Marakon nodded, reared his horse, and leapt into a gallop. Under Issa's light, they reached the keep unhindered. They came to an abrupt halt before the entrance. It was shut, sealed with a great metal door. He locked onto the white figure glaring down from a turret above.

Memory of Karhlusus' laughing head, rolling from his shoulders, haunted him. This time he would kill the wizard *and* the demon king so neither could resurrect the other ever again.

'Karhlusus!' he screamed, and raised the spear.

The demon wizard whirled away in a flurry of robes and disappeared into the keep.

Marakon felt the weight of ages pressing down upon him—the burden of all his past lives and deaths of misery and pain. The fury and longing for vengeance that had burned in him for eternity, now became a beacon of determination and resolve. His justice would be enacted—quickly, simply, and utterly.

'Karhlusus. Come and face your destiny!' his voice rang out.

Laughter came, from all around. The same laughter he'd heard when he'd struck the demon wizard's head off. Above, beyond Issa's indigo shield, Pit Demons massed in great clouds. There came a grinding noise and slowly the metal door began to rise in the same manner as a portcullis. A great gust of dank air burst out and a voice came from somewhere within.

'King Marakazian and his Cursed Knights have come to me once more. What's wrong? Haven't you died enough times already, King Marakazian?' the demon wizard spat out mockingly.

Marakon danced his horse before the black entrance. 'Always afraid, Karhlusus. Always a coward. Even now you hide.'

Magic exploded from the entrance, not seen but heard as a great boom. Knights tumbled from their stumbling mounts. Marakon barely managed to cling to his horse's neck as it staggered. Controlling his steed, he righted himself. His fallen knights remounted.

'Is that the best of it? A coward who fights in the darkness?' Marakon laughed, then spoke quietly to his knights. 'Leave the horses. They'll be safe enough under Issa's shield. That bastard's not coming out to fight.'

He dismounted and secured his horse's reins in the saddle, his knights following suit. In a tight bunch with weapons raised, they moved into the blackness of the keep where the light of Zanufey's moon could not reach.

There were sconces and braziers on the black stone walls, but they were not lit. The place was utter darkness. A greater demon stormed them, its cry piercing. Marakon jabbed the spear into it. Its scream echoed deafeningly before fading into silence. His skin prickled, and he felt as if every hair on his body was raised. He had never been this far into the Murk before, and he longed to leave.

'Light,' Hylion commanded. Pale elven light illuminated the walls.

Several tunnels led away into deeper darkness.

'The spear's humming,' Marakon said, surprised. It gave a low continuous hum, as well as throbbing in his grasp.

'It's hunting,' Ghenath said. 'Hunting for demons.'

Marakon held it forwards and turned left. It hummed less and dimmed. He turned right and it hummed louder and glowed brighter. It was strongest when they neared the farthest tunnel on the right.

'I guess we trust the spear.' Cormak shrugged, and tested his grip on his axe.

'I hate this place,' Lan said. 'It's like one big hellish grave.'

There were murmurs of agreement.

'Be ready for everything,' Marakon said quietly. 'Karhlusus will use all he's got, and that usually means demons, demon tricks and magic, and more demons.'

Howls echoed and three Pit Demons came at them, eyes flaring, teeth flashing. They moved unnaturally fast, but the knights were quick too. There was little room to fight, but their swords drove them back whilst the spear's greater reach finished them off. Their dying howls echoed into silence. Hard-faced, the knights moved forwards.

'Ghenath and I will bring up the rear,' said Hylion. 'With our relics we have a little elven magic. It's not much but we'll assist where we can.'

The tunnel wound lower and forked several times, the spear guiding them each time. Shadows moved around them, but the elven light and light of Velistor seemed to scatter them. A rumbling sound came from ahead. A wall of flame exploded towards them.

Marakon dropped to a crouch behind his shield, flames licking around the sides. He was aware of screaming against the roaring fire. Elven magic moved, dampening the scorching heat, but still his arm burned. Velistor was impervious to the flames, and instead cold light came from it, easing the onslaught.

The flames flickered out and disembodied laughter echoed in the ensuing silence. Marakon yanked off his burning hot shield and checked his arm. The skin was red and blistering beneath his gauntlets, but thankfully still whole. They checked their burns.

Cormak's beard was half singed off, and everybody's face was bright red.

'At least the braziers are lit now,' the dwarf said.

Marakon looked at the flaming braziers and grinned.

'We can't turn back,' Nemeron said when Marakon hesitated. The others nodded.

'We must finish this, one way or another,' said Oria, her eyes hard.

'But using weak magic to fight overpowering demon magic is virtually impossible,' Hylion said, looking drained. 'We must find the gate to the Pit and close it before we can defeat him. Otherwise we'll die fighting greater demons; there'll be so many.'

Marakon nodded. 'The spear is taking us to Karhlusus, not the gate. Hopefully they're in the same place. Can elven magic cloak our presence here?'

Ghenath looked doubtful. 'We can try with the relics we have, but we won't be able to fight at the same time.'

'Just something so we can move around with a little more ease,' he said.

The elves nodded and began casting. Darkness seemed to hug them and they hurried along, winding lower and lower into the keep.

Five more demons came at them, eyes hungry for blood. Marakon struck one between its eyes, sliced across two more and Cormak stabbed the fourth through its neck. The fifth clamped its jaws around Marakon's helmet, but spear and swords plunged into it, taking it down. Marakon snorted out the stench of the demon's breath in disgust.

They carried on without a word. The tunnel opened up into a huge cavern. Marakon wiped the sweat from his brow, and stretched his weary arms. He motioned the others to stay back and peered into the cavern.

Greater demons covered the walls, the ceiling, and flew mid-air in circles like bats. He looked over the ledge, praying elven magic would conceal him well. Karhlusus stood some fifty feet below, before a giant vortex of flaring black and white energy that swirled like a whirlpool in the floor.

Karhlusus had his eyes closed and his arms raised. From the vortex, shadows darted upwards and joined the flying demons.

Marakon's heart was in his throat and sweat trickled down his back. Half-heard whisperings echoed around him and his soul screamed at him to be gone from here. He inched back to the others.

'The gate to the Pit is below.' The knights nodded, their faces pallid. 'Thank the goddess the elven magic is working.'

'We can't hold it for long,' Hylion's strained voice came from the back.

Marakon rubbed his chin. Somewhere in his mind was the memory of how to close demon gates. Or perhaps he should take Karhlusus out right now. He had to do something and fast.

'I can't remember how to close the gate, but we have to stop Karhlusus summoning more demons. Only the spear can kill him.'

Gripping the spear, he turned towards the ledge. Taking a deep breath, he raised the point and aimed it at Karhlusus' heart. Praying to Zanufey, he hurled it.

As the spear left his hand, Karhlusus vanished. Velistor clattered in the place where Karhlusus had been and sprung harmlessly off the floor, wobbling as it did so.

In a blink the demon wizard was beside him.

'Boo,' Karhlusus smiled, his eyes not human but red and demon-slitted.

Marakon shivered and froze, helpless to react as the demon wizard shoved him over the edge with incredible strength. Howling and clawing at the air, he spun down towards the vortex. The gate to the Pit rushed to meet him.

The vortex swallowed him. Soul-draining blackness swirled through every cell in his body. He couldn't breathe or think; everything was scattered.

Things moved. Demons came at him—their immaterial forms flowing through his fragmented body and wiggling through him like worms. Disease filled him from the inside and crazed thoughts infected his mind. Moments from his past flickered, all twisted, confused and evil. Things he couldn't see tore at his flesh. How could he have failed? He screamed.

A flashing length of light spun towards him in the blackness. Demons roared. Velistor. Was it a trick? He reached to grab it anyway.

Sparks flared as his hand touched the spear. It instantly pulled upwards, almost wrenching his arm from its socket. The vortex fought to pull him downwards. Lightning flared between the spear and vortex, tearing him between two great forces. He grimaced and screamed.

He clung to the spear, his ligaments stretching beyond their ability. He could barely breathe. All he could do was endure as the energy fought to balance itself.

'Close it,' he gasped. 'Goddess damn it. Velistor, close the bloody gate!'

To his shock, the spear pulsed in his hand, then he was rushing upwards, simultaneously being pulled up by the spear and pushed violently from below as the vortex began to close.

Exploding into the cavern, he sprawled onto solid rock that had moments before been the vortex.

Karhlusus howled, a horrific demonic sound coming through a human mouth.

Marakon couldn't move as his body pulled itself back together. To his right, white robes disappeared into a tunnel. Above on the ledge, his knights fought scores of greater demons. His momentary joy at closing the gate, the simplicity with which it was done, was swept away as howling demons descended upon him.

The spear hummed, angry and hungry. Whirling it in a circle, demons screamed when he struck. Now the gate was closed, it seemed their forms had become more solid and his spear sank deep into partially solid flesh. Black blood sprayed as gas. Another came at him and one from behind hit him so hard his helmet flew off. Claws raked down his face; hot blood trickled. The spear flashed as he struck back, roaring his rage.

He had to get Karhlusus, before he escaped. No matter how hard he tried to get to the steps leading up, his path was blocked by demons and he fought just to stay alive.

To his dismay, Grazen flooded into the room, brown skin glistening and their eyes wild with fury. But to his astonishment, the Grazen didn't attack them and instead went for the greater demons. Had they turned against their leader? He couldn't spare the thoughts to consider it.

Spinning the spear, he jumped into a space between three greater demons. Claws raked his back and his head, slicing his eyepatch off. He stabbed behind with the spear, heard screams, blinked and steadied himself. It was harder to see with one eye normal and the other far-sighted.

He spared a glance at his knights. They were outnumbered and it didn't look hopeful, but to get Karhlusus, he *had* to leave them. He prayed they would understand. If Karhlusus got away now, everything would have been for nothing.

When a path to the tunnel finally opened up, he ran to it.

A group of Grazen rushed out. They howled at him, saw the spear, shut their mouths, then scrambled past, giving him a wide berth. Surprised, he ran on unhindered, the sound of the battle lessening until it was just a dim noise.

'King Marakazian,' a disembodied voice echoed. Marakon gripped the spear. 'My, we do bear a grudge don't we? Still you think you can fight me—a King of Demons *and* a Master Wizard? You could not then and you cannot now.' As he spoke the voice became less human and more demonic—low, distorted, and struggling with human words.

'You hate to see my power when you lost all of yours,' Karhlusus hissed.

'I care nothing for power anymore,' Marakon said, running forwards, the spear guiding him on. 'I care only for justice and retribution, even if it costs me my life.'

Laughter came again. 'So it will, Marakazian.'

A dark figure filled a doorway. Marakon lunged towards it, but the figure vanished. A swirl of white robes moved ahead and he loped forwards. He was aware he was being led, but with the spear in his hands and Karhlusus somewhere near, he didn't care. At least his knights weren't being harried by this bastard.

'More tricks, Karhlusus? Always afraid to fight?'

He barely finished the sentence when a hundred small creatures flew at him. He thought they were bats, but their bald, black faces and red teeth were demonic. He batted at them uselessly with the spear, their claws slicing easily into his cheeks and forehead before he had time to grab and lift his shield. He swatted what he could, each one screaming as the spear touched.

The demon bats flapped away and silence descended. He wiped the blood flowing into his eyes. The cuts weren't deep but they stung and bled hard.

Moving forwards, breathing heavily, he came to a doorway roughly hewn out of rock—soft, illuminated mist moved beyond it. Cautiously he sidled onwards, flattening himself against the wall. Nothing changed for long moments and there was only the sound of his strained breathing. He stepped into the mist, spear at the ready.

CHAPTER 35

Knights Ascending

THE doorway behind vanished and the mist thickened until he stood within a soup of waist-high fog so dense he couldn't see his feet.

The fog stretched out a long way in all directions.

Damn Karhlusus and his games. If he was going to win, he was going to have to start playing his own games. He moved forwards, shield and spear raised.

'The gate is closed, Karhlusus. Nothing from the Pit can come to your aid. The Shadow Demons have returned to take back what you stole from them. The Grazen have turned on you and the dark moon rises in the Murk. Zanufey's chosen brings justice to your door. It's over, Karhlusus. There's no way out other than to fight me. You can run but Velistor hunts you, and now it is free, it will hunt you forever.'

His voice sounded eerie in the mist, heavy and flat with no echo. It was as if he stood outside in a forest, rather than a chamber. The spear hummed more to the right. He moved in that direction, treading silently.

The mist cleared to reveal not walls but rolling hills, a river and forests spread out in each direction. In the near distance stood a castle and surrounding city. He stared at it. He knew that castle and this place; it was his castle, his land. The City of the Star.

'Recognise it, don't you?' Karhlusus' voice echoed.

'Hah. Nice try. Good illusion, but it isn't real,' Marakon said, annoyed at the emotion in his voice.

'Shall we end this as it began?' Karhlusus chuckled.

A demon materialised before him, twenty feet tall and crowned with black horns. Its face was long, its muzzle longer. Its arms were long, ending in massive claws and held close to its body. Long heavy legs like a toad's yet hard like an insect's, scraped the ground back and forth, pondering him. Dark yellow eyes flashed, vertical pupils narrowed and a long, spiked tail lashed towards him.

Marakon yelled and jumped back as it struck the spear. Light flashed and smoke billowed. It scowled, its face deforming into a hideous mix of demon and human features. It grinned, then became its ugly demon face. It did this continuously.

'Disgusting abomination.' Marakon snarled at King Kull.

Lifting his shield high, he stabbed with the spear. Its tail lashed him back. He sliced at the tail. The demon screeched and smoke plumed from its wound. The wound healed, the skin knitting itself back together. Marakon raised his shield high again. The demon's eyes never left him, never blinked. He could feel his spirit draining whenever he looked into them. He forced his eyes to look only at its chest and lashing tail.

'I can give you a nice death,' the demon garbled. 'Unlike that which your fallen knights have suffered at Baelthrom's hands.'

Marakon hesitated. 'What of those knights?' The demon chuckled. 'Tell me, you bastard!' he screamed and lunged. King Kull dodged the spear easily and circled him, laughing.

'Their souls are in oblivion. Not even demons know where they've gone. But their bodies live on in a fascinating form.'

'Lying demon.' Marakon snarled and drove a flurry of strikes at it, the spear humming and vibrating.

Claws and tails knocked it away though smoke billowed off each strike. He *had* to be hurting it. Why hadn't it attacked him fully? It had to be afraid of the spear.

'So, you're in league with Baelthrom?' said Marakon.

'Let's say we have…an agreement.' The demon grinned then snarled, its eyes widening and nostrils flaring.

'A pact of devils and demons,' Marakon spat.

'Hmm, I think something's missing,' Karhlusus crooned, his face now partially human. He sidled around him just out of the spear's reach and chuckled.

People began to appear. They were dressed in grey-white armour and wore the tabard of the Knights of the Shining Star. Marakon stared, recognising their faces.

'My knights.' He gasped. They were them, but their eyes were grey and empty, dead.

'They're not real, it's just more trickery,' he growled, his heart pounding with emotion.

'Tricks?' Karhlusus said. 'Let's see how unreal you think they are.'

The knights turned to face him and drew their weapons in unison. They scowled and bared their teeth. As one, they advanced. Marakon clenched the spear. They wouldn't attack him, would they?

'They want justice for what you made them do, King Marakazian,' King Kull said, stepping backwards as the knights stepped forwards.

Marakon turned around. There were skeleton knights clustering behind. There was no way out.

The faces of the knights began to wither and age, and the skin peeled and fell from their cheeks—a disgusting sight he couldn't tear his eyes from. Soon he was surrounded by armoured skeletons, reminding him of the Drowning Wastes. He hated that place.

The closest knight swung its blade. He blocked it with his shield and yelled as another stabbed at him. He struck the spear wildly left then right, slicing through bone.

Two screamed, fell and became smoke. A third jabbed its rusty blade in his leg. He grimaced in pain, dropped down and struck up, spear crushing its jaw. It screamed and turned into smoke. His leg hurt to stand on and bled freely but he had no time to stem the flow as another skeleton lunged, heedless of his striking spear. It too screamed, shuddered and became smoke in his face, making him choke.

He whirled the spear faster to create space around him. The skeleton knights fell back. At least they feared the weapon. They were a demon trick, they weren't *real*—and yet real blood trickled from his wound and it hurt. Real or not, they could still kill him.

More came on, their blows clanging on his armour, very hard and very real. He struck again and again. It only took one blow of the spear to fell a skeleton knight, but there were hundreds of them.

The skeleton legion pressed closer. The spear could only do so much. He couldn't fight them all. A sword thrust between his armour plates and he grimaced but was too furious to calibrate how badly he'd been hurt.

'You're not real,' he screamed, lashing wildly.

Beyond the din of their howls and clash of weapons, Karhlusus' laughter echoed.

The spear hummed and throbbed. It was magical. Surely it could do something clever, but he had no idea what. It had closed the Pit gate when he had asked; perhaps a simple command would do?

'Destroy skeleton knights!' he howled, striking the spear's base hard upon the ground.

The ground shuddered and shock waves rippled out from him. The earth rumbled, heaved then quaked, shaking the skeletons so hard they fell apart and disappeared into thick clouds of smoke.

Marakon stood panting and staring at the spear. Didn't it just open gates? Had it tried to open a gate when there was none?

'You'll be a good prize for Baelthrom,' Karhlusus mused, unsmiling. 'I'll ask for more in the reward.'

The demon wizard vanished, then appeared right in front of him, huge and looming. Marakon leapt back too late. Cold demon hands gripped his throat and spear arm and squeezed. He felt his neck cracking and the bones of his arm bending. He couldn't even scream.

'Pity he wants you alive,' King Kull rasped, his breath rotten and sulphuric. 'Your soul would feed me for a long time.'

Claws squeezed harder, Marakon couldn't breathe at all. Every vein in his head he could hear desperately pulsing. His vision blurred, his white eye throbbed, and his face felt like it was swelling.

'You've made a good little spy, King Marakazian. Did you know that? A real pet for the Immortal Lord.'

What was the bastard going on about? He wasn't surprised Karhlusus was in league with Baelthrom, as long as there was something the demon wizard had to gain from it. But did he really intend to give him to the Immortal Lord? And what did he mean, "spy"?

The white spear was doing something in his hand. It had stopped throbbing and pulsating, and now turned cold, as if sensing the life leaving him. The cold crept up his arm, then into his torso, moving ever faster. It burst through the rest of his body, searing his white eye. He arched his back in the intense agony.

The light spread from him and engulfed the demon wizard in a blaze. The demon howled, its skin blistered and bulged then turned white. It flailed and thrashed, tossing Marakon away, and clawed at its own body, trying to fight the light that consumed it.

Marakon rolled, limp and choking. He struggled to his feet, using the spear for support. He staggered forwards, fell to one knee and got up again. It was impossible to aim the spear at the demon as it thrashed, so he ran at it, leapt to avoid its flailing limbs, and plunged the spear into its chest.

The spear and the demon juddered so violently, he was flung aside. He rolled to his feet and stared back. Black smoke poured from its mouth, nose and eyes. The demon screamed so piercingly, Marakon clasped his ears. The spear flared and the demon exploded into black smoke.

Marakon fell to his knees, gasping and blinking in blinding spear light. He stared and stared, but as the smoke dissipated, nothing of the demon wizard remained. Karhlusus was dead? He couldn't let himself believe it. The castle and the hills and forests began to fade. There was silence.

He blinked. Human figures moved towards him in the light. He scrambled for the spear but then squinted at their faces. They were calm and familiar and not attacking. Again, he recognised his long dead knights and then other people not dressed in armour—children, men and women—their eyes alight with life and kindness.

A fair-haired woman came towards him and his heart lurched. She reached down to touch his face. He closed his eyes, tears rolling down his cheeks. Her caress was warm, filled with love, and he knew her touch intimately.

He opened his eyes. She was smiling; they were all smiling. The people nodded then faded into the light. He wiped at the tears streaming down his face.

'Marakon?'

He turned to see Hylion and Oria running towards him. They were all still surrounded by the spear's light. He stood up, took a deep breath and grinned.

'Are you really here?' he rasped, his crushed throat barely able to say the words. 'Karhlusus is gone. By the goddess, the bastard is finally gone.' He sighed, barely letting himself believe it.

Cormak, Lan, Nemeron, Ghenath and Ironbeard appeared with their horses following just behind. They were all bloodstained and battle weary. He embraced Lan then the others. They were solid and real. He laughed.

'Karhlusus is…dead. Gone forever. We're free.' Marakon laughed.

'I can feel it,' sighed Ghenath, closing her eyes in relief.

All their faces were a picture of joy. They cried and laughed at the same time.

'Look,' said Lan, holding up his hand in wonder.

Light, brighter than that of the spear, was coming from it. The others looked at their hands; they were turning into light and then their bodies did too.

'It feels so…pure. So…beautiful,' Oria marvelled.

Marakon looked down, but his body wasn't changing. What was happening to them? Why wasn't he shining too? Then he understood. He looked up, barely seeing them through the tears that blinded him.

'You're free, the curse is gone. For all the thousands of years you've suffered, you can now return to the One Light,' he said.

They smiled at him with smiles of pure wonder, joy and complete freedom. He would never forget it. They were all light now and their faces became indistinct. The horses too were glowing and were now nothing more than horse-shapes of light. Their forms became vertical beams of pure light, then as one they burst upwards.

The light faded and the spear turned dim. He sank to his knees in the gloom that descended, wiping at the tears that fell, wishing he could go with them.

'Marakon?' An unsteady female voice said.

He looked up into Issa's weary face. Her eyes were luminous turquoise, more intense than he'd ever seen a wizard have before. She still looked like a goddess, pale and otherworldly. There was a raven on her shoulder, an ugly little Shadow Demon hiding behind her back, and a black horse watching inquisitively.

She looked about to faint as she knelt before him. He placed a shaking hand on her shoulder, in part to be sure she was real. She gripped his hand in her own. Her hand trembled.

'They ascended. I felt them. Zanufey was here,' she said.

He nodded, vaguely understanding what she meant and too weary to ask more.

Issa had trouble articulating to Marakon what she had been shown by Zanufey in the desert. The blue moon had risen above Carmedrak Rock and its power had filled her—she had become it utterly. Then she'd stood before the trilithon and Zanufey was beside her, serene and divine. The blue moon's power swirled within and through them both.

'The spear is a tool that opens Maioria's gates,' she said. 'It can move down and along through Maioria's natural portals. If held by one who can wield it and used correctly, it can move those assembled quickly between entire continents. What might take months of travelling across land and sea takes only moments to get there via the portals.'

'I remember.' Marakon nodded. Issa rushed on.

'There's more. The spear can open gates that go down to lower dimensions, like the Murk, but not upwards to dimensions higher than this one. Something about frequency. It holds the frequency of this dimension and all the ones below it, but it cannot hold the frequency of the dimensions above.

'That's where the raven talisman is important.' She held it up. 'It opens gates to higher dimensions, like where the souls of the dead go, and also to the astral, maybe even to the ethereal. Do you see how incredible these things are? The raven with the staff is a tool that opens the gates to the stars.'

Marakon blinked, clearly speechless. Issa's excitement wavered as her gaze wandered to his white eye. He'd lost his patch. There was just something wrong about it; it made her terribly afraid. She felt bad feeling this way about his disfigurement and looked away.

'My lessons were too brief. Zanufey went. Then I was here, amongst your knights and the Shadow Demons, and there you were suddenly, kneeling ahead.'

'What happens now? What does Zanufey want? Tell me what to do. Are you ok?' he said, squeezing her shoulder and steadying her when she swayed. She took a deep breath and closed her eyes.

'I'm all right, I think,' she said, though the ground seemed to sway and melt like cheese. 'I'm just utterly spent. Give me the spear.'

He passed it to her. It felt warm and heavy in her hand.

'Now the spear's task is complete, it's trying to take us home,' she said. She could feel it pulling upwards, a bit like Karshur had felt when it had dragged her to the Land of Mist.

She took hold of the raven talisman and slotted it perfectly onto the base of the spear. Magic blazed from spear and talisman. She struggled to hold it as it flared. Marakon shielded his eyes. Storm winds tore at them. She felt movement, or the ground falling away, then every cell in her body seemed to fragment and the wind blew through them. The world was light and shade and a vortex spun with them at its core.

CHAPTER 36

Battle for Carvon

ISSA hoped and prayed for the spear to take them somewhere familiar they all could reach.

The upwards movement slowed and everything grew brighter and felt less dense. A lake and forest appeared, the same lake they had stood before when trying to help Arla. Could there be an ancient vortex, a gateway, here? Why else would the spear have brought them to this place? Perhaps Freydel would be able to discover more.

She sighed in relief. Thank the goddess the spear had brought them to the safety of Carvon. She only prayed Baelthrom was not near. She glanced to the place where Coronos had been murdered with a deep pang of sorrow. The blood had been washed away.

The light and wind vortex calmed. Ground formed beneath her feet. She stared back at the lake. Something was wrong with it. It rippled in odd places, and every now and then a huge splash disrupted its surface.

A familiar, devastating scream cut through the air, making her heart pound. She glanced up and froze in terror, her eyes locked on to the Dread Dragons in the sky.

Moments later, the rest of reality revealed itself. Dread Dragon screams cut through the air, making her knees tremble and give way. Marakon and Bokaard staggered and shook beside her, Maggot clung to her back and Duskar pranced.

'Is that them?' Maggot squeaked.

'Yes, Maggot. Tell King.' Issa gasped.

The screams and yells of soldiers filled the air, deafening. Roaring

Maphraxies spilled around the side of the lake, crashing into King Navarr's army, guards and knights—all wearing the Carvon tabard of a white castle on a blue background. The soldiers dodged around them to meet the enemy, swords raised. Arrows whistled through the air from the forest, thudding dully into their targets.

Issa had no strength to stand, let alone fight, and she panted in the mud, her ears ringing. Hands gripped her shoulders. She stared up at Marakon. He was shouting above the din and looked as exhausted as she felt.

'We have to get away. We are no use fighting in this battle,' he said.

She nodded, dazed.

'They've reached Carvon.' Her voice shook.

Marakon gave a grim nod, and took the spear from her limp hands. He slipped off the talisman and passed it back to her in silence.

Bokaard wrapped strong arms around her and lifted her onto Duskar's back. The big man was soaked in blood and grime, but he could walk all right. Marakon staggered and listed to one side badly, so Bokaard helped him mount his own chestnut horse.

No one said anything as they limped away from the battle, each struggling against the terror and the shame of retreat in their hearts. The king's soldiers, seeing their sorry state, parted to let them pass.

'We have to fight.' Tears filled her eyes. They just couldn't let the enemy take the heart of Frayon.

'We can't,' Marakon growled. He seemed angry, as if he wanted to fight too.

She vainly reached for the dark moon, but its power had gone. She had used it carelessly in the Murk when she should have saved it for here where it was needed most. Why had Zanufey not told her, not helped her? Her real enemy was Baelthrom, not demons.

She looked up at the majestic turrets of Carvon and saw an incredible sight that lifted her heart. A huge golden dragon wrapped around the entire main turret, his tail reaching almost to the ground, and his proud head resting on the tip of the roof as he watched the battle unfold.

'Asaph.' She gasped and pointed. Bokaard and Marakon stared at the dragon.

'The dragons are back?' Marakon said.

'The last Dragon Lord.' She smiled.

A Dread Dragon screamed close. She glanced behind to see soldiers duck and horses flee in a scattering wave as a Dread Dragon swooped low, flaming the forest in a stream of red fire.

Bokaard's horse bolted with Marakon clinging desperately onto its neck. Bokaard held his shield up and dropped to the ground. Duskar stumbled badly and she fell off, feeling Maggot lose his grip on her back. She'd all but forgotten the demon was there. He rolled easily and clawed his way back to her side. Ehka squawked his fury as he wheeled helplessly above.

Winded, she reached for the Flow but there was nothing there.

The golden dragon leapt into the air, a blur of yellow dropping so fast he smashed into the back of the low swooping Dread Dragon. The Dromoorai rider went flying and crashed down into the flaming trees, claymore flailing. The dragons crashed through the forest, flattening the trees and were then airborne once more.

The fire receded and a mass of king's soldiers descended upon Dromoorai, yelling. Asaph and the Dread Dragon flapped their wings and rose, locked in an aerial battle.

Maphraxies ran towards her through the trees, unseen and unhindered by soldiers. How did they get so close, so soon? She reached for her sword, but was half lying on it. She tried to scream but cold, callous hands grabbed her hair and clasped over her mouth and throat so she couldn't even breathe. A blow to the stomach made the world spin and go foggy.

There came intense heat—just bearable—and deep, guttural howls. The hand that had covered her face was wrenched off and she rolled on the ground. Something huge wrapped around her waist and dragged her upwards into cool air.

Struggling to get her wits, her eyes travelled up the massive belly of the golden dragon. Asaph. Tears sprung into her eyes and she realised a part of her had doubted if she would see him again after he'd left with his father's body.

She let the tears fall, let the terror drop, and surrendered to his grasp. Whatever happened, as long as she was with him, there was no place else she'd rather die.

Behind, she glimpsed three Dread Dragons following. Asaph beat his wings harder. The city of Carvon was fast disappearing into the horizon. She felt dragon magic move. It made her woozy. Then they were moving so fast she couldn't keep her eyes open and breathing took all her focus. She barely clung to consciousness.

Asaph smiled at her from above the flames of a small fire he was just lighting. Everything was quiet and calm.

'Sorry about that. I had to get away. When I first experienced flying that fast, I passed out as well.'

She sat up and smoothed back her hair, trying to get her bearings. They were in a small cave and it was dark beyond the entrance. Seeing him made all the horrors of the past few hours fall away. She worried for the others and for Carvon, but exhaustion numbed everything. At least she was with Asaph. Breathing out a long sigh, she smiled and closed her eyes, feeling tears run down her cheeks and being too tired to care about it.

'I didn't know if I'd see you again. You looked so... distraught after, Coronos—I'm so sorry.' The pain twisted her stomach. He came over and sat down beside her, squeezing her arm.

'We've lost Carvon,' she said, her voice hoarse, defeated.

'Possibly,' Asaph agreed, his face grim as he looked into the fire. 'But we had to get away. They were after you and there were too many to fight.'

'I should be there fighting. Zanufey's moon rose, but I was in the Murk. Now all is lost,' an angry sob caught in her throat.

'We always knew they would invade Frayon,' he said.

'But what good is it, me being Zanufey's chosen, me being the Raven Queen, if I can't even stop them? What the hell am I supposed to do?' She wanted to scream. He wrapped her in his arms and kissed her head.

'I don't know,' he said, barely a whisper.

'What's the point?' she said against his shoulder, trying to stop the sobs. 'I can't be what I'm supposed to be. I knew that from the beginning. I want to destroy them all but I can't even help those I love.'

'Shhh, it's not about what you alone can or can't do,' he said. 'We're all in this together. You can't blame yourself. They attacked, somehow. It's like they were led here. Not Freydel, not Navarr, nor any of the wizards and nobles understood why they attacked now. It's as if they knew you were not in Carvon, or even on Maioria. They evaded two units of Feylint Halanoi. This attack was deliberate, to scare us. To let us know how easily they can strike into the heart of the Free People.'

Issa felt cold. 'Did the blue moon rise here?'

'What?' Asaph asked and looked down at her.

'Did it rise here?' she repeated

'No, the blue moon has not risen,' he said.

She sighed and sank against him. 'It rose in the Murk.'

'Then that is where you were supposed to be. Take heart in that,' he said and stroked her hair.

'But I want to be where the Maphraxies are. I live only to destroy them,' she said, the bitterness of missed vengeance a sickness in her stomach.

'No,' he said, capturing her in his deep blue eyes. 'You live for far more than that. You live to live and to love. Don't become bent only on vengeance. Only darkness lies there. I've seen it.'

She sighed. He was right. Vengeance would twist her and she lived for more than just that, but still she longed for it.

'I want us all to be free, that's all. To live lives of joy and freedom and happiness. Not a life filled with death and darkness and war. Do you know what happened to the others?' She thought of Maggot, Duskar, Marakon and Bokaard. He seemed to know what she meant.

'The Maphraxies came straight for you and ignored everyone else. They knew exactly where you were, somehow. When I saw them all rushing forwards together… that's how I found you. I was lucky to get there fast enough.'

Issa stared into the fire. Baelthrom still wanted her. Should she jeopardise everyone's life by being amongst them? The old worries and fears returned. The west coast of Frayon was lost and it looked like the rest of the continent was soon to follow. They had been defeated. Whether or not Carvon withstood the Maphraxies remained to be seen, but she wasn't hopeful.

Sickening worry for Duskar, Ehka and Maggot stabbed at her. And what about Freydel? Maybe his magic would protect him. Ehka would find her wherever she went and Maggot would return to the Murk. Duskar could bolt, no Maphraxie would be interested in a horse and he could fend for himself against a foltoy.

She dared to let herself relax a little.

Asaph's hand slipped from her shoulder and she realised he'd fallen asleep. She snuggled back against him, finding some peace and comfort in the strong beat of his heart. They needed time to rest and recover when there was no time to rest.

At first light they had to return to Carvon and do whatever they could to help drive out the Maphraxies. It would be done. It *had* to be done. But after then, what? Where?

She would call for a council of war, a meeting to discuss what they needed to do—one that involved everyone and not just between the Feylint Halanoi. Wizards, seers and witches needed to attend. Maybe even demons. They had to do something, they couldn't just defend, they needed to attack.

Myrn. The thought popped into her head. She should go to Myrn and learn all the seers could tell her. She nodded her head and stared into the fire. There were great secrets to be uncovered there.

On Myrn I think I'll come to understand many things. And after that, we fight back.

Continued in *Dragons of the Dawn Bringer*

DRAGONS
OF THE
DAWN BRINGER
The Goddess Prophecies

Book 5

Araya Evermore

*AN EXILED KING. A BROKEN DREAM. A SWORD
FORGED FOR FOREVER.*

Issa can trust no one. Her closest allies betray her and
nobody is as they seem. When a Dromoorai captures her and a
black vortex to another dimension rips into her room, she
realises the attacks will never stop and there is far worse than
Baelthrom reaching for her out of the Dark Rift.

The Great Sword of Binding has been stolen and it calls to
Asaph in a vision like no other. Alone he must find it and
awaken the dragons before they fall asleep forever. But the
quest will bring him face to face with the enemy, and to the
very brink of his life. Can he find the sword and reach Issa's
army in time to join the fight against Baelthrom?

The Dragon Dream has fallen and now the Elven Land of
Mists is attacked. Soon there will be nothing left to defend.
Issa must take the offensive and strike into the heart of enemy
lands. War now becomes the Raven Queen's domain.

The world hangs between the darkness and the light but
only the hidden powers of a young woman can save it.

ALSO BY ARAYA EVERMORE

The Goddess Prophecies series:

Goddess Awakening ~ A Prequel

When darkness falls, a heroine will rise.

The Dread Dragons came with the dawn. On dark wings of death they slaughtered every seer and turned their sacred lands to ruin…

Night Goddess ~ Book 1

A world plunging into darkness. An exiled Dragon Lord struggling with his destiny. A young woman terrified of an ancient prophecy she has set in motion.

He came through the Dark Rift hunting for those who had escaped his wrath. Unchecked, his evil spread. Now, the world hangs on a knife-edge and all seems destined to fall. But when the dark moon rises, a goddess awakens, and nothing can stop the prophecy unfolding…

The Fall of Celene ~ Book 2

Impossible Odds, Terrifying Powers

"My name is Issa and I am hunted. I hold a power that I neither understand nor can barely control…"

The battle for Maioria has begun. Issa faces a deadly enemy as the Immortal Lord's attention turns fully in her direction. Nothing will stand in Baelthrom's way—he must destroy this new power that grows with the rising dark moon…

Storm Holt ~ Book 3

Would you sell your soul to save the world?

The Storm Holt... The ultimate Wizard's Reckoning, where all who enter must face their greatest demons. No woman has entered and survived since the Ancients split the magic apart eons ago. Plagued by demons and visions of a strange white spear, Issa must take the Reckoning to find her answers and fight for her soul to prove her worth to the most powerful magic wielders upon Maioria...

Demon Spear ~ Book 4

Demons. Death. Deliverance.

All these Issa must face as darkness strikes into the heart of their last stronghold. Greater demons are rising from the Pit, Carvon is brutally attacked, and a horrifying murder forces Issa and her companions to flee. But despite the devastating loss, she must keep her oath to the Shadow Demons and alone reclaim the spear that can save them all...

Dragons of the Dawn Bringer ~ Book 5

An Exiled King. A Broken Dream. A Sword Forged for Forever.

Issa can trust no one. Her closest allies betray her and nobody is as they seem. When a Dromoorai captures her and a black vortex to another dimension rips into her room, she realises the attacks will never stop and there is far worse than Baelthrom reaching for her out of the Dark Rift...

"Be the light unto the darkness...Be the last light in a falling world."

They had both been chosen: he to save another race; she to save her own from what he had become. Now, both must enter Oblivion and therein decide the fate of all...

BOOKS BY JOANNA STARR

Farseeker

Enlightened. Enslaved. Erased.

Earth, 50,000 years ago before the magic vanished. Invaded by aliens posing as gods, advanced civilisations crumbled. Now, these powerful off-worlders war for control of the planet, and the people who remain no longer remember what they once were. Seduced then enslaved, humanity has fallen...

Free Starter Library

Join the mailing list and get your FREE Starr & Evermore Starter Library available only to subscribers. You'll discover Issa's origin story in my prequel, *Goddess Awakening*, which is not available anywhere else. You'll also get a taster of my latest *Farseeker* series with extra scenes not included in the main story.

To receive this epic free gift, please go to my website below. As a subscriber, you'll also be the first to hear about my latest novels, and lots more exclusive content.

www.joannastarr.com

About the Author

Araya Evermore is the pen name of Joanna Starr - a half-elf and author of the best-selling epic fantasy series, *The Goddess Prophecies*.

Joanna has been exploring other worlds and writing fantasy stories ever since she came to Planet Earth. Finding herself struggling in a world in which she didn't quite fit, escaping into fantasy novels gave her the magic and wonder she craved. Despite majoring in Philosophy & Religion, then Computer Science, she left her career in The City to return to her first love; writing Epic Fantasy.

Originally from the West Country, she's been travelling the world since 2011, and has been on the road so long she no longer comes from any place in particular. So far, she's resided in the Caribbean, United States, Canada, Australia, New Zealand, Spain, Andorra and Malta. Despite loving the mountains, she's actually a sea-based creature and currently resides by the ocean in Ireland.

Aside from writing and working, she spends time talking to trees, swimming with fish, gaming, and playing with swords.

Connect with Joanna online:
www.joannastarr.com
author@joannastarr.com

Enjoyed this book? You can make a big difference…

If you love fantasy books and would like to bring this series to the attention of other fantasy readers, the best thing you can do to reach them is to leave a review.

If you've enjoyed this book, I would be very grateful if you could spend just a minute leaving a review, (it can be as long or as short as you like) on the book's Amazon page.

A heartfelt Thank You in advance.

Printed in Great Britain
by Amazon

79266762R00212